MW01043349

Seven
Wolves
of the
Sun

THE LEGEND

 FriesenPress

Suite 300 - 990 Fort St
Victoria, BC, V8V 3K2
Canada

www.friesenpress.com

Copyright © 2018 by L. A. Walker
First Edition — 2018

All rights reserved.

No part of this publication may be reproduced in any form, or by any means, electronic or mechanical, including photocopying, recording, or any information browsing, storage, or retrieval system, without permission in writing from FriesenPress.

ISBN
978-1-5255-3278-8 (Hardcover)
978-1-5255-3279-5 (Paperback)
978-1-5255-3280-1 (eBook)

1. FICTION, FANTASY

Distributed to the trade by The Ingram Book Company

SEVEN WOLVES OF THE SUN

THE LEGEND

L. A. WALKER

Isobel & Brad
Enjoy the adventure!
Laurie Walker

This book is dedicated in loving memory of my father
Joseph (Barry) Walker
Miss you
(I think you would really like this)

ACKNOWLEDGEMENTS

I THINK IN THE WRITING OF BOOKS, OR IN ANY WON-derful project, it is never only one person responsible for the creation that comes forth. In my case there have been many people who have impacted my life and contributed in some way to the creating and writing of this book.

I have only fond memories of my childhood, especially with my dad. Even though I was a girl, I was considered his first son. Total tomboy. One of the things I remember most, is him talking about how we are all magic with the capacity to do whatever we could think of. I think that is why I lived my life trying everything. The thought that I could not do something, especially because I was a girl, never crossed my mind. So, I thank him for that, and for the music and love that permeated our lives because of him.

My original acknowledgement page started to grow beyond 10 pages as I thoughtfully named my mom, each of my siblings, children, nieces, nephews, grandchildren, and other friends and influences in my life that have impacted the writing of this book, and there were still many more. I know each of you know how grateful and truly blessed I feel to have you all in my life. One of the remarkable things about our family is we always express how we feel to each other. Love is always spoken and shared, and differences are sorted out as they arise. So, when I am expressing my gratitude on these pages to all of you who have touched and enriched my life, I know these words have been spoken to each of you individually and frequently. Thank you for being my foundation, my support, my strength. I love you all very much.

I do wish to take a moment to express a special thank you to my Humber College mentor, Sarah Sheard, for her valuable input during the early stages of this work. This book, and my writing, have improved so much with your guidance. Thank you.

CHAPTER 1

THE MORNING DRIZZLE HAD BECOME A DOWNPOUR. Shista Kian'Huard and his twin, Shista Ko'Resh, heirs to the House of Rhuna, had not yet abandoned their morning ride despite the weather to return to the state house in the city of Kephas. Kian'Huard pulled his hood further over his head and looked over at his brother. Ko'Resh had left his hood back. His hair, which was pulled into a long copper braid, clung to him and acted like a wick that channeled the water in a small river down his back. Kian'Huard knew as much water was running inside the oilskin cape as out and his brother needed to get to shelter before he succumbed to the cold and wet. He reined his horse alongside him and shouted over the storm, "We need to head back to Kephas! I am sure we have been away long enough to avoid duties in the court for the day." For that was the excuse Ko'Resh gave him when they left the warmth and dryness of the state house that morning even though the sky threatened the very weather they now found themselves in.

As Shista, they were expected to attend state functions. More so now as they entered their twentieth year but instead, Ko'Resh would find any excuse to avoid such responsibilities. Kian'Huard's devotion to his twin saw him at his side and, more often than not, suffering the same reprimands from Domini Brin'Toth as Ko'Resh.

Brin'Toth had assumed the role of domini ten years prior. He was in charge of overseeing the education of the royal twins to the duties of the court. Eventually he would provide the tools one, or both, would need to take over as Sharram of Rhuna. Ko'Resh did not make it an easy role.

Ko'Resh ignored his brother and pressed on. It seemed he was looking for something, though Kian'Huard could not guess what. His green eyes remained focused on the ragged hillside that bordered the north side of the road. Without warning, Ko'Resh reined his horse to stop and dismounted. Kian'Huard sighed heavily then followed suit. He had to break into a run to catch up when he saw Ko'Resh disappear behind an outcropping. A chill ran up his spine when he crossed the threshold that was created by the stone and the base of the mountain. An eerie feeling crept over him like a hunger driving him to go deeper along the path before him. He dismissed it to be his desire to get his brother and return home to a hot bath and roaring fire.

When Kian'Huard found Ko'Resh, he was standing at the mouth of a cave. Kian'Huard ran to him and took his arm to pull him back. "We can't go in there." He cautioned him, for he knew his brother well and he was reckless enough to explore a cave without the benefit of proper equipment or supplies.

Ko'Resh shrugged Kian'Huard's hand from his arm and peered deeper into the mouth of the mountain. "Do you not find it curious we have not seen this cave before? We have explored almost every inch of this part of the road since we were first old enough to travel on our own and we have never seen anything like this." His voice was distant and he never took his eyes off the cave when he spoke.

"I admit I am as curious as you, Ko'Resh, but let's go back to Kephas first. We need ropes, torches and dry clothing. We don't know what is in there. A giant lukos could be using it as her den and we have no weapons except our daggers."

Ko'Resh looked to Kian'Huard then back to the cave. "You're right, I know, but I feel very compelled to go in, as though something is calling to me."

Kian'Huard nodded. "I feel the same. I have since I passed the outcropping that shields the cave from view of the road. But I think it is best if we go back and wait until the rain stops. Then we can gather what supplies we need." He did not expect Ko'Resh to agree, given his reckless nature, but, for the moment, common sense prevailed and Ko'Resh grudgingly followed him back toward the horses. When they passed back through the threshold, once more, Kian'Huard felt a cold chill run up his spine. He saw his twin looking around the ground until he found a vertas plant, which their people used to make green dye. Ko'Resh broke open the stem and drew the mark of the House of Althean on the face of the outcropping to make it easier to spot when they returned. They mounted their horses, and Kian'Huard reined his horse to head toward Kephas. Ko'Resh paused a moment to take one last look at the rockface then followed suit.

The next day, Ko'Resh's mood dulled then grew as foul as the weather when the rain grew from a downpour to full-out gale. No one, least of all the young shista, would be leaving the house until it stopped. Often, Ko'Resh remained sulking in his suite or would pace restless and angry through the halls, lashing out at any who chanced to get in his way. Domini Brin'Toth took advantage of the weather and his captive young shistas and made certain they attended several functions associated with the Spring Festival. The festival was why they were in Kephas staying in the state house under the shadow of the mountain rather than in their home in Althean, the great castle that was the House of Rhuna. Many remarked at seeing them in attendance, for they were usually noticeably absent for nearly all functions. This did nothing to improve Ko'Resh's mood and he made no effort to hide his displeasure.

As the days passed with no indication the weather was going to let up, Ko'Resh became even more short-tempered. On one occasion, Kian'Huard happen upon him just as he was raising his hand to strike one of the laundry girls who had the misfortune of being sent with clean linens. She had knocked on his door and when she did not get an answer she proceeded to enter his chamber. Ko'Resh turned on her and growled, "Fool! I did not grant you permission to enter!" He raised his hand to strike her.

The girl shrank back in fear and dropped the linens. Kian'Huard entered the room at that moment and stayed Ko'Resh's hand. "Brother." Kian'Huard did not try to hide his irritation with his brother's actions. "Do not take your anger out on those around you; the rain will let up and we will return to explore the cave." He turned to the girl and dismissed her.

She bowed and expressed her gratitude to Kian'Huard. "*N'othan celib Naid Shista.*" And quickly exited the room, leaving the linens on the floor where she dropped them.

Kian'Huard let go of his brother's arm. "We are summoned to go to the main hall to oversee tonight's banquet."

Ko'Resh ignored him and poured himself a cup of wine. "You may go if you wish. I intend to stay here and continue drinking." He drank down the wine and poured himself another before continuing, "If I do leave my chambers, you can rest assured it will be for more enjoyable pursuits then overseeing a banquet. I believe Madame Tovant has some new talent staying with her

3

that needs to be"—he paused to take a drink— "explored."

Kian Huard could see further discussion would only cause more discord, so he excused himself and left the room, being sure to close the door tightly behind him. He went to the servant wing and left specific instruction that no one was to enter Ko'Resh's chambers and, in fact, that they must be certain to give him a wide berth.

Two days later, Kian'Huard was awakened by the sound of pounding on his door. He rose, still naked, from his bed and opened the door to be greeted by Ko'Resh already fully clothed in his riding gear and carrying two saddle-bags stuffed with ropes and supplies. "The rain has stopped."

"*Nuva daelo maest* to you as well, Ko'Resh." Kian'Huard stepped back from the door and motioned for him to enter then went to his side table to pour himself a drink and fill a plate with fruit and sweet breads. "I trust you are going to allow me the opportunity to eat." He paused and gestured at his nakedness. "And perhaps throw on a little something before we leave. I do not think that cave is going anywhere."

Ko'Resh entered the room and rather grudgingly dropped the bags by the door and went to the table as though he suddenly remembered he was hungry. "I don't know how long the cave will remain visible. What I do know for certain is I have explored that part of the mountain several times and it has never revealed itself to me before."

"Revealed itself?" Kian'Huard stopped dressing and stared at his brother. "That seems an odd choice of words. Are you implying there is some magic about that cave that it decides to whom and when it will reveal itself?"

"I can't say for sure, but I do feel some strange power is associated with it," Ko'Resh replied, his voice trailed and his expression became distant.

"Then, brother, do you think it is wise we go exploring? Maybe some solveige has been cast to trap and abduct the young Shista of Rhuna, ending the line of their father, the great Sharram Kar'Set?" Kian'Huard's tone was more sarcastic than he intended, but he had noticed a change in his twin since they discovered the cave and it was not for the better. Ko'Resh was always the least restrained of the two and much more reckless, especially for one who would someday become Sharram of Rhuna, but since the cave was discovered, his recklessness was tainted with an undeniable voracity that was consuming him.

4

"You mock me, brother, but tell me you do not feel the pull to return and enter the cave," Ko'Resh challenged him.

"I agree, Ko'Resh, I do feel drawn to return, but I am certain it is our adolescent curiosity that draws us, not some renegade Sacerdos'helige with the power of solveige that has selected us for a sinister plan." Kian'Huard tried to soften the mood but, again, noted the tone in Ko'Resh's voice, and the change in his brother. They had been anxious to get out of the court before, but this cave seemed to illicit a sense of urgency he had not felt before and it was obvious to him Ko'Resh was deeply affected. Much more than he would admit. Kian'Huard considered his own reaction to finding the cave. He did feel a certain urge to return but not so strong that if he never returned he would be troubled. Ko'Resh, on the other hand, was obsessed with returning and Kian'Huard knew if they did not go soon, Ko'Resh would go on his own and Kian'Huard could not let that happen. He always looked out for his brother.

Kian'Huard got dressed between mouthfuls so by the time they had both eaten their fill, he was ready. They grabbed the saddle bags and headed to the stables. Kian'Huard expected to be challenged by at least one guard along the way from the state house to the nearby stables but the hallway and outer courtyard were empty. He turned to Ko'Resh. "Do you not find it odd there is no one about?"

Ko'Resh did not respond; he pushed past Kian'Huard and threw open the stable doors. The hair on Kian'Huard's neck bristled. The stable hand was sound asleep, crumpled in a heap in the corner. When Kian'Huard moved to wake him, Ko'Resh stopped him. "Leave him, we must not let anyone know where we are going. He has been made to sleep so we can leave unnoticed."

Kian'Huard dropped his saddle bag and turned to face his brother. "Made to sleep? What have you done? What solveige possesses you?" Fear gripped Kian'Huard.

"Relax, brother, I am not possessed, but I do feel there is someone very powerful guiding me." He quickly corrected himself—"Us, and the secrets that lay within the cave will finally liberate Rhuna and our people. Surely you can feel it." His tone was almost fanatical. Kian'Huard knew there were forces at work causing his brother's obsession. And as much as he feared whatever that solveige was, his love for his brother would see him follow Ko'Resh into the mountain.

They quickly readied their horses and left Kephas for the mountain.

Their route through the city took them through the main square where the market was already bustling with vendors and musicians in celebration of the Spring Festival. It was the first of many through the year but this one always seemed the most celebrated. Even Ko'Resh, who usually avoided any festival or duties assigned to one of his station, agreed to attend. It was three days' travel from the castle in Althean to the state house in Kephas, and each year they, and their father, Sharram Kar'Set, would travel to the city to attend the two-week-long festival. Kian'Huard knew Ko'Resh's interest in the festival was more about the young Rhue women who were ready to let their hair down after a long winter than the celebration of new beginnings and the promise of abundance the festival was really about—he always managed to find a way to be absent from any and all duties related to overseeing the festival.

But it did not matter the reason; they were in Kephas and the strange cave was calling to them. Kian'Huard wondered about the cave being visible now. Ko'Resh was correct. They had explored that part of the mountain thoroughly and that cave was simply never there. The only explanation he had, besides solveige, or dark magic, was that the recent tremors that had been felt over the past months could have loosened rock to expose the entrance. He sent a prayer to Selam for the latter, but he still had no explanation for his unnaturally strong desire to explore its depths or the changes in Ko'Resh.

When they were finally clear of the city boundary they pushed their horses to a full gallop along the muddy road that lead from Kephas to the mountain's edge. In the full light of day, no longer shrouded by rain and fog, Kian'Huard could see the effects of the recent tremors. New piles of rubble had crept closer to the edge of the road and, in some places, he could see where larger boulders had been freed from the mountain face and planted deep into the ground, which had been softened by the recent rainfall. This was enough for him to convince himself the cave was no exception; the tremors had caused the entrance to be exposed to them, though still, the pull of the cave remained.

The journey continued longer than expected, and the resh rose high overhead, warming the air and drying the ground. It was late spring, and the recent heavy rain had finished clearing the last traces of snow and driven the remaining frost from the ground. Early blossoming trees were laden with buds yearning toward the warmth of the resh with promise of fragrant blooms that would later yield succulent fruits. It was warm enough for Kian'Huard to doff his oilskin overcoat. He slowed his horse while he wriggled free of the heavy coat and folded it to stow behind him. He rolled the sleeves of his tunic and gathered his long copper hair and tied it with a leather cord. He noticed Ko'Resh was following suit. They were the first twins ever to be born into the house of Rhuna. It was often remarked how similar they were in mannerisms, but Kian'Huard failed to see it. Physically, they were difficult to tell apart. They were typical of the Rhue, with copper hair and tawny complexions that deepened during the summer months. Both stood just over five measures, which was considered tall for the Rhue. They were lean and muscular and well matched for sparring, which they did often. Both were extremely skilled with bows and blades, as well as hand-to-hand combat. It was also expected of the Shista of Rhuna to study the art of Tae'heb, an ancient form of exercise that trained the body and mind. When used in combat, it was a formidable fighting technique. It was one area Kian'Huard noticed he had a different focus than his brother. He immersed himself in the spiritual and meditative aspects of the form while Ko'Resh's focus was on the combat applications. Though, when they sparred, they seemed evenly matched, which made Kian'Huard wonder if the "meditative" aspect of Tae'heb was not as much a prerequisite as their instructors wanted them to believe.

The call of a bird of prey pierced the air, pulling Kian'Huard from his thoughts, and he nudged his horse to come alongside Ko'Resh. "Perhaps we missed your mark. It may have been washed away by the rain."

"No, I am certain it is near," Ko'Resh replied as he surveyed the area around them. His voice did little to hide the impatience he was feeling as the day drew on and he had not yet found the mark he so carefully drew on the outcropping several days prior. "I need to keep looking." He spurred his horse forward without so much as a glance back at his brother. "You can go back if you want. I intend to find that cave."

Kian'Huard sighed heavily and spurred his mount to follow. Moments later, they were rewarded when the green sunburst of the house of Althean came into view. Ko'Resh barely reined his mount to a stop before he was on the ground and sprinting toward the outcropping. Kian'Huard paused to survey their surroundings. He followed the line of the mountain rising above them then his heart skipped a beat. "Ko'Resh," he called to his brother and pointed toward the mountain, his voice conveying the concern he was feeling. "Look"

Ko'Resh turned and looked in the direction Kian'Huard was pointing. His eyes narrowed slightly and a flicker of concern crossed his face when he saw this particular mountain housed the temple of Osiris. "Does that concern you, brother?" His tone had become caustic.

"Yes, in fact, it does," Kian'Huard responded, trying to keep his tone from sounding confrontational. He knew his brother well, and if Ko'Resh thought he was being challenged that would be all the incentive he would need to blindly rush into the cave with no thought of the ramifications of his actions. He continued, choosing his words carefully. "Think of it, brother; we have travelled this road and explored the countryside as long as we were able to go out on our own. We have never seen this cave or any indication it was here until now. You yourself used the words 'revealed itself to us' when we first found it, and you cannot deny the strange pull it has on us. And now..." He motioned to the temple gleaming white and brilliant in the distance, towers reaching high, carved from the very mountain they were about to enter. "Now we see the cave lays beneath the temple. I just think we should consider we may be inviting trouble." He paused and studied his brother, looking for any indication he was reconsidering.

They both knew all were banned from the temple and the surrounding territory on penalty of death. Only those who were summoned or had been granted audience were permitted to enter the sacred place. Even then, any visitors had to endure a three-day cleansing ritual before being granted access to the outer sanctum. So it had been since the dawn of time. No one but those who dwelt there knew what secrets the temple housed. From earliest childhood, all Rhue children were taught they must never venture near the mountain, let alone the temple. Again, Kian'Huard tried to persuade Ko'Resh to return home, and this time the venom in his brother's eyes was unmistakable. Kian'Huard knew it was time to decide whether to turn back and get help and perhaps leave Ko'Resh vulnerable, or to follow him into the cave and watch his back. By now there was no reasoning with Ko'Resh, and Kian'Huard found his own mind was being cluttered with a driving need to enter the caverns. The need prevailed. He gathered the ropes and supplies they had brought, left the horses to themselves and they ducked into the cave.

The darkness of the cavern engulfed them with an unnatural swiftness, and when Kian'Huard turned to look where they had entered, the passage had disappeared behind them. He paused long enough to light a torch. Despite the heat of the cave, an ice-cold shiver coursed through him. Kian'Huard turned to Ko'Resh. "The way out has closed! What solveige is this! Ko'Resh, I think this is a big mistake." He continued to try to convince his brother they should find a way out, but Ko'Resh was already moving quickly down one of the tunnels and his words fell on deaf ears. Kian'Huard had no recourse but to follow.

The cave system was a maze yet, somehow, there was a sense of direction, of purpose, that pulled them through the endless tunnels. There was no time to mark their path to navigate a way back out. It was, it seemed, going to be a one-way trip.

It took some time before Kian'Huard realized the darkness had faded and they were able to see inside the tunnels without the aid of torches. This revelation left him with an even stronger sense of foreboding, and with no time to investigate the source of the lighting, he had to push his uncertainty aside to stay close to his brother. It reinforced his fear that powerful solveige, dark magic, was at work.

They followed the tunnel and, as they progressed ever downward, it seemed to open up and a soft glow illuminated their path. Kian'Huard looked behind to try to keep track of their progress and to his horror the tunnel disappeared behind them. He called to Ko'Resh, "Brother! The tunnel is closing behind us!" Ko'Resh turned and watched the tunnel walls flow inward and close the passage behind them. For a moment, Kian'Huard saw a flicker of concern in his brother's eyes, but it was so fleeting he thought perhaps he imagined it. They ran their hands over the dusky red stone looking for a trace of an opening or a trigger. None was found. Sick unease balled in Kian'Huard's stomach. Ko'Resh turned on his heel and continued. Kian'Huard struggled with an irrational urge to turn back, even though the path had disappeared, and a wave of confusion washed over him, cluttering his thoughts. He watched Ko'Resh's back grow distant and then felt an almost paralyzing fear when he realized that as Ko'Resh moved further away, the cave walls between them were closing in! If he did not move he would be trapped within the stone! Kian'Huard forced his feet to move and called out to his brother. "Ko'Resh, wait!"

Ko'Resh glanced over his shoulder at Kian'Huard and then disappeared around a corner. Motivated by panic, Kian'Huard scrambled to escape the encroaching prison. He stumbled over the living rock that threatened to engulf him. In his haste, he fell, and as he franticly tried to regain his feet, he felt the ice cold of the fluid rock clutching at his ankle. He kicked his foot free, sending liquid shards in a spray that crackled in the air as they solidified then fell to the floor. The shards bled and grew like some living creature reaching out, determined to devour him as he clawed his way to his feet and stumbled forward through the tunnel. Kian'Huard ran hard and rounded a corner to find his brother standing before an ornate arched gateway carved into the stone.

"I see you managed to catch up, brother," he said, but his eyes did not leave the gate. He ran his fingers almost lovingly over the carvings of contorted faces whose stone eyes depicted the utmost fear and anguish. Stone hands stretched toward the centre of the gate as though they were desperately trying to reach something. Words were carved into the arch as well, some of which were partly covered by the hands. Ko'Resh reached out and brushed his hand across the arch and the brothers jumped back when the hands covering the words moved aside so they could read what was written. Ko'Resh recovered first and moved closer to read in the dim lighting. It was then that Kian'Huard noticed the encroaching rock steadily closing the gap between them. It would only be a matter of minutes before it reached them and there was no direction to turn but through the gate. Kian'Huard was certain his face was beginning to reflect the terror of those embedded in the rock. More faces began to appear and then whispers started, barely audible at first, so he was unsure if they were real or imagined. They quickly grew in volume and intensity, but Ko'Resh seemed oblivious to them.

"Ko'Resh!" Kian'Huard shouted. There was no hiding the panic in his voice. He took his twin by the shoulders and spun him around to face the wall of rock bearing down on them. Ko'Resh glared at Kian'Huard for a moment but his eyes betrayed him with a flicker of genuine fear. He spun around, staring at the cave and the gate as though he were seeing it for the first time. He shook his head to will the voices to silence.

"We need to figure out the key." He was trying to remain calm, and it seemed that what possessed him to bring him to the caves had abandoned him and he was genuinely frightened. For that moment, he was brother to Kian'Huard. He read aloud the words above the gate:

"Dire mareth ko Saal nestor dire nishan"
The blood of Saal holds the secret.

"A riddle!" Kian'Huard blurted, torn between willing the gate to open and watching the encroaching flood of stone ebb nearer with the rising volume of the whispering faces. His mind was becoming too cluttered to think, and he could see that Ko'Resh was also affected. He hammered his fist into the gate and shouted for it to open. The faces in the rock mimicked his shouts and they echoed down the tunnel to the liquid stone that rippled like a pool disturbed by a stone. Then, as the ripples turned back on themselves, two more faces began to take shape and stretched forward from the living rock. Hollow eyes set a sorrowful gaze upon them and mouths cried out tortured screams and, when the faces materialized, they saw themselves, and the mournful howls that escaped the stone-cold lips were their own voices, mocking their fear. Despite their confusion, they knew time was running short. They had to force themselves to focus on the riddle that would open the gate.

Kian'Huard pressed his hand against the centre of the gate and pulled it back in alarm as it sank into the stone. The shock of the icy cold stung his fingers and blisters rose where they made contact. He cursed and tucked his hand into his tunic then noticed that the imprint of his hand remained in the stone.

"Dire mareth ko Saal nestor dire Nishan." Ko'Resh muttered the words out loud over and over. The tunnel was growing colder as the distance between them and the approaching rock apparition shrank. The whispers were no longer incongruent babble but had evolved into a rhythmic chant that ebbed and filled the cavern from barely audible whispers to an ear-splitting crescendo. Each time the liquid death closed another measure nearer, there was an increase in the volume and rhythm of the voices. Their message was clear; they were certain of the twins' impending deaths. Their stone duplicates writhed and shrieked in the advancing icy mire, struggling to free themselves only to be consumed again and again, surfacing and choking out the inky blackness of regurgitated death as though they were experiencing what was

soon to befall the young shista.

Ko'Resh turned, his face ashen with genuine fear. "Kian'Huard," he pleaded, "I am sorry...I..." He did not finish his words as the blackness of the fluid death splashed onto his leg. He panicked and kicked out, sending shards of obsidian in every direction. The wall was within arm's reach when it seemed they were struck with the answer at the same time.

Ko'Resh pulled his dagger and proceeded to draw the blade across his palm. They waited, but nothing happened.

"The blood of Saal holds the secret." Kian'Huard repeated the words, his breath showing in the now-frigid air.

"Ko'Resh! Let your blood fall onto the gate." Ko'Resh nodded and with trembling hands let several drops of his blood fall onto the yawning orifice protruding out from the centre of the gate. Kian'Huard quickly drew dagger and did the same. Stone faces shrieked and arms reached out to embrace the shista in death. They backed away, pressing their bodies against the gate and screamed out in terror as the frigid ooze lapped at their feet and burned its way over their bodies. Their screams were cut off short as it filled their mouths and nostrils, and then blackness engulfed them. Kian'Huard saw the look of absolute terror on Ko'Resh's face and knew his echoed the same. He had a feeling of weightlessness and was thinking "*So this is death.*" And then a feeling of peace replaced the terror of moments ago. Then nothing.

CHAPTER 2

THE NOTHINGNESS EXPLODED WHEN KIAN'HUARD hit the cave floor, landing on his right arm, and felt the sickening crunch of pain that marked a fractured bone. Again, consciousness left him, but only briefly. When next he opened his eyes, he saw Ko'Resh was unconscious beside him.

They had passed through the gate.

Kian'Huard splinted his arm as well as he could with only his dagger sheath and a piece of fabric torn from his tunic and moved to see if his brother was still alive. He let out a deep sigh of relief; Ko'Resh did indeed continue to breathe, and was slowly regaining consciousness.

"Ko'Resh," he whispered, "are you hurt?" Kian'Huard helped him to sit up.

"I am fine, brother." He shrugged him off and stood. "It seems whoever Saal is, he is a relative," Ko'Resh said. His tone seemed distant, and Kian'Huard shrugged it off as a response to what had just happened. Then Ko'Resh noticed the makeshift splint. "I see you are injured." Mock concern tainted his words.

"I will be fine," Kian'Huard replied and tried to quell his growing sense of unease as they stood and surveyed their surroundings.

"I assume we passed through the gate," Ko'Resh stated. He did not wait for a reply; he was already making his way down the tunnel.

"It would seem so," Kian'Huard replied, trying to get some sort of bearing even though he knew it was futile. Then realization struck him. "None of our gear is here." He reached behind to feel his long blade still firmly in place across his back. "It seems only items securely attached passed through with us."

Ko'Resh stopped and turned to face Kian'Huard. "Maybe it ended up somewhere further in the tunnel," he suggested. "We were thrown pretty hard." He motioned toward Kian'Huard's injured arm. "Our gear may have been thrown as well." He began to search the area.

"Maybe," Kian'Huard agreed, but he was not convinced. He noted Ko'Resh still had his dagger, but no other weapons or provisions. "If we don't find a way out, we have no means of survival for any length of time. I'm certain there won't be any game in here to hunt. If we are lucky we may find water, but that won't be enough." He turned to where he thought the gate would have been but there was no trace of it ever being there. He followed the wall, studying it for any signs of a hidden passage that would take them back to the surface, but there was no flaw in the stone wall, no crack or irregularity that would suggest a hidden passage. The only way for them to go was deeper into the mountain.

Ko'Resh watched his brother but did nothing to assist in finding a way out. Instead, he grabbed him by the shoulder and spun him around to face him. "I am not surprised, brother, that as soon as there is some hint of intrigue you try to find a way home rather than continue on the journey. That is so typical of you. Always doing the right thing. Always backing away from anything that may have any possibility of danger or challenge. Always being the practical one, feeling like you have to bail me out when you think I am in some kind of trouble. Well, this time, Kian'Huard, there is no one to run to. Kri'Attole is not here to side with you and help you, once again, pull your careless brother from harm's way. You are going to have to get your hands dirty and follow me. I am going to face this mountain and discover whatever secrets are hidden in these caves. You can come with me or sit here and die!" Ko'Resh did not even try to restrain himself. Years of pent-up frustration poured out of him, spiking his words with venom as he lashed out at his brother.

Kian'Huard was taken aback, but not overly surprised at the onslaught. It was true he was the more cautious of the twins and had indeed enlisted the help of his friend and mentor Kri'Attole to discreetly remove Ko'Resh from certain 'compromising situations.' He drew in a deep breath. "You are right, Ko'Resh. If we are to find our way out, or through, this mountain, we need to work together, and since you have always been the more..." he paused, looking for the right word, "adventurous, I will concede to your expertise in traversing these tunnels." Kian'Huard knew there was no recourse but to forge ahead, so he followed Ko'Resh's lead, not really surprised they did not find their gear as they moved deeper into the heart of the mountain.

They had not gone far when rough stone walls of the tunnel gave way to more polished stone and soon the tunnel opened to a large cavern. The high-vaulted ceiling was supported by columns carved from the rock. The cavern was over two hundred paces across, and from where they stood they could not guess at the length of it for it seemed to stretch beyond what their eyes could see. The distant wall housed many tunnels, each framed with ornate carvings. From their vantage point, Kian'Huard counted more than twenty, but he knew there could be hundreds. In the centre of this great hall there was a long, ornately carved wooden table and one chair, but even as they entered the cavern a second chair appeared. Kian'Huard hesitated at the threshold and reached to Ko'Resh to hold him back. "Did you see that?" He motioned to where the chair appeared. Ko'Resh ignored him and shrugged free of his grasp.

Kian'Huard reluctantly followed Ko'Resh and again tried to caution him as they neared the table and a banquet began to materialize out of nowhere. The aroma of roast beast and fresh breads quickly filled the chamber and Ko'Resh wasted no time in indulging in the feast. Once more, Kian'Huard tried to caution him, but the smell of food and his own hunger drove him to join his brother. It struck him that they had already been in the tunnels for several hours and it seemed would be here for several more.

Kian'Huard drank in the flavor of each bite of food, the smells in the air and the vacuous silence of that great chamber. The room seemed to swallow them and they remained unchallenged as they fed on the bounty before them. When both were fat and gorged, bellies round and aching with their gluttony, they became sleepy. This being a normal response to such content-ment, Kian'Huard did not think anything of it until the urge to sleep became more and more overpowering. The more he tried to fight it, the stronger the urge to succumb became. He saw his brother had already drifted to sleep, seemingly content and without fear as he let the tide of fatigue envelope him. Kian'Huard shook him to try to rouse him, but to no avail. He feared the food was poisoned. He knew he was losing the struggle to remain conscious as his legs gradually refused to carry his weight and wave after wave of sleepiness washed over him till finally the room and his twin brother were some distant memory, his urge to resist had been overpowered and the colorful blackness of dreamless sleep took over.

Kian'Huard felt as though he was floating on a peaceful river, drifting slowly with the current, gently rocking in the buoyancy of his body, suspended weightless in the coolness of the river's womb. He rolled onto his side and breathed deep, as one does when drifting back to consciousness but keeping a toehold in the dream state. He gasped and sputtered, choking on the lungful of water he inhaled. Thrust into total wakefulness by a fit of coughing, Kian'Huard lifted himself to his hands and knees. Cold water swirled around him, the salty taste still bitter in his mouth. Panic set in when he could not find Ko'Resh. He called out, but no response came.

The table was gone and the water was almost to his knees and rising! He waded in the frigid waters, frantic to find Ko'Resh. He followed the pull of the current and called out his brother's name with only echoes reverberating, falling over themselves mocking in response. Desperate frustration set in when the current led him to the mouths of a dozen or more tunnels. There was no way to choose with any certainty which tunnel Ko'Resh had been taken down or to know if he had regained consciousness. Shouting down the entrance of each tunnel only amplified the resounding echoes to a pitch that would have drowned out any response from Ko'Resh. Kian'Huard kicked out at the water, letting fear and anger build, and hammered his fist into one of the pillars. "Ko'Resh!!!" he shouted again. He slid down the pillar deeper into the frigid water and wept at the loss of his brother. The cold had penetrated through his clothing and he shivered uncontrollably. He cradled his fractured wrist to his chest to try to ease the throbbing pain and drew his knees to him while he let the water rise around him, swallowing him and feeding his pain and self-reproach. He was so engrossed in his self-pity that at first, he did not hear the sound of splashing until it was almost on top of him. Despite the ice cold of the water, a bead of sweat formed across his brow. Kian'Huard's hand instinctively went to his blade, only to discover it missing.

"Are you looking for this, brother?" Ko'Resh's voice broke the rhythmic silence of the chamber. He handed Kian'Huard the blade and added, "That was quite a display." The matter-of-fact tones and the smug look on his face sent a shiver through Kian'Huard and his concern for Ko'Resh was quickly replaced with anger.

"You knew I was looking for you and choose to remain silent!" Kian'Huard's voice cracked, partly with the cold and partly with anger. But he had no time to express his feelings of betrayal; Ko'Resh had already turned and started toward one of the tunnels with such definite purpose it seemed he knew the way. Kian'Huard rose to his feet and realized he should get used to watching his brother's back moving away from him. He tucked his blade into his belt and, once again, he followed.

The water was rising swiftly and it was not long before they were forced to swim. There were still several feet between them and the roof of the tunnel, but there was no margin for error. They had to choose the correct exit tunnel or they would drown if the frigid waters continued to rise at that rate. They were beyond cold, and their bodies were moving mechanically. If they did not find someplace warm and dry soon, they would succumb to the cold before they had the opportunity to drown. Kian'Huard was concerned as well that the caverns were filling with saltwater. Even when the tide was its highest, it should not have reached this mountain range. And, though the tunnels held a steady decline, he was certain they had not dropped below sea level. But the fact remained that the sea was flooding the tunnels and the distance between the water and the ceiling was quickly diminishing.

"Ko'Resh, you are certain this is the correct tunnel?" Their feet had left the floor long ago and they kicked and swam with the current trying to keep their heads above the water.

"If you wish, brother, you can turn back." Ko'Resh quickened his pace, putting a physical distance between them that did nothing to rival the growing rift between them as brothers. "You were always the weak twin." Those were his last words before the water forced them to strain toward the ceiling in search of pockets of air, desperate to conserve strength and gulping in as much air as they could with each opportunity. The water was moving faster and since they could no longer touch the floor of the cave they were swept along, their bodies hammered into outcroppings and debris by the current. The salt stung their eyes and wounds until the tunnel opened into a large cavern and the water rushed, swirling toward the centre, creating a vortex that carried them like helpless ragdolls into the raging funnel. Just as Kian'Huard was being swept under, he caught sight of Ko'Resh clinging to an outcropping, and his brother's laughter rang out like a slap to the face as he climbed from the water to the safety of a ledge.

Kian'Huard's lungs screamed for oxygen and still he could not find the surface. His body, battered and bruised, refused to respond to his mind and move his limbs in an attempt to swim. Adrenalin surged through his veins in a last desperate attempt at survival. His lungs forced the last spent air from his body as he burst from the tunnel into freefall. Gulping air between fountains of water flowing over the cliff, he forced life back into his muscles and when he hit the underground river he surfaced quickly and pulled himself onto the rocky shore.

He didn't know how long he laid there. He remembered periods of consciousness mingled with delirium and mindless oblivion. When he was finally alert enough to sit up, his first attempts failed. The pain from his injuries threatened to plunge him back into unconsciousness. His arm was grossly deformed and swollen, the splint long gone. He assessed his injuries to find, with the exception of his broken arm, the rest of his injuries were superficial and, though the saltwater stung, he knew it would also serve to reduce the chance of infection and aid healing. Thoughts of his brother crossed his mind, but he pushed them aside. He would not grieve for him. He would survive to find a way out of there and then deal with Ko'Resh.

He needed to splint his arm again, and this time he would make sure it was properly aligned. He found three small sticks in some of the debris along the water's edge. A few measures away from the water he found a place where a narrow crevasse had formed. He removed his leather riding vest and tunic. The temperature in the cave was hot so he did not need the long-sleeved tunic but he decided to put his vest back on. Using his teeth and good arm, he tore a few strips from his tunic. The rest he folded and tucked into his belt in case he needed more bandages later. He wedged his hand into the crevasse and, after assuring his wrist would remain firmly caught between the rocks, he pulled. Searing pain shot the length of his arm. He clenched his jaw and forced himself to remain conscious when blackness threatened to engulf him. He felt a sickening grind as the bones grudgingly inched into place. Terrible sounds erupted from his throat when, with one final effort, he forced himself to pull harder through the pain and nausea that threatened to overwhelm him and moved the splintered ends back into alignment.

He removed his hand from the crevasse. He struggled with the splint; his hands, wet with sweat, made it difficult to keep a strong grasp. Fumbling with only one good arm and with sweat dripping into his eyes, blurring his vision, he tightened the knots using his teeth and finally securely splinted his arm. It was not till then that he fully noticed the air in this chamber was much hotter than the others. His breath was heavy with recent exertions and the humidity was so thick and hot he felt he was suffocating.

Kian'Huard took in his surroundings. To his right was the waterfall he rode in on. When he saw where it crashed into the floor of the cavern to become a river, instantly, he knew how lucky he was to have survived. Jutting up through the boiling foam were countless shards of rocks. Some were worn smooth by the water's constant motion and others, newer ones, stretched jagged fingers, torn from the face of the cavern wall, yearning to impale anything that fate would send their way. In contrast, only a few measures from the waterfall, the river ran deep and black. The water's surface seemed unnaturally calm so near the chaos that filled its existence mere strides away. He picked up a stone and dropped it into the inky black water. Not even a ripple disturbed the glassy surface when the stone passed through. He decided to maintain his distance. Even the thundering crash of the falls was quickly stifled as though the air itself had swallowed the sound only a few yards from the boil. Unless he was looking directly at it, he would not know it was there, for the silence was complete. Kian'Huard moved several yards downstream in search of a place to rest that offered a respectable distance from the river. In a short time, he found a shelf in the wall that would accommodate him. He gathered dry kelp and grasses that had been deposited along the bank and studied the water lines on the wall to be certain that his chosen crag would not flood if the river should rise while he rested. Satisfied he would be safe, from the water at least, for he did not know what other dangers lurked there, he spread the dried grasses and hoisted himself onto the ledge. The heavy feeling in his chest had abated as he grew accustomed to the atmosphere and the pain in his arm began to subside to a bearable level. Fatigue again threatened to consume him and, since he was too tired to fight it this time, he let sleep take him.

He expected dreamless rest but instead his mind was filled with images, many of which he did not understand. Other images were very definite; his brother was in grave danger yet he was unaware of the threat he was about to unleash on himself. Kian'Huard saw himself trying to stop him and fail.

He saw Ko'Resh change so there was nothing left of the brother he knew. He saw him raise his sword and just as Kian'Huard would feel the bite of the cold metal pierce his flesh, he awoke with such a start that he sat bolt upright, forgetting his surroundings, and cracked his forehead on the unforgiving ceiling. He felt the sticky warmth of blood trickle down his forehead and spat out a curse at his stupidity. He balled up a strip of what was left of his tunic and applied pressure to the wound, taking an inventory of his situation. His boots were sound and both stockings were dry. His short dagger had remained secure, but his long blade had disappeared, along with his water flask. He did not have any idea where he was or how long, if ever, it would take him to find his way out. His head had stopped bleeding and he tossed the blood-stained rag aside then reconsidered and stuffed it into his belt. He did not want to leave any evidence of his passing through there. He scooped up the bedding he had gathered and redistributed it so it looked as natural as possible where he found it. No footprints showed on the bare rock, and the watery evidence of where he had crawled from the river had long since dried. Satisfied he had erased his presence adequately, Kian'Huard began to formulate a plan.

He surveyed his surroundings and noticed a small cave entrance he had overlooked previously. His only other option was to follow the river. He did not relish the idea of being in close proximity to such an unnatural phenomenon. He would avoid the river if at all possible. He considered marking his trail in case the need arose to retrace his steps but decided against it. He did not wish anyone or anything to be able to follow him. He thought briefly of Ko'Resh then recalled how his brother had laughed and saved himself. It confused him that Ko'Resh behaved so but he could not deny the feeling that something greater was guiding them and pressing them to follow a certain path. It was influencing how they thought, and the more Kian'Huard fought it, the harder the unseen force pressed. He was certain Ko'Resh had succumbed to its manipulations. Kian'Huard wondered if he had been more pliant to the force, if it would not have become so strong and perhaps they would have traversed the tunnels together and found a way out. He shook his head to dismiss that train of thought. From the moment they entered the cave and the living rock closed in on them, blocking their exit, Kian'Huard sensed a menacing presence and fought it while Ko'Resh seemed to embrace it and allow it free rein in his mind to guide him toward something and away from his brother.

Kian'Huard ducked into the cave and took a few cautious steps to ensure he could jump clear if the entrance started to close. Nothing. A few more steps and still the path behind him remained open. He let out his breath in a long, ragged sigh and continued deeper into the rock. He followed the tunnel until he came to a larger cavern. Three tunnels branched off. Since he had no idea which to choose, he tossed his dagger and went in the direction the blade pointed. It was not long before Kian'Huard found himself standing at the entrance of another large chamber.

CHAPTER 3

KIAN'HUARD CAUTIOUSLY ENTERED THE CHAMBER, cold sweat trickled down his face stinging his eyes. He blinked and wiped his brow with trembling hands as he surveyed his surroundings. The ceiling yawned overhead, spiked with stalactites that stretched dripping fangs toward the polished granite floor. It did not occur to him till much later that the floor should have displayed an equal abundance of stalagmites. The hair on his neck bristled; this place was possessed of much solveige. It charged the air so there was no denying the presence of an ancient evil power. Once more he found himself with no choice but to move forward, deeper into the heart of the mountain. His scrutiny showed only two exits from this ominous place. The first was the way he came in, back along the tunnel to the place where the water plunged through an opening several measures above the dark pool and then following the river wherever it took him. That thought sent another shiver up his spine. The second possibility was across the cavern. It seemed too easy, but his choices were limited so he made his way toward what he hoped to be an exit.

His footfalls were silent in soft leather boots as he strode the distance across the cavern toward the exit. Ever wary of the shards of rock dangling precariously overhead, he proceeded with caution lest any loud noise or vibration send one crashing. No sooner had the thought entered his mind when a thunderous crash reverberated through the cavern from behind him. He watched in horror as the ceiling began to boil down toward him. Caution aside, he bolted to what he assumed was an exit and dove to safety just as the tide of boulders flooded the floor of the cavern, hurling dangerous shards of debris and thick dust into the air. He strained to run faster to keep ahead of the bone-grinding wall of rock gaining on him. Ahead he could see the tunnel branched to the right. The avalanche was almost on his heels when he dove for cover into the side tunnel. He choked, gasping for air as the tunnel filled with the dust of the passing storm. Still coughing, he gained his feet and backed further down the refuge, waiting till the ear-splitting rumble of the cave-in simmered down to a dull roar then a faint trickle. When he approached the tunnel entrance he could see how tenuous the rock was situated and realized that once again fate had determined what direction he was to take. The thought did not reassure him. He wondered which direction fate had steered his brother. But for some reason, the thought was fleeting, cut off as though it was not time to think such things. Later it would puzzle him how only certain thoughts had seemed to gain footing in his mind.

He turned from the blocked passage and continued deeper into the mountain by the only route available. He felt drawn down the tunnel that was slowly opening up to become more chiseled, gradually looking more like a grand hallway with high, arched ceilings and polished marble floors. Enormous ornately carved pillars supported unimaginably high vaulted ceilings. The stone floor gave way to marble so finely polished it looked like glass. The ceiling was reflected in the smooth depths of the floor, giving the impression of walking suspended over a deep, mirrored pool. Kian'Huard felt a presence in the room. He called out, "Dai nithan rend?" tentatively, at first, since part of him did not really want to know if someone was there and he did not want to trigger another cave in. He waited a few moments, expecting disaster but none came. He called out again, this time shouting, "Dai nithan rend!" His shouts were cut off as though sound was absorbed into the vastness so not even his loudest shout would linger in resounding echoes. In contrast, light seemed to be amplified; though no visible source of light could be discerned, the hall was illuminated and growing brighter as he progressed.

Unease trickled through his mind causing the hairs on his arms and the back of his neck to bristle. His breath quickened. Suddenly he was aware of looking down on himself, and the feeling of separateness sent a wave of nausea through his body. Then his focus changed so abruptly back to looking out from his physical self that he fell to the floor. Nausea overwhelmed him, followed by a searing headache. He retched uncontrollably, but since he had not eaten for so long his stomach was empty and only a fragment of foamy bile marred the perfect floor. He stayed there on his hands and knees expecting to see the pathetic reflection of himself looking back from the polished floor. Expecting to cringe at how filthy and unkempt he had become since entering the cave, he could not even guess at how many hours ago. Again, an electric charge of fear held him. He could see the reflections of the pillars and ornate carvings that covered them and the ceiling. However, even though he stared directly down to his line of vision, no reflection verified his being there. He tilted his head to adjust the angle of the light refraction. Nothing. He squinted into the endless depths of the illusion of a floor, looking for a shadow or some indication that would confirm his being there. Nothing. As he stared into the perfect glassy blackness beneath him, he counted the columns that were reflected there. He studied each carving and found its counterpart right where it should have been in the reflection of the floor. But still he had no echo there.

A shadow of movement in the reflection caught his eye. He strained, staring deeper into the marble pool, looking for a hint of what it could have been, even if it was only a trick of the light. Another shadow passed just outside his line of sight. Kian'Huard leapt to his feet and spun around, hoping to catch a glimpse of what prowled the shadows beneath the smooth surface. Nothing. Again, and always just outside his field of vision, shadows moved with silent stealth among the columns.

"Who's there?" he called out. The emptiness swallowed his words. He reached for the dagger at his thigh and drew it. Something moved in shadow to the left and he turned to face it. Then movement to his right, and he spun and probed the dark corners looking for whatever ghost was stalking him. He could discern movement all around him. Turning and turning, he tried to catch a glimpse of whatever filled the room with such overwhelming presence. Always, they remained elusive fluttering shadows, disappearing under his gaze. Though he could not see what creatures lurked behind the shadowy veil of darkness, he felt their presence like a lover's hot breath on his face, intimate in their closeness and caressing him with the promise of death. His heart pounded and his breath quickened. His body refused to obey his mind's need to flee.

Kian'Huard could sense them closing nearer. The air tasted heavy with animal musk. The illumination that previously filled the great hall had dimmed, leaving only the area around him cast in the palest of light. The unnatural darkness allowed nothing to be seen outside the small circle of illumination. Tentatively, Kian'Huard reached out to the darkness that crowded around him. When his fingertips met resistance, he pulled back. Again, with much trepidation, he lightly brushed his fingers against the darkness. The smooth surface was cold to the touch and gave under pressure then sprung back into place with rings of waves undulating outward like a stone dropped into a still pond. He tested the blackness with his blade, imbedding it fully into the gelatinous air. Instantly his hand burned with ice and he let go of the dagger. It remained suspended with only the frost-covered handle visible. He studied his hand where it made contact with the handle and saw blisters of frostbite forming. He wrapped his tunic over his hand as a makeshift glove, grasped the handle of his dagger and pulled it from the barrier. The cold quickly penetrated the fabric and he had to let it drop. To his dismay, the dagger shattered like glass when it struck the floor.

Then something unexpected happened. The fragments of the dagger pooled into liquid and trickled around, gathering themselves together, reforming then solidifying. Kian'Huard hesitated before he stooped to pick up the blade. He touched it lightly, wary of the possibility of being injured further by touching such a magical thing. The dagger seemed safe enough so, with more assurance, he picked it up and studied it. It was just as it had been before it shattered. Even the nick in the blade where he foolishly struck a rock last season had been reproduced in the blade he held.

Kian'Huard felt the hair on his neck bristle and his heart skipped a beat. The vacuous silence was being penetrated by a shuffling sound; it was no more than a whisper or the soft padding of animal paws. He was trapped and being stalked. Shadows thickened the blackness around him in brief, indiscernible shapes. The unmistakable click of claws on stone approached from all sides. He stared hard into the inky black trying to discern what predator hunted him. A sound from behind caused him to spin around, but too late to see his stalker. Another sound to his right and, as he turned to face what lurked, he felt the brush of icy hot breath on the back of his neck. Again, he spun, dagger at the ready, his breath hard with encroaching panic. Still the harbingers of death eluded him. He could only guess at what creatures would cast such large shadows and walk on padded feet.

"Show yourselves!!" he shouted into the blackness. The words were swallowed almost as soon as they escaped his lips. The blackness thickened before him. A form began to take shape. The gelatinous barrier strained toward him. With nowhere to go, he watched, his back pressed against the back of his leathery prison. Sweat beaded then trickled down his brow. His breath, quick and ragged, escaped his lungs to be frozen in the air before him as the temperature dropped. The beast began to take shape. Kian'Huard's heart pounded, knocking at his chest as though to flee his body. He shivered with fear and cold as the frigid air penetrated his sweat-soaked clothes. His hair froze and hung tight against his head like some strange helmet. The beast pressed nearer, its face, which was of the lukos, was now a hand breadth away. His foul, icy breath filled Kian'Huard's mouth and nose with the bitter, rotting taste of death. The beast curled its lip in a snarl, exposing jagged obsidian teeth. Frost formed on Kian'Huard's face and clothing. It stung his eyes but he dared not blink. Each breath he drew he was certain would be his last as he waited for whatever painful death was in store. Low, guttural growls began to fill the enclosed space. They grew in intensity and were joined by the sound of chanting. At first it was low and subtle, then it grew to an ever-rising crescendo of animal tones and human voice. The beast seemed to hesitate. Its eyes bore into Kian'Huard's very soul, whose ability to fear had long since abandoned him.

The primitive chanting reverberated through the air. It penetrated his being and Kian'Huard realized his breathing and heartbeat matched the constant rhythm. Something within his body began to change. Soft warmth crept from the base of his spine and spread throughout his body in waves of green and gold. The beast had moved off a fraction of an inch, as though reluctant to give up so easy a prey. Light began to fill the chamber. Feeling returned to Kian'Huard's hands and he remembered he still clutched his dagger. He swung out in a great, sweeping arch. The leathery boundary that imprisoned him ripped. The beast let out a long, terrifying howl and retreated further into what remained of the blackness.

Glorious yellow-white light now filled the chamber. The cell that contained him had dissolved into a pool of blackness that gathered unto itself and flowed over the flawless sheen of the marble floor, seeking an escape. The beast had retreated fully into the darkness and then leaped into the pool of black when it passed. Black tendrils stretched, yearning to pull it down. The beast struggled briefly and let out a ground-shaking howl as it was pulled under and totally consumed by the blackness. A blinding bolt of green lightning struck from out of nowhere. It danced across the polished marble floor seeking its goal. Jagged points of green light splashed, reflected off the polished surfaces of the pillars and floor lending an eerie strobe-like effect to the cavern. The blackness seemed to understand what sought it and flowed with greater speed, stretching out into a thin ribbon of a river as it tried to gather speed. The green light arced and bounded over the floor and pounced upon the blackness in an explosion of green fire. The black pool hissed and screamed, it clawed at the floor, stretching long tendrils of itself, searching for a flaw in the perfection of the marble to hide in. The fire held to the blackness, consuming it as day does night until every trace of it had evaporated and the chamber was filled with only purest light.

Kian'Huard was not sure the exact moment he realized he had become a prisoner of the light just as he had been held by the blackness. It encircled him in a warm glow that penetrated the cold ache left by the black beast. Though the warmth felt good, he was still immobilized by that which wrapped itself around and through him. A flicker of panic crossed his mind, coursing through his body like a spark leaping through his nerves. Again, he watched, helpless, as the light gathered unto itself and began to take form. Though this was far less menacing to look upon, uncertainty still remained in his heart as the ghostlike form of a woman took shape in the ever-wavering light. As the form grew into solidity it consumed the light of the chamber, drawing it in to use in the making of itself until only an intense bright spark remained centred at the crown of the woman. Her very being glowed as though lit from within. Kian'Huard shielded his eyes from the intensity of the light but his desire to gaze upon the woman of light drove him to strain to accustom his eyes.

Kian'Huard was struck by her beauty, for she was Rhue, and garbed in robes reminiscent of the ancient rulers whose likeness hung in the great halls. On her head was the crown of the Sharrana of Rhuna. Her hair fell well past her waist in a rich cascade of copper fire entwined with gold beads. Her robe, flawless emerald green, was hemmed with gold threads in an intricate pattern of intertwined knots. Kian'Huard bowed before this woman but he was unable to take his eyes off her. Her eyes were the deepest green and held an intensity he had never before seen. Her skin was pale and perfect, almost transparent with the luminescent fire that formed her. The air in the chamber had warmed. The woman started toward him. Kian'Huard straightened and took a step back. Her voice sounded within his head like a soothing melody.

"Bashar kru Kian'Huard, applenta naeier vance a naidrae adah. Na vodit gan'ern val aevum astra dan breve applenta naidrae chardon…"

"Fear not Kian-Huard, for I have come to your aid. I tell you now that time grows short for your brother. Even now he has come upon that which has drawn you here. You must prevent him from awakening the beasts that call to him."

She was close then. Close enough to touch, but his hand would not obey his mind's command. She reached out to him. Unable to move, he felt a wave of fear wash over him when her hand passed over his shattered arm. The pain subsided and was replaced by an intense heat that centred on the fragmented bone and coursed through his arm. His eyes did not leave hers as the bones knit together. He tried to ask her name but words failed him. Again, her voice sounded in his mind, clear like spring dawn, as rich and soothing as a cool, deep pool.

"Na vodit gan'ern Kian'Huard. Na'danrai rom a dire gaudam dermal bryen naidrae daelo havoth vancent a en faeit. Ga' danine ern ayer…"

"Know this, Kian-Huard. I will return to the physical realm before your days have come to an end. And you will know me. My return will mark the dawn of a new era for your people—for all people who share this world. Much pain will be endured, but the reward shall be beyond measure."

Her gaze left him and she studied the air as though she was listening to a distant whisper. She turned her green eyes back to him, *"Na bashai applenta nith kinsam si haeth cataplet da a'sadan solutisan. Belaine nuner dahn nishan naidrae chardon applenta ar'sadan dain garmort warram. Aram ascendant kru chut ar'sadan myrin a berian. Istmod malvelous dethin fin havoth tralete raba-nialo dain naidrae dermal. Nay'agere gana a vique. Mide alleve amin…. Nay'hast naid bel…. Na'va econsman nim jamire! Acconon haeth Kian'Huard, gan'ast pradef naidrae trumal re gana comrale alvar varaperta val rand ga'bashine!"*

"I fear for our people if this terror should be unleashed. Go now and seek out your brother, for he is in grave danger. He knows not what he is about to awaken. Such beasts should never have found substance in your realm. I urge you to hurry. Time grows short … I have lingered too long! Know this,

Kian-Huard—you must guard your thoughts or you could make manifest that which you fear!"

She drifted away from him as a ghost and her substance wavered and slowly dissipated into the air. Kian'Huard called out but to no avail; the spirit was gone, but her words remained heavy within his mind.

Kian'Huard tested his arm, cautiously at first, then with more confidence. The break had completely healed and strength had returned. He quickly became aware that all his injuries had been healed by her touch, and his heart was filled with a renewed sense of purpose and vitality. His dagger was at his feet and, somehow, his sword had been returned to him. These he gathered and he began again to cross the great chamber, ever aware of an unseen presence; though he could not say for certain, he felt it was the presence of that same spirit.

Soon, another great hallway opened before him even more ornate than the one he had just crossed, with great cornices and figures lining the perimeter, arms stretched upward as though they held the ceiling in place. The muted reds and browns of the stone had been painted with vivid greens and reds and blues. The figures were adorned with gold leaf and jewels of every sort. So taken was Kian'Huard by the beauty and quality of workmanship that at first he failed to notice the tale of terror they depicted.

Then his eyes fell upon a statue of a woman more beautiful than any he had ever seen; it was the image of the spirit he had encountered earlier. And, as beautiful as she was, she was filled with such sorrow that it seemed to flow from the very rock from which she was carved. The legend that was born out upon the rock was of a time so ancient he thought it predated much of Rhuna's written history, but as he studied the walls he realized these events were deliberately omitted, as though keeping knowledge of such things could prevent it from recurring. He could also see that she had been made a prisoner. Though he did not see any indication of battle or invasion; the story told in the walls was of a deep and all-consuming desire. This desire was not shared. He began to understand the true meaning of the pictograph, and he returned his gaze to the statue of the Sharrana. His breath came slow and deep, his heart slowed and he could feel his spirit sink but then he was pulled abruptly from the stone woman by shrieks of agony so horrifying they struck him like a blow. He backed away from the figure, his attention fixed on the corridor before him. The cries of absolute terror boiled through the air. It was then that he recognized the voice of his brother. All fear aside, he charged down the hall with single-minded intent—he had to save Ko'Resh.

CHAPTER 4

KIAN'HUARD BURST INTO THE THIRD CHAMBER SO recklessly he nearly charged off the ledge into an abyss. Around the perimeter was a platform that was no more than four paces across and dropped off into nothing. Kian-Huard moved to the edge and looked down. When he bent over to study the chasm it seemed the platform disappeared into space as though it existed only to be seen head on. It was solid enough when he stood on it, but it disappeared if he tried to see it from any other angle. He backed away from the edge and began to make his way around the perimeter. He studied the centre and saw his brother there, lying prone, seemingly suspended in the air. Over his body vortices were beginning to form. Their spouts were gaping, hungrily hunting the spirits that darted frantically, trying to escape the consuming funnels. The bases of these vortices searched the platform like long, nimble fingers playing over the polished stone, caressing the lifeless form of Ko'Resh as though they were searching for something.

Kian-Huard watched as a fourth vortex formed. It grew from a wisp of nothing and gained strength and momentum as it manifested itself in this dimension. It moved through the air and travelled upward along Ko'Resh starting at his feet and passing through the other three, sparking and drawing more strength as it increased in velocity. The first of these, which was centred over Ko'Resh's pelvis, spun at a slower rate than the other two and as they progressed closer to his head they gained in speed, power and size. The fourth settled into place near his heart. It began to emit a humming sound that reverberated through the chamber. As it grew in size and intensity, the sound emanating from it grew also. Kian-Huard strained to get a better look at what was happening inside the domed area. Though the distance was great, he knew that somehow Ko'Resh had crossed the expanse and he needed to

31

do the same if he was going to stop this.

It was then he noticed something peculiar in the air around him. Every now and then a triangle shape would appear like a ghost, slipping into view then turning on its axis and disappearing. Like the platform upon which he stood, these shapes were of but two dimensions and were only visible when they rotated so their face would catch the light. He reached to grab one but he missed when it turned and slipped out of sight. Another appeared and he caught it. Instantly, three more of the shapes surrounded him. He let go, but too late. The shapes closed around him, boxing him inside. His hands and feet burned. Unimaginable pain shot through his extremities then gripped his entire body. He was aware of a curious slipping sensation. His body felt stretched, thinned out as though to accommodate existing in the two-dimensional space. There was no breath. No heartbeat. His mind still functioned, filled with the terror of what was happening to his body as he slipped from his plane of existence like turning a sock inside out. Then his mind was filled with but one thought—Ko'Resh.

An explosion of light and sound rolled over his consciousness with such intensity it was beyond pain or comprehension. He was filled with an overwhelming emotion that he struggled to identify. As he allowed the emotions to flood through his soul, he realized that he, stripped bare of his physical body, was in the presence of that which formed the foundation of all that is. The feeling that shook his body, that overwhelming sensation, was pure love and joy. He allowed himself to be swept up in that sea of pure, raw love. Only a tiny fragment in some distant corner of his mind remained aware of who and what he was. That tiny fragment was enough to pull him away from the stream of light and back to the pain of being trapped within the tetrahedron. His body barely sustained.

The sound of crashing glass brought him back to full awareness as he was literally thrown from the two-dimensional prison. His body struck a cold, hard surface and instantly started to convulse. His eyes rolled back in his head as seizure after seizure assaulted him. As his muscles began to relax he started to tremble and retch uncontrollably. Blood poured from his nose and ears. His eyes were blind. In some distance he could hear what he eventually recognized as screams. Then he realized it was he who was screaming. Awareness began to trickle back into his tortured mind. His body stopped convulsing and settled into an uncontrollable shiver. He regained his vision to find himself lying next to his brother. The stench of vomit, feces and blood assailed him. His mouth tasted of blood and vomit. His hair was matted to his head with sweat and blood. He ventured to raise himself up but was forced back with a crippling wave of vertigo and blinding pain. He rolled onto his back and breathed deep.

"*Ja'sadete.... NADIRE.*"

The words were unexpected, so at first Kian-Huard that he had imagined them. He turned his head to face his brother.

The venom in his eyes was undeniable. "THEY... ARE... MINE!" The words were forced through a blood-filled mouth and spewed forth in a spray of red. He was grunting, trying to draw breath. His teeth were clenched against the effort and the pain. Each breath sprayed blood and bile.

Kian-Huard saw how much effort it took Ko'Resh to speak and tried to fathom the amount of conviction it took for him to do that.

His own breathing mimicked Ko'Resh's and knew his appearance mirrored his twin.

At first Kian-Huard did not understand what Ko'Resh was claiming ownership of. As his mind cleared, he recalled the strange vortices he observed when he first entered the cavern. He saw that four had settled over Ko'Resh and were in the process of binding with his body and spirit. Each time a deeper link was established, Ko'Resh would let out a terrifying scream that grew beyond what a human could produce to a horrifying, bestial howl. As Kian-Huard lay beside his tormented brother he could make out the details within the vortices that eluded him earlier.

Various sounds emanated from each as they pulsed and vibrated to different frequencies. As each settled over the body they would touch on a specific area and begin probing deep into the tissue. This alone seemed to be the source of much pain. Figures would form then dissipate within the swirling haze, their faces twisted with longing and pain. One face materialized within the vortex. If he could have moved, he would have jumped back with shock. A memory of a legend sprung to the forefront of his mind when he stared into the sorrow-filled eyes that claimed his attention. Sohar Ka'Desh! An elusive spirit heard of only in legend. As the winds within the vortex forced the image of the Sohar Ka'Desh from Kian-Huard's sight so too did it bring into view the vision of his lukos spirit. The beast gnashed and clawed against the ethereal bond that was driving it deep into Ko'Resh.

Kian-Huard turned his face from his brother and stared up at the ceiling of the chamber. He struggled to free himself from whatever invisible bonds held him. He screamed but, though his mouth opened, all that came forth was more blood and spit. His breathing came hard and fast and he found himself choking on his blood. He spit out what he could from his mouth and saw it was clotting. He took this to mean he was no longer bleeding. As he cleared his mouth and airway with several deep harsh coughs he forced himself to relax against the restraints and conserve his strength. It was then he noticed the ceiling of the chamber was covered with an elaborate design. A fresh wave of panic drowned him as he realized what it was. He squeezed his eyes shut and tried to calm himself. A legend, more ancient and unbelievable than the existence of the Sohar Ka'Desh, was depicted across the ceiling of the chamber. The legend of the Sem Lukos Resh. And centremost was an elaborately carved relief of a man sitting in the lotus position with detailed gem work and gold leaf mapping the seven power centres of the body.

The first three of these were glowing brightly, pulsing with light and sound. The next one was growing brighter as the vortex over Ko'Resh became entwined within his consciousness. The sixth showed only a faint illumination, which gradually grew in strength as a vortex formed in its centre. The symbol that represented the sixth power centre began to spin, spewing from it the tortured souls of the beings that it held captive. They yearned and clawed at the air in frantic swimming motions as though they wanted to return to whatever prison had just released them, as though they knew it was better they were imprisoned then to be released into the world. The cavern was already filled with rhythmic sounds and static electricity as it began to resonate at an even higher pitch. The low base tones of the first symbols mimicked a heartbeat and the rhythm of the physical body so much that it was not long until those within the chamber were in sync. As the higher seals opened, the vibrations became more rapid, elevating the physical body to a vibratory frequency that would allow it to be invaded by the corresponding entities. If the legends were true, then Kian-Huard knew he had to find a way to prevent Ko'Resh from taking all the spirits. If Ko'Resh was successful then legend stated he would have the power of a god.

The sixth vortex was already establishing itself over Ko'Resh. There was only the seventh left. Kian-Huard focused all his attention on the seventh symbol. He tried to allow his body to feel the initial vibratory changes as the seal began to open. He focused on the mantra emanating from the seal. It was so very faint at first, but as he opened his mind and body to allow that particular frequency to grow and filter through all the others, he felt the creatures turn their focus to him. His breathing was hard and so rapid he felt like he would pass out. His field of vision narrowed so all he saw before him was the symbol of the seventh spirit. Every detail of the blossom-like symbol etched and burned its way into his consciousness. He felt as though his face were right up against the ceiling of the cavern, that he only had to extend his hand and he would be able to touch the delicate gold petals. An explosion of light blinded him.

Somewhere in the distance a bestial scream shredded his consciousness. He tried to escape what he had brought forth but could not. His body felt as though it was being turned inside out, his soul torn open to force him into alignment with the opening of the Sama Lukos. Pain thundered down his spine then a feeling of being ruptured snapped through his loins. He had a vague awareness of losing something. A burst of red light accompanied these sensations and a deep, rhythmic mantra permeated the confusion in his mind. It was both terrifying and comforting. He felt his body ebb and pulse to the rhythm of the mantra. Though he knew the pain still gripped his body, it was growing distant. The stinging edge of the panic he was feeling reduced to a gut-wrenching ache.

Then a wave of spasms struck his abdomen. He lost his bowels. The stench of the filth mingled with the bitter metallic smell of old blood. He felt as though he would vomit. He was aware that his breathing had grown even more rapid. A violent explosion of orange light erupted from his abdomen. A sensation of being aroused washed over him; it grew to such intensity that it caused pain. He felt vulnerable and exposed, raped by an unseen assailant and he ached for more; so much that he felt it through every inch of his body. Longing filled him, mingled with unimaginable pain and fear. He knew he was screaming, though he could not hear his own voice through the constant chanting as a new voice was added to mantra, this one a slightly higher pitch. While the first focused mainly on the sounds of LAM the new sound reverberating through his body echoed VAM...VAM... The rhythm of LAM... VAM... droned on until his body began to pulse to that rhythm. Though the pain remained, and it had not lessened, he was becoming more able to push it to the back of his mind. He was aware of tears flowing down his face and his physical body sobbing through stale blood and vomit. He knew absolute helplessness and, as each new wave of pain, light and sound rolled over him, a cry of despair escaped through clenched teeth. And he worked harder to shut it out. When he thought he was beginning to tolerate the pain another blast of light and sound erupted within him. This time it was centred at his solar plexus. The light was yellow fire; more intense than any light or colour he had ever seen. A third mantra was added to the ever-present droning—Ram ... Lam ... Vam ... Ram....

The monotony was unbearable, but not as much as what these vocalizations were doing to his body. It felt as though he was being forced open and stuffed with pure, raw energy and at any moment something within him was going to break. His mind was flooded with imagery that defied description. His found he was aware of several lifetimes at once. They babbled and overlapped in his consciousness, all vying for attention but none able to come to the forefront. Snatches of lives and deaths and glimpses of love and hate flashed over each other as he was forced into a higher awareness.

He snapped through an invisible barrier and dropped into nothingness. He was aware of his body's reflex to try to break his fall but there was nothing for him to grab. He waved his arms, reaching out at the nothingness hoping to find some horizon or centre of reference, when a wave of vertigo rolled through him. The empty blackness spun, sucking at his body, pulling him, spiraling through a seemingly endless void. He felt stripped. He struggled to keep that which was being taken when he realized it was his own will. Something was taking control of his mind and body. He continued to fall inward in his mind. Tumbling through his own past then through lives that were tainted with familiarity but that he was unable to recollect. He tried to focus on the images that bombarded his senses. It was as though hundreds of actors were all on the same stage, all playing out their own script.

The confusion was driving him to madness as his mind was torn open to allow this higher awareness that he was not prepared to open himself to. He drew his attention toward a group that he could focus on and found himself looking through the eyes of a mother giving birth. For an instant he became that woman; he felt the pain and rush of emotions as her child drew its first breath. Then he was ripped from that body and slammed into another. This was a fisherman fighting a raging storm and Kian-Huard experienced the man's death as he was swept overboard. He saw his comrades' horrified expressions as he sank below the surface of the violent water to the calm depths below. He welcomed death. But it was not to be, and he found himself within yet another body. As he was thrown into these different entities he knew them. And even more, he knew them to be him. Insanity reached out in anticipation.

A new distant mantra was adding its voice through the din. It acted as a beacon. It drew his thoughts toward it and forced his mind to focus. It guided him through this "ocean of illusions," slicing through the pockets of scattered lifetimes, some very ancient and others not yet lived. It seemed to pull him upward. He felt his mind pressing against an unseen barrier and felt it give under the pressure of his focus. The mantra remained distant and unintelligible but already his body had begun to vibrate to this new song.

The barrier snapped. He felt his ego being stripped away. It was being replaced with something insidious, bestial. His heart quickened and his breathing became hard. He could feel his physical body like some distant projection. He knew he was convulsing. He was vaguely aware of screaming horrible primitive sounds that mingled with sobs of despair when a burst of blue light exploded in his head and thundered down his body, arcing brilliant blue lightning as it struck the area at the base of his spine then began the journey upward. It touched each of the simmering pools of coloured light that had found their place within his being, causing an explosion of light and sound. The blue fire found its place at his throat. Instantly his head went back and his mouth opened and his eyes widened even further. Pure sound resonated from his throat. *Aaaaauuuuummmm*. It filled the chamber; a constant uninterrupted hum that was not reliant upon his vocal cords.

More rapidly than the others, another explosion of light poised over him. This was deep indigo. He had no more urge to try to resist as the light traced a path down through the depths of his spirit then exploded through the other centres as it traveled back up his spine and took up position deep within his mind. He felt a rush of hormones flood his already-taxed body. Then a feeling of calm washed over him. Silence rang in his head. His body was naked and exposed. The temperature dropped. Frost formed on his head and body. His breath froze and fell to the polished floor. He readied himself. Violet light flooded the small circle where he lay. It grew in intensity. He was aware of the giant beast that was closing nearer. Kian'Huard ventured to look up and saw a churning ball of violet fire slowly descend toward him. The beast stalked, restlessly circling in anticipation. Kian'Huard was aware also of the other entity that was being drawn closer. From that entity he sensed an all-consuming power but, under that, he felt pain and remorse. Kian-Huard divided his attention between the violet fire and the creatures that stalked him. He knew he was powerless to stop the progression of what he had started, but as the inevitable became more imminent, panic seized him. A new mantra flowed through the chamber. It resonated off the polished floor and reverberated through the frigid air. It came in a deep, low pitch that caused everything to resonate to that one frequency.

Hum … sa … so … aum …. Hum … sa … so …. aum … hum … sa … so … aum

It filled his mind, and he felt his body begin to vibrate to the frequency of the sounds. The violet fire drew nearer and as it closed the distance, the frequency of the mantra increased. Like tuning an instrument, as the fire descended, the pitch of the voices increased. Kian-Huard lay motionless while his body was further "tuned" to the frequency needed to accommodate the seventh of the Sem Lukos Resh. As the vibratory field was raised, he felt the newly opened power centres in his body become more active until they reached a fevered pitch. He felt separate and as one at the same time.

He watched, as though from a distance, within a dream, as the fire closed the distance and the beast, with its enslaved Sohar Ka'Desh spirit, pressed against the boundary between light and dark. The cylinder of light that imprisoned Kian-Huard had completely filled with brilliant violet. The ball of violet fire rested just above his head. Vortices of different-coloured lights whirled and stretched out from each of the psychic centres that had been forced into an artificial awakening. The green lightning that Kian-Huard had witnessed what seemed a lifetime ago splashed onto the marble floor near the cave entrance. It arched and danced frantically toward his prison. The beast sensed its presence. It knew it had to join immediately. The ball of fire descended through Kian-Huard and exploded in a ball of pure white and violet light at the base of his spine. His body went rigid. The cords of his muscles stood out. He threw his head back and his spine arched as the vortex pushed its way upward through each of the smaller vortices, leaving behind violent churning wheels of energy and power. The beast lowered itself on its haunches ready to pounce, and it snarled and swatted the floor. Its obsidian jowls dripped with anticipation. The violet fire exploded into Kian-Huard's head, blending itself with the indigo vortex that was there at the place of awakening between his brows. Kian-Huard's eyes were wide with madness. The violet ball of fire exploded from the roof of Kian-Huard's consciousness into a vortex of purple and white light. The beast sprang, dragging with it the spirit of the Sohar Ka'Desh.

Kian-Huard's body collapsed. A shriek of frustration rocked through the chamber in an explosion of green electricity. The blackness dissipated.

Silence fell.

Dire Sem Lukos ko dire Resh ja'sadonine beriaed

The Seven Wolves of the Sun had been awakened.

CHAPTER 5

KIAN'HUARD FELT CONSCIOUSNESS SLOWLY EBB BACK and became acutely aware of a significant amount of pain that threatened to hurl him back to unconsciousness. He tried to focus on a place in his mind where he could block it out. He tried to open his eyes but vertigo forced them shut. He drew in a deep, shuddering breath. A faint sound to his right filtered into his awareness. It was his brother. He could make out the muttering whimpering sounds that his twin was making and thought Ko'Resh had gone mad. The thought did not surprise him. He felt as though he himself was very near to madness with the forced opening of his consciousness to accommodate being possessed by the powerful spirit of the Sama Lukos. He could only imagine what madness gripped his brother, who was possessed by the other six.

Kian'Huard ventured once again to open his eyes. He clenched his jaw and fought back the tide of nausea that swept over him. He swallowed hard and forced himself to focus on a point in the ceiling above him. He was vulnerable, and the fear that Ko'Resh would kill him where he lay seemed a very real threat. The vertigo began to subside as adrenaline flooded his system. Ko'Resh was moving. He sensed the movement and then he heard the unmistakable swishing of fabric. Ko'Resh grunted with the effort of forcing himself to his knees. Kian'Huard set his jaw and rolled to his stomach. He raised himself on his arms and saw the bloodied face of his brother. Ko'Resh's eyes burned with hate as he struggled to his feet. Kian'Huard understood his brother's intent. He forced back the bile that rose in his throat as he gained his feet. His breath came in ragged gasps through clenched teeth as pain and nausea and now fear consumed him. Ko'Resh had gained his feet as well. His hand thrust into his side and Kian'Huard could see that he was badly injured.

But this did not prevent Ko'Resh from lunging. The attack was clumsy, and even though Kian'Huard was badly injured too, he was able to sidestep the assault. Ko'Resh hissed and spat blood. Kian'Huard was aware of a light glowing within Ko'Resh's clothing. His breath grew deeper and more rhythmic. It took a moment, but Kian'Huard knew the beings that possessed Ko'Resh had sped the healing process and Ko'Resh grew strong before his eyes. Ko'Resh growled and lunged again at Kian'Huard. This time Kian'Huard was barely able to avoid him.

"You have taken what is MINE!" Ko'Resh screamed across the platform.

Kian'Huard knew he would not be able to avoid another attack. He desperately looked around him for some means of getting off the platform. The distant ledge was several measures away and there was no way he could jump that distance. He backed to the edge of the platform. He ventured a sideways glance at the endless vastness of the depths below. He could not let Ko'Resh gain the power of the Sama Lukos. He took another step back. Ko'Resh advanced, his face was a twisted knot of greed and hate, so much that he was barely recognizable to his brother. Kian'Huard backed even nearer the edge. His heels no longer rested on solid ground. He felt his body sway with another onslaught of nausea. He nearly lost his balance. He quickly regained his centre of gravity. He did not know why he hesitated. Ko'Resh was but two measures away. The air grew thick between them. Ko'Resh sprang at him. Kian'Huard, in an instant of illumination, understood what he saw. He reached out and grabbed at the air, at the same time stepped backward off the precipice. A blinding flash of light sent Ko'Resh into an enraged frenzy.

Ko'Resh shrieked. He rushed to the edge of the platform and screamed out an inhuman howl at losing his quarry.

Kian'Huard clutched the two-dimensional shard, his thoughts consumed with escaping his brother. The device obeyed. It gathered unto itself to form a tetrahedron. It then gathered more unto itself until it formed an octahedron and encompassed Kian'Huard within it. This glowed softly with all the colours of the spectrum and began to slowly rotate. Inside the device, Kian'Huard had no sense of movement as it began to increase speed until the coloured lights became a soft white glow. The device spun faster. As it sped up, the light it emitted brightened to an unbearable intensity then a burst of blinding silver-white light imploded into a deep consuming blackness and disappeared.

Instantly, Kian'Huard was deposited outside of the mountain. He landed hard and was thrown onto his knees from the inertia and rolled several times before stopping. The impact drove his breath from him. Eventually he was able to sit up then bring himself to his feet. To his amazement, he found himself only a few measures from where they had left their horses near the mouth of the cave. A cold chill swept over him when he looked to the mountain in search if the entrance and it was no longer there.

A whinny from the horses drew his attention and he made his way to them. They grew skittish and shied away from him. He approached slowly, speaking in soft tones until he was able to take hold of his mount's reins. He gathered the reigns to Ko'Resh's mount as well. The beast bucked and pulled against the reigns but Kian'Huard held fast while he mounted his own beast with a glance over his shoulder to see if Ko'Resh pursued. He turned toward the city and urged the creatures into a full gallop.

Resh was mid-sky, though Kian'Huard did not know how many days had passed since they entered the caves. He was grossly aware of his own stench and ventured to seek out a stream. He did not stray too far from the road when he happened upon a pool that was fed by a small brook. He dismounted and led the beasts to the water. He allowed them a long drink then tied them out of sight of the road.

He stripped himself of his bloodied and filthy clothing and dove beneath the frigid water. He held himself under the surface as long as possible, emerging only when his lungs felt as though they would burst. He inhaled deeply. The icy water brought clarity back to his mind and cleansed his body. He examined himself and found no visible trace of the horror he had been through. He was wondering if he had imagined it when an explosion of violet fire seared through his mind.

He scrambled toward the shore and crawled up onto the grassy bank. He pressed his fists into his head to ward off the pain and terror that threatened to overwhelm him. He felt a surge of power charge his blood. In that moment he knew, whatever he desired, he could have. He would no longer fall victim to illness or injury; the power of the Sama Lukos would instantly heal his body, he was immortal and powerful. A dark smile crossed his mouth.

He toyed with the idea of harnessing the power of what possessed him. Within the deep reaches of his mind he found the strength to resist what was being offered. He struggled against the power of the Sama Lukos as it tried to force its will onto him. The beast was not easily subdued, but eventually Kian'Huard was able to regain control over his thoughts. He lay prone and naked on the grass while he brought his mind back into focus. Gradually his breathing slowed to a more natural rhythm and his thoughts were again his own.

He rested there for almost two full paces of the resh then rose. He gathered his clothing and washed the filth from them in the pond. The water ran red with his stale blood. Though many stains remained he was able to cleanse the stench from them enough to venture to wear them again. He donned the wet clothing and went to the horses. He checked their hooves for damage after the hard ride and was relieved to find none. He led them again to the water to drink and this time they pulled back. They stomped and snorted as they backed away.

Ko'Resh's mount reared and Kian'Huard lost his grip on the reins. The beast reared again then bolted from the pond. Kian'Huard was barely able to bring his own mount back under control. He led the frightened creature away from the pond and eventually the beast settled. Kian'Huard stroked the horse and spoke softly. When he had calmed the animal, he tied it to a stump and returned to the pond. The water had turned black.

Kian'Huard backed away. A small rodent scurried to the water's edge and drank. Kian'Huard watched it leave the pond and saw it drop onto its belly and writhe in agony. The creature let out a shriek that should not have been possible. It continued to writhe and tear at itself until it was no more than exposed bone and gut. Then it quivered and died. Whatever evil he brought out of the mountain had entered the water when he bathed.

Kian'Huard fell to his knees and retched. His body trembled as he gathered his wits. He forced his legs to support him and ran, stumbling, back to his mount. He could barely steady his hands enough to grab the reigns and climb onto his horse. He tightened his grip on the familiar worn leather and lashed the horse into a full gallop. Tears stung his face as he tried to fathom what they had brought into the world. One thought burned over and over in his mind. He did not want this and was trying to bury that which had possessed him but still, he had caused death. He reined the horse to stop. He was trembling uncontrollably as he slid down to the ground and onto his knees.

He felt as though he had been punched in the gut as realization of what was trapped in that mountain struck him. He struggled to catch his breath and pressed his hands to his eyes while he begged Selam for guidance.

Glimpses of memories of his training in the art of Tae'Heb began to filter into his mind. At first, he didn't understand the significance of the memories and tried to push them aside to clear his mind. But the memories persisted and for a moment he was transported back in time to one of his, and Ko'Resh's, earlier lessons. He found himself looking up at Kri'Attole while he explained to them the principles of an ancient art that, when put into full practice, was a formidable fighting technique. It was designed to tap into the inherent power of the human body and connect it with source energy, or the energy of the creator of their world, Selam. Each level of Tae'Heb was designed to bring alignment with specific energy centers of the body through meditation, vocalizations and exercise. As one progressed through each level, the body would be further tuned to a higher resonant frequency with the ultimate goal of becoming one with the creator. He could vividly recall Ko'Resh's impatience during the lessons. Ko'Resh could not understand the importance of learning about something that no one could ever achieve. Or, if someone did achieve the ability to shape shift or change the weather they would be wise enough not to do it because it would disturb the delicate balance of the world. Kian'Huard Shook his head. He tried to clear his mind but the memories continued. Then he understood the importance of recalling the teachings.

There were seven main power centers within the body, each tuned to a frequency that supported specific functions of the body and psyche. They were known by many names, but the most common in the ancient texts of Rhuna were amladhar, sadishtana, marethna, aneithnat, yanatramda, anya, and sama.

Amladhar was the base or root vortex. It supported self-preservation, personal survival and one's identification with the physical realm. The first of the seven lukos spirits amplified these traits beyond what the physical body could do, even with decades of training. Uninitiated, and without the wisdom of training and focus, this lukos spirit, bound with the higher light being that was the Sohar Ka'Desh, would give one superhuman strength and the ability to alter perceptions in the physical realm and project these perceptions on others. It would also give the ability to control such things as weather and other forces of nature. Kian'Huard shuddered to think one as undisciplined as Ko'Resh could have gained access to such power – and that was just the Amladhar Lukos. Ko'Resh possessed six of the seven.

The second of these energy vortices, Sadishtana, was situated in the naval/sacral area. It controlled sexuality, ability to form relationships, creativity and control. A forced awakening by the power of the second lukos spirit bound with the pure energy of the Sohar Ka'Desh brought about a heightened ability to manipulate anyone. It altered sexual energy to a near-predator state, creating all-consuming desire which could be transferred to non-physical energies to draw to the possessed what was needed to create anything. It altered reproductive DNA to an enhanced state thus ensuring a possible vessel for the beasts should one be needed.

Kian'Huard felt a wave of nausea wash over him at the implications. If Ko'Resh tried to use this energy, knowing how physically driven Ko'Resh already was and giving in to his base impulses, he would become a fearsome predator – perhaps even have the ability to shape shift.

Kian'Huard stood. His legs were weak and he leaned against his horse for support and took a few deep breaths. Another onslaught of memories stuck and his mind moved through the past to recall what the third of the Sem Lukos Resh, Marethna, would be capable of. This energy vortex spun at the level of the solar plexus. It was one of the more powerful energies. At the frequency of a normal physical being, it had the power to connect the physical realm with the energy of higher realms. The energy gave means to express personal power. It brought balance between the three vortices below and the three above. In the enhanced form, brought on by the power of the Sem Lukos, the Marethna vortex would allow the possessed to elicit a persona of extraordinary personal power by drawing energies from beyond the physical to manipulate as a powerful burst of destructive energy or to cause objects, or one's self, to defy the laws of gravity.

Kian'Huard straightened and started pacing the clearing. With the realization of how much power each of the Sem Lukos, individually, was capable of, Kian'Huard grew more disturbed. If two or more were to work in tandem there would be no stopping Ko'Resh. He cursed under his breath and dropped to his knees as more knowledge of the seven was forced into his mind in another explosion of images. Then a new understanding was revealed - the Sem Lukos Resh, once awakened, were an entity unto themselves and could work independently of the host's conscious mind to follow their own agenda.

Kian'Huard did not have time to fully consider what this meant when a green burst of light brought Aneithnat, the fourth vortex, positioned at the heart, to the forefront of his mind. This power center enabled one to see the infinite possibilities of both physical and non-physical realms. It was the integration point for the seven vortices of the body because it held the sacred spark of source energy or soul. It connected with the non-physical energies and acted as a conduit for outflow of desire to be made manifest. Enhanced, it gave the power to manipulate future and past events.

Kian'Huard pressed his hands to his head as images of the fifth vortex, located at the throat, threatened to overwhelm him. Influencing choice and willpower, the Yanatramda Lukos, combined with the Sohar Ka'Desh's pure energy, now controlled Ko'Resh though vibration and tone; they would be able to bend him to their will. They would enable him to summon the power of the others to their bidding. Ko'Resh was no more than a puppet, but Kian'Huard knew his twin was under the illusion he was in control.

The sixth lukos, Anya, located between the brows, controlled intuition and enhanced precognitive abilities. If not properly tuned, could cause Ko'Resh to become delusional and act out his delusions using the power of the seven.

Kian'Huard had taken their Tae'Heb training seriously and had some control, and much more discipline than his twin; and he feared what he could do if he summoned the Sama Lukos. He recalled what he knew of the seventh, the Sama, which was located at the top of the head. This energy vortex spun very rapidly. Under natural conditions it acted as a conduit, channelling the source energy down through the other energy centers to the root. It was designed to maintain a connection to source and to inspire a loving and harmonious existence while living in the physical world. His connection to the Sama Lukos and its Sohar Ka'Desh brought understanding and, perhaps, a bit of hope. The Sama Lukos was a necessary key to maintaining balance and alignment between the host and the other six of the Sem Lukos. Without its influence, Ko'Resh would have great difficulty harnessing their power with a coordinated effort. Kian'Huard hoped they would be in constant competition for dominance without the Sama Lukos to bring them to true alignment.

Still, he feared, despite possessing the Sama Lukos himself, it may not be enough to counter even a disorganized onslaught from the other six. He also understood he did not want what possessed him—Ko'Resh did. Ko'Resh planned to use the power.

Kian'Huard stood and clenched his fists, focused his attention and cleared his mind. He strode across the clearing toward his horse. He had one resolve. He had to stop Ko'Resh.

Kian'Huard reined his mount to stop when the city came into view. The day was hot and sweat beaded his brow. His clothing had dried quickly and the leather of his tunic, which was usually buttery soft, had become stiff. He studied the road ahead and behind for any trace of Ko'Resh. He saw nothing that would indicate Ko'Resh had passed this way. He then turned his attention to the city. Everything was quiet on the main road and the farms that dotted the surrounding land were bustling with activity. Kian'Huard's heart skipped a beat. The farmers were harvesting!

Kian'Huard was certain that at the most only a day or two had passed since they entered the caverns. It was mid-spring then. If the farmers were harvesting, then at least four full cycles of rhuna had passed! He slid from his mount and guided the beast off the main road. He found a rocky prominence and climbed it to get a better view of the city and try to determine how long they had been gone. It didn't make sense. Why would the horses still be tethered outside the cave? Why had no one found them and taken them back to the stables? And how could the beasts be well? There was not enough fodder on that hillside to feed them for more than a day or two. He scanned the city. The gate was heavily guarded. Kian'Huard wondered about that; usually only two of the sharram's guard kept watch. He counted six. He studied the outlying buildings and noticed others of the sharram's own guard posted around the city's perimeter. Very few people could be seen.

From his vantage point he could make out the market square. Usually the markets were brimming with life and colorful clothing but Kian'Huard could see they were nearly empty. There were few vendors and even fewer people walking among the booths. Those he did see hurried to gather purchases then wasted no time in leaving the area and shutting themselves in their houses. Small battalions marched through the cobbled streets dressed in full combat regalia. The city had the appearance of being under martial law. He scanned the city to try to figure why there was such a high level of alarm. He looked toward the state house. It rose like a fortress above the smaller dwellings of the village. The only other building that rivalled it in stature was the ominous Temple of Osiris, which was carved into the side of the mountain.

Separating the two buildings was a vast square that housed gardens where one could find the most exotic of plants and flowers. Huge dome-shaped structures made of clear blown silica panels sheltered the more fragile of the plants from the harsh cold season. This square and the market plaza were the focal point of the city. But now even the groundskeepers who were always present in the garden square had abandoned their stations. A horn sounded from within the state house walls, drawing Kian'Huard's attention. It played a long sorrowful note then paused, followed by two more blasts, and it took a moment for Kian'Huard to recognize it was the death wail of Rhue. The low, sad tone reverberated through the city walls, calling the people from the safety of their homes to the streets to pay homage to whomever it was that had passed in the royal house. His thoughts immediately went to his father Sharram Kar'Set. It was then he noticed the banners rolling in the breeze atop the towers and as he looked more closely at the details that had escaped him earlier, he saw that all the buildings displayed the black and green pattern of death and life intertwined in an overlapping knot that had no beginning or end.

They were never close; his father had distanced himself from his sons since their birth. He blamed the innocents for the death of their mother and could never find a way around that pain in his heart. But when the sorrowful sounds of the mourning song of Sharram Kar'Set reached Kian'Huard's ears he wept at his loss, for after death there was no way to mend that which was broken when he first drew breath in this world.

He leaned against a rock, pulled his knees to his chest and buried his head in his arms. The stress of what he had endured beneath the mountain and returning to find the city in mourning broke him. He let the tide of emotion take him and mourned the loss of his father.

He did not hear the approaching footfalls and was caught off guard when the unmistakable cold metal of a blade touched his neck.

"Rise and be known." The voice was coarse and authoritative but held a ring of familiarity. The words were punctuated with a slight nudge of the blade.

Kian'Huard raised his head toward the guard.

"Selam!" The guard stepped back as though he had seen a ghost. He kissed the back of his right hand and touched it to his forehead—a gesture made to ward off evil and invoke protection from Selam. "It cannot be!" The surprise and fear in his voice was a stark contrast to his burly appearance.

Kian'Huard knew this man. He rose to his feet and addressed him by name. "Kri'Attole!"

The guardsman had already regained his composure and bowed before Shista Kian'Huard. "Forgive me, Naid Shista, for the city is in mourning." He rose and studied Kian'Huard intently as though he expected some form of trickery. The suspicion in his heart was openly apparent.

Kian'Huard lowered his head. "It seems that my father has passed from this life."

Kri'Attole hesitated. "It is not your father's passing we mourn … It is you and your brother's."

When Kian'Huard did not respond, Kri'Attole continued. "After you disappeared, we searched everywhere for one full turning. Eventually your father was convinced by the elders that it was time to end the search and declare his sons dead. That was early in the turning when the cold was leaving the lands. It was still another three full cycles of Rhuna before he finally gave up. It was only last rise that he called for the horns and raised the Banners of Passing."

"Kri'Attole, listen to my words. For me, the passage of time has been different. We have been gone only days. Some dark solveige is at work here!" Kian'Huard felt a shiver pass through him. He wondered at that which possessed him and how or when it would awaken and take control of his mind. For he was certain that was the eventual end. He wondered what suffering he would impart when the time of awakening came.

Kri'Attole sensed the turmoil within Kian'Huard. He slapped him on the back. "Let us return to the castle and bring these glad tidings to your father." He turned toward the road then stopped and faced Shista Kian'Huard. "And what of your brother, Shista Ko'Resh, what fate has befallen him?" His face took on a serious note.

"I am uncertain of my brother's fate. We were separated some time ago and I have not been able to find him." It was not entirely a lie. He knew that Ko'Resh was essentially lost to them. Still, he avoided making eye contact with Kri'Attole, for he had known Kian'Huard since birth and was his confidant and teacher, picking up where his father severely lacked. It was he that Kian'Huard always would turn to when he needed to discreetly deal with Ko'Resh's indiscretions. He worried that Kri'Attole would sense the lie and Kian'Huard was not ready to speak of what had happened in the caverns. He was still uncertain himself.

Kri'Attole did sense reluctance but surmised it to be unexpressed grief or shock from whatever it was that happened these past seasons. He did not press further. He knew that Kian'Huard would come to him when the time was right and they would deal with whatever demons he was fighting together. His mind remained troubled, however, at Kian'Huard's insistence that mere days had passed since they left the city. He hoped that information would not come to be common knowledge.

They set out toward the road and met with the three other guards who were assigned with Kri'Attole. Their reaction at seeing Kian'Huard was much less restrained than Kri'Attole's. They made no effort to hide the reflex gestures to invoke protection from their god, Selam. Though they were trained at battle and were the fiercest warriors of Rhuna, these people were highly superstitious and no amount of training could dispel those beliefs. For certain, in their eyes, they saw a ghost.

"Enough! You behave like women!" Kri'Attole growled.

"But he was lost!" one of the group spoke out, but he quickly regretted his outburst.

"Obviously there was a mistake, for here he stands before you. Flesh and blood. Alive and well." He gestured to Kian'Huard to come forward and took him by the shoulder, giving it a shake. "See? He is as real as you and I and is still shista, heir to the Kingdom of Rhuna! Show your respect!"

With that, the men bowed low to their young shista. Kri'Attole grunted with satisfaction and mounted his ride. Kian'Huard and the others followed suit.

"There will be feasting in the city tonight!" Kri'Attole said as he reined his horse to the city. The beast reared up onto its hind legs, neighed and pawed at the air. Kri'Attole laughed a deep hearty laugh, "You see, Shista Kian'Huard! Even my horse wishes to celebrate your return from the dead!" He spurred the horse into a full gallop, leaving the others to do the same.

50

Kian'Huard found himself caught up in his mentor's enthusiasm and raced after Kri'Attole. The wind in his face felt good. He felt alive. He was acutely aware of the beast beneath him and the rhythm of its hooves striking the ground. His body swayed with each galloping stride, muscles flexing and stretching in tune with his mount. His breathing matched that of the beast. He let out a whoop and urged more speed from the horse. The creature leapt into a full-out gallop and closed the distance that Kri'Attole had gained. Soon they were alongside each other and the familiar competitive spirit that Kian'Huard and he shared flared, and they raced toward the city.

"You have grown slow in my absence!" Kian'Huard shouted. He spurred the beast again and pushed past Kri'Attole. A genuine smile erupted on his face when he looked over his shoulder at his friend.

They did not slow even as they approached the city gate. What few pedestrians were there scrambled from their path as the pair tore recklessly through the narrow streets. The guards that were posted at the gate had no recourse but to move hastily aside when Kian'Huard and Kri'Attole thundered past.

Even in his disheveled state, his people had recognized their shista and word had spread like wildfire through the inner city until it reached the ears of his father, even before they had come to a halt before the castle entrance.

Sharram Kar'Set stood just where the great oaken doors were flung open. He watched, expressionless, as the pair strode across the great hall to bow before him. "Arrest them."

Kian'Huard looked into his father's face as the guards pulled him to his feet. He tried to pull free but was not able. Kri'Attole was also abruptly dragged to his feet by two more guards.

"Father, do you not know your own son?"

"My sons are dead, just as their mother is dead." Sharram Kar'Set's words were ice.

"I am Kian'Huard! I live! Can you not see with your eyes that I stand before you?"

"I see you would want me to believe my son lives, but my eyes will not be fooled but such solveige!" The ice in the sharram's voice turned venomous.

"Your eyes do not deceive you, Father. I do live. If you would but trust he who stands before you and grant me a chance to tell you of what has befallen your sons these past months!"

"My Sharram..." Kri'Attole tried again to shake himself free. "Have I not been your loyal servant? Have I not known your sons since the day they first drew breath in this world? Do you not think that I would know them as my own and be able to see treachery with my own eyes?" He had raised his voice more than he had intended to his sharram.

"Perhaps you are blinded by what you want to be true?" Sharram Kar'Set made a dismissive motion and the guards started to marshal them toward the exit.

"No! Wait!" Kian'Huard shouted as he tried to break free from his captors. He was able to grab a dagger and slashed across one of the guards' arms. The man let go of Kian'Huard to stem the flow of blood from his arm. Kian'Huard followed through on the slashing motion to bring the blade downward and imbedded it into the thigh of his other captor. Kri'Attole followed his lead and was able to break free one arm and retrieve a short sword from the guard on his left and brought the hilt down on the face of the other, rendering him unconscious. Thus armed, the duo fought back the remaining three guards. The skirmish ended quickly. The sound of more guards about to storm the great hall could be heard through the doors. Orders were being shouted as an alarm was raised. Kian'Huard turned to face his father to try to convince him that he had indeed survived.

He stared deep into his father's eyes. He took a step back. Too late, Kian'Huard was drawn deep into the dark-green eyes shadowed with evil. The deception that was his father wavered like heat waves rising from the cobbled streets. His father's face became twisted and distorted. The trim grey/red beard faded. The neatly braided hair shrank back into filth and disarray. The green silk robes faded to tan leather and then Ko'Resh stood before him, his face twisted in mockery. Before Kian'Huard could have Kri'Attole witness his brother's deception, Ko'Resh again took on the form of their father.

"Kri'Attole! That is not my father!" Kian'Huard shouted. "It is Ko'Resh! He is using powerful solveige to deceive our eyes!"

The doors burst open and guards stormed toward them. The pair readied their weapons. Kian'Huard watched as the men approached. With Kri'Attole at his side he knew that many of these men would die. He knew he and his companion would eventually be taken captive. He frantically tried to think of some other means of escape. A vaguely familiar feeling began to rise within him. Terror struck his heart as he understood what was awakening within his mind. He shook his head to clear his thoughts and force the beast back to the depths of his subconscious. But he was not yet strong enough or able to control the power that was trying to manifest, and the beast forced its way to the forefront. His mind contained one thought—escape. He watched, as though from a distance, the guards scrambling to take up position within the hall. He watched their movements slow until they stopped. Many frozen in place mid-stride, faces contorted with the exertion of entering into combat.

Kian'Huard spun on his heels, surveying the chamber of human statues. Movement caught his eye. He turned to face Ko'Resh. There was no mistaking the hate in his eyes. Their minds touched, connected as brothers and twins but more, as that which possessed their souls and was divided between them yearned for release and to be reunited. A swirl of mist formed at their feet and shrouded them from the room. They threw their heads back, each letting out a fierce howl. Their bodies became rigid as the power they wielded pushed its way up through their bodies and exploded through them in a shower of bright light and sounds. The drone of the mantra that imprisoned them in the chamber drummed in their ears once again, forcing their bodies into a higher vibrational frequency to allow the power of the beasts to manifest. Ko'Resh grinned through clenched teeth at the adrenaline rush. Kian'Huard struggled in vain to fight against the emergence of the Sem Lukos Resh. He focused his mind on one single thought: he envisioned the power as the great beast that it once was and lay it down in his mind as though to slumber. His breath came in ragged gasps as he fought to regain control of his mind and body. Gradually he could sense the beast losing ground. He felt the fire within his body relax.

Ko'Resh laughed and made a grand, sweeping gesture with his hand. Kian'Huard was thrown through the air and slammed into a distant wall. His body fell to the floor in a heap. He tried to push himself up onto his hands and knees. Ko'Resh made another gesture with his hand and Kian'Huard was spun over onto his back. His breath was forced from him as though a great weight pressed down on his chest. His eyes bulged and blood oozed from his ears and nose. With a sense of utter helplessness, he allowed the re-emergence of the beast that was within. He understood all too clearly that he had to fight Ko'Resh with all the power he possessed or else Ko'Resh would kill him and take the seventh power unto himself.

The beast was easily summoned. Kian'Huard felt the surge of base human instincts and emotions flood through him. He felt the power rise from deep within to surface in his mind in an explosion of white and violet light. His body glowed with the energy that poured through him. He sprang to his feet and faced his brother. He needed only to think of Ko'Resh being thrown across the room before he saw his twin hurling through the air to slam against one of the marble pillars. Ko'Resh hit the floor hard, gathered himself onto his hands and feet like some primitive beast and launched himself at Kian'Huard. Something was changing. As Ko'Resh bounded across the floor he moved as the lukos. His body lengthened and his shoulders narrowed and hunched inward. His face grew long and wide and blood dripped from his mouth as canine teeth forced through his gums. He lunged at Kian'Huard, and the force of the impact threw them both to the floor.

Terror caused a rush of adrenaline to flood Kian'Huard's body. His breath grew quick and deep. His mouth went dry and his heart thumped hard against his chest. Pain started to build beneath his skin. His muscles spasmed hard and he felt a ball of fire explode at the base of his spine and travel upward. As it moved through him he convulsed as each of his power centres were forced open to receive something he did not desire. He cried out in anguish when he realized that he too was changing. He tried to focus his mind to stop the process. Blood trickled from his nose and ears. He clenched his jaw tight as though the act would prevent the teeth he could feel forming beneath his gums from erupting. He tossed his head from side to side, focusing his will upon his body. Strangled cries escaped through bloodied lips. His own teeth fell from his mouth as the bestial canines forced their way to the surface, gleaming long and bloody in the ethereal haze.

Kian'Huard's mind came into sharp focus. He suddenly knew that what he saw was not real. Time stood still as he surveyed his surroundings. Those who were present in the great hall were as statues of living flesh, and some, such as the guards that were summoned, were frozen mid-stride when they stormed in to defend their sharram. The swirling mist that ebbed through the chamber clung to those within, encircling them in a paralyzing fog. Then his gaze fell on his brother. Ko'Resh, the only other who was not affected by the mystical bondage, was rapidly closing the distance between them. His eyes held more hate than Kian'Huard thought could be possible. He knew one thought consumed his brother's mind – to gain control of the Sama Lukos that Kian'Huard possessed. Only then would Ko'Resh be able to summon unto him the absolute power of the Sem Lukos Resh. Kian'Huard forced his mind to dismiss the illusion of the fearsome lukos that shrouded Ko'Resh and the image dissipated, leaving only his brother charging toward him, sword at the ready. He knew he had to act quickly.

Ko'Resh seemed bent on killing his twin brother; he struck swift and hard, slashing at Kian'Huard with his short blade. Kian'Huard jumped back and drew his blade, and in one motion blocked Ko'Resh's advance. Ko'Resh let out a harsh growl. He clenched his teeth and swung again at his brother. Kian'Huard blocked this and found himself launching his own attack. Part of his mind was acting in self-defense, but something insidious was taking over and an undeniable desire to slay his sibling was gaining a strong hold. He attacked vigorously and his brother responded in kind. The sharp clang of steel on steel rang through the great hall as the brothers lunged and parried. They advanced on each other and retreated through the maze of human statues. Ko'Resh slashed violently at Kian'Huard and his swing missed his brother and sliced through one of the guards who happened to be trapped in time beside him. The twins stopped and stared. Kian'Huard watched with mixed apprehension and abhorrence as the man's head teetered forward then stopped, suspended by the mist that entrapped him. A fountain of red erupted from the gaping wound then it too came to a halt when it contacted the imprisoning fog. An amused smirk twisted the corner of Ko'Resh's mouth at the sight of the slain guard and at Kian'Huard's reaction to it. Kian'Huard was backed into a corner. His breath was quick and hard. Ko'Resh did not appear to be winded. It seemed he drew strength from that which he possessed and it flowed through him in an endless stream of power.

≫ ≫ ≫

Ko'Resh advanced on his brother. Thoughts flooded his mind as the creatures that stirred within him added their wisdom and experiences to his. At first, they came in a trickle of images and ideas, but as he relinquished his control to the power of the six, the thoughts and images swept through him in an overwhelming tide that drowned him. His vision blurred as he continued his advance on Kian'Huard. He shook his head to try to focus. Fear filled his mind. All six of the spirits he possessed were vying for control. They were affecting his own ability to control his body and his step faltered. His arms were no longer his own and he watched in horror as his blade slid from unresponsive fingers and fell to the floor. His knees buckled. He tried to push himself up onto his knees but his arms failed him. He managed to roll himself onto his back. His breath became labored. The beasts continued their fight for dominance, oblivious to the effect they were having on their host. His eyes were wild and terrified when he looked up at Kian'Huard.

"Help me!" The words were a mere whisper, breathed out by the young man that was Ko'Resh before he was possessed.

>> >> >>

Kian'Huard stood over his brother and stared into his dying eyes. He held his blade at the ready, unsure of what to expect. He was certain of some form of trickery.

Ko'Resh's eyes dimmed. His body seemed to shrink. Kian'Huard lowered his blade. A final rasping rattle escaped Ko'Resh. Kian'Huard dropped his blade and fell to his knees beside his brother.

How much time passed while he knelt beside his brother he did not know. He was swallowed up by grief and fear. A movement of shadow and light caught his eye. He looked to his brother's fallen body. The mist that entombed the others in the room was moving, swirling faster among the people and drawing itself together to form a shroud around Ko'Resh. Those who were freed of the mist fell to the floor in crumpled heaps, seemingly alive but unconscious.

The mist continued to gather over Ko'Resh. It wrapped itself around him, lifting him to float a few measures above the floor. Kian'Huard fell back and pressed himself against the wall. The mist divided itself into six. A faint glow started to form at Ko'Resh's head. The glow brightened and formed into a pulsating ball. It continued to compress into itself, growing brighter as it shrank in size until the light was a blinding yellow white that looked like a miniature sun. Kian'Huard was forced to shield his eyes against the blinding orb, but he still saw it take up position at the top of Ko'Resh's head. A loud crack snapped the air as the orb plunged into the top of Ko'Resh's head. The room went dark for a moment then brightened and Kian'Huard could see the ball of fire as it passed down through Ko'Resh's body then settle briefly at the base of his spine. Then quickly it retraced its path back upward, leaving a trail of mini explosions as each of the power centres that were occupied by the six spirits ignited and sprung to life. When the fire again reached the top of his head, Ko'Resh's body shuddered and he drew in a sharp breath. His eyes snapped open and still contained that same wild look of fear. His breaths were deep and erratic. He rolled to his belly and clawed at the floor, trying to crawl closer to Kian'Huard. The fear had been replaced with hatred. Kian'Huard struggled to his feet and pressed himself against the wall. He side-stepped, trying to distance himself from Ko'Resh. He did not turn his back on his brother as he made his way along the wall toward the exit.

>> >> >>

Blind hatred fueled Ko'Resh as he struggled toward his brother. He forced his body to respond to his mind's demands as though it were a hostage to be tortured into compliance. His movements were jerking and uncoordinated as he pulled himself to his feet and took a few staggering steps toward Kian'Huard. His physical body screamed in pain as muscles received mixed signals from different consciousness all vying for control over the frail flesh form. His head twitched and his eyes rolled as he tried to focus the physical optical receptors at his prey and make sense of the imagery that was bombarding the overtaxed brain. Then his jaw went slack. His fingers went dusky and his lips cyanotic. In trying to gain control of the physical, the spirits interrupted the autonomic systems and the feedback loop that would have caused the diaphragm to contract and draw air into the lungs was broken. Ko'Resh's body teetered and a puzzled look sprung to his face. All at once his body shuddered and drew in a loud, sharp, gasping breath. He staggered forward a few more steps and sputtered in another gulp of air. He blew to force air out of his lungs. Again, his body lurched forward as the beasts began to assimilate better control over the musculature. He drew in another deep breath, this one more controlled. Another step toward his prey; another deliberate breath.

≫ ≫ ≫

Kian'Huard started to move away from where he was rooted as he saw that with each step forward the beasts gained better control over his brother's body and the movements became more deliberate and better orchestrated with the body systems.

Around him were the beginnings of movement throughout the great hall as those who were bound outside of time were released. He saw their movements start slowly then speed up as they were reintroduced to the normal flow of time. The guardsman who fell victim to Ko'Resh's blade slumped slowly then crumpled to the floor. A moment later his head was released to time and fell beside him. A nearby woman screamed and ran to the man. She cradled his body to her breast and gathered his head. "No … Selam … Nooo!" Her words forced their way through grief-laden sobs. She ignored the blood that now covered her and stroked her husband's hair away from his face. She prayed franticly to Selam to restore her husband to her and held his head in place as though it would somehow reattach itself. Another woman came to her and tried to pull her away from the body. There was a brief struggle then the bloodied and weary woman was detached from her dead husband and led from the chamber.

This distraction took only a few moments, but it was enough time for Ko'Resh to sufficiently close the distance between himself and Kian'Huard and launch an attack. Kian'Huard caught the movement just in time to block a savage blow then another.

Ko'Resh advanced, swinging his sword wildly, and Kian'Huard had no recourse but to maintain a purely defensive stance. He was being forced back toward a narrow opening that would prove fatal if he were to be corralled there. Ko'Resh lunged and overstepped himself. That gave Kian'Huard a split second to sidestep from his fragile defensive position to one that would allow some offensive maneuvers as well. The tide of the fight had turned and the twins fought on more equal footing. This somehow amplified the intensity of the duel and the pace quickened. Swords flashed in shafts of light that shone down through the roof, arcing explosions of electric rainbows ringing with death lust. Sparks flew from steel on steel as they parried each slash. They had always been well matched when sparring and this day seemed no different except that Ko'Resh had already died once. And that which awoke with his first breath of second life was entwining itself around his will, sharpening his vision, heightening his already deadly reflexes and fortifying his endurance. Power was growing inside him. He held firm his jaw and focused his attention on the man before him who he no longer recognized as brother. That which fed him denied him the ability to think freely. It was driven by a single purpose—to reunite all of what it was even to the death of one who became an unwitting vessel dividing their power.

Ko'Resh fought with renewed savagery and again Kian'Huard found himself struggling to maintain an effective defense. And he was growing tired. Ko'Resh seemed to sense this and intensified his attack. Kian'Huard summoned all his will forth and focused what strength he had left on deflecting the onslaught of razor-sharp steel. He felt warmth descending through him. He felt himself grow distant from what he perceived as his body. He was vaguely aware of his movements as he continued his battle against Ko'Resh. He panicked and fought that which guided his hand. He faltered in his parry and Ko'Resh carved a long line into his right arm. The force within his mind exploded through him and assumed complete control. Though he was aware of his movements and felt the bone-jarring clashing of blades, he had no power to control the battle for his life, and with renewed energy flowing through him he advanced his attack and again the battle was on even ground.

The twins fought endlessly as mere puppets to the forces they had awakened. Their bodies were fueled with the lust and hatred of thousands of years pent up within the entities they had unleashed. The great hall was suspended between time and space when the full power of the Sem Lukos Resh spewed forth. Though divided, the effect on the world surrounding the bearers was no less dramatic. It was as though the hall was torn from the very foundations and flung deep into space. None who ventured to enter the hall from within the castle were able to penetrate the barrier that engulfed it. Those who tried to force the heavy wooden doors were thrown with such ferocity their bones shattered. Within the chamber, time hurried and ages passed then cycled back upon themselves. At whatever time the battle ended, so then would the victor find themselves, be it centuries in the past or some unseen future.

They were aware, Kian'Huard and Ko'Resh, of the changing of the world beyond the boundaries of their stadium. Though they had no time to lend focus to what was taking place beyond the clashing of swords, they were aware of brief glimpses of seasons superimposed over a sea of churning stars.

"ENOUGH!"

The deep voice resonated from nowhere and everywhere; it surged through their bodies in a penetrating wave of irrefutable power.

The twins were thrown apart

Kian'Huard landed hard and struggled to catch his breath. He saw no trace of Ko'Resh. Vacuous silence filled the great hall. Kian'Huard raised himself from where he lay, lifting his head. His arms trembled with the effort as he struggled to his knees. He was soaked with sweat and his body felt drained. He focused on his breathing. He was vaguely aware of voices and the clamor of people running and the scrape of a sword being drawn. There was a ringing in his ears that was gradually clearing to be replaced by pounding. He was aware that the pounding was not in his head but upon the great wooden doors. The shouts became more intense and a final thunderous hammer against the doors threw them open in a splintering crash. Guardsmen swarmed the chamber, searching every corner. Ga'Etan, Kian'Huard's domini and mentor, rushed to his aid and helped him to his feet. He studied his young charge's eyes and took a step back. He muttered a prayer under his breath and touched his forehead with his medallion.

"You must go to the temple at once, young Kian'Huard!" His voice did little to hide his fear.

Kian'Huard followed obediently, his mind clouded with remnants of the powerful spell he had been under. When his steps faltered, his guardian quickly supported him and though Kian'Huard was not certain, he thought he saw fearful reluctance in the man's eyes when his hand made contact to steady him. As soon as he felt Kian'Huard had gained his balance he let go his support and repeated the prayer for protection, again touching his medallion to his forehead.

"What of my brother?" Kian'Huard said, his voice echoed his own fear.

"I know not of your brother. Only you were in the chamber when we finally brought down the doors," Ga'Etan replied. He hesitated for a moment then continued, "You were gone for many seasons, Sire. We had lost hope of finding you. Your father…" His voice trailed.

"What of my father?" Kian'Huard stopped and turned to face the man. He saw great pain reflected in the man's eyes and felt a deep sorrow welling up within him as he feared the worse.

Ga'Etan met his gaze. He searched for the right words to tell him of his father's strange illness that came on suddenly the day the twins went missing. How it progressed quickly and deformed the great sharram until he was not recognizable then finally took his life. "He is gone," was all he could manage.

"Gone?" Kian'Huard was confused.

"He fell ill and passed from this life..." He did not finish

Kian'Huard turned on his heel with a new wave of emotion that gave him strength and headed for the king's chamber. "If my father has passed from this life how is it Ko'Resh was able to trick everyone into believing he was our father?"

"Naid Shista, it was many seasons ago your father passed to the spirit realm. He is no longer in his chambers. His body was returned to Althean and has been laid to rest beside your mother. I know you wish to go to him, but first it is imperative you go to the temple!" Domini Ga'Etan started after him.

Kian'Huard ignored him and strode down the empty corridor. He was vaguely aware of Ga'Etan rushing to catch up. His thoughts were racing. Not only could Ko'Resh assume another form, but he could also have people believe what he wished. Kian'Huard would not be able to trust what his eyes or thoughts were telling him.

The significance of the empty corridor did not dawn on him at the time. He continued in his purposeful stride for several moments before he realized he did not recognize his surroundings. He was not sure when Ga'Etan stopped following. He halted and drew his sword. The hairs on his neck bristled. The corridor remained empty. Smooth stone walls rose to a vaulted ceiling and tall stained-glass windows lined the outer wall at even intervals, reflecting the ancient architecture that his kingdom was renowned for. But there was a taint to the air that gave him pause. A feeling of expectation flooded him though he could see no signs of threat. No footfalls sounded any approaching enemy. He continued to advance more cautiously, his blade at the ready. He focused to slow his breathing and calm the pounding in his ears, keen and alert to any sound that might betray an enemy.

The silence that returned baffled him and set him on edge. He knew there was no time that the corridors were deserted in the state house, save a brief period through the night but never for more than a half phase when a guard on watch would pass through on rounds. And where did Ga'Etan disappear to? He was very headstrong and determined to have Kian'Huard go to the temple. Why would he give up the chase? Unless…

A flash of metal caught his eye just in time for him to parry the intended death blow. Behind the sword, his brother grinned and delivered another well-executed advance. Kian'Huard understood Ko'Resh fully intended to kill him to retrieve the seventh spirit. Kian'Huard was at a disadvantage—he did not wish to harm his brother if he could help it. He avoided the deadly slash of razor-sharp steel and spun on his heel and ran. It took but a moment for Ko'Resh to register that Kian'Huard had fled and he pursued. Blinding rage filled him and he screamed a blood-curdling howl that echoed for what seemed an eternity through the hollow passage.

Kian'Huard was becoming fatigued. His mind was not making sense of what he was seeing. His heart could not grasp the hatred his brother now held. He ran down the unending hall wishing that he followed Ga'Etan's command to go to the temple.

The passage spun with a sickening twist. The walls melted and swirled together then opened up. Rocks grated and reformed themselves. A large chamber appeared before Kian'Huard. He swayed as his focus adjusted to allow his mind to assimilate what his eyes were telling him. Several priests looked up at his abrupt intrusion. Some of the younger priests were unable to conceal their shock and fear and quickly muttered prayers of protection. The elders fixed their steady gaze on him. There was no mistaking the severity in their expressions.

Kian'Huard's vision blurred, and black spots appeared before his eyes then consumed his vision. The cold stone floor greeted him. Pain shot through his head.

CHAPTER 6

SORELIGE KABIT DEL'ARRAN'S HAND STOPPED MID-PEN stroke. A ripple radiated outward from deep within the heart of the mountain that housed the Temple of Osiris in the land of Rhuna. He felt the colour drain from his face and his heart pound. He laid his pen on the wooden desk beside the scroll he was working on. He knew where the twins, Shista Kian'Huard and Shista Ko'Resh, were.

As shista, heirs to the throne of the House of Rhuna, their disappearance several weeks prior had left the kingdom distraught, and, as more time passed without even a trace of the young men to be found, their father, Sharram Kar'Set, reluctantly gave up the search and the country was plunged into mourning. Sorelige Kabit Del'Arran pushed himself from the desk and exited his private library. He moved quickly through the dim corridors of the inner sanctum of the Temple of Osiris. It was one pace till reshfall, and the others of his order would be readying for evening meditations. He doubted anyone else would have taken notice of the subtle energy wave that swept through the mountain. It was extremely ancient and none lived who would have been trained to detect such energy. Except him.

As sorelige, highest authority in the Temple of Osiris, only he had knowledge of the Sem Lukos Resh. His earliest education to the position of sorelige was given deep within the temple catacombs where he learned the ancient secret Helige, magic that permeated all of Mythos, and how to control it. He learned too of solveige, or dark magic, that existed as well. Though it was not part of his education to his role of sorelige, except to know it existed, he made a point of learning all he could to control the power of the solveige. It helped to ease the burden of being segregated. Only one sorelige could be present within the temple at any time. Once the current sorelige selected his surrogate, he was taken deep within the temple to where all history was stored and the indoctrination began. The chosen would remain within the catacombs until his predecessor died and then he would be summoned to take up the position of sorelige.

The indoctrination process was grueling, and Kabit Del'Arran was not a man easily alarmed, but he knew the implications of the energy that was released. He would have to ready the others of his order if there was to be any chance of containing that which he believed had been released. If his fears were confirmed and the young shista had indeed found the chamber containing the Sem Lukos Resh, he would have to act quickly to prevent the power contained within the seven spirits from becoming fully manifest. He mumbled a quick prayer to Selam. Only destruction and terror could come from summoning the Sem Lukos Resh back to the physical realm.

Another four full cycles of their moon, rhuna, passed before the royal twins found their way back to the city of Kephas. They were locked in a battle over possession of the Sem Lukos spirits. By fate or design, the spirits were divided between the two shista, preventing full integration. This meant the seven were not able to work in synchrony, which would greatly reduce their power. This would work in Sorelige Kabit Del'Arran's favour except that they would need more of the Sacerdos'helige from the inner temple to perform the binding over two instead of one. The Sacerdos'helige were called. Everyone knew the tones to maintain the binding spell. Sorelige Kabit Del'Arran was ready.

They did not have long to wait. Shortly after their return, the shista continued their conflict into the corridors of the state house. They were distracted by their intense focus on destroying each other.

Sorelige Kabit Del'Arran drew forth from within himself a powerful invocation. He let its strength build then focussed his intent and unleashed it onto Kian'Huard and Ko'Resh. The effect was immediate when his thoughts overpowered the mayhem the shista had created with a resounding command— "ENOUGH!"—and the fighting ceased.

Ga'Etan had lured Kian'Huard into the hallway and Ko'Resh had followed. Sorelige Kabit Del'Arran invoked the tones to alter the physical makeup of the castle and readied himself, and the others, to transport the young shista.

As soon as Kian'Huard fell unconscious under the powerful solvieg of the inner temple priests, they gathered the lesser apprentices to enter the mantra and add strength to the binding they had containing the twins. They were able to capture Ko'Resh in his moment of fury just when he was about to deliver a fatal blow to his brother. It was luck, or destiny, that they were able to intervene. The powers that Ko'Resh had taken into himself were not fully developed and were not synchronized. Had he but a few more hours he could very well have been impossible to contain.

Kian'Huard struggled against the beast within him, making it difficult for the beast to gain a foothold. They could only transport one twin at a time and Kian'Huard's struggle offered them the time they needed to capture and bind the two. Had Kian'Huard allowed the spirit of the Sama Lukos to freely take his consciousness he would have been lost to them. They would have had to choose between the twins and they knew the essence of Kian'Huard was stronger than that of his brother but retrieving his soul from the Sama Lukos would have been very difficult and no one was certain if Kian'Huard would remain intact. Ko'Resh was very difficult to capture and bind. Only the disorganized competition for control by the six lukos spirits gave them an opportunity to capture him. If even two spirits were working collectively, the priests' power would not have been enough. They maintained constant vigil over the twins as they lay in a state caught between worlds. No less than seven inner sancta elite Sacerdos'helige maintained the drone of a binding mantra at all times. As each tired, another would commence the mantra. The Sacerdos'helige would remain outside the chamber until his entire being, both physical and nonphysical, resonated fully and completely with the vibration of the binding mantra. He would introduce his harmonic to the inner circle, synchronizing his breathing so there was never a gap in the drone of the binding spell. Then, the Sacerdos'helige being replaced would slowly remove him/herself from the tight circle, all the while maintaining the precise harmonics until he was beyond the chamber walls.

Only the most disciplined of the Sacerdos'helige were permitted to participate in the binding of the twins and the Sem Lukos, for the sight that befell their eyes took absolute focus and concentration; even the slightest shift in focus would compromise the binding, and the spirits gave a spectacle that challenged the most adept of the temple initiates.

The binding was so powerful that it crossed beyond the third and physical dimension, beyond the fourth and into the fifth. The twins lay side by side, but with enough distance between them to facilitate positioning of the Sacerdos'helige between them. Each twin was encompassed in a glowing orb that oscillated with the tones of the mantra. Colors shifted over the surface of the orb and swirled like mini galaxies of small rainbows over each of the occupied power centres. Ko'Resh's body twitched constantly and plumes of bright colors and energy flared from him and became caught up in the churning vortices that marked his kialthean power centres. The six occupied energy centres exploded with the amplified power of the lukos spirits. Each made itself visible while it struggled to gain control of Ko'Resh's power essence, conscious and unconscious mind and soul. The ongoing battle played out visibly within the churning vortices of each kialthean. Deformed, etheric forms of lukos dove and devoured the energy vortices but were not able to bind fully and would be thrown against the binding spell perimeter. The perimeter blazed brilliant white and silver/aquamarine when the unworldly creatures slammed into it. Vicious snarls and angry howls echoed with each failed attempt. The beasts would claw at the boundary and leap toward the Sacerdos'helige. Their venomous anger continued unchecked.

And the boundary held.

Kian'Huard's unconscious form played out a similar scene with the exception that only his crown kialthean was occupied. This, however, was a most powerful centres and the connection to dimensions outside time and space were challenged by the Sama Lukos. It had a more controlled approach to breaking the binding. It stalked the perimeter of the binding field, testing the strength and abilities of each of the Sacerdos'helige holding it, seeking out the weakest link. Bestial anger flared each time it was not able to sway the focus of one of its captors. It would only take the slightest imperceptible waver in focus, a slight variance in pitch in the mantra, droning without pause, for the Sama Lukos to gain the footing needed to possess the adolescent. He filled the mind of Kian'Huard with visions of power and eternal youth but the young shista continued his resistance within his mind. When the Sacerdos'helige became aware of the mind struggle within Kian'Huard's consciousness, they erected a second powerful barrier between Shista Kian'Huard's fragile consciousness and the Sama Lukos. This sent the unearthly creature into a fit of unchecked anger. It threw itself relentlessly at the barrier, lashing out with huge paws, claws unsheathed, looking more solid than etheric as he swiped and clawed at the circle. The Sacerdos'helige never faltered and the circle held.

While the most disciplined of the temple's initiates maintained the circle, the remaining apprentices and scholars scoured ancient texts and scrolls to find the means to re-bind the Sem Lukos Resh to the cavern. Many cycles of rhuna passed and they found nothing of any use. The inner circle holding the barrier never faltered. The world outside the inner sanctum moved through seasons and time.

At first, the people of Rhuna held vigil and would lend prayer to the plight of their young shista. But as seasons progressed, they gradually returned to their routine lives. The Sacerdos'helige did not have that luxury. The discipline necessary to maintain the barrier allowed no other thoughts to enter. The hold they had on maintaining the barrier and preventing the Sem Lukos Resh from fully occupying their young shista was more at risk with each passing day. Eventually the human nature of the Sacerdos'helige would demand reprieve from the soul-draining burden of maintaining the barrier. Finding a solution before that eventuality was paramount. Though not helpful thus far in presenting a solution, the ancient texts were very clear about one thing: the power of the Sem Lukos Resh was beyond comprehension. It could, when fully aligned, conquer even time and space. When the host gained the ability to harness the power there was nothing beyond his grasp. Thought became a weapon that none could combat. The terror that Saal, the creator of the Sem Lukos Resh, imparted on the people and the land was clearly depicted in the writings. But the words paled when one saw the tapestries and renderings of the horror that was Saal. Most of that era was removed from the history texts for fear that one day Saal may return and remember that which he created.

When after nearly one full turn of seasons had been completed, news came from the scholars.

A young mage discovered a single scroll of text in a secret cubby behind a stack of writing supplies. He was reaching beyond the reams of paper and bottles of ink when he overextended his reach and fell into the stack. Paper and ink tumbled. All eyes turned to give a harsh but silent reprimand for his carelessness. When he foundered with trying to right himself he noticed a cavity in the stone wall. Curiosity piqued and he reached in to discover a single aged scroll. The papyrus was so fragile that a small corner fell away when he removed it from its makeshift vault. He stood on trembling legs and handed the delicate relic to the Sorelige Kabit Del'Arran, who gently placed it on one of the many writing tables in the library. Not a soul breathed as he gently unrolled the parchment. It was written in the ancient tongue and bore the seal of the highest of mages of that era. The document did indeed tell of how the holy ones were able to entrap the Sem Lukos Resh. It described how Saal tried to evade capture and the exorcism of his creations from his body and soul. But one thing in the text was clear—in the present state, with the Sem Lukos Resh divided between the two shista, there was no way to remove the beasts.

The atmosphere in the chamber fell from hope to utter despair. It hung like a thick veil of caustic smoke smothering all light. Sorelige Kabit Del'Arran left the scroll and went to the window overlooking the courtyard. It was spring again. He recalled that it was spring the last time he ventured to look outside at the world he struggled to save. Only one decision could be made. But that choice did not destroy the Sem Lukos Resh, it only postponed the inevitable. For how long, there was no telling. He drew a ragged breath and let it leave his body in a long sigh. He did not turn to face the others but kept his head down when he spoke.

"We must kill Kian'Huard and Ko'Resh."

Gasps and murmurs filled the room instantly. Two of the younger Sacerdos'helige whispered a protection prayer and touched their medallions to their foreheads. The others' faces echoed emotions from sorrow to anger and disbelief.

One ventured to object, but the holy man raised his hand to silence him and the others.

He addressed the group. "I do not make this decision lightly. How long to you truly believe we can continue to maintain the barrier? Another season … a phase of rhuna … a pace of the resh? We are, and have been for some time, on borrowed time. We have exhausted all options and studied every scroll to the last." He made a motion to the tattered parchment on the table.

The young man who discovered the scroll cried out. He moved across the room and began pulling down the shelves and emptying their contents onto the floor, not concerned if he was damaging priceless scrolls. "NO!" he cried out. "We have to keep looking! Maybe there is another secret chamber somewhere!" Two of the others restrained him.

The elder took the young man's face in his hand and had him look into his eyes. "Young Sa'Evan." He softened his voice, but the authority in it remained undeniable. "None of us wish to harm our own, but there are no other scrolls and we are running out of time. We are but human and the creatures that we are dealing with are more than that." He lifted his gaze from the boy to address all in the room. "I do not know for certain that killing the shista will be the final solution. It may only slow the inevitable. These beasts have been released. They will continue to haunt this world until a vessel is found that will contain them. We have learned from the parchments that only a descendant of Sharram Saal can be a possible vessel. There are no other heirs if Kian'Huard and Ko'Resh are..." He hesitated. "Killed. The line of Saal will be ended. The Sem Lukos Resh will roam our world searching endlessly but will have no power here."

Sa'Evan shook himself free of his peers, straightened, and drew in a breath in readiness to say something, but then his shoulders fell and he studied the stone floor.

"What is it?" Sorelige Kabit Del'Arran could see the conflict behind Sa'Evan's eyes.

Sa'Evan hesitated then his words came out in such a rush no one could understand what he was saying.

"Gain control of yourself and your thoughts, Sa'Evan! It is pointless to rant if none can understand what it is you are saying."

Sa'Evan drew a long, shuddering breath, calmed himself and started again very slowly. "What if there is another child?"

The mages drew closer; Sa'Evan became suddenly very uncomfortable with their attention focused on him. He faltered.

"If you have some knowledge, then speak it now!" The elder was not unkind, but his tone was authoritative and commanding.

By now the young mage was completely unnerved. He had hardly expected to be the only one who knew of Ko'Resh's ... his thoughts were interrupted.

"Sa'Evan! What is it you are trying to say?"

"There may be a child of the royal line." He blurted the words and hoped he would not have to speak anymore.

"What knowledge do you have of this?"

The room echoed absolute silence. Sa'Evan cleared his throat and swallowed. Sorelige Kabit Del'Arran could sense the boy's unease and impatience was becoming the new flavour in the room. "Shista Ko'Resh may have a child, um, children." He did not dare look up from his study of the floor and continued, "I have seen him with many young females and I know that at least three are with child. If they are of his seed, I do not know, for these women have provided ... comfort "—he blushed—" ... to many men. And given the ... um ... friendly nature of our sharram, can we be certain he has no protégé outside the castle walls?"

If the silence was deafening before, after his statement it went cosmic. Not even a breath stirred. The air went still and, as if on cue, the resh dipped to the point on the horizon that bent the light into the red end of the spectrum and flooded the chamber.

Sorelige Kabit Del'Arran broke the silence with a deep, indrawn breath and let it out slowly. The boy was right. "We are doomed," he whispered. He gathered the fragile, ancient parchment, gently rolled it and placed it into a copper cylinder. He tucked it into an inner pocket in his robes. He turned a stern gaze to Sa'Evan. "We will discuss your penance later, should we survive and there is indeed a *later*. For, in speaking of what you know, you admit you have been sneaking out of the temple late at night and following the shista and spying. And going to the tavern and drinking. And breaking your vows. Which, though each offence is enough to have you expelled from the temple on its own, combined, may be considered treason. However," He paused and let his voice soften just a bit. "If you had not violated your vows then you would not have known about the possibility of another child who carries the line of the House of Rhuna. I will take that into consideration when next we discuss this matter."

The sorelige turned from the young man and left the room, his heart heavy with the knowledge that what had been put in motion was destined to be played out. He wondered at the timing. Indeed, the planets had come into an alignment that altered the very vibration of Mythos and would allow a convergence of physical and non-physical entities to co-mingle. But this was only a partial alignment. The true total alignment would not take place for several

70

hundred years, around 2,500 if the charts were correct, and he knew they were. So why the Saal chose to release his creations at his time eluded him. If he did decide to kill the young shista to remove the Sem Lukos from them, he would have to minimize future potential hosts. That would mean close monitoring and control over the House of Rhuna and any bastard children that may be potential hosts. In his understanding of the Sem Lukos Resh, he knew not all born of the House of Rhuna would hold the specific genetic marker that would allow them to be taken. He needed a way to "see"—to determine if someone held the genetic code that would make them a threat then they would take any children who posed a threat and sequester them in the temple to live out their lives. He would have to act fast; he could sense those who held vigil over the shista were beginning to feel the strain from the weight of responsibility thrust upon them.

He gathered ten of his most adept Sacerdos'helige to his chamber to hold a secret meeting. There they formulated a plan and brought forth the decree that allowed the Sacerdos'helige to enter any dwelling in Rhuna and remove any children they determined held the mark of the beast. The ten he trusted to this act were able to look into the essence of another and see what traits they embodied from their parents. Thus, The Cull came into being.

CHAPTER 7

SORELIGE KABIT DEL'ARRAN FOLLOWED THE CORRI-
dor down to the deepest part of the temple where the two shista lay. He chastised himself for not considering the obvious—the line of Saal would have
threads throughout the kingdom. He himself knew of several bastard children brought into the temple to be kept hidden. Their mothers believing the
infants died at birth. If Sa'Evan knew the truth of his own lineage he would
be overwhelmed by the implications. His mind was weak, like his mother
who drank too much and often came to the temple to receive medicines to
cure an assortment of illnesses sprung from her promiscuous lifestyle. When
Sharram Kar'Set went to her chamber in a state of drunkenness, the child
Sa'Evan was created. Kar'Set brought the woman to him and she remained
in the temple until the child was born. She was, however, too weak to bring
the child into the world and died as he took his first breath. Sa'Evan knew no
other life than that of the Sacerdos'helige. His penchant to sneak out and frequent the taverns was another indication of his connection to the monarchy.

Sorelige Kabit Del'Arran doubted the Sem Lukos Resh would be particular about their vessel if they were abruptly evicted from their current bodies.
He knew there was no way to remove all potential hosts. He also doubted
ignorance of one's lineage would offer any protection from the spirit beasts.
The thought of a frail mind like Sa'Evan being possessed by such creatures
did nothing to quell the sorelige. He knew it was only a matter of time before
someone faltered and the barrier that contained the shista and the creatures
would weaken. He paused for a moment then reconsidered his destination.
Instead of following the tunnel deeper into the mountain to where the two
young shista lay, he slid his hand along the smooth wall to find a latch and
pulled. A narrow entrance opened and he slipped through. He followed the

dark corridor for several hundred paces before it opened up in front of him. Only he knew what lay beyond the entrance.

He approached the first outer vestibule. Inside, he barely took notice of the deep emerald color of the polished stone inlaid with geometric patterns of the purest copper. The stone was very rare and the amount that had to be mined to create the chamber was a testament to devotion by the creators. It was longer by two than it was wide and the ceiling arched high above more than twenty measures. It was designed to amplify sound and create a feedback that would resonate through the very cells of whomever was in the chamber and elevate their vibration to bring them into a higher state of awareness. He took a deep breath and cleared his mind of all thoughts. He reached out in his spirit and embraced the light that was his higher nature. When he felt it fully present he crossed to the centre of the chamber. He drew in a deep breath and let it out slowly and with control. A second breath pulled in and out. The third he drew in even deeper, and as he exhaled he began a low pitch note using the sound of "a." The sound left him and resonated through the chamber. As it reverberated on itself it amplified in volume, taking on a life of its own. He then drew his breath and increased the pitch and the sound of "e" sprung to life. The two sounds mingled and bounced from the sheer walls. He continued with "i" and added 'o' and "u." With each vowel he increased the pitch of the note, creating a harmonic resonance that pulsed to life in the polished stone around him. The sound created an electrical charge that coalesced on front of him. He moved back from the centre of the chamber to allow what he had created take form. At first it was a slight glow in the air, barely perceptible to an initiate, but he knew what to look for and watched as it quickly gained substance. The sound took on an etheric glow as well. Each vowel resonated at a different frequency and glowed with soft hues of color that were undetectable with human eyes. But Sorelige Kabit Del'Arran had been trained for many decades and was able to see the color of sound and drew these colors to him to raise himself to another level of consciousness.

The ball of electricity that was forming in the centre of the chamber grew in intensity. It gradually took on a more defined shape. As it neared the critical frequency, the geometric outline of a tetrahedron churning in the air in front of him sharpened. With each harmonic plateau increase in frequency and color, the shape spinning in front of him morphed and doubled into a more complex structure. The gateway continued to form in front of him. He resisted the urge to step back when the structure of light and sound energy pulsed mere inches in front of him. The next harmonic shift would expand the gateway to completely fill the chamber. When that happened, the copper inlays would take on the charge and re-focus it to the centre of the chamber and the gateway to move him beyond the current time and space would be complete. Then he could transport himself to any place or time at the speed of thought. He knew there were many such chambers scattered throughout the stars and on many worlds, built by an ancient race in the time of Saal.

When Saal created the seven beasts, all other creation ceased and the Rhue found themselves plunged into a world of struggle, pain and separateness. For it was then the land shook with such ferocity and lowered Rhuna to below the level of the sea and a great wall of mountains rose up around the country that offered protection from flooding but also separated Rhuna from the rest of the world, as much for the protection of the world as for the Rhue. Over the centuries courageous, or foolish, youth challenged those mountains, only to be taken by them. It was thought at that time that this chamber had been destroyed. Ancient writings indicated it was the intent. But it had survived, and so too did the scrolls that gave direction on how to activate the gateway. These scrolls were only known to two living souls at any time. Each generation would pass the knowledge to his successor in a highly secret ceremony. Then the successor would remain in solitude deep within the temple to be tested in his strength of character. Even after proving himself he would remain secluded until the death of his predecessor. His first duty would be to locate the gate room and initiate the opening. He was forbidden to fully open the gateway on his initial sounding. The experience of the raw power of the chamber could prove overwhelming for many and time saw a few sorelige taken by the vortex, never to return. It took a very disciplined mind to wield the power of the sound gate. It took even more discipline to maintain mental control and find your way back.

The sorelige Kabit Del'Arran planned to use the gate to move through time to see if he could find the missing knowledge needed to remove the beasts from the young shista and return them to the crystal prison from which they were released. It would be a dangerous task and, if he were not fully focused, could result in changing the history of his world. One misplaced thought could even prevent the beasts from being exercised from Sharram Saal so many eons ago.

He knew the time he wished to visit and the location of the crystal chamber that would contain the beasts. He focused his attention on that exact time and envisioned himself being there. He thought of a tunnel just beyond the chamber to prevent being noticed when he appeared.

The harmonics in the gate room reached the next convergence pitch. His thoughts were locked to the time and place he wished to travel. And he knew in an instant he had arrived.

CHAPTER 8

A RIPPLE PASSED THROUGH THOSE WHO HELD VIGIL over the young shista. All but one held their focus. The one faltered but regained control within the blink of an eye; it was enough. The imperceptible flicker was all the great beast needed. The mage's throat was torn from him by the ghostlike creature. Though the others in the chamber believed they held strong, the beasts saw the weakness and struck with full animal fury. Not one remained alive. The beasts entered their hosts and forced them to consciousness. Barely aware of their surroundings, they were driven to follow the control of the Sem Lukos Resh.

They made their way from the chamber to the upper levels of the temple. A trail of bloodied and broken bodies marked their passing. They exploded into the light of the resh at its zenith. They shielded their eyes from being temporarily blinded and pushed on, guided by the animal instinct possessing their will. They were aware of shouts of disbelief around them and angry outbursts when they knocked down some unfortunate person who could not get out of their way. One man stood up to them after seeing his wife knocked to the ground. Swift was the retaliation of the Sama Lukos that possessed Kian'Huard. The man fell to the ground clutching at his throat while his life bubbled from him. His wife gained her feet and rushed to him. This was rewarded with another swift slash from Ko'Resh and she too fell. The crowd parted to allow them passage.

The shista, still barely aware of their surroundings, staggered through the street until they found two horses. They mounted them and spurred them into a full gallop out of the city and away from the temple. That which possessed the young monarchs touched the spirit of the horses. It gave them unnatural speed and ability to sense where pitfalls might be so they ran at full gallop with no regard to where each footfall may land. This enabled them to escape the city before the alarm could sound to close the gates.

The brothers followed the road for a brief time then headed across country. They rode the creatures hard until they were near collapse. They dismounted and the beasts withdrew from the minds of the horses. The horses screamed and kicked out. They reared and pawed at the air, and their nostrils flared with the fear that was now allowed them. They stomped and pounded the ground with both front hooves. Their mouths foamed and their eyes were white and wild. They screamed again and then bolted, quickly putting distance between themselves and their unnatural mounts. Kian'Huard and Ko'Resh were led to find shelter in an abandoned shack. The beasts drew them into a deep, unnatural sleep. Then they began the process of fully integrating themselves into the psyche of the young shista. They snarled their resentment of being separated, but for now, they were free.

The integration proved very difficult. Had the seven been released into one body, the Sama Lukos would have overseen the process and brought the other six into alignment with the host by increasing the frequencies of the host power centres to the point where the corresponding lukos energy could "tune" itself to become one with the host. The Sama Lukos also acted as the alpha, for the Sem Lukos were of an animal nature and in nature, every pack has an alpha to ensure the wellbeing of the pack. While the twins were in close proximity the Sama was able to assert itself to maintain the seven. However, when the twins were separated by more than a few measures, the six that possessed Ko'Resh resumed their struggle for dominance even at the expense of their host. It would take an enormous amount of willpower for Ko'Resh to remain sane if he were separated from his brother. Such strength of will he did not seem to possess.

Kian'Huard woke first. He sat up and looked over at his brother and felt relief he was alive. He tried to recall how they came to be there but the memory eluded him. Ko'Resh stirred beside him. He looked much worse, with his disheveled appearance and drawn expression, than Kian'Huard, though neither showed any outward injuries that would suggest they had been in any form of combat at all. "Ko'Resh." He moved closer to his brother. "Ko'Resh, wake up."

Ko'Resh stirred slightly and moaned. Kian'Huard shook him by the shoulder. "Ko'Resh, wake up!" Again, Ko'Resh moaned then he opened his eyes. Kian'Huard saw a darkness shadowing the depths of the green eyes that stared back at him. He pulled back slightly and tried not to let Ko'Resh see the fear he was feeling.

Ko'Resh sat up and held his head in his hands. He glanced toward Kian'Huard. "Usually when I wake feeling like this there is a naked woman and an empty wineskin beside me." He looked around at the run-down shack. "I see neither." He turned his attention to Kian'Huard. "But I do see my brother looking as though he lost his favorite hound. Tell me, brother, why so despondent?"

Kian'Huard was a little taken aback. Had Ko'Resh forgotten all they had been through over the past cycles? Or was this another of his games to take him off his guard? Kian'Huard played along, "You do not recall how we came to be here?"

"Brother, what I recall is you and I entering a cave outside Kephas and then waking up here," Ko'Resh replied. There was a note of sincerity in his voice that was nearly enough for Kian'Huard to let down his guard. Nearly.

"I was hoping you remembered how we got here because I too cannot remember anything after we entered that cave." He lied, but he did not feel Ko'Resh was being truthful about what he recalled. "I don't recognize this place. I am going to take a look around and see if I can tell where exactly we are." He rose and looked around for something to use as a weapon. He was hungry, and by the length of the shadows across the floor, night would be upon them soon. Unless they were very close to a village, they would be spending the night here so they would need food, water and a fire.

As with all houses in Rhuna, this small shack had a fireplace that dominated the north wall. He ducked his head in and strained to look up the chimney to be sure it was clear of bird nests or other debris. He let out a sigh of relief when he saw a small circle of blue above him. He noted a fire starter hung on a nail beside the fireplace. He searched around the shack for anything more that might be of use and found a bow and a few arrows laying atop a shelf. He tested the gut to be certain is was not too dry or rotten to draw. But good fortune was not his that day; the wood of the bow was cracked and the gut all but crumbled when the least bit of tension was placed on it. The arrows were old, but appeared sound enough for small game, but they were virtually useless without the bow. They would not be having meat tonight, but he had a sound knowledge of what plants were edible. With any luck he could find something to satiate their hunger. He turned to Ko'Resh. "You rest for now while I scout. If you feel up to it, perhaps you can get a small fire started and with any luck I will have dinner when I return."

Ko'Resh nodded in agreement and lay back down. Kian'Huard studied him for a moment before ducking under the low door frame and out into the afternoon sun. At first, he was a bit disoriented because with the evening sun full in his face, the North Wall Mountain range should have been visible somewhere to his left. But it was not there. Instead, the land seemed to drop off all around him. The careen of a sea bird caught his attention. Then slowly the sounds of the wind and sea began to register. The rocky terrain and sparse grass left little guessing. Somehow, they had travelled across the entire country to the farthest tip of Rhuna where it towered well above the sea. That explained the abandoned shack. None had ventured to live in this remote part of the country for several generations. The land was not fruitful, and there was no access to the sea for fishing. He moved closer to the edge of the point to look out over the water. Far below him on his left was the Sea of Cippus where he could see several vessels in the distance making their way back to port at the end of the day. To his right was the Aevitas Ocean and, not too distant on the horizon, he could see, jutting from the ocean depths, thousands of shards of rock that had been pushed up from the sea bottom, effectively separating Rhuna from the rest of Mythos. Legend spoke of Saal creating such evil that those who created the world caused Rhuna to be separated rather than destroy the entire world of Mythos they had newly created.

A cry from the stable brought his attention back to the present. He hurried back to find Ko'Resh thrashing about, his body straining in some sort of fit. He rushed to his brother and rolled him onto his side. Ko'Resh's face was red with strain. Spit sprayed from his mouth as he struggled to breathe and his eyes rolled back. Ko'Resh reached to his brother. "Don't leave me," he pleaded.

Kian'Huard held tight to Ko'Resh. "I will not leave you, my brother ... I promise."

Gradually the seizure began to subside and Ko'Resh's breathing returned to normal. His body relaxed and he slumped in Kian'Huard's arms. A strange golden-violet mist surrounded the two as they huddled together in that shack with the late afternoon sun bathing them in dark shadows. Kian'Huard felt something of himself been drawn out into the mist, lending strength and order to the tortured body of his brother. He did not understand the significance of what was happening at the time but soon it became clear how inseparable they had become.

The night had grown cold and damp even in the shelter of the abandoned shack, so when Ko'Resh had settled back into sleep, Kian'Huard used what little broken furniture was there to start a small fire, but it would not burn for long. He fashioned a torch from the broken remains of a chair and some rags and lit it with the fire then ventured out into the night in the hopes of gathering more fuel. He had noticed what could have been a small barn nearby so he went to scavenge what he could to burn. He also knew that Rhue tradition would have the settlers start a small garden with a hardy strain of capann, a tuberous root crop that was a staple in every Rhue home, alongside the barn. If the plants were able to take root, then there should be some there for they would continue to grow even after they were no longer being tended. His torch was beginning to burn low as he checked the south side of the barn, for that was the most common site for the beginning garden at a new homestead. He was quickly rewarded by the sight of several leafy plants. The ground was soft enough for him to dig with his hands and he quickly unearthed several large capann. He stowed these in his pockets and went into the barn in search of fuel for the fire.

Again, luck was on his side. Though there were very few trees in this part of Rhuna, the previous tenants had managed to store a significant supply of firewood. Kian'Huard gathered as much as he could carry and headed back to the shack. As he neared the entrance he could hear Ko'Resh moaning and thrashing about. He dropped the firewood and rushed into the shack to find his brother in the throes of another seizure. Kian'Huard once more ran to Ko'Resh's aid and again, the golden-violet mist surrounded the twins and Ko'Resh's seizure calmed. Once he was certain the fit had passed, Kian'Huard brought in the firewood and stoked the fire. It was not long before the cold was pushed back from the small hovel and the fire had a deep bed of embers. Kian'Huard brushed as much dirt as possible from the capanns and placed them in the fireplace near a pile of embers then returned his attention to his brother. "I have found some food for us."

Ko'Resh moaned and tried to sit up.

"Rest for now. I will wake you when they are ready to eat. I have not seen a well or any water yet but will look at first light. For now, we are safe and warm." He sat beside Ko'Resh and divided his attention between his brother and the flickering dance of the fire. His mind replayed the events of the past ... how long? Weeks? Months? He was acutely aware of the prison the Sacerdos'helige had trapped them in, and their bloody and violent escape. And the horses ... but how could the beasts have carried them so far? They were more than a month's journey from the Temple of Osiris and from what he could recall, they travelled no more than ... he was suddenly struck by the realization that he had no recollection of how much time had actually passed; just a memory of riding at full gallop and then waking here.

Ko'Resh stirred beside him. His color had improved and when he opened his eyes Kian'Huard could see his brother was more alert. He pulled the capanns from the fire, juggling each on a pair of sticks to place on a rag between them. "Dinner is served." He gestured to the slightly blackened vegetables.

Ko'Resh looked at the capanns then back at Kian'Huard. "Cooking is definitely not your forte, brother." He gave a brief smile. Kian'Huard could see he was still very weak from the seizures and, for a moment, he could almost believe he had his brother back.

Ko'Resh sat up and picked up one of the charred roots, moving it from hand to hand and blowing on it to try to cool it enough to break open. Kian'Huard followed suit and soon they had devoured the entire lot.

"Do you know where we are?" Ko'Resh asked.

Kian'Huard realized it was only he who had been outside and each time he returned to the shack they had no conversation because Ko'Resh was having a seizure. "Yes, we are at the farthest tip of Rhuna. Durgess Point."

Ko'Resh looked around at the shack. "I can't believe someone tried to homestead way out here."

"Tried and gave up."

Ko'Resh nodded and raised himself to stand. "Lucky for us, I suppose. But how did we get here? It is what, a month's journey from the temple?" He swayed a bit, losing his balance.

Kian'Huard scrambled to his feet to steady Ko'Resh. "At least a month, and I don't know how we got here."

"Thank you, brother. I'm still a bit weak, it seems." Ko'Resh leaned on Kian'Huard for a moment then straightened. "I need to relieve myself." Kian'Huard hesitated in letting go of his arm. "I appreciate your concern, but I think I can manage without your assistance."

"I will be here if you need me."

Ko'Resh opened the door and a chill draft swept into the cabin. "I'll be fine, you keep that fire going." With that, he ducked out into the night, letting the door fall closed behind him.

Within moments Kian'Huard heard a bang coming from outside. He rushed outside to find Ko'Resh once more thrashing about with a seizure. Then it dawned on him. "Brother, whatever spirits possess us, it seems they do not wish to be separated." He dragged his brother back into the cabin and made him as comfortable as possible. "Can you understand me, Ko'Resh?" Ko'Resh gave a weak nod and Kian'Huard continued, "I am going to try something. Are you ready?"

Again, Ko'Resh nodded. Kian'Huard stood and moved toward the door, all the time watching his brother's reaction as the distance between them grew. Once he was roughly ten measures from Ko'Resh, Kian'Huard could see his brother's eyes begin to roll back. He quickly closed the distance and Ko'Resh's body relaxed as he knelt beside him. "It seems we are to be inseparable."

"Is does seem that way, Kian'Huard." Ko'Resh's voice was strained with fatigue.

Kian'Huard threw more wood on the fire and settled beside his twin. "Tonight, we need to get some rest and tomorrow we can figure out what can be done to remove these spirits and get our lives back."

Kian'Huard looked over at Ko'Resh to find he had already fallen asleep. He closed his eyes and after some time, he too drifted to dreamless sleep.

Kian'Huard gasped, struggling for breath, his throat tight and a great pressure on his chest. He flailed his arms as he was pulled back to wakeful panic. His eyes opened wide to find Ko'Resh sitting atop him, hands securely circling his throat. Kian'Huard struggled to push Ko'Resh from him. A piece of wood caught his eye. He reached to the log, straining to wrap his fingers around it. Black spots swirled as his vision blurred from lack of oxygen. His fingers found the edge of the log. He forced every last ounce of his strength to pick up the log and bring it down on the side of Ko'Resh's head. It was enough to cause Ko'Resh to loosen his grip and allow Kian'Huard the opportunity to throw his brother from him and scramble to his feet.

"Ko'Resh!" He gasped. "What are you doing? You know you cannot be separated from me!"

"You are mistaken, brother; I cannot be separated from the Sama Lukos. But it can be separated from you and I can unite it with the others within me." His tone was as cold as the ice in his eyes.

Kian'Huard bolted for the door. He meant to put as much distance between them as he could to bring on another seizure in Ko'Resh. He hoped to incapacitate him long enough to restrain him and maybe figure out a way to free them both from this nightmare.

He burst from the shack into the full light of day. Temporarily blinded, he ran with no idea of direction. He could hear Ko'Resh following. When his eyes adjusted to the sunlight he could see he was running full-out toward the cliff that rose several hundred measures above the raging surf of the Aevitas Ocean. He didn't have long for his plan to work before he would run out of land. He ventured to look to see how far behind his brother was.

Ko'Resh was charging at him like a mad beast, his eyes burned with hatred. Kian'Huard's heart sank. Ko'Resh was more than far enough away to spur a seizure unless … he was faking it when they were testing the theory in the cabin.

Suddenly Kian'Huard stumbled, catching his foot on a rock. He tried to roll as he fell to land back on his feet but fell hard on his side, knocking his breath from him. He struggled to force air back into his lungs while scrambling back to his feet, aware the edge of the cliff was very close, as was Ko'Resh. He had to survive at all cost; he could not allow Ko'Resh full reign of all seven of the Sem Lukos Resh. He did not know if killing his twin would mean he would be taken by the six spirits that currently possessed Ko'Resh, but he had no time to ponder—Ko'Resh was upon him.

Ko'Resh slammed into him and knocked him to the ground. Kian'Huard used the momentum from his fall to carry himself into a roll and out from under Ko'Resh. He scrambled to his feet in time to sidestep another lunge from his twin then follow through with a sweep of his leg to take Ko'Resh off his feet. Ko'Resh easily avoided the attack and once more threw himself at Kian'Huard, making full body contact with a bone-jarring thud sending both sprawling on the ground. By this time, they were precariously close to the edge of the cliff. One moment of distraction and one or both would plunge to their death. Kian'Huard reached out to push himself back from the edge and to his horror the ground gave way beneath his hands. His eyes popped wide as he fell forward and saw the loosened rubble hurling toward the sea. In a panic, he struggled to roll back on to more solid ground but he was not fast enough and Ko'Resh was upon him unleashing a flurry of blows to his head. Kian'Huard felt the sharp pain of bones breaking under the barrage, tasted the blood that poured from his mouth and head.

He was growing weak and losing ground. "Ko'Resh … stop … please." His plea was weak and went unheeded by his brother. He knew he was losing and, for a brief moment, imagined what it would be like to fall so far and shatter upon the rocks below. Somehow that thought gave him renewed strength. He rolled to his right and managed to shake his brother from him. He scrambled wildly away from the edge of the precipice, all the while trying to gain his feet. Once more Ko'Resh was quickly upon him. Kian'Huard rolled onto his back and kicked out at Ko'Resh's legs to take him off balance. He dug his hands into the soft soil to gain as much leverage as possible. The soil crumbled in his hands and he took it up and threw it at his brother's eyes.

Ko'Resh staggered back, trying to clear his vision. He lost his direction and stumbled, half blind, toward the edge of the cliff. Without pausing to think, Kian'Huard scrambled to his feet and threw himself at Ko'Resh. The two fell. Kian'Huard hit the ground with a jolt. He felt his right arm being wrenched and his shoulder dislocated. It took him a moment to realize Ko'Resh had gone over the edge and was clinging to his wrist. Through searing pain, Kian'Huard rolled onto his stomach. For a moment their eyes locked. Kian'Huard could feel Ko'Resh's grip slide.

"Brother," Ko'Resh pleaded

Kian'Huard tried to reach him with his other hand but the ground began to crumble beneath him. Panic and self-preservation set in as he tried to wriggle back onto more solid ground. The pain in his arm was almost unbearable. "Hold on, Ko'Resh. Don't let go!" His mind raced trying to think of what he could use to save his brother. Ko'Resh's grip slid once more. He barely had ahold of him. Kian'Huard reached down with his good arm but Ko'Resh was just beyond his reach. Again, his hand slipped. "No! I can't lose you!" Kian'Huard cried.

"Save me, brother!" Ko'Resh's voice held true panic as he reached to find something solid to grab hold of but instead sent more rubble hurling to the raging surf. His efforts only served to further loosen his grip and then lose it entirely.

Ko'Resh's eyes widened with horror, his hands frantically grabbing at the air as he fell.

Kian'Huard watched, helpless, as his brother fell away from him. He screamed until he had no more voice. He backed away from the edge and collapsed. For a while he considered joining his brother but something held him back. Instead, he lay there curled in a fetal position and wept for what had been lost.

He did not know how long he lay there, undisturbed by man or beast. He had expected the six spirits that possessed Ko'Resh to find him and take over his body once his brother had died as Ko'Resh believed would happen. But none came. So he lay there a little longer until pain and hunger forced him to get up. He knew with the power of the Sama Lukos he could return to claim his throne and destroy all who would stand in his way, but that was not his true nature; that was Ko'Resh. He would not return to the castle. His would be a life of solitude until he died, or he found a way to remove the beast that lived within him. He considered returning to the temple but then recalled their bloody escape and decided against it. He would most likely be killed on sight. He looked around. He would stay there at the cabin until he regained his strength, and then he would head to the mountains to live out his life.

CHAPTER 9

KIAN'HUARD SLOWLY MADE HIS ASCENT TO THE TOP of a mountain where he had constructed an observatory centuries ago. He had made the journey every season for as long as he could remember; and perhaps a bit longer. His pilgrimages had become more frequent of late, performed with each phase of rhuna as she rose in the evening sky. Each time he made his way to the observatory he tried to convince himself what he was seeing were the imaginings of an old man who had outlived his time in this world.

But each night when he charted their position, his fears were confirmed. The planets were shifting into an alignment that had not been seen in over two thousand years.

The man paused for a few moments. He laid his walking staff against one of the rock outcroppings. The corners of his mouth turned up into what could have been mistaken for a smile. Not a smile, but a moment of melancholy as he remembered a distant time when he could traverse this hillside without the aid of the staff. He looked down in the direction from whence he came. The land fanned out beneath him, beyond what his eyes could see, in a living tapestry of greens, gold and reds. The land was rich and the people gentle. Their country was cut off from the rest of Mythos by impassable mountains that dominated the north and west. Where the mountains met the sea at both the eastern and westernmost boundaries, the foothills quickly gave way to towering shards of volcanic rock that had been pushed up from the depths of the sea, completely enclosing the entire country with an impassable barrier. The mainland, a crescent-shaped peninsula, reached like a crooked finger into the green-blue water. It was said that it was those who created this world who did this for, according to legend, a great evil was brought to Mythos by one who dwelt in the land of Rhuna and, instead of destroying the whole of the people, it chose to separate them.

He knew the legend to be true, though many had, once again, forgotten. For he kept the evil at bay and hid himself away in the mountains. Even though Rhuna was cut off from the rest of Mythos, the people continued. Despite their solitude, Rhuna was prosperous and her people were skilled farmers and trade smiths. They had few soldiers, for there was no need. A royal guard existed, no more than a thousand men and women trained in the ancient art of Tae'Heb. Everyone born of the House of Rhuna was trained from their earliest years in this form. The memory of the fortress that was the House of Rhuna initiated a chain reaction of thoughts and Kian'Huard's mind wandered through the long path that was his life.

He recalled his brother and a time when that which lay restless within him did not possess his soul and he was a free man. As the centuries passed, he understood more about how they came upon the entrance at the base of the mountain, how they were led by an unseen force deep below the Temple of Osiris and to the chamber of wolves. Once there, they were powerless to stop the long-imprisoned spirits from taking their bodies and the bloody battle that ensued. He did not want the life that was thrust upon him when he became possessed by the Sama Lukos. His brother relished the power the six spirits he thought he possessed gave him. But that power was only an illusion, for they held their own agenda and it did not involve the seven being divided between two physical bodies. They pitted the brothers against each other in an effort to bring the seven together as one. But they were not successful. Something in the division of the embryo in the creation of identical twins also divided the gene that was created by Saal that allowed the physical body to contain the power of the Sem Lukos. Another child would have to be created. One that brought the gene back into a single body.

Kian'Huard realized such a child would have to be the product of Ko'Resh's sire and his own combining. He recalled his noble heritage and how he chose to abandon that life and seek the refuge of solitude after he did the unthinkable and murdered his twin brother. He thought that was the only way to break the thread that was woven into their bloodline. That act of violence forged his decision to leave the royal court and relinquish his right to be Sharram of Rhuna.

Kian'Huard pulled himself from his ruminations. Evening was fast approaching and he needed to be ready to measure the procession of the planets at exactly the right moment.

He sighed heavily and shook his head as if to shake loose the thoughts and have them scatter, like startled mice, back to the far reaches of his subconscious. A long braid of copper hair fell across his shoulder. He pushed it back and this time a faint smile crossed his face—to think that one as old as he would have anything but a sparse amount of grey hair. Indeed, it seemed that having his soul possessed had some advantages in longevity and slowing the aging process. But those advantages were quickly outweighed when he outlived everyone he grew up with. It was another factor in deciding on a life of solitude. He had witnessed many changes in his land and its people. He had, at times, chosen to interfere to cause events to play out to a particular end and many times questioned his reasoning for such manipulations. He was never quite sure if his thoughts were his own or if the manipulator was also being manipulated. Of one thing he was certain—the night he mated with Sharrana Mura of Rhuna under the guise of her mate Sharram A'Rhan, his actions were not his own and he was powerless to stop it. That was the last time he knew a woman.

It was in that moment that he became aware of his brother's continued existence and obsession to somehow return to Rhuna and reunite the Sem Lukos Resh. He also became aware that it was his brother who manipulated him into going to the Sharrana. He felt the connection between the six spirits his brother possessed and the seventh that possessed him grow stronger as the time when the possibility they could become reunited in one embodiment drew near.

After many centuries Rhuna would again be accessible by way of the sea. This, he assumed, would be how Ko'Resh would return. He was certain his twin thought of little else for all these years and had devised a means of achieving this seemingly impossible task. The constant reminder that Ko'Resh did survive plunging into the sea and continued to survive until he reached land elicited a sense of foreboding that was impossible to quell. He wondered what havoc his sibling had created to maintain power and control. What manipulations had taken place? How much history had been tampered with to satisfy Ko'Resh's lust to return to Rhuna? How many innocents died at the mercy of the beasts that controlled Ko'Resh?

Did Ko'Resh even realize he was being controlled, or was he still under the illusion that he was the master and not the slave?

Kian'Huard sighed heavily and rose from where he rested. He studied the evening sky as it changed from powder blue to deep indigo. The resh dipped lower on the horizon in an explosion of gold and fire that licked the mountaintops in a final blaze of glory before succumbing to the pull of morning that beckoned on the other side of Mythos. He scanned the opposite horizon for the first silver glimmer of the rhuna, rising nearly full. The darkening sky slowly began to reveal constellations that had remained unchanged for eternity. He smiled, finding humor that at least the stars were older than him.

It was then he became aware of a presence and not a heartbeat later knew it to be Sharrana Nahleen, one of the few people whose company he enjoyed. She would catch up to him soon, so he settled his ancient bones back down on the rock cut, smoothed his green robes over his knees and waited. He divided his attention between the sky and the path below.

The night sky, though it had become progressively more ominous with each moon cycle, never failed to fill him with a sense of awe at its infinite beauty. The planets, which were normally scattered throughout the panoramic view, had ebbed closer to an inevitable alignment which was sure to change the very essence of all who dwelt on this small world called Mythos. Some would be more affected than others. Sharrana Nahleen would be affected most of all. This thought brought Kian'Huard much anguish knowing, though he possessed much power, he was helpless to change that which was about to unfold. He straightened, knowing she was about to arrive.

In that moment the physical world around him seemed to stand still. A feeling of dread knotted his stomach and boiled upward through him. His heart skipped a beat and began to pound in his chest as a force, driven by bright white light, exploded in his head. He drew a sharp breath and sprang to his feet, his gaze intent on the east. The Sama Lukos was stirring inside his mind. Centuries of meditation and learning to control his thoughts enabled him to keep the powerful spirit dormant but somehow it had pushed its way into his consciousness of its own accord. He struggled to clear his mind and focus his attention to suppress it when the image of his twin brother Ko'Resh appeared. Kian'Huard clenched his teeth and focused all his mental energy on regaining control. Still, the illusion of Ko'Resh grinned at him from within his mind mouthing one word… "Soon."

At that moment, Sharrana Nahleen rounded the corner. He saw her falter in her step. Kian'Huard knew she had been touched by the spirit of Ko'Resh.

Her hand went to her stomach. "What was that?" she asked. "It was as if something passed through my mind, like a restless ghost or spirit, then it was gone." She paused for a moment. "It was menacing and dark like…" She didn't finish. She looked over at Kian'Huard, and his haunted expression stopped her mid-sentence.

Kian'Huard's body was rigid, his vivid green eyes focused somewhere deep within himself. He was partly aware of her words, but much of his attention was on pushing the beast within him out of his conscious mind. With one final, determined effort, he suppressed the Sama Lukos and regained control. The image of his brother dissipated. He became weak and slid back to rest on the rock. Nahleen rushed to his side and assisted him to sit. He could see at once her face was full of questions and knew the time was at hand to begin to educate Sharrana Nahleen to her destiny. He felt a great sorrow encompass his heart as he looked into her face and saw his same vivid green eyes gazing back at him. He had hoped the curse of his family line had been broken with the death of his brother, prayed the part of the gene that Ko'Resh held within his bloodline was lost forever, making it impossible for the Sem Lukos Resh to become united within one physical body. But alas, now there was no doubt his brother somehow managed to survive, and his genetic line as well.

He himself had been manipulated through the centuries to continue his genetic line and Nahleen, Sharrana of Rhuna, unknown to her, was his great-granddaughter, heir to the Sem Lukos Resh and a fate that would see her destroy all that she loved. He did not fully understand how Ko'Resh survived his journey across the Aevitas Ocean nor how he intended to return with his progeny to perpetuate the line and bring forth a Sheth Child. But in that moment, he understood Ko'Resh's obsessive determination and came to the disturbing realization that somehow that was exactly what would happen. And he unwittingly played his part as well over the generations, for Nahleen stood before him and within her was that same gene that caused him to awaken the Sem Lukos Resh many centuries ago. How she would learn to despise him in the time to come.

≫ ≫ ≫

On a serpentine path snaking through a dying forest on the opposite side of this world, a man, identical to Kian'Huard in appearance, save his unkempt manner, descended the incline to the base of his chosen hillside upon which he had earlier charted the progress of the same planets. This man was not filled with the same sense of foreboding as his counterpart. He relished the impending alignment. In fact, his entire existence was spent in anticipation, planning for what was about to unfold. As the time grew near, the beings he possessed became more restless. He could feel their strength build as the procession of the planets drew nearer to alignment and he was drawn to perform certain tasks that satisfied the need to perpetuate his line. Forced copulations with members of the House of Krit had brought forth a child who carried the genetic code needed to complete the Sheth Child. That child grew to be one of the most powerful and respected leaders of the Krit people, Sharram Rhandor. But Ko'Resh remained unable to understand how he was to return home to his beloved Rhuna and take Rhandor with him. He had created a drought that ravished the land to spur Rhandor to seek his counsel. This proved to be a painstakingly slow process. He needed a more direct approach. He knew even the strongest mind would become malleable when it is consumed by a strong emotion such as grief.

That morning, as rhuna was setting on the western horizon and the resh curled its golden orange fingers through the Illuna Mountains to launch herself into a naked sky that spanned a scorched and dying land, he gathered the power of the lukos spirits and reached out in his mind to touch his brother. Even as the thought entered his mind he knew that his brother was aware of his presence. He let a feeling of pseudo-victory wash over him. He was aware that somewhere his own physical body remained clutching a tree branch as he swayed drunk and drooling with the power he was unleashing. His breath came in passionate gasps, heavy with the power-lust that enveloped him. He then became aware of another presence. His eyes widened with greed and revelation as he knew the essence of the nature of the entity. His mind consciousness left his brother and swept through the woman. The pleasure he felt was almost sexual as he passed through her, touching her soul and knowing that she was the one and soon, she would be his.

His consciousness slammed back into his physical body with such force that he was knocked backward and staggered to keep from falling to the ground. He was almost giddy with excitement at discovering without a doubt the woman did indeed exist. Like a weaver creating a tapestry one thread at a time, centuries of planning and manipulating were coming together and forming a viable picture.

With the drought in full bloom and the people of the country of Krit starved and dying, it was time to initiate a chain of events to bring the final player into the game. Ko'Resh used the power he controlled to summon to him a man-child. This he had done many times before but this child was one whose loss would be a devastating blow to the entire nation. The child he summoned was Arlon, Shista of Krit, Sharram Rhandor's only child and heir to the throne. Taking the boy would be the final card played to bend Sharram Rhandor to Ko'Resh's will. The loss of the child would stir emotions no other loss could elicit. Those emotions would cause chemical changes in the brain that were necessary for Ko'Resh to infiltrate Rhandor's mind and make him receptive to Ko'Resh's control. He focused his thoughts on bringing the child to him. As he entered his hovel and closed the heavy wooden door he knew the boy had resolved to leave the fortress during the night to cross the desert separating them.

≫ ≫ ≫

Shista Arlon paced, unable to hide his frustration. He knew his father, Sharram Rhandor, only intended the best but he felt his over-protective attitude was extreme. But how he turned a blind eye to the plight of their people he could not comprehend. How many more Krit had to become ill or die before action was taken? He should have acted when Arlon's mother, Rhandor's mate, Sharrana Rasala, was claimed by the sickness. He wondered if his father understood the loss Arlon felt when his mother died. He was unsure if he was angrier at her death or at his father for his apparent lack of anger.

Why could he not understand his son's need to do something to avenge her death? He was certain the plague and drought were caused by the dark solveige possessed by the one named Ko'Resh. How could his father not know this? Why did he not mount an attack and rid their country of the sorcerer?

Arlon was certain their world would right itself once Ko'Resh was killed. But his father disagreed and forbade him from acting on his anger. He instructed him to remain in his chambers and even posted a guard to ensure he would not leave. It infuriated him to be treated thus. He was in his sixteenth full turn. Old enough to begin the rite of passage to manhood. Yet he had been humiliated and sent to his room in front of the court like a young milk-fed.

So, he paced in his room. His thoughts boiled like a dark cloud between what was and what he desired to be. Some commotion at his chamber door drew his attention and he turned to see his manservant, Bartus, enter. He was about to reprimand him for coming to his chamber unbidden but the words caught before they were spoken. In that instant, a plan sprung to mind.

A smile touched his lips as the plan became cohesive. He motioned for the door to be closed and studied Bartus carefully. He knew he could trust him with most anything but this was different. This meant deliberately aiding in countering a direct command from the sharram himself. He considered if he had the right to ask such a thing of Bartus.

When Bartus entered the room, Arlon could see in his eyes he, too, had an agenda. He watched as Bartus drew a deep breath to calm himself and steady his resolve. "Naid Shista." He bowed. "Know that I am forever and always your servant and the words I speak come from a heart that aches of loss and fear." He raised his head and forced courage that he did not feel into his voice. "I believe I am able to assist you in leaving your chamber to cross to the outer village and avenge your mother." His voice belied the fear Arlon was certain he felt for proposing they defy the sharram. "You know I think of you as brother; your mother raised me as her own when my parents were killed and I was left orphaned at barely eight full turns and had no relatives who could take me in. We grew as siblings until the demands of your education to the court separated our stations. Understand I have the highest respect for our, your father and do not wish to appear…" Arlon stopped him. He knew what Bartus was going to say and wanted to spare him the moral dilemma of actually uttering the words that, if overheard by the wrong person, could be considered treason. Arlon knew others often commented about how similar he and Bartus were in stature and appearance. They could almost pass as siblings. As they grew older, some of the similarities faded but their build and hair color were very close. Once Bartus was of age and officially became manservant to his long-time friend he did adopt the traditional complex braid that was woven into his long black hair to signify his station in the castle. Shista Arlon wore his hair loose and it trailed well past his shoulders to mid-back. The most significant difference in the two were their eyes. Bartus' eyes were the deep ebony customary to the people of Krit while Shista Arlon saw the world through the strange blue-green eyes that only one other of their people was known to have. His father Sharram Rhandor.

"Do not say any more, Bartus. I too have been considering a means to escape these walls. It is best only I speak the words aloud."

The two sat on the floor and Arlon explained what he intended to do. For the plan to work, Bartus would have to braid Arlon's hair to match his own, a task he was not exactly adept at. They would have to exchange clothes and with any luck, Arlon would be able to pass by the guards and escape the castle. He would have to keep his eyes down but they were certain this would work. Bartus remarked he often walked through the castle unnoticed; none saw past his braids.

Shista Arlon studied his friend and confidant. He knew what strength and courage it took for him to even suggest they act against his father. Retribution would be swift and very unpleasant. More so for Bartus. Arlon weighed the fear of this retribution against his driving need to cross to the place past the city of Gaelen where the one who possessed the dark solveige lived. He knew if he was to leave, it would have to be that night; rhuna would rise nearly full and provide enough light for him to see but remain in shadow enough to escape unnoticed through the streets. If he waited until rhuna was at full cycle her light would make him far too visible. He closed the distance between them, took him by the shoulders and looked him in the eye. "Do not fear retribution from me, Bartus. I shall not betray you to my father. I know that your words are driven by love for my mother." He let go Bartus' shoulders and turned toward the window that dominated the south wall of his chamber. He could see the tension leave Bartus when he spoke those words.

The plan seemed sound and Bartus had earlier taken the liberty of stowing a sack with supplies under the root of a tree where they spent many afternoons as youth. There were only a few horses remaining that were not so sickly they could not be ridden. It seemed it would be too much a temptation to ride such a significant amount of meat through a starving country but they decided to take the risk. Arlon was healthy and quick enough to be able to abandon the beast and escape should any ambush occur.

Bartus' hands trembled as he gathered his master's hair into braids that defined the rank of manservant. For a moment they doubted their resolve as Arlon's hair was pulled back off his face, exposing his chiseled features. Bartus had expected this and had enlisted the expertise of one of the girls he kept company with. She showed him how to apply darker shades of powder to mask certain features while enhancing others.

Thus, he was able to diminish the appearance of Arlon's higher cheek bones and soften the bridge of his nose. It was not enough to make him appear as Bartus, but enough that, with a quick glance in the dark of the corridor at night, he might not be recognized as Shista Arlon. They knew most would see the braids and not give him a second look unless something caused suspicion.

Bartus assessed his work; "Remember to keep your head down and do not speak unless absolutely necessary. If you must speak then do so as low-born. Muddy your accent and draw out your words."

Arlon looked at Bartus and shook his head. "You don't talk like that"

"No, but it would be interesting to hear you natter like Drogal down at the stables." His attempt at trying to break the heavy air fell a bit flat.

Arlon cleared his throat. "Hey you tharrr boy…dun ya be trryin tu be gittin thar harses outta me stables within ou my seein tharrr good an rready!" Arlon tried rolling his r's to mimic Stable Master Drogal rather unsuccessfully.

The two young men laughed, but it was strained and quickly swallowed by the gravity of what they were about to do. Arlon was almost certain Bartus' role in this would not go unnoticed or unpunished. He was also certain Bartus knew this as well.

Arlon straightened and pulled the hood of his tunic up around his head. He reached his hand to his friend. It did not seem enough of a gesture. He pulled him in and hugged him. A sense of foreboding filled him. At that moment he knew they would not cross paths again.

He pushed himself from the embrace and turned to the door. He motioned to Bartus to get into the bed and pull the covers. He took one last look around his chamber and knocked on the door to signal the guard.

He felt his heart skip a beat when the latch was pulled and the door opened. He kept his head down, pushed his way past the guard and hurried down the hall. It felt like an eternity passed before he heard the door closing behind him and the latch drop into place. He forced himself to breath as he made his way through the empty corridors and out to the stable. He thought it curious that Drogal was asleep and did not stir when he entered or when he gathered his saddle and led his horse from the stable. He walked the beast for some distance before he saddled him. He mounted and reined him to head to the back pasture where the old tree held his supplies. He had no second thought about what he planned. He was driven by a blinding certainty. He did not give a moment's pause to consider how easy it was to escape the castle completely unchallenged or that he did not encounter anyone at all moving about. He urged the beast into a quick trot and then a gallop in the direction of Gaelen.

The road was well travelled before the drought, and he made astonishing progress. He found himself passing through the town at first light still veiled in the shadow of predawn. A strange mist circled around him like a shroud. Odd creatures appeared in the swirling fog then would disappear so quickly he could not be certain his eyes did not deceive him. He passed through the village unchecked. He kept the hood of his tunic pulled well over his face and saw people moving from the shadows, cautious but curious, until the heat of the day forced them back. He dismounted and tied his horse. He would walk from here and leave the beast to the village. He was not far beyond the gate when he heard the horse shriek. It was quick.

He strode headlong toward his destination. He knew soon he would come face to face with the sorcerer who caused his people so much pain; the one who took his mother from him.

His resolve remained strong when he forced open the door of the hut. The stench that assailed him was overpowering. He staggered back and bought his hand to his face to cover his mouth and nose. He did not see the man behind the door. Too late, he saw movement and tried to react. He felt a sharp blow to his head. Shista Arlon fell into blackness.

CHAPTER 10

ACROSS A VAST DISTANCE OF DEADENED SOIL, A MAN, great in stature and great of noble heart, strode with deliberate purpose. His heart ached with pain and fear. Yet only his god would know of this fear, for he hid it even from himself and it was this fear that bound him to this world and caused him to allow another to rule his soul.

As this man neared the end of his journey, each footfall echoed silently in the rising and settling of the dust of this new desert. Those who kept watch spied his approach and a signal was passed through the village.

Even if he were accompanied by a great procession, his arrival could not be more pronounced and though he walked alone, he walked with the hearts and souls of his people. Their devotion was unfailing. He was Rhandor. He was their sharram. As he approached the village, those who still had strength made their way to the street to greet him. Even in their sick and weakened state they bowed low as he passed. Any other time they would have pondered why he strode deliberately toward the hut south of their village but they saw the boy-man arrive, shrouded in secrecy two days earlier. They heard his cries of agony and buried his tortured body. Those who performed this task went mad within hours and hurled themselves from the cliffs that rose to separate the village from the sea, ensuring the identity of the adolescent would remain a mystery.

They knew soon someone would come.

They did not expect Sharram Rhandor, unescorted. And upon seeing him it was scarcely a heartbeat before rumor circled that it was Shista Arlon who was buried by the roadside. Then disbelief, desperation and defeat consumed them. They could not accept the idea that Rhandor would send his own son. But they did not know, nor could they, that Rhandor did not know until too

97

late that Arlon stole away into the night to seek out the man who possessed solvieg—the dark powers. And Arlon himself did not realize that he was summoned and his will was not his own. He was unaware that he was a tool necessary to carry out a plan to draw Sharram Rhandor into the grip of the one who summoned him.

Anyone whose mind was not clouded from the pains of hunger and remained inclined to take notice of such things as posture and gait would have seen that Rhandor was deeply troubled. He strode barely noticing his kinsmen. His strong hands were balled tightly into fists turning the knuckles white. His square jaw clenched in anger and disgust, an air of desperation, unfamiliar to the man, echoed in his blue eyes.

And so it was that Rhandor, Sharram of Krit, the single member of the procession, tread through the village of Gaelen and onto a dirt road that ushered him past the place of the dead where a fresh mound of dirt, already dried to dust in the scorching heat, beckoned his attention. He thought it odd that with the death fires burning someone would take the time to bury a body. His stomach tightened but his pace did not slow. He desperately wanted to be on time, but the sick pain behind his heart told him he was already too late to save his son. He pressed on. His eyes remained focused on the recent grave. As he watched, a hot gust of wind blew past him to the dry mound and picked up a column of dust. His pace slowed as the column moved through the deadened trees and onto the road. It took up position in the centre of the road and came to a halt before the man. Then came a long and painful howl that froze Rhandor's blood, and for the first time in as long as he could remember a tear escaped him. The wind shifted and the column of dust moved to engulf him. It bit vengefully into his eyes. It filled his mouth and nose, leaving a bitter taste, and prevented him from drawing a breath. Pain like nothing he had ever experienced slammed through his body. He stopped his march and knew the pain to be anguish and remorse. It filled his heart beyond what he ever imagined possible. The wind ceased and the column collapsed and when he looked at the dust it was not dry soil but ash. In that moment, visions exploded in his mind as though he was seeing through someone else's eyes. He saw himself approaching the door to Ko'Resh's hut and pushing it open. At once he knew he was seeing as Arlon. He saw movement then a period of blackness. The visions returned through a fog but he could see Ko'Resh, through Arlon's eyes, standing above him and saw the flash of metal and felt the bite of steel running down the length of his right leg. He was aware of screaming and being restrained. And the smell, the terrible unmistakable stench of rotting flesh. His vision flickered then he saw what Ko'Resh held secret beneath his robes when he lifted them and exposed his own flesh rotting from his bones.

Rhandor fell to his knees and pressed his hands to his eyes to try to stop the visions but they kept coming as he felt the flesh being carved from his son's body to be grafted over the decaying flesh that was Ko'Resh. He felt bile rise in his throat and did not try to stop it when the full realization that his son was skinned alive burned its way into his mind.

When pure raw emotion was all that Rhandor knew, Ko'Resh invaded his subconscious and planted a subliminal suggestion that would grow in strength and remain hidden from Rhandor's consciousness. This was the final thread Ko'Resh needed to weave to draw Rhandor completely under his control. Once placed, the spell would wind itself around Rhandor's will, unnoticed, until it was firmly established and then Rhandor would be no more than a puppet to Ko'Resh.

Rhandor lifted his head to the sky and cried out. He cursed the name of Selam for allowing such things, and his shame and sorrow were great for he was unable to save his son and it remained uncertain whether he would fail his people as well. He gathered his strength and pushed back the memory of his son when the wail of a woman claimed his attention. He stood and faced the village. The people had heard his outburst and fallen to their knees. They prayed and wept for they believed that what they feared had truly come to pass. Shista Arlon, heir to the throne, was dead and Sharram Rhandor had been powerless to prevent it from happening.

Rhandor faltered. He looked south beyond the village and imagined, in the distance, the walls of the city of Jordan to the south. Looking east and north he saw the Illuna Mountains. Once covered with a lush canopy, they now lay barren. Naked shards of rock strained toward the sky as though begging relief from Selam himself. Where once a thundering waterfall fed life to his people, a jagged, ugly scar remained. It slashed the face of the mountain and tore open a gash in the land that shred it in two. In all directions lay nothing but wasteland. Dry desert and fire. Fire that burned constant, fueled with the bodies of Krit taken there by wagons from the nearby cities and villages. A new wave of anger and frustration washed over Rhandor. To the east lay the Sea of Sagares and even those waters no longer supported life. Dead sea creatures that once fed the seaside villages and promoted trade with the nearby countries of Norval and Sambahar littered the shores and cliffside. A villager, in an act of desperation, drank from the sea and died an agonizing death. And to the west, the endless Aevitas Ocean. Even if hope could be found beyond the huge expanse of water he doubted anyone would be able to set aside generations of superstition and legend to attempt to journey into that unknown. Many believed the drought and the poison waters to be the work of the one Rhandor now sought. That man was Ko'Resh.

There were still two paces journey to reach the hut of Ko'Resh. Rhandor looked to the sky. The resh was past its zenith and there were but five paces till darkness and the rising of rhuna. He hoped he would be well away from this place by then. His thoughts returned to Ko'Resh. Some said that name meant "of the resh," but this was a man who harbored no light; only the black of solvieg surrounded him. Rhandor glanced again at the place of the dead where he was certain his son's body lay and wondered of the boy's spirit. Had it died also? He squashed the thought of what the afterlife may hold for one who died as Arlon. He forced himself to turn away. He corralled all thoughts except those feelings of contempt for Ko'Resh and continued his journey.

As he neared the hut the unmistakable stench of death assaulted him. He looked to the east. The resh was now past the sixth pace. His gaze was drawn one last time beyond the dirt road, even beyond what his eyes could see, to where the gravesite lay. He imagined the golden light of the evening resh touching the mounds of dry dust and prayed the souls of those beneath had moved on to the afterlife as heroes and warriors even though many were too young to know battle or even the first stolen kiss from a maiden.

He paused outside the door and listened to the sounds from within. He wondered at a rhythmic hissing that was punctuated with the sounds of papers rustling. Rhandor drained himself of all thoughts of what happened behind these clay walls and made himself void of all emotions save his hate for the man within and his own need to save his world. He still had three paces of resh-light before dark. Much evil lurked here.

He pushed open the rugged wooden door. He did not bother to knock or announce his arrival before entering. A myriad of strange and familiar scents assailed him, tainted by the unmistakable stench of rotting flesh pushed by a wave of cool air. He found it strange that the air within the hut was much cooler than the stifling heat outside. The dim glow from a smoky oil lamp prevented darkness from engulfing the windowless, one-room hovel. Rhandor surveyed the room; his gaze paused briefly on an assortment of colored vessels filled to varying levels with liquids and vegetation. The centre of the room was dominated by a large table covered with many papers and more vials. To his right were shelves with more of the same. To his left was a filthy, unmade bed. Rhandor quickly averted his eyes, unsure of why, then let his gaze rest on the form of the short man directly ahead of him working with his back to him at the only other piece of furniture in the room, a small desk littered with even more paper. Rhandor's hand went instinctively to the dagger on his thigh, touching the hide-wrapped hilt. He toyed with the idea of imbedding the blade in the man's back.

The resh dipped lower on the horizon, drenching the hut in a blood-red glow through the open door. He took his hand from the dagger and again suppressed his anger. He pushed the door closed, allowing it to slam with a loud thud. The blast of air from the sudden movement nearly extinguished the weak flame of the lamp. Still Ko'Resh did not look up from his work or acknowledge the sharram's arrival. It was distasteful enough for Rhandor to feel that he needed to illicit the help of one he had nothing but contempt for, but to be ignored and kept waiting only fueled his frustration. Again, his hand brushed the hilt of his dagger and again he wondered at his restraint at following through on his instincts.

The hissing sound that Rhandor heard earlier proved to be the sounds of a strange device in one corner of the room that was moving cool air into the filthy hut. He watched the man's back as he continued to ignore him and shuffle through a heap of parchments, keeping a select few in his left hand. The others he carefully added to a pile on his right. Rhandor realized that though the hut was filthy, everything in it was in some kind of order. Only when Ko'Resh seemed satisfied he had what he wanted did he turn and acknowledge Rhandor.

"You find me offensive yet you seek my help, Sharram Rhandor," Ko'Resh said. He studied the giant man's face as though trying to probe his mind, confirming that what he planted earlier was indeed in place.

"I have nothing but contempt for you, Ko'Resh, that I do not deny. And you would be correct in assuming that I would as soon slit your throat as see the likes of you survive while many more deserving of life die."

"Ah, my sharram, and who is it that determines which of us is more deserving?"

"I doubt that I am *your* sharram," Rhandor growled down at Ko'Resh. "As for who deserves what—I am sure time will make that distinction." Rhandor glared contemptuously at the man. "You know why I am here. And I am more than certain you have a solution."

Ko'Resh's eyes fell back to his work. "Yes, but ..." he muttered to himself.

"But what!?" Rhandor's jaw tightened.

He turned to hide his face from Rhandor and absently arranged some papers. "It seems the answer lies almost beyond our reach." He glanced up at Rhandor, making brief eye contact as though assessing his strength then quickly shifted his gaze to the door

"Almost?" Rhandor repeated, his scowl deepening.

Ko'Resh ignored him. He brushed past the giant Krit and started through the door. He motioned for Rhandor to follow. Rhandor obeyed, eyeing Ko'Resh's unusually short stature as he followed him into the hot night air. He was glad to be out of the closeness of the hovel and the terrible stench that permeated the air. The resh had set but the night offered no relief from the stifling heat, which was in stark contrast to the cooler temperature of the hut. Rhandor knew it was some form of dark magic that controlled the temperature of the hut and this knowledge gave him a perverse sense of hope that such power could turn back the drought and famine and save his people. He also harbored the idea that it was this very solvieg that caused the drought in the first place. For now, he would bide his time and humor the short man and, when he knew his people were safe, justice would be served.

And what of this man called Ko'Resh? It had been rumored among the people that the wizard was not of Krit. Rhandor had no trouble in believing such a rumor. Many times, Rhandor pondered the strange man's existence. So little did anyone know of him except that he was very old. Many legends spoke of one with the same name, but it seemed almost inconceivable that they could be speaking of this same man. That would make him centuries old. The unnaturalness of that concept made the hairs stand up on the back of Rhandor's neck as he found he was consciously accepting that the man he was now following was indeed the same man. His appearance, however strange in stature to the Krit, seemed ancient, yet he possessed all of his teeth and his hair was a long, thick unkempt nest of a copper hue.

Rhandor recalled his vision at the gravesite and repulsion filled him when he remembered what abomination lay hidden beneath the filthy robe. Ko'Resh stood barely five measures; the shortest Krit woman stood at least six. Rhandor tried to picture the man locked in union with a long Krit woman. The thought repulsed him. Apparently, it was distasteful to the twisted mind of Ko'Resh also. But, nevertheless, some strange blood mingled with the noble blood of Rhandor's ancestors, turning his eyes blue, away from the deep ebony of his kinsman. Some, in the deepest reaches of their minds, believed Ko'Resh went to the Sharrana Yara, Rhandor's mother, and caused her to see only her mate at a time when his father was away and Rhandor was the product of that union. They cursed his blue eyes to the elders. Some believed them to be an omen and said he would bring death to the people of Krit. Others thought the blue fire was a sign of greatness. Krit women found them alluring, so he found in his adolescence. But as he surveyed the wasteland that was Krit, he felt he was cursed. Even as he held his mate, Sharrana Rasala, and she drew her last breath, her death brought on by a sudden illness at the earliest signs of the famine, he believed his existence was a curse. Shista Arlon's death cemented that resolve. And as they continued to walk through the night ascending the same path Ko'Resh travelled with each phase of rhuna, Rhandor glared down at the back of the man and wondered.

As a child, Rhandor had heard the legend of Rhuna, a land beyond the Aevitas Ocean. Rhuna, named after the light in the night sky was only that, Rhandor told himself, a legend. The people were said to be as beautiful as Rhuna herself. Their skin pale, their hair, the copper fire of the resh at morning rise and eyes as green as a field of new grain. A legend? Rhandor glanced at Ko'Resh now struggling beside him. Green eyes glared back. Though it mattered not if such a land existed, for none had ever crossed the endless waters and none would. Superstition lay heavy on the Aevitas Ocean; so much so that even the mention of venturing beyond sight of land caused even the most stout-hearted to call forth protection from Selam. For a brief moment he was filled with doubt at so daunting a journey, but again his thoughts seemed to be taken from him and dulled so he stopped questioning and allowed himself to believe in the possibility that Ko'Resh would be their savior.

Ko'Resh stopped briefly and turned to Rhandor. "You wonder too many things, Sharram Rhandor." He returned his attention to the narrow path and continued ahead. "Too many," he muttered and let out a deep sigh as though he had just laid down a heavy burden.

Rhandor hid his unease at the insinuation that Ko'Resh had known his thoughts. A lucky guess? Ko'Resh would have him believe otherwise.

They arrived at the village gate retracing the path Rhandor had taken earlier. As they passed the place of the dead where Arlon's body lay, Rhandor felt the sorrow welling in his heart threatening to once more consume him. Something within him once more turned his thoughts and numbed his mind to his emotions.

They passed through the village of Gaelen via the main thoroughfare; at this time in the evening the streets used to bustle with people finishing last-minute commerce or couples enjoying an evening out. Families often strolled through the main square, children marveled at magicians and acrobats, all feeling safe and carefree. Parents worked together to monitor the children though it was hardly necessary as no danger lurked here. Colorful clothing that defined the Krit merchants flowed over tall, lean bodies. Dark, thick hair adorned the heads of Krit women who were rumored to never cut their hair through their lifetime. Many had tresses well past their waist. Men wore their hair long but most found it more practical to cut it short or keep it well bound in braids down their backs. Stately and proud was their affect, but at the same time they were a very giving and peaceful people. However, when raised to arms, if provoked, they used swift and deadly force. Both men and women were highly skilled warriors and this was common knowledge throughout Krit and the nearby countries of Norval and Sambahar.

This night no children romped in the square. In fact, the children were the first to die. Unnaturally quickly they succumbed to whatever magic squeezed the life from his land. No vendors pawned their wares, no bright clothing rustled to the rhythm of an impromptu street band. No laughter rang through the streets. Only the stench of death remained and the only music was the bitter wail of mourning that ebbed through the deepening night.

And Gaelen was not unique. All of Krit suffered the same fate and no one knew how to stop it. Even the elders were taken by surprise when the famine struck, let alone the almost mystic disease that swept through the kingdom simultaneously. History told of other times when famine and plague ravaged the land but the people had warning—the signs were there and the elders had the people prepare food and medicines to help protect them and better weather these natural disasters. Even the early winter stores they had begun to gather were ravaged by some unknown blight that rendered them inedible. The plague was unnaturally swift and thorough, thus the elders looked to unnatural causes, and many fingers pointed to the one unknown— Ko'Resh. But to what end did destroying the people of Krit serve?

Rhandor wondered of the other creatures that shared this world. The domestic creatures had all succumbed shortly after the children. His thoughts turned once more to his son Arlon and an empty pain he knew could easily consume him began to creep into his heart. He felt the pressure of something intruding on his mind. This time he knew he was not imagining it. A gut feeling told him to discontinue his train of thought. He felt a strange conflict within him. He glared at Ko'Resh who straightened and turned to return the stare. For a moment there was a wordless exchange between the two men then Ko'Resh appeared to nod as though coming to some conclusion, and with an overconfident smirk he again turned his back to Sharram Rhandor.

The unlikely duo continued their trek in silence throughout the village. No one seemed to take notice as they passed. It was as though a shroud hid the pair from onlookers.

Rhandor assumed this was more of Ko'Resh's solvieg.

≫ ≫ ≫

Ko'Resh encouraged the silence, for it offered him the opportunity to continue to invade Rhandor's consciousness and, as Rhandor allowed his mind to wander, it became easier for Ko'Resh to channel thought patterns and manipulate where Rhandor's thoughts were carried. This enabled him to reinforce Rhandor's belief that he needed Ko'Resh.

The last distance of the footpath to the summit where Ko'Resh kept his crude observatory was quite steep, causing even Rhandor to become slightly winded. The combination of heat and lack of adequate nourishment had begun to whittle away at the sharram's strength and endurance. Though, even in his decreased capacity, he was still a formidable match for most adversaries. This brought Ko'Resh's thoughts back to his encounter with the woman during his last pilgrimage up this mountain. He wondered who she was but knew intuitively that she had to be the Sharrana of Rhuna. No other bloodline was capable of sustaining the power of the Sem Lukos Resh. The seven spirits needed the strength of the royal blood. He thought of his own progeny, Sharram Rhandor, and hoped he carried enough Rhue blood to bring what was divided with the birth of identical twins back into one soul. It was not so much the bloodline as the ability to sustain the power he sought that became divided somehow with the division of an embryo so many centuries ago. And perhaps adding Krit blood to the mix would strengthen the bonds between the Sem Lukos Resh and the embodiment that would try to contain such power in one being.

It was possible indeed; it had been accomplished many, many centuries ago when Saal, the creator of the Sem Lukos Resh, walked the soils of Rhuna. It was Ko'Resh's desire to create such a being again and transfer his soul into that body. After killing his brother and reuniting the Sem Lukos Resh, he would be the most powerful being on the planet. He needed to control the giant Krit because he knew Rhandor would never take the sharrana against her will and Sharrana Nahleen would never give herself to Rhandor. But that was inconsequential, as there was no way she could fend off such a man, and by the time they arrived on the shores of Rhuna he would have complete control over Rhandor. He saw no way he could fail. Soon all would be his.

"Tell me, Ko'Resh," Rhandor growled. "Why do we take this evening stroll? Surely we did not come into the heat of this night to gaze at the stars?" He made a sweeping gesture toward the heavens not even trying to hide his animosity.

"Yes, Sharram Rhandor," Ko'Resh replied too matter-of-factly, his tone blaring with overconfidence. "We did indeed journey to this hilltop to observe the heavens."

Rhandor's hand reached out and grabbed Ko'Resh by the throat. Ko'Resh's eyes bulged, partly because of the pressure on his throat but more in surprise because he did not see this coming. Rhandor continued to squeeze and a smile blushed faint on his lips. Ko'Resh's flesh compressed under Rhandor's vice-like grip. His pulse bounded.

Ko'Resh stood on his toes trying to gain some height to relieve some of the pressure but he lost his balance and was struggled to regain his footing as well as draw in a breath. He summoned the power of the first spirit of the six he possessed. He felt the familiar stirrings as the spirit breasts, which lay at the base of his spine, coiled like a ghostly serpent, began to awaken. They wound their way upward through his physical and ethereal self and unleash their god-like power, amplifying what was created in the forced combination of the spirits bound to each other and to his own soul.

A mantra began to chime, first in his conscious mind, then quickly and steadily deeper, until his whole body vibrated with the sounds as they resounded over themselves

Lam Lad Au Ram, Lam Lad Au Ram, Lam Lad Au Ram…

He felt the surge of power of the first spirit as it rose within him. He felt the primal lust and trembled as a flood of energy swept through him down from the top of his head to the base of his spine before rising again to settle like a ball of fire, light and sound slightly above the base of his spine. He became connected and separate at the same time, to Mythos and himself. He was consciously aware of all aspects of his body; he felt his breath as it entered his lungs and the molecules break down and bond with his blood and he felt the carbon gasses as they were expelled. Every beat of his heart pulsed outward like a pebble dropped into the centre of a tranquil pool in an electric wave ever-expanding from its epicentre to beyond his physical being. He focused on the vortex that was opening, allowing more energy to flow. He felt the first stirrings of the creatures, bonded together in a perverse triad that blended the masculine, feminine and savage animal that existed in all, but became bastardized and amplified as it spewed forth within Ko'Resh, giving him power. It altered his connection between his body and the physical plane of existence. It opened a floodgate that controlled the adrenal glands and caused his physical strength to increase beyond human capability.

With his strength amplified thus, he was able to pull Rhandor's hand from his throat as though he was merely shooing an insect and dropped to the ground. The power continued to build. Ko'Resh rose to his feet and had to steady himself while he let it wash over him in an overwhelming tide of black/red color and sound. He raised his eyes to meet Rhandor's and drew himself up, and though he was considerably shorter than the giant Krit, at that moment, he seemed as though he was so much more.

≫ ≫ ≫

Rhandor unconsciously backed down. He stared at the man before him, but no thoughts would manifest. He watched, as though from a distance, as the form of a great beast, not unlike the lukos that stalked the once-lush forests of Krit, rose from somewhere within Ko'Resh and shrouded him in a ghostly vapor. He saw the forms of other creatures and at first, he did not recognize them. He watched their sorrowful dance as they struggled to break free of the bonds that imprisoned them, harnessing their spirit essence to channel power through the beast to which they were enslaved. And as he watched, he knew them to be Sohar Ka'Desh, a legendary creature that was both beautiful and alien to look at. Rarely seen by any, it was said the Sohar Ka'Desh were pure energy beings who descended into the physical realm to maintain balance on the planet. They came to counter the darkness that had been created when the world began. It was said, because their energy was so pure, that they were not able to remain in the physical realm so when they descended to walk upon Mythos, they become joined with the spirit of a lukos. For every Sohar Ka'Desh there was a lukos spirit guide, which was why they were able to avoid being seen. If one was fortunate enough to see a Sohar Ka'Desh, they would also see the lukos joined to it. Such a sighting was said to be a good omen among the peoples of Mythos.

Rhandor took a step back in an effort to break whatever hold Ko'Resh had on him. His thoughts were fragmented as he struggled to regain control. A sense of vulnerability crept into his psyche as the last strands of free will sought to abandon him.

≫ ≫ ≫

Ko'Resh toyed with the idea of pressing further into Rhandor's mind and taking total control but restrained himself knowing he needed Rhandor to exhibit an aura of control to his people when the time came. He allowed the first of his beasts he summoned to probe Rhandor and watched as his aura changed in response to the mutated energy field as it invaded his very soul. Ko'Resh saw the wheels of energy throughout Rhandor's aura spark, flare up and then return to almost normal as his creatures swept through leaving a trace essence of what had passed. Ko'Resh saw it as a good omen that Rhandor did, in fact, carry enough Rhue blood to bring about the Sheth— the chosen one.

This accomplished, Ko'Resh restrained the beast he had summoned and allowed Rhandor to regain his consciousness. He was having a difficult time harnessing the awesome power he had unleashed. This was the first time he allowed any of the spirits to manifest so near their full potential. The wave of power was exhilarating and overwhelming. His body responded with a primal sexual response that was unexpected at first but as the power centre's opening evolved, he understood the natural progress of his feelings of desire and being disjointed from his surroundings yet connected to all that is and more. As further knowing flooded his ancient body, he became rejuvenated with this knowledge and his interconnectedness with many planes of existence at once. His greed for more power caused him to hesitate in restraining the beast. There was a moment of conflict as the spirit creatures fought for freedom and he struggled to restrain them. A spark of fear shot through Ko'Resh's body when, for a brief moment, he thought he would not be able to subdue them. He felt panic begin to rise within him. He pushed harder with his mind and focused on his desire to control the raging power within him.

He envisioned the serpent-like power conduit coiling and drawing to itself the lukos spirits and imprisoned Sohar Ka'Desh into a vortex of black and red. It spiraled lower and tighter until only a small wheel of white light glowed dimly at that place near the base of his spine. His adrenal glands slowed their outpouring of hormones to a normal level. His heart rate returned to normal and his erection subsided. He swayed, nearly losing his balance. His mind filled with conflicting emotions of fear and excitement. The raw power of what he possessed was becoming clear to him. He smiled and nodded to himself. Once he claimed the Sheth Child and the seventh of the lukos spirits that his brother had, he would indeed be an invincible force. He turned his attention to Rhandor, who had the appearance of one recovering from a night of heavy drinking. At that moment Rhandor seemed small. Ko'Resh knew he could end his life with the flick of his hand. Soon enough, but for now, he needed Rhandor to bring forth the Sheth Child. He pushed past the giant and continued the journey to the observatory, beckoning Rhandor to follow. He charted the movement of the planets and reviewed his calculations in silence. When he finally spoke, it was not necessarily directed at Rhandor and he most certainly did not expect any response.

"The planets will be aligned within two full cycles." He studied Sharram Rhandor, not oblivious to the ruler's excellent physical condition, and felt a stirring within him. He was not sure why he could be moved by the sight of the great man, save the knowledge that he would be the key to gaining ultimate power over all he desired.

"This alignment," Rhandor growled, "I trust will somehow provide the tools to end this drought?" Rhandor's venomous expression left little to the imagination.

Ko'Resh hid his unease over what had happened earlier. It continued to elude him how Rhandor was able to accomplish that feat and how it took the full power of the Amladhar spirit vortices, the first of the Sem Lukos Resh, to subdue him. Even now, Rhandor seemed to retain an unacceptable level of free will that threatened to overtake Ko'Resh's hold and jeopardize his plans.

"Yes, Sharram Rhandor." He found himself using Rhandor's formal title and chastised himself silently when he realized he had given just the slightest bow. "As you have already correctly surmised, I am not of your people. My homeland lies on the distant shores of the Aevitas Ocean. Since the dawn of time my home, Rhuna, has been closed off from the rest of Mythos. When the planets come into alignment there will be a great quaking of the land and that which separates Rhuna will fall into the sea. When I return to Rhuna, I will claim what was denied me many eons ago and I will have the power to end your people's suffering. Long have I desired to return home." The last sentence was spoken as his gaze swept the heavens and seaward toward his home land of Rhuna then to her namesake, the moon rhuna, glowing silver and all but full in the stifling heat of Krit.

He sighed heavily, shook his head and wondered at the moment of melancholy he just experienced. It seemed that as the time drew nearer he was having these episodes more frequently. At first, he brushed them off, not believing them to be more than an imagined wave of nostalgia, but during the past full cycle of rhuna these episodes became a little more frequent and much more definite. He shrugged the feeling off and pushed past Rhandor to start his descent and return to his hut. "Come, Rhandor." He turned briefly, looking back over his shoulder with a feeling that he forgot something. "We have a long journey ahead of us and much to do to prepare." With that, he continued down the same path they travelled earlier.

Rhandor followed obediently. His affect gave the appearance of submission.

CHAPTER 11

KIAN'HUARD GATHERED HIS ROBE AND REACHED FOR his walking staff. "Come, Naid Sharrana." He beckoned her to follow. "I have something to show you and much to explain." He sighed heavily, his voice barely audible as though he wanted to avoid speaking. He fixed his eyes on hers and felt a sense of loss building in his heart. Nahleen helped Kian'Huard to his feet and handed him his walking staff. He knew she had questions but they would have to wait until he completed his task for the evening. They continued the remainder of the journey in relative silence. His silence stemmed from knowing what needed to be done and what the cost would be. He needed to find the right words. He knew she could sense his emotions, but there was no way for her to imagine what could disrupt their peaceful existence so much that it would illicit such overwhelming feelings, and he had no words with which to comfort her.

As they approached the observatory, which was carefully concealed within a rocky crag in the face of the mountaintop, Kian'Huard took a moment to pause and drink in the view. The resh was all but gone, leaving only a thin strand of mauve thread weaving itself through the mountains that bordered the country of Rhuna on the north and acted as a pedestal for the city of Kephas that housed the Temple of Osiris. The land spread out before them from this vantage point like a giant tapestry filled with patchwork farmland and tidy rows of houses and shops in the towns dotting the land as it stretched a yawning arm to the sea that bordered the bulk of the kingdom. The capital city of Althean, which housed the castle, rose like the hub of a wagon wheel. All roads eventually made their way to the city centre and the public gardens that Althean was famous for. The rich, deep-blue velvet of the evening sky was beginning to surrender the first crystalline shards of starlight as its color deepened with the loss of resha, now visiting the opposite side of her world. Their moon, rhuna, was now beginning to emerge from the embers of the setting of the resh. As the face of rhuna that was turned toward the sunken orb of their sun came into the correct alignment, it exploded in orange, red and purple fire. The effect was breathtaking, as though the back of the small planet had burst into flame that pushed it up into the sky. As the resh settled further to bring the first strands of dawn to the opposite side of Mythos, the shift in alignment turned the front of rhuna into a half-globe of liquid silver fire that swirled at the equator to blend with the orange fire below. No matter how many times Kian'Huard watched this celestial exchange, he was always captured by the beauty of the stark silver-and-orange planet rising full into a black, diamond-studded sky.

That night, as he watched the cosmic ritual unfold as it had since the dawn of time, he focused his attention on the dread that rose in the pit of his stomach. He watched Nahleen as she too was captured by the beauty before them. He cleared his throat to nudge Nahleen from her thoughts. "Come," he said and motioned for her to follow him into the observatory. Nahleen took one last moment to drink in the beauty of rhuna rising, nearly full, in the east, and shining down on her namesake, the country of Rhuna. Then she turned and followed Kian-Huard into the mountain.

>> >> >>

They climbed a stairway carved into the very rock itself, passing deeper and higher into the mountain. The passageway remained illuminated though no visible means was evident. This always intrigued Nahleen, though she never thought to ask Kian-Huard about it and tonight was not the time to ask. The air inside the mountain remained warm and dry, another anomaly that would remain unchallenged but evidence indicated some form of magic was responsible. Her thoughts strayed to what she experienced earlier as she came upon Kian-Huard on the footpath and the intense feeling that swept through her. A shiver coursed through her and she pushed the feeling aside as realization that her life was about to change dramatically overwhelmed her. She reached out a hand to steady herself against the rock wall and paused for a moment while she gained her composure. Kian-Huard stopped and turned back to face her. He said nothing, but the look on his face echoed through the mountain tunnels like a desperate, remorseful howl. Nahleen gasped as their eyes met. The wordless exchange took only moments, but she was filled with so much emotion and it lingered heavy on her heart for the remainder of the ascent.

The observatory remained unchanged for as long as Nahleen could remember, and in this time of great unease, its familiar surroundings provided her with a superficial sense of comfort.

Kian-Huard motioned for her to sit on one of the two roughhewn wooden chairs that were placed on opposite sides of a similarly constructed, neatly organized table to the right of the entrance. The centre of the huge chamber was carved, somehow, out of the heart of the mountain and was filled with the viewing instrument created by Kian-Huard many centuries ago. It was through this device made up of cylinders and lenses that he was able to chart the progress of the planets and study the wonders of the heavens. And though he had spent more than one person's lifetime in doing so, he still remained filled with a sense of awe and wonder at the infinite complexity of the universe.

Nahleen sat. obediently. Even though she was the Sharrana of Rhuna, she harbored a great deal of respect for the ancient man and only he could ever illicit this kind of staunch obedience. She felt a closeness to him, almost familial but deeper, that she did not share with any others. She knew in her soul they shared a bond that was more than the sum of both their beings but remained unsure of the nature of that bond. And that night, as she sat across from him at the wooden table worn smooth from centuries of use and studied his ancient face, something in his tone and the sadness in his eyes told her that bond would soon be tested.

Kian-Huard rested his hands on the table, folding and unfolding a handful of yellowed parchments as he groped for the right words to begin to tell Sharrana Nahleen of the true nature of their existence. His eyes met hers again and he turned his head to one side and nodded to himself in an act of confirmation.

"Do you know how old I am?" he asked. His voice, though soft and gentle, shattered the overwhelming silence.

Sharrana Nahleen could not restrain the puzzled look from her face. She thought the question a rather strange start to a conversation, and the answer eluded her.

"Sharrana Nahleen…" he started, his eyes fixed on his hands folded in front of him resting on the parchments. Closer scrutiny showed the tension he was feeling. He sighed again. "Nahleen…" His voice softened further, almost to a whisper. He forced himself to relax and lay his hands flat on the table, unconsciously patting the parchments as he searched for words. "*Bend-het-seten.*"

"But that is impossible!" She objected, but the look in his eyes told her otherwise. "How?" was all she could manage. That was more than two millennia!

"For sure, Naid Sharrana, it is an extraordinary tale. Much have I done, much have I seen and much, I find, I am soon to regret." His voice was filled with sincere emotion.

Nahleen tried to swallow, her mouth suddenly dry and her heartbeat heavy in her chest. She remained quiet, her jaw set, looking more regal than she felt, and waited for him to continue.

He cleared his throat.

"Naid'kia modet applenta astendo
Naidan asan modet applenta tranest
Naidan eithne astra d'ai codentair
Applenta naid eith vida Rhuna
Applenta naid eith vidorn Sharrana
Applenta naident "

My soul aches for freedom
My body longs for rest
My heart is torn
For my beloved Rhuna
For my beloved Sharrana
For myself

He stared into the distance, focused on a time barely remembered but impossible to forget; the turning point that changed his life forever.

"I will tell you now of a time many seasons ago when two arrogant and foolish adolescents entered a place they had no business going. Too arrogant to understand, or even care, for they were twins, born as shista. Our mother, Sharrana Irial, died in childbirth and our father, Sharram Kar'Set…it is said that his soul died that day as well, for he loved her beyond words, beyond life.

So it was said among the people.

"Ko'Resh and I, though raised in court, were rather undisciplined for future leaders. Our father, though physically present, was little more than a shadow of a man giving little substance to life. The people of Rhuna were patient and understanding for many years but expected their sharram to eventually rally and again be the great ruler that he was. As my brother and I grew to adolescence it became increasingly apparent that our father was all but dead. Ko'Resh and I were growing further apart and adopted vastly different lifestyles. By ten full cycles, when we should have been assuming minor duties in the court, Ko'Resh was frequently absent, often being discovered by our guardians in some very compromising circumstances. Many times, a large sum of currency was needed to rectify his wrongdoings.

"The more truant he became, the closer I stayed with him to try to bring him back or at least be there to summon the help that inevitably was needed to bail him out." Kian-Huard's green eyes echoed the pain of a distant wound that could never heal. But there too was seen great wisdom as only could be gleaned by one who death had forgotten to take and who had lived an unimaginably long time.

Bend-het-seten: 2,500 years.

Nahleen, in her very soul, knew that he spoke the truth, but her mind continued to struggle with the concept that a man could continue in a single existence for so long. Always suffering the pain of the loss of those close to him till he decided on a life of solitude. She was unsure which was more difficult a choice. Nahleen reached out a comforting hand to him across the table and felt a familiar comfort herself as the soft warmth of his hands encompassed hers. They remained thus for a moment as each gathered their thoughts and readied their hearts and minds for that which was yet to be told. Nahleen sensed something insidious loomed close in the future, smothering hope, waiting to shatter the peaceful existence her people had known through recorded history. It felt like a gnawing hunger, craving something, and she felt she was the one who would be devoured when the hunger was finally sated.

≫ ≫ ≫

Kian-Huard studied the Sharrana's face, and her delicate features belied her incredible strength and the power she held in her position. The same copper tresses that adorned all Rhue cascaded over her shoulders in billows of curls when not confined to the restraints of a braid. And her eyes were bright, full of life and intelligence and fueled with the passion that was inherent in these people. He reluctantly released Nahleen's hand and rose from the chair to stretch his legs. His gaze passed over the familiar surroundings of the observatory. He knew every nook and crevice in the cave. Every subtle shade of brown, grey and red forming their random patterns in the rock walls, the table he had hewn from a single tree and the chairs that had worn smooth over the centuries. A few shelves lined with books and papers. Most were charts he had made himself of the progression of the stars and planets over those same years. Last, his eyes fell on the centre of the cavern. It was filled with the device he created to watch, more closely, the subtle changes in the heavens and the planets that escaped his sight without it.

It did not take him long; only as many years as two lifetimes to understand the intricate balance and interactions of these unseen bodies and events on his world. He walked over to it and ran a hand over the polished metal tube. He lightly touched one of the many adjustment levers that eased his maneuvering the heavy device to different areas of the heavens and then to subtly adjust the distance between the lenses to bring his subject into focus. The cylinder contained three lenses that he crafted himself from the finest silica sands available. He then began the tedious task of carefully grinding the lenses into just the right shape to refract the light and magnify the distant planets. He had also fashioned several different eyepieces to further amplify his subjects. Looking up revealed that the top of the mountain was missing and, in its place, he erected a dome of the clearest glass, through which the farthest extreme of the viewing device protruded. The entire dome and telescope were mounted on a system of pulleys, rails and gears that allowed him to easily maneuver the entire structure to face any direction at any altitude. It was the culmination of three lifetimes' work for the skilled smiths who participated in his project. None of whom knew what the strange requests were for, but each worked with diligence and excellence, passing on skills and specifications as they neared the end of their time. And all under his watchful eye and with little or no explanation of what the finished project might be. As each piece came together and was assembled he spent more and more of his time here, inside the mountain, away from his kinsmen. Until that night.

It took him many phases to understand how he came to be in the bed of Sharrana Mura and how she saw only her husband. With that understanding came the sickening knowledge that Ko'Resh was most likely still alive and that he was, somehow, able to manipulate him into taking the sharrana. Nahleen's mother was the product of that night. He turned, sighing as he did so, and studied the face of Nahleen, Sharrana of Rhuna, and saw his own vivid green eyes. She had the same delicate features as her mother and the same strength of will that proved necessary on more than one occasion. She would need that strength now, and more. He watched her brow furrow as she tried to anticipate his thoughts and saw the flicker of confusion cross her face. To anyone else she was the epitome of control and dignity, but he knew her well. As well as he knew himself, and he was well aware of the conflict she was experiencing.

"Nahleen, I fear your life here in Rhuna is about to change beyond repair." His hand that rested on the polished cylinder fell to his side in an act of succumbing to his now-sorrowful mood. He returned to sit across from her. "I tell you now of the folly of two young men who, in selfish pursuits, damned many and unleashed a power that could consume all we know."

"The day broke clear after three of rain in mid-spring and the ground was still soft and smelled musty of recent snow cover. In my mind's eye I remember so many years ago as if it was only last rise." And so Kian'Huard told Sharrana Nahleen of what happened those many centuries before.

CHAPTER 12

NAHLEEN LISTENED TO KIAN'HUARD, AND ON OCCAsion she would interrupt him to have him clarify a point, but for the most part she remained silent until she fully understood the implication of what he was telling her. The first alignment he spoke of had happened some 2,500 years ago, but it was only a partial alignment that allowed the passageway to the chamber of the Sem Lukos to be visible to Kian'Huard and Ko'Resh. They had a specific quality within their bloodline that allowed the Sem Lukos to possess them but, since it was divided between twins, the seven could not achieve their full power. The past centuries had been devoted, by fate or design, to creating a vessel that would be able to reunite the divided blood and create a Sheth Child that would be able to contain the full power of the seven. She was that vessel and somehow, Ko'Resh was going to return to Rhuna and bring with him the sire to the Sheth Child.

That thought caused a wave of betrayal to wash over her and she felt weak and drained as she pushed herself from the table and stood up from her chair. She could not keep the fear she felt from showing in her eyes. Not only was her destiny to unleash a terrible menace on the world, but her friend and confidant had orchestrated it. He manipulated the House of Rhuna to bring forth a child—her, that would be the vessel that would see the evil that was Saal returned to the physical world. She became lightheaded then angry. Her thoughts were interrupted by the offering of a hot beverage. She turned on Kian'Huard and threw the cup. "Tea will not fix this!" She paced the room for a while, swallowing the anger and betrayal she felt. Then she turned to him. "How could you do this?" Her voice shook with emotion.

"You must understand, I had no choice, I am usually in control of my physical body but when a task needs to be completed that I refuse to do,

119

the Sama Lukos takes possession of my body and sees that the task is done. You need to know that I refused to go to your grandmother, but I was not in control at the time." He returned to her side and turned her to face him. "I wish I could change what has been set in motion but I cannot. The alignment that is taking place now is a full alignment of all seven planets and our moon. They will remain thus for two years. The power being released by this alignment has more effect then the previous. Saal is able to interact within this physical realm. Over the past months I have felt his presence more and he is able to make himself visible, if only for a short time. He will return to Mythos, of that there is no doubt, for there is none in this world who can stop him. And he comes for you. The child you will bear, he will take as his physical embodiment and the bride he chooses is you, for you are the incarnation of his beloved Majha." Once more he offered her a cup of tea.

Again, she refused, but he left it there knowing her stubborn nature.

His face softened somewhat. "I wish there was another way to bring you to understand, but I fear time is of the essence. Ko'Resh is mounting an invasion and, when the alignment pulls down the walls that for so many centuries have separated Rhuna from the rest of Mythos, Rhuna will, once more, be accessible. This will happen in less than three years." He moved from her side and once again sat across from her.

"Child." His voice was soft, and though the word implied naivety, she knew he only meant it as endearing, and she knew also that his many centuries of life and his control over the beast inside him gave him a wisdom that no other living soul could imagine.

"Please drink. It will take the cold from within your soul and fortify your physical body."

She pushed the cup aside. He pushed it back

"I must insist, Sharrana Nahleen. You have been given information very few can endure and you must replenish yourself. This tea will do you no harm, of that I can assure."

She took the cup he offered her. In her heart she still trusted him. She knew if he wished her ill harm than she would be powerless to stop him. She brought the cup to her lips and smelled the aroma of mixed herbs. She detected a combination of many she could recognize but there was a sweet overtone that she could not quite place. She went through her inventory of herbs and spices in her mind to see what resonated, but she could not place the sweet, heady aroma that wafted from the beverage.

Kian'Huard smiled, as he watched her analyze the tea to identify the herbs that made up the brew. All of them but one he knew she would easily recognize. The one would not be found in the land they call Rhuna. Again, he encouraged her to drink. The tea had strong healing and fortifying properties and she would need to drink it on a regular basis from then on. The one herb also had properties that would help free her mind to encompass a way of thinking that defied reality. He would be very careful in measuring and preparing her tea. Too much herb and she could form an addiction to it and her mind could become lost in the euphoric properties.

But first, she had to drink the initial dose.

She took a tentative sip. The warm fluid had subtle flavor that did not leave a bitter aftertaste. She found it pleasant and sipped more of the brew. Kian'Huard allowed himself to relax. They remained in thoughtful silence until she finished her tea.

Nahleen felt slightly light headed but did not feel any alarm considering the events that had just taken place. She lifted her gaze from the empty mug and studied the face that now seemed to belong to a stranger rather than her beloved mentor and friend.

"After you and your brother escaped the monks ... what happened?"

He cleared his throat to begin. "Nahleen, Naid Sharrana, I remain your humble servant, but I must have you understand that time is no longer on our side. It is enough to say that we hunted and fought each other over many years and much of the kingdom. It still brings me pain to recall how I did finally believe I had slain my brother by casting him from the cliffside. I know this pales as an explanation, but understand you have been told what is most important. The darkness has been growing these past millennia and is preparing to emerge and claim what it needs to become manifest in the flesh." He shifted in his chair then stood.

"I have much I need to teach you during the next full turn of seasons. I believe it would be best for you to gather some of your belongings and stay here in these caverns with me during your tutelage. You can instruct your domini to manage the court in your absence."

She started to object. He raised his hand slightly to stop her. "I fear you have no choice in the matter. If you wish Rhuna to survive that which is coming, you must be prepared. What is about to befall our world is beyond anything you have been taught before. You will need to learn much over the next seasons to be fully prepared to fight this powerful foe."

"And are you that foe or my trusted friend, Kian'Huard?" Her words were barely a whisper. She did not lift her gaze to his. She did not really want to hear the answer, for she already knew. He would change and become that which he had so long fought against.

He did not answer. He turned from her. "Go now, Sharrana Nahleen, and gather what you will need for an extended journey. Tell no one where you are going. Bring your weapons as well, for you will be learning how to be more effective with them."

Nahleen rose from the table, and vertigo forced her to steady herself for a moment. When it passed she left the chamber and followed the tunnel. When she felt fresh air on her face again it was full dark. She had been away for a whole day.

Nahleen made her way down the footpath back to the city. She kept her head down to avoid attracting attention to herself and she breathed a prayer of thanks to Selam when she reached the castle uninterrupted. For a moment she considered staying. A strong feeling of anxiety clenched her chest as if in warning. She pushed back the fear that threatened her and continued to her chambers to gather what she would need. It was becoming clear that whatever path she had been placed on, she was destined to see it to completion.

When she had packed as much as she thought she could comfortably carry she took the servant passage to the kitchen. It was well past midnight and she was certain no one would be up and about to notice her. She raided the larder of some crusty bread and filled the last remaining corner of her duffle bag with dried fruits and cheese. Her water skin was kept in a small closet next to the main kitchen. She filled the skin and two others as well then changed her mind and emptied one and replaced the water with wine from last season's vine.

She felt weighted with more than her provisions when she made her way to the stable to say goodbye to her horse. He trotted to her and began rooting through her clothing looking for the treat he knew would be there. "You are certain I brought you an apple! Well perhaps I forgot this time?" Argus tossed his head as though he understood and circled the stable in a show of displeasure. When he returned she pulled an apple from her cloak and gave it to him. She scratched his head while he chewed the tart fruit, sending a glob of slobber to land on her hiking boot. She barely noticed and buried her face in his mane. She loved the musky scent and felt the heat of him close. She would miss him. He sensed her sadness and nudged her with his nose. She kissed the soft muzzle then turned and left. She knew he would be there for her when she returned and would follow her as though she never left. Such was the devotion of the beast.

When she returned to the cavern she hesitated briefly then entered. She followed the winding corridor deep into the mountain until she was again in the chamber that housed the large viewing device. Kian'Huard appeared from behind the cylinder and nodded. His expression was almost one of surprise that she had followed his instruction. She wondered about her devotion to him. After the day's events, and the fantastic tale he told of power and betrayal, she should have never returned to the cavern. But she did return, for good, or ill, to be trained to fight a foe who may turn out to be the man training her.

The following day was spent training and retraining in weapons and hand-to-hand combat. She was already a master at Tae 'Heb since she had been training since she could walk and the moves were second nature to her. She knew they were defensive moves but had never used them in any practical application, nor had she ever sparred with another student. It was too awkward for the others to strike out at their shista when she was young and, when she inherited the throne, there were none who felt comfortable sparring. Also, her domini would not allow her to indulge in such "boorish, adolescent behavior," as he put it. She smiled when she thought of how he would react if he saw her getting thrown to the mat by Kian'Huard. This, in itself, surprised her immensely. Despite his ancient age, he was very nimble and his strength was equal to that of a man … much younger.

Kian'Huard seemed to notice her levity. "I am amusing you?"

"Not at all." She feigned a frown. "I was just imagining what my domini would do if he saw me now. I imagine he would be quite beside himself."

Kian'Huard smiled, "Yes, he would." His eyes softened for a moment then he made a quick sweep with his staff. She parried, once, twice, then was able to land a quick blow that took him off balance.

He regained his footing. "I think that is enough for today Nahleen." They had been sparring since first light and it was past last pace before evening. He pointed to an opening in the cliff face. "In there you will find a hot spring. It has many soothing and healing properties which you will find of value, especially as your training progresses. Everything you need is already in the chamber. I will brew some tea. You can find me in the observatory when you are ready." With that, he turned to the opposite face of the courtyard and left her standing there.

She watched him move away from her then focused her attention to the area around her. She wondered at how such a place could be found within the mountain. It was surrounded on all sides by the green-grey stone that was native to Rhuna. She studied the smooth walls, looking for tool marks that would indicate the courtyard was manmade, but none could be seen. She counted her paces from one end to the other; there were more than three hundred, and it was as wide as it was long. A small garden on the south-facing side provided fresh vegetables and a small stream of water cascaded down the centre of that same wall. Its source was unknown, and it sprung from a crevasse about thirty paces above her. The water was cool and clear and seemed to flow endlessly into a small pool. The opposite end of the pool was built to contain the water, but when it reached capacity it flowed through a small stone drain and out of the courtyard. The passage to the observatory was at the far eastern side of the south wall and the passage to the hot spring was directly opposite it on the north wall. The remainder of the courtyard consisted of well-packed sand and was obviously built as a training area.

A rack of assorted weapons was assembled under an overhang on the west face that provided enough shelter even in a torrential downpour. Nahleen wondered where the water would run off. She explored the base of the walls to find several drains lined with stone and covered with metal grills. She studied the openings and thought they were large enough for her to fit into if she felt she needed to escape. She tested the grill on the drain at the farthest wall away from the observatory. She felt the heavy metal shift slightly. She thought, if she needed, she could lift it enough to squeeze through. She wondered what would cause her to have such a thought.

What Nahleen could not see was the web of copper and gold that lay deep beneath the surface, meticulously placed there by Kian'Huard centuries ago in an intricate pattern that acted as a conductor to harness and focus the energetic field that pulsed through all of Mythos. The configuration created conditions that were conducive to raising one's personal vibration and allowing one to utilize the power that was inherent in all who lived on the small planet, but very few, if any, knew how to truly harness that power. The field also allowed Kian'Huard to transfer energies to Nahleen as well as thought waves to guide her and to open her mind to be receptive to, and aware of, other dimensions that co-existed with their world. This was knowledge given to Kian'Huard by the Sama Lukos and, though many times he fought to abandon the project, the beast had its way and the arena was built.

When Nahleen made her way to the hot spring, any thoughts of escaping quickly fled. The tunnel opened abruptly before her. The walls soared high into shadow beyond light that poured in through arched openings high above her. The walls rose straight up and were polished so no foot or handhold could be seen. There was no way to scale these walls. She felt trapped. If there was a way from this place other than the main tunnel, she did not see it. It was a vulnerable position in the event of an attack.

She further studied the grotto. The centre of the chamber was occupied by a steaming pool of clear water. Stairs were carved into the stone and the pool was given shape to look more manmade than a natural occurrence. Fresh linens were piled on slabs to her left and a tray of fruit and breads was on a low table carved from the bedrock beside the pool. She saw her skein of wine had been placed there as well. Nahleen wasted no time throwing off her dusty, sweat-stained clothes and descended the few steps to the pool. She tested the water with her foot. It was hotter than she expected but not too hot to slowly immerse herself. She found several areas carved below the waterline to provide seating. They were at different levels so one could be as immersed as one wished. She wasted little time sinking in up to her neck. She found a seat that accommodated her and let the hot mineral water relax her tense muscles.

She moved to explore more of the pool and found herself losing her footing. She sputtered and came up for air then deliberately dove under the water to determine the depth of the pool. She pressed down until her lungs ached and forced her to the surface. She gasped and gulped in a lungful of air. The pool was much deeper than she expected. She swam to the table and dried her hands before breaking off a chunk of bread. She realized how famished she was and stuffed herself on bread, cheese and dried fruit, washed down with gulps of wine. Once her hunger was satisfied, Nahleen allowed herself a few minutes' indulgence to sink herself on one of the lower seats in the hot spring and sipped at her wine. She relaxed into the hot water and eased the tension from her muscles, closed her eyes and let the mineral water infuse her body.

She tried to clear her mind but was not able. So many images sprang to the forefront. She tried to control where her thoughts wandered but repeatedly found herself following scenarios that would play out, each ending with her own destruction. She did not know where these thoughts originated. Before her experience in the observatory with Kian'Huard she was never predisposed to have such destructive imaginings and was always able to find her centre and clear her mind. Now her thoughts seemed to have a life of their own and, as time passed, they became dark, as if her mind was turning against her.

She became aware of the lengthening of shadow in the grotto and rose from the pool. She quickly dried herself and donned the undergarments and warm fleece robes necessary to ward off the cold damp of the mountain nights.

Evening was full upon them when she made her way to the observatory, which now served as kitchen and living area. A corner of the room was sectioned off by a makeshift curtain that defined her sleeping area and afforded her some privacy. A bed of sorts was constructed with reeds and animal skins. Beside the bed was a small wooden box where she stashed her few belongings and clothing. Her weapons were kept in the training arena save her small dagger, which she secretly kept hidden under the head of the bed. Kian'Huard slept on the floor behind the viewing instrument.

Nahleen combed her hair and gathered it into a loose braid, which she coiled and tucked loosely around her head. As usual, several rogue curls escaped and fell over her face. She did not bother to try to tuck them back in place; she had come to realize it was a futile act. She sighed and made her way to the worn table where Kian'Huard waited with a fresh pot of tea.

When he saw her approach, he poured her a cup of the steaming brew and placed it across the table in front of him, indicating he wished her to sit. She noted that he did not pour himself a cup but already had hot tea in front of him. She inhaled deeply as she sat, trying to detect the aroma of his beverage, testing the air for subtle differences in what was placed before her and what he had made for himself. She was not able to discern a difference but also knew she was not likely to, given the distance she was from the tea. Also, the strong, spiced aroma of her beverage was overpowering.

She sipped the tea, letting the warmth flood her. The herbs did have a soothing effect and she chastised herself for her suspicions. She recalled the drainage tunnels and asked Kian'Huard where they lead. He told her the tunnels and the courtyard were there when he discovered the cave many years prior. He had no real reason to try to find where they led as they always functioned and there was never a reason to check. She wondered if he was being truthful or if he was hiding something.

CHAPTER 13

NAHLEEN'S TRAINING CONTINUED THROUGH TO harvest. She returned to the city on a few occasions to ensure there were no pressing matters to attend and to reassure her court she remained available and in control.

During her time in the city she indulged herself in spending time in the stables with Argus. Initially he greeted her with enthusiasm and his customary prancing and rooting through her cloak for an apple. As the days grew short, her visits were less enthusiastically received. His bearing was more cautious, as though he did not know her. Her last visit left her confused and more than a little dismayed.

Argus pranced around the corral, circling her. He ran at her and stopped short of colliding then tossed his head and stomped. His head dropped and he turned an eye to her and studied her. He whinnied and moved off again, circling the corral, keeping a watchful eye on his master. Again, he charged her and stopped short, dropping his head as though in submission and nudged her … hard. Nahleen quickly caught her balance and for a moment actually felt in fear of him. He backed away from her and she could see he studied her again. He went to her and shoved her with his giant head then again backed away from her, throwing his head and snorting. He pawed at the ground, his eyes wild, then reared and let out a guttural cry and galloped from her. He leapt the fence and raced into the pasture.

Nahleen stood frozen through the entire episode. Argus had never behaved in such a manner and she most certainly had never felt fear in being with him. She wondered if her absence had changed him. Or had she changed so much in her absence that he no longer recognized her? Whatever caused his behavior, it was certain he did not fully recognize her or he feared something about her. Her heart grew heavy at the thought. She wondered what could have changed to elicit such feelings from the beast. She stared after him until he crested the small hill in the main pasture and passed from sight. She knew he was safe there, so she did not feel the need to go after him but she would let the hand know to bring him in at evenfall. She tried to understand what had happened. She knew her outward appearance had not changed, except she was physically much stronger as a result of the past months of training with Kian'Huard. But that was not what spooked Argus. There was something less tangible that only the intuitiveness of the beast could see. Her thoughts went to Kian'Huard and the beast he said was within him. She wondered if that bestial energy had somehow attached itself to her. She did not feel any different; no primitive animal tendencies surfaced within her. But for certain something had changed.

Her thoughts continued probing the idea that her time with Kian'Huard was causing some form of energy transfer between them as she made her way to her chambers to gather fresh clothing and a few supplies before returning to the mountain. As she packed, it occurred to her to remain at the castle. She had no reason to continue to abandon her duties on the word of an old man who could very well be stricken with a weakness of the mind that comes with advanced age.

Nahleen unpacked and summoned her handmaiden to inform her she would be remaining in the castle and would be attending supper. The girl bowed and hurried to inform the kitchen. Nahleen sat on the settee by an open window and drank in the cool evening air. A slight breeze brushed against her face and toyed with the strands of hair that had escaped the combs and pins. She let out a long, heavy sigh. She tuned into the sounds coming to her from the courtyard and the more distant rumblings of the city. The echo of horse hooves punctuated with the distant call of merchants vying to convince the crowd theirs was the best and least expensive of fabric, breads, preserves … whatever their wares. The city had a pulse, a vibrant life that was tangible even from where she sat.

The resh was setting behind the castle, throwing shadows of spires and towers over the courtyard. The trees, already aflame with autumn red and orange, burst gold when the long rays of resh touched them as it sank below the horizon. Nahleen reached for her tea. There was none. She pulled back her hand and hesitated a moment, curiosity piqued. Her brow furrowed slightly as she realized this was the same time each evening Kian'Huard would make her tea for her. She found herself craving it, and she dismissed the craving as merely a habit that had formed through staunch routine over the past months. She moved from the window and prepared to go to dinner.

It had been several months since Nahleen was present for a meal at the castle and the entire staff outdid themselves to show how they missed having her. No sooner was she seated than fresh bread and cheese was brought to her. Wine glasses were never empty. The air about the dining hall was almost one of celebration. She had invited her domini and the other heads of state present at the castle to join her. Sitting among her people, she felt a warmth she had not felt for some time and she realized she missed their company. Her time with Kian'Huard was quiet and full of a depth of purpose, which weighed heavy. This night brought laughter and conversation and a comradeship she truly missed.

By dessert, Nahleen was basking in the normalcy of the evening so much that she barely noticed the slight tremor in her hands. She passed this off as over stimulation in comparison to the past months of near solitude, and possibly the wine. She found herself wanting tea, but when this was brought to her it did not satisfy her need. She realized again she was craving the brew Kian'Huard was making for her each day. She'd had the tea three times a day at the same time, and it was hours past the time she would have had her evening drink. It occurred to her that Kian'Huard was drugging her.

Her domini noticed her change in affect. "Is all well, Sharrana Nahleen?"

"Yes. I suppose I am no longer used to our wine. It has been some time since I have shared a glass. It seems to be making me a bit sleepy. I think I shall retire early." She held her hands to her lap to quiet the trembling, which was growing more noticeable. She excused herself from the table and bid goodnight to her guests. As she addressed each of them she again realized how she missed being at court.

When she made her way back to her chambers the tremors were becoming difficult to conceal. She broke into a cold sweat. She quickened her pace and breathed a sigh of relief when she closed her door behind her.

"My lady."

The words startled her so she jumped. She spun to see Adele, her chambermaid, standing ready with her nightclothes.

"I did not mean to startle you, Naid Sharrana." She gave an awkward bow, not sure how to proceed.

"I know." She motioned for the girl to relax. "I fear I have had a bit too much wine," she lied. Nahleen crossed the room to the divider where she began to remove her clothing. Her chambermaid draped the nightclothes over the screen and gathered the lavish gown and undergarments to be laundered.

"Will you be needing anything else, my lady?" Adele inquired through the screen

"No, that will be all for tonight, Adele. I think a good nights' sleep in my own bed will do me the world of good." She came from around the screen to see Adele turning down the comforter on her bed, and suddenly she was overcome by a wave of exhaustion. She crossed the room and watched Adele leave by the servants' passage.

She barely noticed the door closing when she laid down and gathered the soft, down-filled quilt over her. She felt a rolling in the pit of her stomach. She squeezed her eyes shut to stop the room from turning. The tremors in her hands had increased to body shakes. Cold sweat beaded over her body and a deep chill crept through her. She became aware of a presence but was too engrossed with trying to ease the nausea threatening to erupt to fully take notice. She felt warm hands lifting her head from the pillow. She fought down another wave of nausea but this time without success and her stomach emptied onto the floor. The hands supported her as she struggled with the pangs of her withdrawal. When the retching subsided, she felt her head raised once again and a cup of warm liquid pressed to her lips. She smelled the spiced tea and turned her head away. The hands insisted. She tried again to refuse the beverage but felt it being poured slowly into her mouth. She tried spitting it out but inhaled it when she took a breath. This sparked a coughing fit. Her body ached and she grew weak. Again, the beverage was offered and she reluctantly drank from the cup. She tried to focus, to see who it was that was able to enter her chamber, but her eyes could not focus on the form that sat in shadow beside her. She felt the effect of the drug washing through her and tried to fight it, but the drug was too strong. Soon her body began to relax. The cold sweat dissipated and the vertigo subsided. She felt herself being pulled into darkness. Peaceful black engulfed her. She was vaguely aware of being laid back down and the comforter being pulled up.

Morning dawned bright and painful for Nahleen as the first threads of waking wove through her mind, forming a web of recollection that created more questions than answers. She ventured to open her eyes but daylight cut into her head like a dagger forcing them shut. She tried to turn to sit but vertigo threatened her with a wave of nausea, so she remained curled in a fetal position, eyes closed, trying to recall the events of the previous evening. She was certain she did not drink so much wine to be rendered unwell but recalled feeling cold and having hand tremors then body shakes. Then another memory crept to the forefront. She tried to focus, but it eluded her. The memory of spice played in her subconscious yet she remained unable to recall what occurred after she left the banquet hall. She grew frustrated at her memory lapse. A rustling sound pulled her from her thoughts and gave her impetus to once again open her eyes. She did so slowly, one eye at a time, drawing the cover up to block the light pouring in the window but still allowing her a vantage in the direction of the sound. She made out the form of her chambermaid Adele and felt enormous relief.

Adele heard movement and turned to her sharrana. "*Nuva daelo maest naid Sharrana.*" Nahleen saw her hesitate as though she were going to say more, but the look on Adele's face changed abruptly from duty to concern as she quickly crossed to the window and closed the heavy drapes.

"Thank you, Adele." Nahleen always appreciated her handmaiden's instinct for knowing what to do … and her discretion. Though there were very few incidents where such discretion was necessary. Nahleen pushed back the covers and motioned for Adele to assist her. She raised herself to sit on the side of the bed. Adele steadied her until she was able to get her balance.

"Can I get you some tea, naid Sharrana?"

The word tea triggered her. She felt bile rise. She struggled to keep from vomiting. "No thank you, Adele." She paused then added, "I would like a glass of cold water, if you would."

Adele gave a short bow and turned to leave. She hesitated and turned back to Nahleen, obviously torn between fetching the water and leaving her very unwell sharrana alone.

Nahleen sensed her unease and motioned to the girl. "I will be fine." She forced a faint smile to reassure Adele. "I will lay here until you return." She settled herself back down in the bed. This satisfied the girl and she hurried from the room, gently closing the door behind her. She was in such a hurry to gather the water and return that she did not notice the shadow that shrank into the corner behind the wardrobe as she passed.

CHAPTER 14

NAHLEEN DRIFTED INTO AN UNSETTLED STATE; SHE was neither awake nor asleep. She was aware of the room around her, but also of something else. A presence, at first no more than a shadow, that had been lying in wait in the dark corners of her chamber. When the shadow emerged, had she been awake and alert, she would have known it to be Kian'Huard and would have known who brought the tea through the night. But the effects of the drug and the soft mantra that softly filled the room lulled her into an altered state, a different place of being. She could not bring her mind to understand the other place. It was there, she could see it in her mind's eye, as though through a mirror, or flipping over a coin. Both sides existed at the same time, together yet separate and vastly different.

She felt she only had to change how her mind interpreted that time and space and she would be able to shift from the world that housed her room, the castle and her kingdom to the unknown place that was forming in the mist of her mind. Slowly she felt herself letting go of the world she knew and her focus shifting to the alternate reality. Shadows became more cohesive to form shapes that gelled into a landscape dotted with monolithic structures. Fog rolled around her, dampening her hair and clothing. She was aware she still wore her bedclothes, though her bed had given way and she found herself standing bare foot on a grassy path. The path was lined with a stone fence that stretched before her as the world formed.

She became acutely aware of the salty taste of the air and the feeling of sea spray on her face. The air was neither warm nor cold but a chill swept through her. She felt compelled to move along the path. The fence, which was low enough to easily climb over, framed both sides making the path wide enough for a wagon though no ruts gave evidence of the roadway ever being used.

The grass was low-cut and manicured, which she thought strange since no structures that could be interpreted as buildings were to be seen. As she made her way along the path she strained to see through the fog in what direction the sea lay. She listened for the sound of the surf crashing but any sound was swallowed by the heavy air. Scattered about the landscape were stones set into the ground in strange patterns. Some stones were only as large as a loaf of bread, while others rose with great purpose several measures into the air. Some were so tall their pinnacle became lost in the heavy fog that dominated the countryside. A corner of her mind whispered for her to leave that place.

Nahleen tried to change her focus back to the reality that was her bedchamber. Panic rose within her when she could not.

A sound so faint she barely heard it caused her to turn, for no other sound colored that place. Before her stood a giant lukos. She had seen other lukos before but this beast towered over her, his shoulder level with her head. He brought his head down to stare into her eyes. Terror held her in his gaze. As though sensing her fear, he took a step back. He lowered himself to the ground, never relinquishing his gaze. Though the air was heavy with moisture, his thick black fur remained dry. In contrast, her hair lay matted and dripping and her clothing clung wet to her body. He did not carry the animal scent she expected from such a creature. His was almost pleasant. Not of animal musk and rotting breath but of outdoors and … warmth. He remained motionless save the expanding of his chest with each breath and kept his eyes focused on her.

Her terror waned slightly as the moments passed and he did not attack. Eventually a calm resignation replaced the fear as she stood before the great creature. He sensed the change and lowered his head to rest on massive paws, his gaze never straying. His indigo-blue eyes transfixed her and drew her in. Her body responded to some force that caused her to move toward him. She was close enough to feel the soft moist heat of his breath. His nostrils flared slightly when he exhaled and tiny droplets formed on the surface. Even with his head resting on his paws his eyes were level with hers. She was close enough to touch his snout if she were to reach out her hand. His fur was black. She saw no shading, no variations in the color.

She tentatively reached toward the beast, aware that in such close proximity he could easily rip her apart before her brain would even have the opportunity to fully realize what was happening. She expected him to growl or swipe at her but instead he remained still. Her hand paused midway, waiting for a sign that she had crossed some unseen barrier. Nothing. She moved in closer, past the great head to his shoulder. Her hand brushed lightly against his fur. She expected his coat to be coarse and wiry but instead it was incredibly soft. She grew bolder and ran her fingers through his luxurious coat. He turned his head to watch her in silence. She began to feel a link forming between them. She pulled her hand back and moved away. She studied the creature, and he her. Too late, she realized what had taken place.

She felt her body bend to his will as she moved beside him and climbed onto his back. He stood and she nearly fell. She righted herself and buried her hands in the thick fur to grab a hold. When he seemed satisfied that she would not fall he turned to the path and launched himself into a full run. Nahleen panicked and clung to the beast. She buried herself against him, feeling his body moving in a fluid rhythm. She allowed herself to move with him. She lifted her face to the wind. The stone fence that bordered the roadway continued and she looked past it to the surrounding fields. Small shrubs and trees now dotted the landscape, dispersed among the stone monoliths that flew past her line of sight so quickly she could not discern any details, just fleeting glances. She was beginning to feel exhilarated at riding this creature. Her heart pounded, seemingly in concert with his footfalls. She knew he was running hard, but his breath remained steady and unlabored.

As they passed through the countryside the fog began to dissipate and she could see a great body of water to her right. The sharp scent of salt made her believe they were near Cippus Sea but the landscape was unfamiliar. She knew of no other saltwater near Rhuna. Notably, the air lacked the undertone of decaying fish that one would expect so near the sea. It occurred to her there were no gulls circling the surf; indeed, no sign of animal life could be found. Ahead, a fortress began to materialize through the fog. Even at such a great distance she could see that it was formidable in size. Her beast continued, unchecked in his race, to carry her toward their destination. The fortress rose from deep below the fog, stretching high, carving into the rockface consuming the great mountain as though it needed to be even more impressive than the mountain itself. It climbed to the summit and crowned it with towers and spires, many of which remained hidden in the clouds. It became clear this was their destination.

They continued toward the mammoth fortress and she realized how far in the distance it was. Its massive size belied the distance between them and it seemed several hours passed before they gained the appearance of drawing closer. Nahleen was aware of time passage, but the resh did not progress across the sky.

She became uneasy as they neared the fortress. It engulfed her entire field of vision. The beast she rode upon slowed to a trot then a quick walk along a narrow path that ran as far as she could see beside the fortress. There appeared no break in the wall, no visible entry points, when the beast suddenly turned. She felt swallowed by the stone walls when they entered through a narrow arch, which she was certain had just appeared, into the outer courtyard. She looked behind them to see the passage closed by the formation of a stone wall, seamless, with no indication of where the arch had been. Nausea crept into her gut. She had seen a similar occurrence. She pressed to recall. A hot flush of fear washed over her when the images given her by Kian'Huard when he and Ko'Resh entered the mountain cave came to mind. The walls narrowed around them. The air smelled stale and of damp stone. Though no visible source of light could be seen, the passage was illuminated enough to make out details of the sameness of the stone arching around them. There was no room for panic. She fought the primal instinct of flight and forced herself into a fragile calm.

Nahleen sensed a subtle change in the beast. She leaned forward, straining to see if there was any clue to where they were going but only grey-black stone arched ahead of them, framing the passage that rose in a steady incline and curved left, deeper into the fortress. Behind, the walls closed, choking off any escape route. She could feel tension increase in the muscles along the creature's back. His shoulders tightened and his smooth gait became choppy when he increased his pace. She was forced to lean into him and hold deep into the thick fur to keep from falling. She noted it was becoming difficult to breathe. They had been climbing steadily since they entered the fortress and the air was beginning to thin, though this did not seem to affect the beast.

Nahleen felt a subtle tingling through her body. It radiated outward from her solar plexus and pulsed in a steady rhythm from the depth of her core to encompass her whole body. At first, she didn't realize her breathing and even her heartbeat echoed the steady pulsing of the energy penetrating her.

Her body seemed to grow lighter as the intensity increased. She noticed the energy grew in frequency and intensity as they climbed higher into the fortress. She wanted to panic but was unable. Her mind was clouded with colors and imagery that she could not identify. She felt as though she was looking through another's eyes on a life that was not hers.

The corridor turned to the left and opened into a vast chamber. Pillars carved of purple and white quartz towered upward beyond her vision. The perimeter of the great hall was lost on the horizon. The floor appeared to be made of the purest clear crystal. She looked for any flaw in its perfection and saw none. Though there was no visible sign of living beings save her and the beast in the chamber, she could feel a strong lifeforce pressing near. Again, the natural urge to flee was stolen from her. The great beast that bore her lowered himself so she could dismount. She hesitated. He shook his head slightly and gave a short growl. Nahleen slid from the creature's back. When her feet were firmly on the floor he launched himself. The air cracked and the beast shattered into thousands of tiny fragments of purple light. These were sucked into the opening and the space closed behind to leave Nahleen alone in the vast chamber.

Nahleen studied her surroundings. Never had she seen such an expansive structure. She could not imagine how long or how may craftsmen it would take to build such a thing. She was overcome by the enormity of her surroundings and her solitude. She had felt some odd comfort in the beast's presence. The feeling she had before the beast disappeared of another unseen lifeforce grew stronger. The air before her began to waver like heat rising from stone. The wave-like pattern gathered to form an oval shape, its borders a thread of golden, purple light that swirled like smoke. The inner circle grew intensely bright and Nahleen had to shield her eyes. The light lowered in intensity and a form took shape within the light of the oval. She could do nothing else but watch as the shape of a man began to coalesce from, and within, the light. The urge to run gripped her but she suppressed it. There was nowhere to run to.

As the man took form she brought herself to focus on what was unfolding before her. She felt a warmth wash over and through her. She felt her chest encompassed in a deep emotion. Her breathing had become deeper, heavier. When she was able to discern a face, she felt a deep bond form even though the man did not look familiar to her. She saw in his eyes a depth of emotion beyond words. And she saw pain there as well. His body was nearly fully materialized when the process ceased. The oval of light surrounding him gathered in to lay against his form, shrouding it with a ghostly light of purple and blue. Then the light gathered to him and dimmed. She could see his features more clearly. He was Rhue, of that she was certain. His copper hair and vivid green eyes were proof enough of that. He was perhaps one measure taller than her. He held himself with the countenance of the House of Rhuna.

His garb was intricately detailed with a pattern that intertwined over itself. She could not discern the fabric the overlay material was woven from, just that it was finer than anything her people were capable of. His copper hair was gathered at the crown and pulled back off his face and secured with a gold buckle, leaving the rest to fall well past his shoulders. To Nahleen, he was both beautiful and menacing. His calm affect did little to mask the storm of emotion that raged behind his eyes. Nahleen found herself drawn to him. Their eyes locked in a deep exchange. She grew frightened but was unable to avert her gaze. He drew her into him, never touching her physically but with a command of power that could not be refused.

He moved to study her. She remained riveted in place. She became very self-conscious under his scrutiny. She forced herself to stand tall, a mannerism ingrained during her adolescent years. She held her chin up and straightened her shoulders. She was keenly aware of his presence, though he was now behind her. She stood her ground, though her mind was screaming to run from that place. The rhythmic pulse that had begun in the passage and intensified when she entered the chamber had taken on a new frequency. It resonated through her body. She was beginning to feel lightheaded and was afraid she would faint. She clenched her jaw and steadied herself.

He moved to stand before her. The wordless exchange continued. He reached out to touch her but seemed unable. This fortified Nahleen. She took a step back.

Again, he reached toward her. It was her turn to study him and she saw pain. Within the depths of her mind, thoughts were forming. She knew these were not hers. At first, she could not understand the thoughts, though she could sense intense emotion associated with them. She was told to allow her mind to relax though no words were spoken. She realized he was speaking to her from within her own thoughts.

"No," was all that could escape her. His power overwhelmed her and she felt him inside her mind more intimately than any other person should be. His thoughts poured into her consciousness in a wave of abstract ideas, concepts and emotions.

"Stop..." she gasped, "this is too much..." She pressed her palm to her forehead to block out the flow of sound and imagery. "I ... can't ... process this," she stammered. She felt the pressure of his thoughts ease. His face showed genuine concern then her mind was freed. Gradually a concept formed and she understood he was trying to communicate to her and he would remember to send one idea at a time.

"Who are you?" She reluctantly relaxed and opened her mind to allow him to respond. She struggled with the concepts that flashed within her mind's eye. Glimpses of lifetimes, of passion and power. "I don't understand."

She felt him shift in her awareness as he unlocked another part of her brain; one that processed speech. Then his words flowed into her and she was overcome by what he spoke of.

"Nayer vancai, Naid Sharrana, me en mide ko hegat redalt"

"I come, my sharrana, at a time of great change." His voice reverberated deep within her mind and soul.

"Nayer vancai applenta jan"

"I come for you"

"Mae dire hegat Lukos bae dire evaienes dain rand Na'vai raslad applenta tem arm"

"As the great lukos from the emptiness in which I have lived for so long"

"Gan'ernine nayeh anin"

"You knew me once"

"Gana sadonine dire lume a naid arlden"

"You were the light to my world"

"Mae'en goslamire elitvalarn"

"Like a delicate candle"

"Dernan nier dern dire evaelum"

"Pushing back the darkness"

"Ern vanisolent churel me naid kia"

"Now loneliness gnaws at my soul"

"Naid modeth astra furmai"

140

"My hunger burns"

The form of Saal moved close to her. Her skin prickled with the pulse of energy that radiated from him. She felt his desire as a tangible thing, pressing its heat into the core of her being. She tried to block the wave of longing from becoming her own but, like a predator seeking its prey, his consciousness found what was locked deep within her own ancient history so many lifetimes ago and pulled it forth. She gasped as the full emotion of their past together ruptured from where it hid and spilled over her. Her physical body responded to his mental intrusion. A great aching feeling of pain and desire flooded her. She clenched her jaw to fight his intrusion into the most intimate part of her soul. And he continued ...

"A tatere gan' mae anon ateram"

"To touch you once again"

"Mae en rham"

"As a man"

"Cortire a cortire"

"Flesh to flesh"

"Haeth emord astra faeit sinth"

"This pain ends soon"

"Tam jamdupri ga'certu naid faeit"

"So long ago you saw my end"

"Dire bash val darthenire nith vidire econsman"

"The fear that shadowed our love still lingers"

"Astra dai sati a macerai naid bevrainier"

"It is enough to ensure my existence"

"Naid asan nikru tam alvanai apersigne dain cortire"

"My body cannot yet be made manifest in flesh"

"Endal naid eith vidorn althea dai alvar mae'an thadain an asan"

"Until my beloved creation is reunited within one body"

"Dire mide astra dai me praesto"

"The time is at hand"

"Astra dai susurrus dain ko afra"

"It is whispered in the wind"

"Tem dan astra dan"

"So shall it be"

"Nayer Sadai Saal"

"For I am Saal"

"Ko altheaneir ko dire Sem Lukos ko dire Resh"

"The creator of the Sem Lukos ko dire Resh…"

"I know you as Majha, for you are my mate and have been for eternity. Since life began on this world. We were there, as creators, with the others, so long ago the knowledge has been lost. But my desire for you remains, unchanged, as it was since first we descended to the realm of flesh and blood."

Nahleen closed her eyes to try to shut out his words but they resounded within her mind. Her heart pounded as she became overwhelmed with the raw emotion that drove his dialogue. She began to realize it was that emotion that was focused to bring her to that place. Some part of Saal, though imprisoned by a force she had no understanding of, was gaining strength and able to manipulate energy just beyond the physical realm. It was how he was able to focus his desire to draw her here. But he was not yet strong enough to fully manifest in the flesh. She could sense he knew a time was at hand when he would be able to transcend his prison. The alignment Kian'Huard told her of was more than a physical alignment of planets; it would be a conduit for a powerful energy that would alter the vibratory frequency of Mythos and create an alignment of energy that would allow him to return.

Nahleen did not understand how she knew this information. She felt Saal's presence in her mind, but a deeper connection had formed, giving her access to all that he was and all that he desired. She tried to break the bond but was unable. She became aware that even with the shift in energy he would not be able to descend to the flesh as he once did but would need a vessel.

Horror gripped her as she came to fully realize his intent. She summoned every ounce of her strength of will and tried to shut him from her mind and soul. He grew agitated at her efforts and forced himself deeper into her psyche. She resisted and cried out for him to stop. He pressed harder. Nahleen continued to fight his invasion. She drew strength from deep within. She filled her every thought with the desire to return to the castle and be away from this place. She felt her body hum with the power she was invoking. She knew what she was doing was effective when she felt Saal withdraw from her. She sensed his fury and faltered briefly, losing her focus. He pressed to regain his connection with her. She panicked briefly, but once more found her resolve and brought her desire to escape him fully into focus. She felt his essence begin to fade from her consciousness.

He lashed out at her, filling her mind with horrific images of death and torture to try to break her focus. The images were so realistic it seemed as though she was living and dying through each. She could feel the bite of steel when a life on a battlefield was taken, watched in horror through the eyes of a mother as her child drowned and she was unable to save him. The images rolled through her. She forced herself to remain focused on her desire. She pushed the distractions to the back of her mind and when her desire to return to her bedchamber was complete in her mind and all aspects of her being aligned with this one desire, she felt herself become as a column of pure white energy. Saal's anger and frustration resounded through the empty chamber with such force the columns cracked and began to collapse. Nahleen remained focused and disappeared from the chamber. Saal let loose his temper and destroyed that place he had created to bring his heart's desire to him.

>> >> >>

Nahleen found herself back in her bedchamber. Her nightclothes were soaked with sweat, her breathing heavy with the exertion of her escape. She sat up in bed and surveyed her room for any hint that Saal had followed her. Part of her understood what had happened and how she was brought to that place but the memory began to fade. She recalled how Saal invaded her mind more intimately than any physical assault and the intensity of emotions that overwhelmed her. She knew they were his, but she felt them as though they were her own. She tried to push these out of her mind but they remained as vivid as when she stood before him. How she came to be there and how she was able to escape eluded her.

The resh had begun to rise, chasing shadows from the city and burning the last of the dew from the gardens. Nahleen reached to pull the cord to summon her handmaiden then changed her mind, preferring to remain undisturbed. She needed to collect her thoughts and make sense of what she had experienced. She reached to pour herself water to wash and found the jug empty. She noted how neat everything in her chamber was, as though no one had been there for days. The gown she left out to wear this morning was no longer set out for her. She looked in her wardrobe to find it had been hung and put away. There were no fruits or breads set on her table nor was there any water or wine. She reached to summon Adele when the girl breezed into the suite.

It was a moment or two before she noticed Nahleen watching her. She became flustered and apologetic, lowering her head and muttering several apologies for not having the room ready for her return, but complained that no one told her the sharrana was returning.

Nahleen motioned her to stop. "You say I was away?"

"*Vae* Naid Sharrana." Her face did little to hide her confusion at the question.

"I understand this may not make sense to you, but I must ask, how long was I gone?"

"Naid Sharrana, you were gone from here for three nights."

Three days she was away, though she did not recall physically leaving her chamber. She thought what she experienced was no more than a very vivid dream. Apparently, she was mistaken. The idea that she had indeed encountered a being who called himself Saal had many implications. The memory of the intimate interaction sent a wave of unease through her. She recalled how he spoke through her mind rather than verbally. The invasion into her mind left her feeling exposed and vulnerable, feelings she did not wish to experience again. Reluctantly, she knew her only recourse was to continue working with Kian'Huard. Perhaps with the new information she has been afforded, he would be less secretive. She needed to seek his counsel about Saal and how he told her she was his mate so many years ago. Was it even possible? How could he know her as Majha? Indeed, she had many questions for her old friend.

Nahleen called for Adele to set out her clothing and bring her fresh water. She also directed her to bring breakfast along with hot tea when it occurred to her that she had been, she assumed, three days without the drugged tea. She wondered at that, given the strong reaction she had when she was delayed in having one dose. Perhaps the tea had served its purpose in opening her mind enough to be pulled into the other world by Saal. That would be another matter to discuss with Kian'Huard. Such behaviour was treasonous.

When Adele finished setting the food on the small table beside the window Nahleen dismissed her, "Thank you, Adele, you may take your leave now." She knew the young woman was nearly beside herself with curiosity and most certainly this conversation would be the subject of much discussion in the back kitchen, but Nahleen had other, more important, matters to attend. She dismissed Adele again when the girl hesitated. Adele nodded once then left Nahleen alone with her thoughts.

CHAPTER 15

RHANDOR FOLLOWED KO'RESH AS THEY RETRACED their path to return to the hut. Night was full upon them but rhuna, shining full in a cloudless sky, provided enough light for travel. She cast eerie shadows on the road as her light passed through the ragged remains of a forest that once grew lush and thick from the foothills of the Illuna Mountains through much of Krit. The village of Gaelen was carved deep into the heart of the woods. The buildings were constructed from logs and lumber cut from the site when trees were cleared. When the earliest settlers put down roots here the first structure built was a massive log building that served as the central gathering site. Some logs were from trees so big around that three men could not touch hands if they encircled the trunk. It took nearly two full years with all hands working to complete the massive structure that towered nearly as high as the trees themselves and encompassed an area that could contain all the citizens of Gaelen should the need arise.

Once the structure was built, the artisans took over and began laying intricate carvings of various flora and fauna into the massive beams and pillars that supported the structure. The outcome was breathtaking and left no doubt to the skill of the Krit builders. Everyone who lived in or near Gaelen would gather there for all manner of governance. It also housed the Chamber of Gathering where the residents, and any travellers, congregated for ritual prayers and sharing. It was a place of free speech and of sharing ideas and concepts. It was also to give thanks and homage for the bounty that all enjoyed; it's corridors and great chambers had always been bustling with activity but now it lay empty. Radiating out from the Chamber of Gathering were paths that lead through gardens and a communal orchard. The orchard thinned to make way for the market square, and streets formed into neighbourhoods and the neighbourhoods became Gaelen. Rows of wooden clapboard or log houses sat neatly on yards adorned with fruit trees, vegetable gardens and flower beds. Backyards joined together and the outermost perimeter was fenced to pasture what livestock the neighbourhood raised. Vibrant clothing that reflected the colours of beautiful flowers flowed through the streets of Gaelen, adorning Krit merchants and patrons. Children were free to roam unburdened with concern. The music of commerce ebbed and flowed through the street, each merchant singing out his cry to entice you to purchase his or her wares. Often, purchases were made in appreciation of the song more than actual need for the item. Such was the joy of playing the game of the market.

After the ravages of the drought, dust and death remained to colour the landscape and the streets were void of song. Rhandor was not used to feeling out of control. It gnawed at his heart that he felt compelled to seek out the solveige possessed by Ko'Resh. He felt he lost something of himself in dealing with the sorcerer.

The Flumen River flowed nearby and was a major trade route used to ferry their goods to the Sagares Sea. From there they could journey south to Jordan or north and east to Raglan or any of the other port cities and villages that dotted the coastline. The western border of the village overlooked the Aevitas Ocean. Few souls were brave enough to voyage beyond land-sight when sailing this water. When this plague struck, all ports were quickly shut down and any vessels seeking port were turned back. Many remained out at sea as long as possible in an attempt to avoid contact with the infected, but the vessels were not designed for long-term voyages so the crew quickly ran out of food and supplies and were forced to put into harbour or choose an equally slow death by starvation on the open sea.

It seemed almost impossible how selective the plague was, for none who were not of Krit were affected. The drought halted at the border. Disease ravaged the Krit, but none of the neighbouring lands fell into illness. Again, Rhandor wondered at what would bring such devastation and more importantly, why. He found himself pushing aside his thoughts and continued following Ko'Resh. Into what destiny he did not know, but he felt compelled to continue.

The air remained still and hot. Rhandor felt perspiration bead across his back and neck but the dry, thirsty air took it from him as soon as it formed. His muscles had begun to cramp from dehydration but, for now, it was tolerable. He looked at Ko'Resh walking beside him and wondered if he too felt the pain of lack through his body. Outwardly he showed no signs of suffering from dehydration or hunger. It occurred to Rhandor that Ko'Resh was indeed in possession of a great power. Whether it be the solveige of darkness or helige, sacred magic, he did not fully know, but he was resigned to use whatever power it was that Ko'Resh possessed to bring prosperity and health back to his people.

Rhandor suspected Ko'Resh was aware of his thoughts. He feared Ko'Resh possessed a power that allowed him to manipulate his will and invade his innermost thoughts. Rhandor drew on his own inner strength, and he recalled his attack on Ko'Resh. Alarm pricked at Rhandor when Ko'Resh's hand moved to touch his throat where the sharram had grabbed him.

As they neared Ko'Resh's hut a flicker of shadow caught Rhandor's attention. He tried to focus on what caused the movement, scanning the grove of trees that lined the short path from the road to the hut. His body tensed, alert to any sign of movement. His pace slowed, but no movement disturbed the shadows.

Rhandor noticed Ko'Resh's back straighten and grow ridged; he saw his eyes focus in the trees, darting from shadow to shadow, straining to see. "What has you alarmed, Ko'Resh?" The hair on the back of his neck bristled, triggering his own primal instincts. "What stalks us?" His hand went to his blade while he scanned the path ahead and turned to look behind for anyone or thing that may be following. Sword drawn and body on alert, he probed the night. A branch snapped to his left. He spun and raised his blade. Something moved in the shadows. He tensed, ready to strike. "Show yourself!" he commanded.

Again, the snap of dry branches underfoot sounded just beyond sight within the shadows. Rhandor strained to listen. The uneven crunch of footfalls on the dead underbrush was unmistakeable. As they neared, Rhandor could make out dry, raspy breaths. It was clear that whoever approached was having difficulty. Rhandor focussed in the direction of the sounds, trying to get sight of who approached. His back was to Ko'Resh. Another bout of staggering footfalls brought a shadowy form into view. At once Rhandor could see the small form of a child. He sheathed his sword and went to the boy, who collapsed onto the side of the road. Rhandor gathered the child from the ground and pulled his water canteen from his belt. The child could not have been more than eight full turns. He offered the child some water but the child coughed and spat up thick black blood. He gasped, straining to catch breath, his eyes wide with fear. Rhandor helped the boy to sit forward. The boy gasped and thrashed his arms like he was drowning, trying to draw air into his diseased lungs. The tortured little body went rigid for a moment then collapsed into a limp bundle in Rhandor's arms.

A dim glow of orange light caused Rhandor to turn to face Ko'Resh in time to see the light swirl and disappear within him. "What have you done?" He forced his words through clenched teeth. He stood, still cradling the dead child, and raised himself to his full height. There was no mistaking the venom in his glare, so much that Ko'Resh took a step back. Rhandor looked back to the child. He suffering remained etched in the small, still face. Death had not erased the fear that encompassed the child's final moments. "You did this?"

Ko'Resh looked hard at Rhandor. "There was nothing that could have been done for the child. How he survived this long when the children were struck down first by the plague is disturbing. Had we tried to help him it would have prolonged his suffering. He was already too far advanced with the illness. It was … merciful."

Rhandor could see Ko'Resh was waiting for his reaction. He looked again to the face of the child and the great man's affect relaxed. Ko'Resh exhaled; he had been holding his breath waiting for Rhandor's response. Rhandor was still holding the child. "We will give him a proper burial." His tone begged Ko'Resh to argue.

"Yes, of course, naid Sharram." Ko'Resh gave a slight bow. Rhandor thought he saw a flicker of fear in Ko'Resh's eyes. It occurred to him that though Ko'Resh possessed great power over those around him, somehow part of his own mind remained free of that control. Rhandor thought Ko'Resh would be striving to search out and corral that part of his consciousness to bring him fully under his control. He made a silent vow to himself that he would fight such control. Rhandor stood almost two full measures taller than Ko'Resh. His physical strength easily surpassed Ko'Resh's. But mind control was foreign to him, and he was not sure how one would protect oneself from such an invasion. Rhandor was known throughout his kingdom for his sharp mind and diplomacy. He hoped it would be enough, for his knowledge of solveige was very limited.

He was compassionate and fair. He was not quick to arms but would defend his people with whatever force was necessary. There was a long-standing peace between Krit and the neighbouring countries of Norval and Sambahar. Occasional skirmishes erupted when small bands of malcontents threatened the outlying villages. He met those with decisive action and they were quickly resolved.

Rhandor carried the child's body to a small burial plot they passed a short distance prior. Tools lay where last they were used when the dead became too numerous for the grave diggers to tend. That was when they lit the fires. Many still burned and the stench of burnt and decayed flesh lingered heavy over much of southern Krit where the population was greatest. On occasion, a sharp wind would sweep across the land from the sea and carry the smoke and stench with it, but even the sea air had lost its crisp, salty odour and was fouled with the taint of death.

Rhandor took up a shovel, dug a small pit and gently placed the body. He kissed the back of his hand and touched it to his forehead and then the child' in a gesture of respect and blessing. He did not understand why he felt so compelled to bury this child except perhaps it gave him a sense of closure to care for another's when he was not able to do so for his own son. A tight burning sensation closed around his heart. He clenched his jaw and brought his emotions under control. This was not the time to mourn. He gently filled the small grave with soil and said a blessing over the soul of the child and surveyed the burial grounds. Hundreds of new mounds dotted the area. It filled him with anger and remorse, but he did not allow himself the luxury of these feelings and pushed them aside. When he restored Krit and gained revenge on whomever it was that brought such devastation to his people, then he would mourn all who had perished.

"Naid Sharram." Ko'Resh broke the silence. "I must urge you to continue our journey. You have done what you can for the child and we must not ..."— he seemed to choose his words carefully—"delay, for there are many who live that need you as well."

Rhandor straightened and turned to face Ko'Resh, his heart filled with resolve to find the solution to their plight. He looked down at the man before him. "Yes." He gave a slight nod. "It is time to serve those who remain and bring this treachery to an end." With that, he turned from the burial grounds and started back along the path toward Ko'Resh's hut. Ko'Resh hurried to follow, his shorter stride forcing him to push to keep up with the sharram.

The duo continued the remainder of the trek in silence. When they approached the hut, Ko'Resh moved to stand in front of the doorway. He motioned with his hand and muttered a few unintelligible words. The frame around the door briefly glowed with a soft blue light and the door opened. Ko'Resh entered and motioned for Rhandor to follow.

Rhandor, hesitated then ducked his head and entered the hut. The door swung closed behind him leaving them in darkness, for no windows were built into the walls to allow any light, or any curiosity seekers, to penetrate the hut. Rhandor gradually could distinguish a table before him then more of the hut became visible. He saw Ko'Resh held a globe that glowed softly, illuminating the interior of the hut. Ko'Resh motioned for him to sit at the table that stood in the centre of the room. Rhandor complied. Ko'Resh poured two large goblets of water from a clay jug he kept beside what looked to be a small well dug within the walls of his hovel. Rhandor took the water and drank deep. He did not fear poison. He was certain if Ko'Resh intended to kill him he would already be dead. No, Ko'Resh needed him for some reason and he intended to find out what that reason was.

"I have played along with your charade long enough, Ko'Resh. It is time you explain to me how I can save what is left of my people." He placed the cup onto the table and glared at Ko'Resh. He was not prone to displays of anger, but the evening thus far had taxed his patience. He forced himself to remain calm while he studied the wizard. For truly that was what Ko'Resh was. Rhandor hoped whatever solveige Ko'Resh possessed was enough to save his kingdom.

Ko'Resh sat in a chair across the table from Rhandor. "As you know, I am not from your lands. I was brought here by circumstance and treachery from a land on the far reaches of the Aevitas Ocean." He paused and took a drink.

Rhandor studied his face, searching for small "tells," such as poor eye contact or restlessness, that would indicate Ko'Resh was lying but he saw none, so he waited patiently for him to continue.

"The treachery came from my twin brother, Kian'Huard. He stole from me my birthright and then sought to destroy me to claim all for his own. I managed to escape him, but he hunted me relentlessly. When he found me we fought, even though I begged him to stop, that said we could share the power of what we had and rule our lands side by side as brothers. He would have nothing to do with it. Unfortunately, his greed and hatred were more powerful than my love of my brother and he was able to best me. He struck me such a blow he thought I was dead then he cast me from the cliffside and into the sea." Ko'Resh paused again to take another drink, cleared his throat and continued. "Circumstance, or fate, however you wish to define it, intervened and I was spared death and brought to your lands. I do not recall how I was able to survive the journey across the Aevitas Ocean or even the fall from the cliff. By all accounts, I should have perished. But I remained alive and when I came to shore near Gaelen I was able to find food and shelter and my body recovered. I hesitate to tell you how long ago that was for indeed it sounds far too spectacular to be true, but nonetheless I do sit before you now and I fear my sibling has discovered I am alive and has found where I have been hiding." He emptied his mug, rose to refill it and offered Rhandor another. Rhandor's eyes narrowed slightly, and his head gave a nearly imperceptible tilt to the left. An expression of concern wrote itself across Ko'Resh's face. In that moment, Rhandor thought he sensed the taint of deception in Ko'Resh's words.

Rhandor declined the offer of water. He wondered at the odd contrast of fear and power that Ko'Resh displayed. For certain, he did possess much solveige but as time passed, it seemed to Rhandor that perhaps Ko'Resh's power was diminishing. He knew not if the tale Ko'Resh told was true, but he did know there were no others of his colouring or stature in Krit or in Norval and Sambahar. He recalled a very ancient text he was forced to read as a young shista. He found it rather boring and skimmed over most of the writing but recalled some mention of land beyond the far reaches of the Aevitas Ocean and of a people of fairer colour with hair of copper fire. But the land was cursed by the gods and none were to venture there on penalty of death. Now he wished he had paid more attention to the scrolls…

Ko'Resh returned to sit across from him. "I believe my brother has brought this devastation to your people using that which he stole from me." He took another mouthful of water. "We must journey to Rhuna, my homeland, and retrieve the power from him and use it to repair what he has done."

Rhandor sat back in his chair and studied Ko'Resh. What he suggested seemed impossible but, as his logical mind tried to dismiss the impossible, the web of control Ko'Resh had woven into his psyche moved to take possession of reason and he found himself asking what they needed to embark on such a journey.

Ko'Resh chose his next words carefully. Centuries of waiting and planning were coming to an end. Soon Rhuna would be his and he would possess the final link to ultimate power that was stolen from him so long ago. But first he needed Krit and the resources the country had at its disposal.

"Sharram Rhandor, we will need to commence work right away. Krit will be known as the country that cast aside superstition and fear to cross the uncrossable sea. We will build vessels the likes of which have never before been seen in all the kingdoms of Mythos. Your people will go down in history as the first to rediscover the lost race of the Rhue. Unfortunately, time is not on our side. We have much to do and only three full cycles to complete the ships and ready an army. We need to start immediately to ensure the vessels are completed on time." He paused for a moment and gently probed Rhandor's mind to ensure the link remained strong and unnoticed. Satisfied, he continued, "To facilitate this I suggest you make me your second. Advise your people they must take orders from me as though they were coming from you."

Rhandor's brow furrowed slightly at some internal struggle as he slowly moved his head from side to side. After what seemed an eternity his face softened, his eyes lost some of their sharpness and he nodded in acquiescence. Ko'Resh stifled the grin that threatened to emerge. His heart raced. He had Rhandor. The Krit were his to rule.

"I will gather what I need and we can leave for Jordan tonight." His words came almost in a rush while he piled his many parchments onto the table to bind them together and place in a small case. He did not bother to gather any of his clothing or other personal items. He would not need them. After centuries of living in a near-impoverished state, Ko'Resh was finally returning to the lifestyle that was denied him and he planned to make the most of it. He closed the case that contained all his research and charts of the procession of the planets along with what knowledge he could recall that he was taught as Shista of Rhuna. So many centuries waiting for this time and now he feared there would not be enough time to make all the preparations. He summoned Rhandor to follow as he left his hovel for the final time.

CHAPTER 16

IT HAD BEEN THREE DAYS' TRAVEL SINCE RHANDOR and Ko'Resh left the hovel and journeyed back through Gaelen where they found passage on a small vessel that was travelling south on the Flumen River to where it met the Sagares Sea. From there they would have to disembark to find a larger vessel that would carry them south in the Sagares Sea around Sentinel Point and into Pacina Bay to finally come to port in the Krit capital, the city of Jordan.

The port should have been alive with activity but fishing boats remained moored and abandoned at the pier. Nets lay in crumpled heaps dockside, and barrels that should have been overflowing with fish lay empty. The crisp salt air was tainted with the stench of death, for no part of the country of Krit was unscathed by that which Ko'Resh unleashed. Very few Krit could be found manning the port, so it took longer than usual for their small ship to dock and its few passengers to disembark. Checking for citizenship papers was overlooked, for there was no one to perform the task. The street that ran the length of the docks was all but empty, and it took Ko'Resh several minutes to find a carriage to carry them to the castle which rose, with undisputed majesty, in the centre of the city. It did not bother Ko'Resh that they saw the stone fortress rising above the bare branches of drought-ravaged trees or that he was the cause of such devastation. He was too rapt in his own greed and power lust to see beyond his own desires to what damage he had done to the delicate balance of the planet herself.

Their arrival at the castle held very little pomp since most who served had died from the plague. Ko'Resh wasted no time in having Rhandor sign a decree declaring him domini. The title gave him authority second only to Sharram Rhandor himself. He was shown to the guest suite, which occupied one of the upper wings in the fortress. Traversing the corridors to his suite, Ko'Resh saw that no expense was spared in its construction. The stonework was almost comparable to what could be found in Rhuna. The stones were carved to fit nearly seamless and careful consideration had been made to ensure the colouring in the stones in each section of the castle matched. Coloured glass windows let flow natural light and painted the walls with reflections of intricate mandalas and ancient rulers. Clever use of the natural variances in the stone created a colour scheme that easily identified different areas of the castle as well as creating a huge bas relief on one whole wall within the great hall of a historical depiction of the line of rulers of the Kingdom of Krit. The floor of the great hall was polished marble and when looked at from the upper balcony that spanned the north and east walls, one could see it was, in fact, a map of the kingdom. Rich tapestries were in abundance through-out the fortress, for the Krit loved colour and filled their lives with as much as possible. As much as Ko'Resh took note of the vibrancy of the castle, he remained filled with purpose. A small part of him considered remaining in Krit and conquering the outlying countries through Sharram Rhandor but he pushed those thoughts aside. He would return to Rhuna and claim his birthright. Kian'Huard would pay for his treachery.

Ko'Resh found his suite to be of equal grandeur and designed to ensure any guest who stayed there would be impressed, from the huge fireplace that dominated the northern wall to the near floor-to-ceiling arched stained glass windows pieced together with the purest coloured glass he had seen. Though he could not be certain the windows in the palace in Rhuna were not equal or even finer, he was a young man then and it did not occur to him to take note of such things. With free reign, Ko'Resh could begin his preparations but first there was one thing he wanted. He called for the manservant assigned to him.

Ko'Resh did a double take when the young man entered his chamber, for he so resembled the young shista who he had taken to a painful death not even a full cycle prior. He quickly regained his composure. "Tell me your name."

"I am Bartus." The young man looked back at him with eyes darkened with the pain of loss. He spoke with the fluid, melodic accent that was native to Krit but his voice lacked spark and was filled with indifference.

Ko'Resh assumed he was most likely raised in the fortress and was servant to Arlon. He pushed back the swell of energy that was beginning to pulse within him. The beasts could sense fear and pain within the young man. They were trying to reach out to bring his fears to life. For that is what the Aneithnat Lukos, centred at the heart, would do. It would amplify fears and bring them to fruition and draw strength from the power that was released while the subject died the death they feared the most. Ko'Resh relished the feeling, the rush of power that swept through him when they took another victim. But not this day. He could not afford to indulge himself, or his beasts—they had to complete their mission and return to Rhuna to bring the seventh, the Sama Lukos, to join with them.

Ko'Resh motioned to the ornate bronze tub that stood just to the left of the fireplace. "I wish to bathe before dinner." He then seemed to notice his clothing for the first time in several years. "And I wish you to bring me attire befitting a sharram."

Bartus bowed then left. It was only a few moments later that several servants entered through another entrance discreetly hidden behind a tapestry to bring hot water for the tub. Ko'Resh wasted no time doffing his ragged clothes and sinking deep into the water. He studied the patchwork of flesh that covered his body, recalling each of the victims as he peeled their flesh from their bones to cover his own rotting flesh. Arlon was the last contributor to the collage of suffering that Ko'Resh wore.

Over the centuries he found, though he was gifted with what seemed to be immortality, the beasts he possessed lacked the essential harmonics that would bring them to work in tandem. So, while on occasion they managed to cooperate when driven by a definite purpose, they failed to rejuvenate the body on a continuing basis. As parts aged and failed, Ko'Resh would need to "harvest" replacements, resulting in a patchwork effect when the tawny-coloured flesh of young Krit boys replaced his own rotting flesh. The application of new over old was not always streamlined, and his body was covered with bulges where flesh overlapped flesh and the new bonded to the old. This caused him to keep himself covered from neck to toes lest anyone noticed. Once bathed, Ko'Resh dried and donned a robe then called for a barber to trim his hair and shave his beard. Even after bathing, the taint of rot and death still lingered on him. He was about to summon Bartus to see where his clothing was when the young man entered carrying a bundle of green-and-white silk bordered with gold embroidery.

Bartus bowed and handed the clothing to Ko'Resh. "I apologize for taking so long, but there are few in Krit of your stature, Domini Ko'Resh. These belonged to Shista Arlon when he was an adolescent. I hope they will serve until our tailor can make you something more."

Ko'Resh took the clothing from Bartus. "Yes, these will be sufficient for now." He turned from Bartus, dismissing him with a flick of his hand, and placed the clothing on the bed.

Bartus hesitated. "Do you wish assistance with dressing, Domini Ko'Resh?"

"No, that will be all."

Bartus bowed and exited through the hidden servants' door.

Ko'Resh stared for a moment at the quality of the silks and workmanship. A crooked smirk crossed his face to know these belonged to Rhandor's only child, the child whose life he took. When he opened his robe, he saw the triangle-shaped scar that was etched into the flesh that so recently became his. He remembered seeing the distinctive mark when he drew his blade through Arlon's living flesh and fashioned it onto his body so the mark lay visible on his lower abdomen as a trophy for him to admire. He threw the bathrobe aside and dressed himself in the clothing of the dead shista. When he looked at himself in the mirror, he saw Sharram Ko'Resh of Rhuna.

CHAPTER 17

KO'RESH WAS ENJOYING HIS LIFE IN THE GREAT FOR-
tress of Jordan. He relished his rule. It was almost enough to ease his bitterness at being cast from Rhuna and living so far from his native people. So
much was taken from him by his brother. He recalled the journey through
the caverns and how, at the last moment when his birthright was nearly fully
bestowed on him, his brother stole the final and most powerful of his spirits.
His time was nearly at hand. His return to Rhuna would see him take the
throne and gain revenge on his brother.

Ko'Resh, now second in command to the sharram, was free to move
about the fortress. He had woken several days earlier from a dream that was
so much more. It was as though he was present with another, a great sorcerer
who was showing him something. The directions were very specific and came
with a warning that if he did not follow the directions precisely the results
could be disastrous. To re-enforce the fact, he was blown up several times in
the dream state and was able to experience his body being torn and mangled
quite vividly.

Ko'Resh woke in a cold sweat, and he pushed aside the warnings that
flared within his mind and crossed the room to the chamber pot to relieve
himself. Used to being alone, he did not think to wear his robe until Bartus
entered. Too late, he tried to cover himself. Bartus took one look at the
deformed body and the colour drained from his face. He bowed and excused
himself then bolted from the room. Ko'Resh knew Arlon and Bartus had
shared a past and Bartus, most likely, knew of the scar. He may have even
been the cause of it. And there was no doubt in Ko'Resh's mind that Bartus
noticed that same scar on him. It appealed to his twisted sense that Bartus
knew and was not able to do anything about it.

Ko'Resh finished dressing and left his chambers in search of something. Initially he was not certain what it was he sought, but as he moved through the corridors winding through the vast fortress, he found himself standing before a large, ornate oaken door. The instant he saw it he knew it was what he was looking for. He did not spend any time admiring the ornate designs carved into the solid wooden slabs or noticing the intricate details of the enormous metal hinges. He grasped the latch, threw it back and pushed open the doors. His heart skipped a beat—he had found his apothecary. At once, the overwhelming stench of death assailed him. It seemed no one thought to attend the mages when the plague descended so they remained locked within the chamber in a heap of decayed flesh. He held a cloth to his face and entered the room, stepping over the bodies that lay just inside the threshold. He wasted no time in summoning guards to remove the bodies and, while they carried out their gruesome task, for many of the bodies were so rotten they fell apart when the men tried to lift them, he took inventory.

The main chamber was circular and at least thirty measures across. The ceiling towered high overhead and light poured in through a dome that was supported by eight columns carved with many runes and markings, most of which were unfamiliar to him. The base of the columns framed four doorways, each facing one of the cardinal directions. The north doorway was the one he had entered through, and the other three led to smaller chambers, each very similar in design to the main chamber but with different purpose. One housed a supply of herbs and minerals, some of which he recognized, though many he didn't. Another was a library of sorts, with shelves stuffed with books and scrolls and a reading table in the centre of the room. The third chamber he found most interesting and he wondered if Sharram Rhandor knew such a place existed within his castle walls. The room held cabinets and shelves with many metallic instruments such as blades and clamping devises. The centre of this room held something even more sinister—two raised cots equipped with restraints and darkened with the stain of years of blood that had been scrubbed, but not removed entirely, before it penetrated the wood fibers. Ko'Resh wondered at what experiments the Sorelige of Krit performed within these walls.

By the time he finished his preliminary survey of the chambers, the guards had removed the bodies and two women had been given the arduous task of scrubbing the stains from the floor and cleaning the rest of the chambers.

It took two full days, but finally he was able to start his work. Armed with his newfound knowledge, he proceeded to rummage through the available supplies. He carefully measured and re-measured powders into a metal bowl. His hands trembled slightly with excitement. The first attempt cost him his eyebrows in a flare-up. For the second he was more cautious, but the mix was weak and the powder just fizzled. For the third attempt, he measured carefully and stood back. The explosion shattered nearby glass and the force of the blast threw tools and shards of glass across the room, forcing Ko'Resh to drop to the floor to escape injury. He stood and surveyed the damage, managing a true smile and thanking that which he possessed for the knowledge. He knew the ratio to mix. He had Rhandor summon metalsmiths and provided them with diagrams to manufacture several dozen large, round vessels. He summoned miners to go to where the volcano slept and gather what he needed. Others were sent back to the mines for coal. Some he sent to the caves in the mountains nearest the sea to harvest bat guano, but he did not know if that would be enough for his needs. He needed the elements in large quantities and in short time. Then an idea occurred to him.

Ko'Resh called all who wished to receive extra rations to gather at the centre plaza just before the setting of the resh the following evening. Though he used Rhandor as a figurehead in dealing with the nobles from the outlying territories and neighbouring countries, he was able to directly control the local population as Rhandor's new advisor. He made his way to the plaza and was not surprised at the crowd that gathered. Many were engaged in conversations, guessing at what they could be asked to do. As he walked through the crowd he could overhear bits of conversation and it seemed most were willing to do almost anything so see their families fed and get a start on preparing for spring planting. But first they had to make it through the winter.

Ko'Resh made his way to a makeshift platform and climbed the three steps. He paused to survey the ragged group that assembled before him, their eyes full of expectation and need. He marvelled at how quickly such a fierce and noble people could be brought to their knees. It fed his ego and gave him an even greater sense of confidence. He knew he had not even begun to tap into the full potential of his power. When he did, none would have the power to defeat him. Not even his brother for, unlike Kian'Huard, Ko'Resh was not afraid to summon the power of the Sem Lukos and learn what abilities he could culture. He returned his attention to the crowd and raised his hand for silence. A hush quickly filled the square and all eyes turned their attention to the man before them. He heard mutterings as many wondered at his copper hair and shorter stature but, for now, acceptance ruled and previous rumours of him possessing dark solveige and turning it on them had been quelled.

"I have called you here under the authority of Sharram Rhandor." He filled himself with the essence of authority. "There is a need for a certain material and your sharram wishes all to assist in creating it." He paused while murmurs circulated through the crowd. He saw heads nodding with affirmation. Once again, all turned their attention to Ko'Resh, anxious to play their role in aiding their beloved sharram. Ko'Resh continued, "I am sure you are all aware of the great vats that have been erected just north of Jordan between us and Gaelen." Another wave of affirmation swept through the crowd. Ko'Resh knew the construction of the holding vats was the topic of much rumour, with as many ideas of what its use was as there were people telling the story.

"All who are able are to gather as much manure, straw and ash as possible to fill the vats. Everyone is required to collect their urine and take it to these vats as well." A new wave of chatter rolled through the group. Ko'Resh could hear sharp retorts followed with the unmistakeable rise in tone when a question was asked. He let them puzzle with his plans and create their own theories before once again raising his hand to summon them to silence. "This decree is by order of Sharram Rhandor." Silence fell over the crowd. "Rations will be increased according to amount of product each of you brings. Your contributions will be weighed before being added to the vat. Each measure will increase your ration by one-tenth."

Some faces showed disappointment at how little they would gain compared to the amount of work it would take to gather and haul even a few measures of waste. A spattering of conversations could be heard, some voicing complaints, others reminding the complainers that they could be overheard and possibly punished for speaking out. Gratitude for the increase in rations was not overabundant. Speculation regarding the need for human and animal waste was another topic that passed through the now-thinning crowd. Despite mystery and disappointment surrounding the order, the people of Krit eventually went their separate ways. Dark was descending upon the city, providing a small amount of relief from the day's heat. Ko'Resh maintained control over the weather, ensuring small amounts of rain fell, enough to afford a glimmer of hope but not enough to quench the thirst. Days remained nearly unbearable until now. Ko'Resh knew he would have to manipulate the weather enough so the people could actually leave the shade of their homes and gather what he needed.

When the square had emptied of people he summoned the power of the Amladhar lukos, the spirit that brings forth frequencies necessary for survival. His body swayed slightly and a shudder ran up his spine. He felt a surge of energy commence at the base of his spine. The energy expanded and took on a red glow. It began to rotate and a vortex formed. His breathing became more rapid when the demand for oxygen increased. He allowed the spinning vortex of energy expand to engulf him. An eerie red glow emanated from within his body, originating at the base of his spine and outward. The Amladhar Lukos awoke and a ghostly apparition of the great beast began to emerge from the centre of the vortex. Another shade formed. It was the Sohar Kadesh who was bound to the lukos, its sorrowful form locked in an eternal struggle for freedom. Ko'Resh revelled in the surge of power brought on by the awakening. His breath came deep and ragged and his eyes opened wide with greed and power lust with what he controlled.

His world was within that vortex. He was the epicentre of the power, aware of the spirits that circled him, and they were at his command. His thoughts became theirs. The great lukos turned his massive, ghostly head to him. He swatted at the ground with his massive paw then raised his head to howl. The beast knew this was not his true master. But he knew he had to succumb to the role until his master returned. Ko'Resh, blinded by power, failed to see the charade. He commanded the beast heed him and made known his intent to alter the weather enough to allow for industry to commence.

The beast complied. The Sohar Kadesh that was bound to him searched with his consciousness to the corresponding energy vortex of the planet. It balked at the idea of altering the delicate balance of energy that maintained the basic eco-logical harmony, but the solveige that had been created to bind him to the will of the physical vessel they occupied was strong and he had no choice but to reach with his consciousness and bring forth the change. They swept over the land as a dark cloud, churning with the intent to bring rain to the dying lands of Krit.

Ko'Resh sensed the task had been completed and summoned the spirits beck to him. The great lukos snarled and swatted at the air as it was drawn inward into the vortex. The Sohar Kadesh was pulled inward with it, radiating the deepest of sorrow. Circling the outer event horizon of the blood-red vortex, his ghostly form stretched and wavered, reaching out longing for freedom, unable to break the bonds that imprisoned it. Ko'Resh struggled against their will. He was able to concentrate and focus all his attention to containing the power he had unleashed. Gradually, he felt the energy slowly subside and the vortex of energy shrunk, pulling in the last remnants of the Amladhar Lukos and the Sohar Kadesh eternally bound to it. When the final traces of the wheel of energy faded and his body returned to normal, a shudder ran through him. He staggered slightly then gained his balance. His heart still pounded with the release of adrenaline. He calmed his erratic breathing and then brought his heartrate back to normal. For a brief moment he wondered what control he would have when he unleashed all six. Even after so many centuries, he had never summoned more than the first three of the six Sem Lukos that he possessed. He should have been concerned, but his arrogance did not allow it. They were his to control and when the time came they would obey. He surveyed the now-deserted square. Night brought an unnatural silence to the city of Jordan, for the streets were emptied of people and no commerce was carried out after nightfall since the drought. Even the insects and night birds had abandoned their song in the wake of the devastation that was brought to Krit.

Ko'Resh felt a subtle change in the air. A gusty wind swept through the street, picking up dust and litter. The smell was unmistakeable. Rain was coming. Ko'Resh pulled his cloak close around him and headed back to the castle. There was one more piece to put into action for him to complete his goal. He needed a ship. In the morning he would head to the shipyards in Jordan.

CHAPTER 18

THE KRIT SHIPYARDS WERE RENOWNED THROUGHOUT the eastern continent for their highly skilled ship builders and innovative designs. Quite often Marius, the master builder, would receive requests from wealthy clients to design and build unique vessels that would distinguish their owner above others. That reputation brought him tradesmen from all over the continent in hopes they would be granted an apprenticeship under Maruis' tutelage.

He, and his apprentice Endrede, were Krit and every bit the typical example of Krit physique. They stood head and shoulders above most of the others who worked in the shipyards. Their black hair was long and straight and well kept. Endrede chose to weave his hair into the complex pattern denoting his position as a ship builder. The front of his hair was pulled from his face in several rows of smaller braids, which came together at the back in a weave that formed one larger braid. He fastened it at the nape of his neck with a metal clip shaped like a half-circle engraved with a boat and oars signifying his trade. His braid fell below his waist, and a brown cord was woven into it to signify he was an apprentice but nearing the completion of his apprentice-ship and would soon be able to work independently of his master. His sharp features and well-chiselled jaw gave him a very distinguished profile and his lean body was toned and fit and the bronze colour of his skin was deepened by many days working outside in the yards. His dark eyes usually held a glint of mischief, but that had dimmed after the loss of his family to the plague. When word of the illness reached him, he rushed to his family's homestead to bring them to stay inside the shipyard compound but when he arrived at his home, his parents and siblings had already succumbed to the illness that ravished the land.

Marius matched Endrede physically, though his features were softer with age and wisdom. He was the master builder. He had had the privilege of being mentor to many outstanding apprentices but Endrede was, by far, exceptional. They had an instant bond when Endrede's father first brought him to the shipyard hoping he would be allowed to learn the trade. He told Marius he felt his son showed promise as a builder, and he was right. Within one full turning of seasons Endrede had moved beyond manual labour to assisting with concepts for ship designs. And his designs were sound.

Marius recalled the day Endrede presented a ship design that surpassed anything ever constructed. It was a massive vessel capable of transporting hundreds of men and enough supplies for several months' journey. Marius studied the plan, scrutinizing every support and beam. The plan was flawless. "How did you come up with such a plan?" He was truly puzzled; Endrede was very gifted, but this was beyond exceptional. The plans contained elements not employed in any vessels currently constructed because there was no need. "How could you know how to do this? I have shown you what I know, but this surpasses even my knowledge."

Endrede did not look up at his mentor; his eyes remained fixed on the design laid on the table before him. "I had a dream," he told Marius, his voice no more than a whisper.

"A dream?"

"Yes. It was so real, and in it I designed and built the most magnificent ship ever seen on Mythos. Then the plans came to me." He looked up at Marius as though searching for permission to continue. Marius nodded and motioned for him to have a seat. "The first night I was shown the hull and how it would need to be shaped and the ribs and structure. When I woke in the morning the memory remained so strong I felt like I had no choice but to draw it." As Endrede spoke, his excitement grew and his words came out in such a rush Marius had to get him to repeat some of what he said so he could fully understand. Over the afternoon Endrede explained how the dreams came to him each night for the past eight or so, each detailing a different part of the ship from hull to cargo holds, crew cabins, masts and sails. As he studied the drawings in front of him, Marius could see no detail was exempt from the visions that were given Endrede.

Marius rose from the table and poured himself a drink. He offered one to Endrede. "I commend you, Endrede, for your work, but there has never been such a vessel built and I do not foresee there ever being a need. No one has ventured beyond sight of land on the Aevitas Ocean; superstition and legend have seen to that." His face softened when he saw Endrede was clearly disappointed but he continued, "Even if we were to embark on building such a vessel, we do not have the manpower needed to construct such a ship; the yard itself would need to be expanded and a new rail system would need to be built to accommodate a vessel this massive." Marius carefully rolled the drawings and placed them in a hide tube. "Should there ever come a day when the people overcome their fear of the sea, then we will build your ship, Endrede. Until then, may I keep your plans here with me? I wish to study them further. I believe I can learn a lot from what you have drawn." Endrede nodded, and Marius knew he understood the concerns about the cost and manpower.

One phase of rhuna later, Ko'Resh came to the shipyards and called a meeting with Marius, who greeted him with reservation. He had heard countless rumours of the copper-haired domini, many of which were gruesome accounts of child mutilation and solveige. But Ko'Resh was domini, and that title demanded respect so he bowed and gestured for Ko'Resh to enter. "I am honoured, Domini Ko'Resh, please come in."

Ko'Resh barely acknowledged Marius as he strode into the office. He did a quick survey of the room then turned to Marius, who was still standing at the door. "You will build me three ships."

"Yes, of course, Domini. Do you have a design in mind?"

"Indeed, I do." His tone went from forced cordiality to cold and bitter. "I wish to cross the Aevitas Ocean with an army." He crossed the room to look out the window that overlooked the shipyards and went on to describe exactly what it was he wanted.

Marius thought it was not coincidental that Endrede had furnished him with just what he needed to complete the task. He called for Endrede to join him and Domini Ko'Resh.

Endrede was elated at the good fortune of seeing his masterpiece come to fruition and was even more so when Marius made him overseer of the project. Work commenced right away, and word was sent to Sambahar and Norval for any and all shipbuilders and aspiring apprentices. Fear and superstition were set aside; the people needed a focus and they would need as much help as possible. Manpower was in short supply, as the drought had taken its toll on Krit resources.

This was how Oran and Strouthem of Norval came to be working the ship-yards of Krit. Marius liked both men the minute he set eyes on them. Though Marius was shipmaster builder of Krit, he quickly discovered Strouthem had the knowledge and demeanour to oversee the entire yard and the diplomacy to liaise between the tradesmen and labourers that came to Krit to work on the massive vessels. The rumour of the giant ships had spread quickly and many left their homes and villages to be part of the massive undertaking. So, in the spirit of democracy, he gladly turned the reigns over to the Norvalian.

At first it amazed Marius how smoothly the construction was going and how many skilled hands were at the ready to participate in the construction. Until today. He had just finished reviewing his plans for the next phase of construction and signalled the crew on the first ship to proceed. He stared up at the framework of the giant ships, which looked more like the skeletal remains of some monstrous sea creature. The ribs, which would serve to support the first layer of boards curved up and out, were forced into place and held by a complex structure of beams, braces and scaffold. The scaffold also served to keep the ships from leaning and supported them where the bottom curved up and around the main fixed rudder that would serve to keep the ship on a straight path through the water. The ships would be steered by a complex system of ropes and pulleys that would move the second rudder under the stern.

Dozens of men and women crawled over the scaffold, each working on a specific part of the structure. He watched Strouthem them through whistles and hand signals like a conductor synchronizing an orchestra, bringing all the different trades to one goal. He turned from the first ship and focussed his attention on the second. The builders worked with military precision and rarely was there an idle minute waiting for the crew ahead to complete their section before the next could begin. Satisfied with their progress, he turned to head back to the main office when something caught his eye. Light played along the main support beam. At first, he thought it a trick of the eye. He looked to the resh. It was nearing midday, but it was on the wrong side of the shipyard to cast light on that section of the ship. Then the enormous beam that served as a brace to the scaffolding on the second ship began to splinter under the weight. Marius heard the sickening sound and scrambled to safety. He hollered to those near the beam to get away, but the men atop the massive structure were well beyond earshot. All he could do was watch, helpless and horrified, as the beam collapsed, taking with it several dozen men.

With the centre scaffold missing, the ship began to list, threatening to crush the fallen men. In a heartbeat all hands rushed to erect a temporary brace. Ropes bigger round than a forearm and steel pulleys the size of grain barrels were hoisted and slung in an attempt to re-right the ship. Only then could they take tally of the casualties. Marius sent Strouthem to the fortress in Jordan to inform Ko'Resh. He did not relish the idea of being another man short, even if only for three days, but Ko'Resh needed to know and perhaps he would be able to find more builders to ensure his ships were completed on time.

CHAPTER 19

A COMMOTION OUTSIDE HIS ROOM COMMANDED Ko'Resh's attention. He recognized the voice of the young guard he posted outside the room to prevent his being disturbed. He was telling someone that they were not to enter and to stand down. The argument was quickly growing and just when Ko'Resh reached to open the door the unmistakeable sound of a sword being drawn brought silence. He opened the door to see his young guard, sword drawn and posturing toward one of the tradesmen he had left to supervise the building of his ships. The man's face was ashen and he did not attempt to hide his emotions. "Domini Ko'Resh,"—he gave a slight bow and continued—"There has been an accident at the shipyards." His eyes darted from Ko'Resh to the guard still pointing the sword at him. He shifted nervously as though getting ready to bolt at the slightest indication he would be run through.

Ko'Resh allowed a brief moment to revel in being referred to as "Domini"—second to the sharram—then quickly turned his attention to Strouthem, the master tradesman he had recruited from the nearby country of Norval. He was typical of the people of his country, lean and robust, but fairer of colour than the Krit, although tawnier than the Rhue. He stood a head taller than Ko'Resh and the young Krit guard stood much taller than Strouthem. The men of Norval traditionally kept their hair and beards long but well-groomed, usually adorned with intricate braids and some bead-work. It was easy to distinguish the married men of Norval by the elaborate braid work their wives would do. It was a more effective way of ensuring others knew of their marital status than by the traditional ring. "Tell me," he demanded. He did not try to conceal his growing agitation.

Strouthem gave another short bow, more of a bob of his head to prevent his eyes from leaving the steel blade poised less than a measure from his throat. "The main scaffold has let go on the second ship. I fear many lives have been lost…"

Ko'Resh interrupted. "What of the ship? Does it remain intact?"

"Yes, but there are many injured and …"

Again, Ko'Resh interrupted him, "Get more men and rebuild the scaffold. You must not fall behind. I want those ships completed on time!" His words came with such venom even the young guard took a step back.

"But, sir … there are no more men to be found." Strouthem took a step back at the look of rage that clouded Ko'Resh's face. In fact, it seemed to radiate from him and fill the area around them with a palpable energy that pricked at the skin and sent a shiver of fear coursing through Strouthem. He unconsciously took a step back.

Ko'Resh's temper flared, but something prevented him from lashing out at the man. Strouthem watched, frozen in place, as Ko'Resh's face contorted at some great internal struggle. His eyes glazed over and he threw his head back. His body lurched side to side with the internal conflict. He went rigid then abruptly his body went flaccid and he collapsed to the floor.

Strouthem moved cautiously toward Ko'Resh. He motioned for the young guard to assist. "What is your name?"

The young man nervously moved closer. "I am called Almeric." His attention was divided between Strouthem and Ko'Resh.

"You can put that sword down. I am no threat. I need you to assist me. Your master has had a fit. It is not uncommon among many people, but we need to assist him."

Almeric looked down as though noticing the sword for the first time. He let it fall to the floor. The crash of metal on stone echoed endlessly through the corridor. The young guard looked as though he was going to bolt. Ko'Resh had started another bout of convulsions and began foaming at the mouth.

"Tear off a piece of his robe," Strouthem told Almeric. He did as he was instructed and handed the fabric to Strouthem, who folded it several times. "I am going to try to open his mouth. When I do, put this between his teeth like this…" He demonstrated what he wanted done. "Can you do that? We need to prevent him from biting his tongue and it will help him breathe."

Almeric nodded. Strouthem handed him the cloth then pressed his fingers against Ko'Resh's lower jaw, forcing his mouth open. Almeric quickly wedged the cloth between Ko'Resh's teeth when another wave of convulsions swept through him. His eyes rolled back and his body arched and went rigid. Blood and spit trickled from the corner of his mouth. Strouthem rolled Ko'Resh on his side. "You need to get the physician," he told Almeric. "Leave me your vest."

Almeric complied and hurried down the corridor. Strouthem folded the vest and placed it under Ko'Resh's head. He removed his own overcoat and placed it over Ko'Resh. The seizure had ended, but Strouthem knew Ko'Resh's body would be very frail and he would need much rest after such an episode. He knew this because his own son suffered from such fits. They took him to every healer they knew of but none were able to help. His wife became so overprotective of the child that his spirit failed. No child could bear being separate from the others, unable to play freely. The illness took much from him, but an overzealous mother took his love of life and when he could no longer bear the loneliness he took what little control he had left and took his own life. His mother never recovered from the loss and she blocked off her heart and drove Strouthem from her. He remembered as though it were yesterday how he pleaded with her, but she had turned her heart to stone and away from him, never trying to understand that he lost his son as well.

The sound of approaching footsteps drew him back from his ruminations. The active seizures seem to have ceased and he removed the rolled fabric from between Ko'Resh's jaws and used the corner of it to wipe the spit and blood from his face. He could see where Ko'Resh had bit his tongue and had no concern for the wound. He had seen worse. A group of men rounded the corner. Two were carrying a stretcher, a third was a healer in the employ of the sharram and the fourth was young Almeric. Carefully they placed Ko'Resh's limp body on the stretcher and took him to his chambers.

Strouthem excused himself to return to the shipyards. Something about what he had witnessed remained unsettling; as though there was more happening than just a seizure. His instincts were on full alert. He quickened his pace. Night was closing, and he did not relish the idea of being on the road after dark. He found shelter for the night in a room above a well-lit tavern. Sleep did not come easy with the noise filtering up from the patrons below; and what sleep he managed to get was riddled with nightmares of being hunted. When dawn broke, pulling him from yet another disturbing dream, he gladly left the confines of the small room and gathered his pack. If he had a mount, it would take him only half a day of hard riding to reach the shipyards, but most horses had perished in the plague so he had to make his way back on foot and prayed he would reach the shipyard before nightfall.

When finally, the familiar landscape gave rise to the sight of the walls surrounding the yard ahead, he gave thanks to Selam for his safe return. The resh had dipped low on the horizon, causing him to pick up his pace. The glow of the shipyard lights in the distance gave him comfort. He let out a long, ragged sigh and drew his oiled cloak closer around him. A twig snapped to his left. "Who's there?" he called out. Silence fell. The crickets ceased chirping and the song of a night bird was replaced by the sound of his heart beating hard against his chest. He swallowed and drew in a deep breath to calm himself. *"Your mind plays with you after what you witnessed. There is no threat."* He brought his breathing under control. He strained his ears, listening for any indication he was being followed. No sound penetrated the night. Dark had fallen fast. He continued toward the glow of the yards.

This time the sound was directly behind him. The unmistakeable crunch of a heavy foot on gravel. He did not look behind; he broke into a sprint. The sound of someone or something in pursuit rang above his pounding heart. He began running, forcing as much speed as possible into his legs. His stalker followed suit. Strouthem could hear the breath of his pursuer and the pounding of heavy footfalls closing. He forced himself to move faster, frantic to reach the safety of the company barracks. Terror overtook him and his body responded. Adrenaline coursed through his veins, super-charging his muscles. He ran, blind with fear. And his hunter closed in. He could see the buildings that skirted the shipyard and make out the shapes of the workers inside. He could hear murmurs of conversation with the occasional staccato of someone yelling over the crowd. Hot breath caressed the back of his neck. He cried out in terror. He legs were failing him. His mind jumbled with new horror when he smelled the animal scent. The door to the nearest barracks was nearly within his grasp. He screamed when something swatted the back of his legs. He stumbled and slammed hard into the unyielding wooden door. His breath was knocked from him, but he managed to wrench open the door and burst into the room, nearly falling to the floor. He quickly regained his balance and slammed the door closed behind him, throwing the bolt and securing the lock. His dramatic entrance brought instant silence to the barrack and all turned to face him.

CHAPTER 20

IN STROUTHEM'S ABSENCE THEY HAD BEGUN THE grisly task of removing the dead and injured from the wreckage. Marius felt overwhelmed at the sight of even more death, as though Krit had not yet suffered enough, but he kept his focus to be an example to the others and they were able to remove the bodies and tend the wounded. Only then were they able to completely fortify the supports. The number of dead was over a dozen and the injured, twice that. It would be impossible to make the deadline with such a diminished workforce. Marius, Endrede and Oren were discussing the accident, trying to understand how the scaffolding could have given away. Marius listened while the others, once again, went over the events that led to the accident. They had been debating for the past hour how to continue construction and whether to take time to honour the dead when the sound of someone slamming the door halted their debate.

As one they turned to face the door.

"Master Strouthem!" Oren exclaimed. He rushed to Strouthem with Endrede close behind. They wasted no time in assisting Strouthem to a chair. "Bring me water," Oren shouted. He took one look at the face of his friend and paled. Strouthem's eyes were wild. His mouth opened and closed, but only disjointed, indiscernible whispers escaped him. "In the name of Selam, what has happened to him?" He checked a wound on Strouthem's temple. It bled profusely as head wounds do, but applied pressure was sufficient to stem the flow. Other than that, he found no further evidence of physical injury.

"What solveige is this?" Oren whispered. "I have seen Master Strouthem in much worse shape and have never seen him behave thus." He looked up at Marius, who handed him a basin of water and a few clean rags. "This wound is not that severe to rattle his mind." He indicated the gash on Strouthem's forehead, which he had cleaned of blood. He rinsed the rag and began to remove the blood that had run down the side of his head. Strouthem continued to moan and babble incoherently, and his eyes remained unfocussed and wild. Oren leaned closer to listen and see if he could make any sense of Strouthem's prattle. Suddenly, Strouthem grabbed at him. Oren avoided being grabbed by the throat, but Strouthem was able to grip his clothes and pull him closer. His eyes barely focussed and no recognition flickered in his wild stare. His breath was foul with the stench of fear. Oren pushed back, trying to free himself, but was held firm in Strouthem's grasp, the injured man's mouth opening and closing as though he was trying to say something.

"What is it?" Oren asked, unable to hide the fear form his voice. "What has driven you to such madness?" His voice was a choked whisper.

Strouthem eyes darted around the room then back to Oren. His panicked state seemed to be increasing. His grip tightened and he pulled the man closer. He grunted with the effort of trying to formulate words. When finally, the words came, they were forced from his throat accompanied by spit and blood, harsh, as though it caused him great pain to speak. "LEAVE... THIS ...PLACE!" His eyes fixed intently on Oren, filled with fear and desperation. His body convulsed and his eyes rolled back. His grip on Oren relaxed and then he went limp.

"Help me get him to a bunk," someone shouted as they pushed Oren aside. The men grabbed Strouthem and laid him on one of the bunks. Strouthem's face was pale, but his breath was slowing to a more regular rate.

"Selam!" Oren gasped. "What solveige possesses this place?" He pushed himself from the bed where his friend lay and backed away, never taking his eyes off Strouthem. "There were rumours among our people of powerful solveige possessing this land and its people. We were warned not to come here." His voiced cracked. "But the lure of the great ships was too enticing so we ignored the warnings." He looked around at the men then back to Strouthem. "Forgive me, my friend. I am sorry for convincing you to come to here. This is my fault." He retreated to his cot and sat down, shaking his head from side to side, blinking back tears that threatened.

"Had it not been for me, he would not have made the journey from Carden. Even despite other warnings, we still came." He glanced over to where Strouthem lay. "When we arrived in Raglan, it took every bit of

Strouthem's bartering prowess to secure a boat. No one wished to cross to Krit with rumour of plague and solveige. It took a full three paces of resha and fifteen silver pieces before we could gain passage with a small vessel travelling south and west across the Sea of Sagares. When we landed in Jordan, the devastation was obvious. We should have turned back then, but once more I convinced Strouthem to continue. The stench of burnt flesh, waste and decay hung in the air so thick it choked our breath and we held rags to our faces. People were sparse and any we encountered were filthy and ragged. Emaciated bodies hovered in the shadows, watching as we passed by."

The men knew of the difficult journey they had in coming to Krit, for every one in that room, save the Krit themselves, had the same journey, the same warnings that went unheeded with the lure of building the great ships. And though none wished to be reminded of the choice they made and the journey they took though the city of Jordan and the land between the harbour and the shipyards, they let Oran continue, for they knew he needed to speak the words to be able to reconcile himself with what happened to Strouthem. They knew the Krit who watched them from the shadows as they passed through the city held resentment toward them because when the plague struck the borders were closed. The Krit were left to their sufferings. Now, with the promise of fortune, the curious and opportunistic were returning to the devastated land to profit from their misery.

It seemed the others were right to fear the darkness that swept the land. Oren looked to Endrede and Marius. "What solveige possesses this land?" His voice carried the fear that flooded his heart.

Marius sighed; he had no words of comfort for the young Norvalian, for he had none for himself. The plague that ravished the land was swift and merciless, yet there were pockets of areas that were not affected. His shipyards were one. A great wall had been erected around the yard decades earlier to prevent adolescents from taking sport in daring each other to climb the scaffolds and walk the towering main beams when two young men died falling from them. The tragedy prompted the building of the wall surrounding the entire shipyard and a significant amount of land that was being used to grow vegetables. When the plague struck, it was with a heavy heart Marius closed the yard off from outsiders in an effort to keep the illness from sweeping through them as well. When the drought was realized it was already too late to be of any assistance to his fellow countrymen and he made the difficult decision to keep the gates closed and save as many as were within the confines of the shipyard as possible. He was overwrought with guilt knowing they had a well that was not contaminated—so much that each evening he would fill several buckets with water and put them outside the gate. At first the water was taken and the empty pails left. But within a few short weeks, when he checked the pails in the morning they remained untouched.

And the silence grew. He shuddered, recalling how the normal sounds of a flourishing city grew quieter, then the undertone of suffering rose above the diminished city soundscape, quickly replacing it with the wails of the death lament. This too subsided, until only an occasional cry could be heard. Then the silence came. Marius recalled the night he and the few dozen men and women within the walls of the shipyard were taking their evening meal. Though they despaired at the suffering that reached their ears, there was a twisted comfort in knowing they were not alone, that some hope could remain. The sounds carried across the distance of dead land and if they climbed the scaffold they could see the fires burning to the north and west outside the great city of Jordan. When the silence fell it was as though the whole of Mythos had disappeared and they were alone. Not even the cry of a night bird or howl of a scavenger broke the stillness of death that cursed the land of Krit. They all left their barracks and made their way to the centre of the yard, each caught in a moment of fear and uncertainty, exchanging looks of pain and loss. Though the plague was real to them and the suffering of their kinsmen a burden they all shared, the silence that engulfed the land had a tone of finality that broke them. They gathered in a group and prayed to their god Selam for the souls that no longer walked among them. Many had family outside the wall. The silence brought death to their loved ones and took all hope from the living. They joined together in the lament of the dead, and the sorrowful tones echoed from the walls of the shipyard and spilled into the night for none to hear.

Marius recalled that night, living that moment once more, when he looked into the pained eyes of young Oren. How did one give comfort when they had such need of it themselves? He reached to Oren and placed his hand on his shoulder. "I am truly sorry, Oren. I can't tell you what has taken this land. I don't know, but I fear there is a greater purpose to what has been happening,

178

whether for good or ill, and only those who are necessary to the cause will be spared."

He was beginning to see a greater picture as more outsiders ventured into Krit. It was as though any who would be needed to continue in certain trades were spared the worst of the devastation. He heard rumours of a battalion of Krit warriors, over a thousand in number, who were training in the Illuna Mountains when the plague struck. They were reportedly returning home when an avalanche trapped them high in the mountain where food and fresh water remained plentiful but out of reach to those in the lowlands. He heard of other areas as well that remained unspoiled. Then he heard of what had befallen Shista Arlon and a shiver of fear ran through him, for that news also brought with it the knowledge that the strange man who lived north of Gaelen was now advisor to Sharram Rhandor. If there was anyone in Krit who possessed such solveige to make manifest what has come to Krit, it was Ko'Resh. Marius wondered at what power the one called Ko'Resh had to be able to bring himself to be second to Sharram Rhandor. He kept his thoughts guarded for fear they would be known to anyone other than himself.

He brought his attention back to the young Norvalian. "Know that you are most welcome to remain with us. We will assist you to tend to Strouthem. I do not recommend you try to return home, for it is a long journey and should not be attempted alone, and I have none to spare to accompany you." He looked about the room at the ragged group of Krit, Norvalian and Sambaharan. Each had known loss that day. "I say this to all of you. I cannot deny there is some power afoot that I can not explain. Whether by misfortune or intent, we suffered great loss this day. I do not know what Master Strouthem stumbled on to bring about this madness of mind, but I do know Ko'Resh is in need of these vessels and therefore in need of us. I do not know what demons he battles or the purpose of these great ships. I do feel certain he wishes to journey deep into the Aevitas Ocean, for there would be no other need for such vessels. As shipbuilders we have embraced the challenge of building ships that rival any that have ever been constructed. I say we continue our work, if not for the craft but to see them carry the one named Ko'Resh from these lands." He surveyed the group, and many nodded in affirmation. Some remained uncertain. Small conversations percolated through the barracks. The tone of the room was initially divided, but gradually coalesced into agreement to continue the build. Some for the craft, some to rid the land of Ko'Resh and some for rear of reprisal if they abandoned the work. Whatever the reasons, all present were staying.

"We need to find more men." A voice from the back of the room rose above the others.

Everyone looked to Marius for an answer. "At dawn I will go to Jordan and send word with any who are travelling to call for labourers. But now we must get what rest we can. Dawn breaks in five hours." He turned to Endrede and Oren. "Help me tend Master Strouthem. You can send for someone to return him home in the morrow. Endrede will assist. But tonight, we must make him comfortable and try to understand his ramblings. Perhaps we can gain some insight to what haunts him, and what may be in store for us should the ships fall behind." He spoke trying to hide the trepidation that welled within his own mind.

Oren approached Marius. "It is our custom to prepare and bury our deceased before resh rises on the day following death."

Marius could see the conflict in Oren. A deep need to follow his tradition versus fear of venturing into the dark of this night. Marius could have forbidden him from leaving the safety of the barracks, but something told him Oren needed to tend to the burial of his comrades. He asked for volunteers. Two others from Norval who understood the ritual rose to assist their countryman. They gathered what they needed and ventured out into the night. While they prepared the bodies, none noticed the dim glow radiating from within the hulls of the ships.

CHAPTER 21

KO'RESH FELT HIS RAGE BUILD AT THE NEWS Strouthem gave. He sensed the collapse of the scaffold was not accidental. He could feel an intrusion; someone or something just beyond his awareness was present, penetrating into the field of energies he possessed, stirring them into action. His focus changed from Strouthem to within his own being. He reached into his mind to find the intruder. White-hot pain crushed his thoughts. He was aware his body convulsed in some distant reality. The intruder remained elusive to him, but he could feel the savage power of the six lukos entities and their Sohar Ka'Desh respond to the pull of who or what called to them.

Ko'Resh became almost frantic—his mind raced, probing his innermost consciousness, reaching to pull back the six he so jealously coveted. They were his and nothing was going to take them from him. Energy surged through his body, loosening the threads of reality to which he clung with desperate intent. His physical body went limp and crumpled to the floor when his spirit was pulled from it by some powerful force. He found his consciousness transported away from the castle. He was aware of seeing the land beneath him whip past as he travelled at incredible speed. For a moment he was pulled up, defying gravity, past the life-giving blanket of atmosphere and thrust into the cold dark void of space. Panic set in, but even as he began to thrash wildly he realized he was unharmed and he calmed his mind. He looked at the blue-green planet beneath him and felt awe at the frail beauty of it.

Then his attention shifted to the shipyards, and in an instant, he found himself flying along the roadway near the outer barracks in time to see Strouthem racing, in sheer panic, toward the door of the first building. Then he saw the source of Strouthem's terror. He watched with detachment as a ghostly phantom drove panic through the man, latching onto his soul and touching his mind just as he stumbled into the door. The body twitched, mouth still screaming, functioning on primitive reflex, his eyes vacant echoes of the terror he knew. Ko'Resh felt drawn to whatever it was that so easily snatched life and, once again, he was instantly transported to where his thoughts focussed and he found himself standing in the hull of one of the vessels. He was not alone. An ethereal light coalesced and swirled. It gathered unto itself to create the form of a man. Something about the being before him elicited a feeling of familiarity and fear. His initial reaction was to escape from that place. He focussed his attention on returning to the castle where his physical body lay weak and prone. The entity before him prevented his leaving.

Ko'Resh felt a ripple of fear course through him. He had been in the astral plane before, and no one should be able to manipulate his thoughts or actions. But he was being held. He set forth a strong desire to return to his physical body but still the power of the one before him prevented it. Another wave of fear brought an arch of static blue light to play over his spirit form, a charge of conscious desire unable to be made manifest so it was released as pure energy. He was aware the energy passed over and through his astral body down to his etheric body and thus affected his physical with another wave of convulsions. He drew his attention back to the being before him.

"Nay'ernai ren gan'sadine."

"I know who you are."

"Saal"

No words were formed, for none were needed in this realm. Thoughts were true and pure to the intent of the spirit wielding them. They would flow forth from their origin to be received by whomever was tuned to be receptive.

Ko'Resh levelled his gaze, and his eyes locked on the vague form of a face that wavered before him in vortices of blue, green and pale-yellow light. He said, "I know you cannot bring yourself to be manifest in flesh. You do not have the power. I have control of that which you created and they obey me. Once I return to Rhuna and Sharram Rhandor mates with Sharrana Nahleen, I will take the child for myself and reunite the Sem Lukos. Your time with this world is finished. I am the power that takes and creates. You have lingered too long, beyond the physical realm, separate from the flesh that you so deeply lust after. Now you will watch from here as I take this world as mine."

Saal's thoughts penetrated deep into Ko'Resh's mind clear as the spoken word. "You think you control my creation? If it were not for me they would have destroyed you long ago. Who do you think stayed your hand when you sought to let your wrath be unleashed on the shipmaster? Who do you think has shown you how to use the power of the six who dwell within you? Who directed you to bring about the Sheth in Sharram Rhandor? Who do you think saved your wretchedness from perishing on the journey from Rhuna to the land of Krit? *You have no power* save what I allow, and you will do my bidding to ensure Sharram Rhandor reaches the shores of Rhuna. The accident at the shipyard was caused by your brother and could have been worse except I was able to intervene and direct the Sama Lukos, preventing the beam from shattering completely. Many lives have been lost and your workforce is greatly reduced. I have caused the mountains to shake and the pass that was blocked is now open, freeing those who were trapped. They are travelling home now and will return in one more day. It is the missing contingent of Rhandor's army, one thousand men whom I have kept beyond the reach of the famine you created. They return now to take their place on the ships to Rhuna. They have with them a rephaim. It was found injured in the rubble that sealed the passage through which it was trying to escape. When the battalion returns you are to take the rephaim into your care and see to it he is able to make the journey to Rhuna. Make certain all who know of its existence forget. I will need him when you return to Rhuna. Rephaim are strong and are able to find their way even in the darkest of places."

Ko'Resh balked at the words driven into his mind by Saal. He held himself defiant to the implication that he had no power over the six energies. They were his, and he was not about to let Saal take them from him at any cost. He would take the rephaim because it suited his purpose to have creatures able to traverse the darkness of the catacombs to search out any who would take refuge there, but he would not relinquish his control over the entities within him.

Saal continued, "It is to be hidden within the cargo area of the ships. They are cave- dwellers and are unaccustomed to daylight." With that, Saal made a dismissive gesture and Ko'Resh found himself thrashing about in his bed as though he was falling from a great distance. He gasped and sat bolt upright.

Pain shot through his head at the abrupt reunion of body and spirit. He flung the covers aside and sat on the edge of the bed. Perspiration soaked his hair and bedclothes. He cursed under his breath that he had to do Saal's bidding. That would change once the Sheth Child was born and he took it for himself.

≫ ≫ ≫

Kian'Huard had found he could watch Ko'Resh by entering a deep meditative state that allowed his spirit to leave his body and travel where his mind would focus. Though he could not interact with those around him, he was able to monitor the progress of the ships and knew it was only a matter of time before Ko'Resh would return to Rhuna. It was by chance that he discovered he could call the Sama Lukos to journey with him. He had been in a meditative trance and felt the familiar ripple through his physical body as his attention shifted and he felt the freedom of rising above himself. He always looked for the "silver thread" that connected his spirit to his body while he was absent before he would set his intent on where he would journey. That night he noticed a second thread intertwined with his. He followed it to see it connected with the etheric form of the Sohar Kadesh that was bonded to the Sama Lukos. He wondered what power they would have, if any, in the astral plane.

His intent that night was to check the progress of the ships so he focussed his attention on journeying to the shipyards of Krit and in an instant knew he was there and so were the Sohar Kadesh and the Sama Lukos. He wondered if it were possible to summon the Sama Lukos to destroy the ships in this realm or if they could act upon the physical plane in the hope of preventing Ko'Resh from seeing his plan to fruition. He fixated his attention to calling forth the power of the creatures. Because they were outside the physical body, the energy formed, gradually increasing in intensity as a vortex of pure white light just below him. He watched as the vortex grew in size and intensity. He made clear his desire to destroy the ships and, as the power reached near peak intensity, he easily visualized a weakness in the main support beam of the centre ship.

At first, the Sama Lukos and its imprisoned Sohar Kadesh played along the length of the beam, causing it to begin to splinter. The weakness in the wood spread outward and along the length of the beam. The energy created by the Sama Lukos followed the cracks in the wood, filling them with a pulsing white glow. Kian'Huard reached out with his mind, entering the very fibres of the wood, coaxing them to weaken further and separate. He sensed the beam was about to shatter, and then something changed—Kian'Huard lost the ability to control the powerful energy he had unleashed. He tried to refocus his thoughts, to force the Sama Lukos to comply with his order, but the beast defied him and stopped the destruction before the beam shattered. Then Kian'Huard became aware of a presence. Saal!

Fear gripped him when he understood what had happened. The alignment of the planets was now sufficient for Saal to interact on an energetic level with the physical realm. He was losing what tenuous control he had over the Sama Lukos. He knew he would soon have no power over the beast. He withdrew from the ship and beckoned the beast to follow. He did not expect it to obey but, for some reason, it did comply and returned to a more dormant state. Time became shattered and for a moment Kian'Huard lost his bearings. He sought out the silver thread that connected him to his physical self. It was a safeguard he practiced whenever he became disoriented in the astral plane. He was able to refocus on the shipyard but could see some time had passed since he encountered Saal.

The ships were righted and night had fallen, but he was not sure how many days had passed in the physical realm. A movement caught his attention. A man was heading toward the shipyard. Kian'Huard knew he was one who was overseeing the building of the ships. He called forth the Sama Lukos and made clear his intent. Soon he could see the shadowy figure of a giant lukos in pursuit of the man. Kian'Huard mustered all his attention on the man. He did not wish to take a life, but if he could frighten them enough, perhaps superstition would take over and delay the build. He watched the ghostly form of the giant lukos pursue the man, and just as the beast was about to pounce, the man disappeared into one of the bunkhouses in the shipyard. Kian'Huard knew those who were constructing the ships were merely pawns in Ko'Resh's game. He meant no harm to them, but also knew he needed to stop Ko'Resh at whatever cost.

Kian'Huard pulled himself from the ether world and returned to his physical body. He awoke as though from a vivid dream, but he knew otherwise.

185

He knew the events had really happened and he was quite shaken by them. He also knew Saal would do whatever it took to ensure Ko'Resh returned to Rhuna with his protégé Sharram Rhandor to take Sharrana Nahleen and reunite the Sem Lukos Resh.

CHAPTER 22

NAHLEEN TOOK HER MORNING MEAL IN HER ROOM, leaving specific instruction not to be disturbed. She needed time with her thoughts. The sting of betrayal pricked at her when she poured her tea, and her thoughts went to Kian'Huard. She needed answers. Answers she knew he held. She considered going to the Temple of Osiris. Surely with what she had experienced these past seasons she could beseech the knowledge of, the sorelige, guardian of ancient magic and overseer to a cult of the highest order dedicated to protecting the long-forgotten secrets of Rhuna. Neither choice gave her comfort, but she was determined one would give her the knowledge she sought—at what cost would be determined. She recalled the vision she shared with Kian'Huard. If there was any accuracy to what she experienced, then the sorelige was very much involved in the events that occurred those many cycles ago, and those in the temple kept a record of everything. She finished her meal, opting for water instead of tea, and donned her riding gear. She packed a small sack with a few essentials. She would travel light, and alone, though she was certain Domini Val'Raslin would object loudly. Which he did.

"Naid Sharrana, I cannot abide you going on so dangerous a journey. You yourself have said there is a traitor living in the mountains. The old man. What was his name?"

"Kian'Huard."

"Yes, him. What if he has a secret army he has been training in that mountain? You did say there was a hidden training facility there, right?" Domini Val'Raslin was beside himself with anxiety. He was a slight man and rather frail in appearance. He had spent his entire life in service to the royal court and did not participate in many physically demanding endeavours. So the thought of Nahleen travelling across country alone was beyond reason for him.

"Yes, I did, and I am certain there is no army. I was there alone, and there was no sign that any others had been there for some time, if ever." Nahleen tried hard to keep her frustration in check.

But Val'Raslin was not letting up. "At least take an escort."

"I can travel faster alone."

"Naid Sharrana, please." His tone was almost pleading. "You are being unreasonable. I have looked the other way while you were away with that 'Kian'Huard' in the mountains and now you tell me he was drugging you! Then there was the time you disappeared for three days with no recollection of where you were." His face was getting flushed as his frustration rose.

Nahleen remained silent while he spoke, and her mind briefly wandered back to her meeting with Saal. She had told everyone she had no recollection of where she was, but in fact she recalled every moment of it very clearly. She sighed. "Okay, I will take an escort, but only one guardsman."

Nahleen could see relief wash over Val'Raslin; his shoulders relaxed and the furrow between his brows disappeared. He gave a slight bow and she saw a faint smile touch his lips. "Thank you, Naid Sharrana." He straightened and then his face became very serious. "Please be careful." He paused and fidgeted nervously. "I have heard something is going on at the temple. I can't say for sure, but there have been reports of the Sacerdos'helige riding in to villages and taking most of the able-bodied and leaving only the weak or frail. I sent three scouts to gather information and report back, but they have not yet returned."

Nahleen grew concerned. "It sounds as though the sorelige could be gathering an army. But that does not make any sense. Rhuna is impenetrable from the outside, and there are no divided factions within our lands that would warrant building another legion of soldiers outside of the House of Rhuna, unless they plan to take the castle."

Domini Val'Raslin nodded. "We should proceed with caution but not jump to any conclusions. As soon as I hear from the scouts I will send word to you. If the sorelige is gathering an army, then we need to find out his intent. No one knows for sure how many are housed within the temple, and if the rumours are true, he has added more than a thousand to his numbers during the most recent cull. More than enough to take the castle, in fact; he would be able to take control over the entire country."

Val'Raslin took Nahleen by the hands and turned her to look at him. He had served her family for two generations, entering the court of her father just before she was born. He had watched her grow into the woman who stood before him, a strong and compassionate sharrana. He let out a long sigh. "Please be careful, Nahleen. I know something is coming but cannot yet say what it is." He let go of her hands and turned to the window. "The Temple of Osiris is very powerful. Sorelige Garret Del'Tolan is reputed to be one of the most feared of temple leaders in known history and no one knows what his agenda could be. He keeps himself apart from the others and is only seen publicly when absolutely necessary. He shares nothing of his plans with anyone. Even the highest of the Sacerdos'helige know nothing of his true intent."

Nahleen shook the feeling of dread that swept through her. Her experiences with Kian'Huard and Saal gave her a pretty good idea of Sorelige Garret Del'Tolan's intent. She felt certain the sorelige knew of the planetary alignment and how it would affect Rhuna, making the country once more accessible to the outside world. And she was also certain he would have knowledge of the Sem Lukos and her role, however unwilling, in facilitating Saal's return to Rhuna. She knew he meant to destroy her or the Sheth Child, or both, by whatever means necessary. She hoped to meet with him—perhaps they could find an alternate solution. It was a huge risk, but one she was willing to take. "Thank you, Val'Raslin, for your service, and more importantly, your friendship and devotion to myself and my family. You have given me a lot to think about and your words will not go unheeded. But you need to understand, if I am going to find answers, they will be in the temple and I need you to manage the court in my absence."

Domini Val'Raslin gave a bow. He would continue to oversee governing Rhuna in her stead. When he left the room, Nahleen called a messenger to her and sent him to find Kian'Huard and deliver to him a summons that he meet her in Kephas. Before she met with the sorelige, she intended to meet with Kian'Huard and then decide if she would turn him over to the temple.

When preparations were complete, Nahleen went to Argus. She recalled her last encounter with the beast and how he reacted to her as though he saw something menacing in her, so she had the stable hand take Argus to a nearby paddock for her to approach him. Dew still lay heavy on the ground, soaking her soft leather boots and leaving a dark trail of wet where the fine mist coating the ground was crushed into long, watery lines. She could see where Argus and his keeper tread between the stable and the paddock. She also saw another set of footprints. As Nahleen neared the paddock she saw Dar'Kayel, head of her royal guard, a term of surrender to her domini for his peace of mind.

Dar'Kayel bowed low as she approached. "Naid Sharrana."

"Dar'Kayel, I see you have been chosen to accompany me at Domini Val'Raslin's insistence."

"For certain, Naid Sharrana. I insisted on being your escort." He smiled. "It saves me from the rigors of training our new recruits. So very green they are, I fear I would dispatch one or two had I remained."

"Well, for the sake of Rhuna's young men, and my domini, it seems we are stuck with each other." Nahleen had reached the paddock. She searched the field to find Argus prancing, head and tail held high, showing off for Dar'Kayel's mare. She turned to Dar'Kayel. "Please, call your mare and wait here. The last time I was with Argus he acted as though he did not know me, or saw something about me that distressed him. I would like a few moments with him to be sure he is not going to be difficult."

Dar'Kayel gave a short bow and whistled for his mare. She wasted no time in galloping to him. He attached a short rope to her harness and walked her out of the paddock and out of sight of Argus.

Nahleen entered the paddock, closed the gate behind her and moved toward the noble beast who had situated himself at the far side. She stopped in the centre of the field and waited, head down, for him to come to her. Horses did not know human hierarchy; they knew devotion and authority, but these had to be earned. Her last encounter with Argus was disturbing, almost frightening, when the large creature charged at her, stopping short of bowling over her then bolting from the stables. Standing in the field, she felt very exposed and was trusting whatever shrouded her from him had dissipated and he would come to her. She was pulled from her thoughts at the sound of hoofs approaching from behind. She drew a deep breath and calmed herself, relaxing her shoulders and keeping her head dropped.

She could feel he was very close, and she could smell his familiar animal scent and feel the heat of his body radiating from him. She heard him paw at the ground, snort, then turn and gallop away. Nahleen remained motionless; she knew she needed to regain his trust, so she continued to wait. The next time he approached, he came toward her on her right side. She could see him just inside the range of her peripheral vision. His head was down and every few feet he would stop and cock his head to study her. He continued to advance, taking his time, as though testing her, looking for a trace of what he sensed before. Then he was close enough to brush against her with his soft nose. He snorted when he inhaled then he nuzzled her, pushing against her hand looking for the treat he knew would be there.

Nahleen let out a sigh of relief and reached into her pocket to pull out an apple. Argus gladly took the fruit and rewarded Nahleen with his customary glob of slobber on her boot. She stroked his long face and neck then led him across the field to be saddled, feeling somewhat comforted by his acceptance of her, though it raised even more questions. These creatures were very perceptive—he knew something was not right and responded to it, and after her encounter with Saal it changed. Whatever shrouded her had left and the coincidence that she was no longer drinking Kian'Huard's tea did not escape her.

Nahleen finished readying her mount and addressed Dar'Kayel. "You will ride with me to the city of Kephas, and from there I will go to the Temple of Osiris alone."

She could see he wanted to object but thought better of it, and instead he swung onto his horse and reigned her toward the castle gate. He paused while Nahleen mounted Argus and brought him alongside. "Shall we, Naid Sharrana?" He motioned toward the road leading through the gardens of Althena and outward beyond the city. She clicked her tongue and coaxed Argus into a trot. She allowed a smile to surface at the joy of riding, the freedom and exhilaration she felt when she and Argus moved as one, and a small amount at Dar'Kayel's company. He was known for his humorous monologues when on long rides and perhaps some humour was what she needed.

CHAPTER 23

NAHLEEN AND DAR'KAYEL RODE THROUGH THE square. As her people recognized her and word spread, they gathered to bow low and pay their respects. They slowed their rides to a gentle walk. Children scurried to snatch flowers from willing venders and the occasional garden to present to her as she passed. Each she took with respect and patience, never showing the pressing need she felt to be out of the city.

"They love you."

Nahleen turned to Dar'Kayel for him to repeat his words, but the clamour of children vying for her attention swallowed them.

"The children." He spoke louder and reigned his horse to beside her. "They are very drawn to you."

"I suppose." She looked about at the young, eager faces surrounding her, each hoping she would notice and acknowledge them. "All children want to see their sharrana; it is exciting to them to imagine life in the royal court."

"No, Naid Sharrana, it is *you* they adore, not your title. You treat them as equal. Your reputation for kindness and fairness evokes loyalty beyond what your rule would dictate." He gave a crooked smile and bent to retrieve a flower from a young girl no more than ten full turns. "And being seen with you boosts my popularity as well." With that, he nudged his horse forward and left before Nahleen could reply and before he could see her smile at his boldness.

They had made their way through the main square and onto the road that lead out of the city. The crowd had thinned and they made good time. Spurring their horses into a quick trot they reached the Calligavi River as the resh was beginning to dip low on the horizon.

"We will make camp here," Dar'Kayel stated as he reigned his mare left of the road and down a small embankment that sloped onto a small plateau and dismounted.

The area was along the riverbank, with enough grass for the horses to feed before the forest took over. They were off the road enough to be aware of any travellers, but out of sight as well. Dar'Kayel wasted no time in erecting Nahleen's shelter and then his own. When he finished he saw that Nahleen had gathered firewood, constructed a pit and had a small blaze burning. A wry smile crossed his face. The sharrana was definitely not a frail, privileged waif. She was known for taking charge and leading by example, even if that example meant getting her hands dirty. The great flood two turns ago proved that when all who could, gathered to fill sacks with sand to protect the low-lying homes. When they were called together, Sharrana Nahleen was among the first to take up a shovel. If there were any whose loyalty wavered before, there were none after that. She was a remarkable woman and, even without her title, Dar'Kayel knew she would be just as remarkable.

"Naid Sharrana." He gave a bow. "The resh will be setting soon. I trust you will be safe here if I scout the nearby woods for some small game."

"Of course, Dar'Kayel" She had gathered more wood and was piling it near the fire. "Go hunt. I will tend the fire and have it ready for your return." She picked up a small metal pot. "I will set some water to boil for tea."

With that, he gave a quick nod, gathered his short bow and ducked into the forest. Just a few strides beyond the boundary where the grassy riverbank ended and the forest began, Dar'Kayel paused and inhaled deeply. He loved the scent of the forest, the spicy crisp of the canopy mingling with the deep musty tones of the fungi and decay of the forest floor. He appreciated the balance of nature one saw within the confines of the woods. And these were old forests. The people of Rhuna knew to be respectful and manage what wooded areas they had. Some areas, like the one he was in now, were very old. The canopy towered high overhead and was so thick it nearly blocked all the light of resha. The forest floor was soft and lush with moss and layers of fallen leaves. Bright-coloured fungi sprouted on fallen branches, vying with the moss to claim any nutrients released during its return to the soil.

Dar'Kayel stepped quietly, deeper into the forest, alert to any movement that would indicate prey was near. He readied his bow. A flock of blackbirds took flight in a frenzy of feathers and disgruntled squawks at his intrusion.

This startled a small hare into bolting. Too late, the creature realized its mistake. Dar'Kayel's arrow found its mark and the hare fell. He approached the animal and gave thanks to its spirit for giving its life to nourish his own. It was small, but not too small to provide enough meat for himself and Nahleen. He skinned the hare to keep the scent of blood away from the camp and retraced his path to the clearing.

The shade of the forest deepened as dusk fell. When he finally broke into the clearing, the resh had all but set. He saw Nahleen had a well-established fire burning with ample embers to roast the hare. She had set a pot of water to boil as well and was just adding aromatic leaves to brew for evening tea. She started at the sound of branches snapping underfoot when Dar'Kayel exited the woods.

"Naid Sharrana, forgive me if I startled you." He gave a short bow and moved to skewer the hare on a makeshift spit.

"Not at all, Dar'Kayel." She nodded toward his catch. "I see I am not to be disappointed by your hunting prowess this evening."

He chuckled. "Indeed, Naid Sharrana. The creature practically threw itself on my arrow in its haste to serve you."

Nahleen shook her head and gave a short laugh. "I am sure that is exactly how it happened, Dar'Kayel. Now, if you are finished with your tale of 'little adventure' I will relieve you of your catch and get it cooking." She took the spit and cradled it between two Y shaped sticks she had sunk into the ground to suspend it above the embers.

They ate and engaged in some small talk. Though Dar'Kayel was more than a little curious to why Sharrana Nahleen was going to the Temple of Osiris, he kept his curiosity to himself. He would protect her, that was for certain. But he was not immune to the tales and superstitions surrounding the temple and, despite his reputation for valour, he worried he would not be able to protect Sharrana Nahleen from what was rumoured to lay behind the temple doors.

"Dar'Kayel, your thoughts run deep," Nahleen said.

"This is true, Naid Sharrana; however, not so deep to distract me from ensuring your safety."

"Of that I have no doubt." She studied him intently across the glow of the low-burning fire then continued. "There are questions burning within you that you hesitate to ask."

194

"That I do not deny," he responded. "But such questions are not for me to ask."

The mood grew sombre. As though in response, the fire dimmed, masking their faces with an eerie glow that pulsed across their features, distorting lines and casting deep shadows. The distant careening of a night bird split the air. Dar'Kayel reached and threw more wood to feed the flames. The fire responded, greedily lapping a long orange tongue over the length of the log, setting it ablaze with its all-consuming hunger.

"Your questions need not be asked, Dar'Kayel. I shall tell you what brings me to seek out the council of the Sorelige Garret Del'Tolan of the Temple of Osiris."

One could not hear mention of the temple without instantly being bombarded with a myriad of childhood images of cloaked Sacerdos'helige snatching children from their mother's arms to be indoctrinated into the spiritual life of the temple. The fortunate of the initiates would be trained to become Sacerdos'helige, the more public figures in the temple. They were also the ones who rode into the countryside during a cull and took children from their families. The less fortunate of the taken were never seen again; they were the ones who were taken deep into the mountain to be the keepers of the past. These were images brought to life by older children telling tales to terrify the younger siblings. Tales reinforced by adult rumour and drunken barroom banter.

And there were the Culls.

This lent credence to the wild tales of baby-snatching. It was true—every five to ten full cycles a group of Sacerdos'helige would leave the temple, travelling in covered carriages that were shuttered to hide those within. And those riding alongside were shrouded in heavy, dark-green, almost black, cloaks with hoods that were pulled over their heads. Slats, only large enough for them to see out, were cut into the face of the hood. Their eyes were further disguised by heavy kohl liner. They travelled throughout Rhuna and selected children to be taken into the Kialo-Raslaine. Age did not seem to be a determining factor, for some were taken as infants while others as young adolescents.

Dar'Kayel still vividly recalled the day they came to his house, though it was many cycles ago. He was a child of five full cycles and his brother was seven. They were at evening meal, himself, his parents and his older brother and younger sister, no more than a babe in arms, when the door burst open. His father reacted quickly at the intrusion even before he knew who it was. He had taken up his long sword and held it ready while he positioned himself between the door and his family. Dar'Kayel still remembers the pain on his father's face when he realized who had entered their home. How he let his sword fall and his stance go from defender to submissive all within a breath of time. He remembers his mother crying, "No" over and over when the men pulled the three of them from their parents.

They studied his sister first then returned her to their mother. She clutched her daughter to her chest and tears of joy and anguish flowed from her while she watched them with her sons. Dar'Kayel was next. He stood before the menacing form, forcing himself to appear unafraid through a quivering lip and full, wet eyes. He could still feel the icy cold touch of the Sacerdos'helige when it took his face in its grasp to bring him to look into the deep-green pools that stared out from behind the shroud. He remembered those eyes, for one could not forget such a thing. Even as a young boy, he knew the Sacerdos'helige was pushing its way into his mind, rummaging through the essence of what he was, searching for something that would tell it whether he would take Dar'Kayel from his home and family or leave him. Though the process took only a few moments, Dar'Kayel felt himself pulled through what life he had lived in his short five cycles, what potential his future life held, and, most confusing for a small child, what lives and deaths he had already experienced.

When the sorelige finally let go of his face and released his mind, he nearly fainted. He was aware of his father nearby but he did not come to him until the Sacerdos'helige moved away. His brother was not so fortunate. The hooded intruder took his brother's face and barely a moment passed when he let him go then nodded to the other. Then they took him. Dar'Kayel recalled screaming, "No!" and trying to run after them, but his father prevented him. His father held him so tight he could barely breathe and he felt the wet of his father's tears as they fell onto his cheek. He never saw or heard from his brother again.

Nahleen watched Dar'Kayel retreat into his thoughts, reliving some painful past. "You lost someone to a cull?"

"Yes. I was a child of only five cycles." He paused and poked at the fire with a stick. "They took my older brother." He threw another piece of wood onto the fire to distract himself from his thoughts. He had not recalled that night so vividly for many cycles. "I have not forgotten my brother or what happened, though time had dulled the pain and faded the details. But tonight, something has changed, making the memory especially strong. It is as though our journey to the temple has brought the memory forward. I can recall that night as though it were only yesterday." His thoughts turned inward as he struggled with the emotions that welled from the wounds of that distant memory.

Nahleen poured tea and handed a cup to Dar'Kayel. She drew in a deep breath. She had to share what she knew, and what she feared, with someone. She took a sip of her tea, letting the warmth flood her and the aromatic herbs relax and help clear her mind to find a starting point. The Sacerdos'helige were formidable, that was true, but deeper within the temple another sect of keepers dwelt. None but a few Sacerdos'helige of the highest order within the temple itself and the current sorelige knew of the existence of the keepers of ancient sacred magic. They dwelt within the mountain, never venturing out into the world. Of the children taken in the cull, few were taken to serve in the repository, usually the youngest, for they could more easily adapt to the solitude and darkness of the mountain. It was rumoured the keepers were so pale they were almost blue for lack of light. Their hearing was extremely acute to compensate for decreased visibility. Their eyes were dark, losing the green pigment genetic to the people of Rhuna from the relentless dark of the caverns.

History was passed from one generation to the next. Each segment of the past could be found in one of the thousands of small chambers branching off from the endless tunnels. The chambers were always carved with their length running east and west and the dimensions were always the same: 17 measures in length, 8.5 measures in width and 9.5 measures high. The interior of these chambers was polished granite. The only furnishing within the chamber was a stone slab supported on short granite pedestals that served as a table. Silk-covered cushions provided seating for three. Within these chambers sat two of the Sacerdos'helige. The giver of the knowledge always sat on the east side of the table facing west and the receiver of knowledge sat on the west facing east. The third seating was on the north side of the table facing south. This was for those who sought knowledge specific to what that particular chamber was designed for. Much of the interior of the mountain was an enormous human repository, a honeycomb of passageways and chambers. The deeper into the mountain, the more ancient the knowledge. Nahleen knew she would have to traverse to the deepest reaches of the mountain to obtain the information she sought.

"Dar'Kayel, I will tell you what I seek in the temple, and why. Know that I speak the truth, no matter how impossible it may sound."

"It is not my place to doubt you, Naid Sharrana."

"Maybe so, but what I am about to tell you defies belief, even for myself, and I experienced it."

With that, she put more wood on the fire. She went to her pack and pulled out the flask of wine. She tossed the last of the tea from her cup and filled it with the wine then handed Dar'Kayel the flask. "Drink, Dar'Kayel. Perhaps the wine will take the edge off reason and you will know my words be true."

He took the flask and poured himself a cup, drank it down then poured another and waited.

Nahleen studied him across the fire, his handsome features accented in the bright glow. Had she ever decided to take a mate, he would have been among the men considered. Rhuna was a small country, cut off from the rest of their world by impassable barriers. Any ancient concept of only marrying royal blood was long ago dismissed. The House of Rhuna would select candidates based on physical traits as well as such qualities as integrity and intellect. She was past her thirtieth cycle and she had not yet considered a union. Though it was not unheard of, she was definitely one of the few exceptions. She took another drink from her cup. "Do you know of the man who dwells in the mountains?"

"I have heard rumour but have not chanced upon him."

"He is Kian'Huard. I have known him for several cycles and have recently learned he is of distant royal blood."

Dar'Kayel's eyes met hers and they locked for a moment. He waited for her to continue. When she did, she spoke almost non-stop for several paces of rhuna. At first, her words were guarded as she tried to convey her experiences with Kian'Huard and the truth he told her of her own lineage and how she was to be the vessel that brings forth the Sheth Child, which would bring about the destruction of much of Rhuna and quite possibly the rest of Mythos. As she spoke, caution was set aside and her descriptions of the past events became more detailed. Dar'Kayel listened intently to her words, and he only interrupted her if he needed clarification. Midway through her oration he rose and paced around the fire. She could see in his face he was trying to assimilate what she told him. She knew all children of Rhuna heard the myth surrounding why their country was separated from the rest of the world. But myth was easily dismissed. Now she was telling him the myth was indeed history and a great and fierce power was loose upon their world. And she was not yet done. She saw his tension rise further when she told him of her meeting with Saal.

"Naid Sharrana, how am I to protect you against such a foe?"

"I do not tell you this to seek your protection, Dar'Kayel. I tell you so you are warned of what is coming so you can protect our people." She stood to face him. "So you can protect them from me." She returned to sit once more across the fire from him and let out a long sigh. "There is more." She focussed her attention on the fire, not wanting to make eye contact. "Kian'Huard has a twin. His name is Ko'Resh and he has been living these past centuries in a land across the Aevitas Ocean. He has been constructing great ships that will bring him home to Rhuna, and he brings with him an army greater than what we can possibly defeat. He also brings their sharram. He is the one who is intended to father the Sheth Child and give Saal the vessel he needs to return to this realm."

He started to object but Nahleen stopped him. "I want you to swear you will take my life if they indeed do come in search of me."

Nahleen watched Dar'Kayel fight back his frustration. She knew everything that he was, everything he knew, his sword, his life, was committed to protecting and serving her above all else. What she was asking was almost inconceivable to him.

"I fear you have put your faith in the wrong man, Naid Sharrana. For I cannot believe myself capable of carrying out such a request." He bowed slightly, his internal conflict easily read. "If I may take my leave, I will find a suitable place to keep watch." His voice held a strained calm.

"Of course, Dar'Kayel." She watched him stride toward a small knoll that would offer clear sight of the road, their camp and the forest edge. His posture was rigid and his stride long, exposing the conflict he was trying to hide. She knew him well enough to allow him time with his thoughts. She also knew, when the time came, he would do as she asked.

Sleep did not come easy for Nahleen, and she lay awake and restless through most of the night. She suppressed the urge to seek out Dar'Kayel for company. She sensed he was not yet ready to engage in any conversation. For certain, she gave him much to digest in one evening and so much seemed beyond possibility. When dawn finally broke clear and cold, she rose to find a small fire burning and water set to boil. Nahleen looked about but could not see Dar'Kayel. The sound of a twig snapping at the edge of the forest claimed her attention in time to see him emerging with a small bundle. He strode over to the camp, and his mood seemed lifted.

"*Nuva dalo maest*, Naid Sharrana." He gave a bow as he spoke the traditional morning greeting and placed the bundle on a stump that served as a makeshift table.

"*Nuva dalo maest*, Dar'Kayel." She returned the greeting but was curious at his shift in mood. She did not think a night spent on guard, alert to danger, would serve to put his mind at ease with the knowledge she had given him, nor the task she had put on him. "You seem in good spirits this day, Dar'Kayel."

"Indeed, Naid Sharrana, I had much time through the night to consider all you spoke of last evening and, though much of it I do not fully understand, I trust in you and will continue to honour my pledge to serve you." He paused for a moment then continued, "I cannot truthfully say I will be able to do as you have asked. Understand, my life has been devoted to your protection. However, should a time come when you become a threat to our people, and I am certain there is no other recourse but to comply, I will be swift and merciful."

Nahleen nodded. She could see the struggle and pain in his eyes. It was a terrible thing to ask of him. But she feared the day may come that she was glad she did ask.

Dar'Kayel broke the silence. "Enough darkness. Let us enjoy the bounty I have found for our morning meal." With that, he opened the package to reveal a veritable feast of wild berries and fruits.

Nahleen smiled and took cheese and bread from her travel sack to add to the meal. Though the mood had lightened, there remained a brooding undertone of pain in Dar'Kayel reflected in his eyes and affecting his posture, giving him the appearance of one carrying a heavy burden.

They broke camp as soon as they finished eating and continued on their journey to the city of Kephas. Few words were spoken and they maintained the horses at a steady, quick pace. It was still two days' journey to the city and the latter part of the journey through the foothills would be most challenging. Once they crossed the Calligavi River they followed the road on the eastern shore north toward the small village of Rainer that was nestled where the river divided. The west branch of the river was fed from high in the mountains, and the east branch flowed from somewhere beneath the Temple of Osiris. A tributary of the east branch flowed through the city of Kephas. It was regarded as sacred and none dared drink or bathe in the water.

They reached Rainer by dusk on the second day of their journey. Rainer, like most towns in Rhuna, was built from stone. The outlying houses were nudged closer together as the landscape changed from farm land to industry. Almost all structures in Rhuna were made from stone carved out of the mountains. Lumber and agriculture were meticulously managed to keep the ecosystem viable. Their forbearers had the insight to realize they lived in a closed system and laws were put in place to protect and manage their resources. The main industry in the town of Rainer, aside from the local markets, was hospitality. The town streets were laid out to bring travellers through the market square and into the main thoroughfare. As with all towns and villages, a centre square lay at the heart of the town and the focal point were the gardens. The Rhue loved beauty and colour, and they expressed it through nature. Along the route into town, stone houses displayed well-manicured gardens, each trying to outdo its neighbour. Window boxes overflowed with vibrant displays that drew the attention of all manner of songbird and butterflies.

It was not long before news of Sharrana Nahleen's presence passed through the village and the townspeople made their way to the street to greet their sharrana. Children gathered flowers to lay on the road before them. Nahleen and Dar'Kayel dismounted. He took the reins from Nahleen to lead her horse while she met with the people.

It took nearly two full paces of the resh for them to make their way to the centre square, and night was near full upon them. The crowd slowly dissipated, leaving the market to the last of the vendors closing their shops for the night. Nahleen and Dar'Kayel found a small inn and Dar'Kayel tethered the horses in front of the inn then accompanied Nahleen to the entrance. The sounds of conversation and music spilled onto the street when Dar'Kayel opened the door. Nahleen blinked at the brightness as her eyes adjusted from the shadowy cover of dusk into the brightly lit tavern. A few patrons were engaged in a boisterous drinking song when one noticed Nahleen making her way across the room to the front desk. He loudly shushed his friends in the middle of their refrain and stood holding his hat over his heart and began the anthem of their sharrana. It was only moments before everyone in the tavern had joined in, leaving Nahleen feeling quite honoured. She turned to Dar'Kayel. "I believe I am quite safe here. If you wish to tend the horses, I will secure us rooms."

Dar'Kayel bowed slightly and turned so only she could see and hear him. "And I believe you are blushing, my revered and gracious sharrana." He joined in the song with the other patrons.

Nahleen smiled and shook her head. "And I believe you are out of tune, Dar'Kayel, so maybe you should tend the horses before you are arrested for treason for your butchering of my anthem."

"As you wish, Naid Sharrana. I live only to serve you." With that, he made a deep flourishing bow, flashed his best smile and left the inn.

The owner of the inn, a chubby, spirited woman, scurried to the counter, tucking her blouse and smoothing her skirt and trying to fix her hair at the same time. She appeared quite flushed at having Nahleen in her establishment. "Naid Sharrana, how can I serve you?" The woman bowed while she addressed Nahleen.

Nahleen smiled at the woman's nervousness. "I need lodging for myself and my guardsman for the night. I would prefer adjoining rooms." Nahleen was certain she would be safe but did not wish to tempt fate. She would feel much safer with Dar'Kayel in the next room.

"Yes, anything you wish, Naid Sharrana. I have my best rooms available." The woman went to a cupboard and retrieved two keys from their hooks. "If you will follow me." She gestured for Nahleen and headed to the stairs that led to a hallway with a balcony overlooking the tavern on one side and several doors on the other. The woman, once she became comfortable with the idea of having Sharrana Nahleen staying at her inn, became quite chatty. She was nearly falling over herself at the honour. She called her two sons to carry Nahleen's travel pack and to draw water to her room for a bath. She spoke nonstop about her life and how her late husband and she had built the inn and how she has managed to keep it up with the help of her sons since her husband passed. Though Nahleen was exhausted, she remained courteous and gracious to the woman, but could not be more relieved when the innkeeper finally closed the door behind her and Nahleen found herself in welcome silence.

Moments later there was a knock at her door. She cautiously opened it to find Dar'Kayel standing before her. She let out a long sigh of relief. "I trust the horses are well tended?"

"Indeed, Naid Sharrana. And were you able to secure separate lodgings for me or am I to spend my night downstairs in the tavern loudly singing your praises with the other patrons?"

Nahleen paused a moment. "I believe it would be misuse of my authority to subject those unsuspecting loyal subjects to any more of your singing." She laughed and handed him the key for the adjoining room. "I believe it is in the best interest of our country for you to get a good night's sleep and leave the barroom ballads to those who are clearly more talented. I am in no mood for a revolution."

Dar'Kayel bowed slightly and clenched at his heart. "Your words cut deep with truth, Naid Sharrana. I will retire to my room." He straightened and his tone lost its levity. "You need only call out and I will be at your side."

"I know," she replied. Their gaze lingered for a moment before Dar'Kayel turned to leave. He paused to make sure her door was closed and he heard the lock turn before making his way back down to the tavern. He took a table that afforded him a clear view of the stairs and waited. When he was tending the horses, there were rumours among the stable hands of strange happenings at the temple. He was told someone would be arriving late this evening from Kephas who may have more information.

Once Nahleen closed and locked the door, she wasted no time immersing herself into the bath, letting the hot water soothe and relax her. The past two days' ride was hard and the next day would be even more strenuous when they ascended the mountain that housed the temple.

When she finally retired, sleep came in restless waves, interrupted by Dar'Kayel's distinct off-pitch vocals mingling with a myriad of drunken singers and the rhythmic foot- stomping and cup-banging that accompanied most drinking songs. When dawn broke damp and grey, she did not feel rested and the cold penetrated to her bones.

Nahleen was anxious to get back on the road. She dressed quickly, brushed and braided her hair and stuffed several pieces of fruit and bread into her travel sack. She filled one flask with wine and the other two with water and set out to find Dar'Kayel. When she opened her door, she was startled to see him before her. He looked amused at startling her.

"I see you are ready to leave," he said as he eyed the pack slung over her shoulder. "I anticipated an early start and have readied the horses."

"Your intuition does not fail you this morning, Dar'Kayel." She moved into the hall and quietly closed the door behind her. "Let's make haste in leaving this establishment before our hostess wakens." She did not dislike the woman, but she was in no mood to be bombarded with her ceaseless chatter. Besides, they still had another days' journey to the city of Kephas and the Temple of Osiris and she could feel the weather beginning to change. She did not relish spending a full day on horseback in the rain. She sent a silent prayer to Selam to hold off the rain until they made the temple.

As they made their way through the town of Rainer Nahleen thought the main square seemed somewhat empty, even for the early hour. She dismissed it to the grey sky and threat of inclement weather, but something in the back of her mind would not accept that reasoning. She shook off the notion and spurred her mount to a quick trot, leaving Rainer behind.

They continued their journey east under the constant threat of rain from a steel-grey sky and it was not until the city of Kephas was in sight that the wind shifted, the temperature dropped and the clouds released their burden in a torrent. Nahleen had drawn the hood of her oilskin cape up over her head moments before the downpour started and she watched the landscape disappear behind a veil of water. The horses slowed as the roadway became slick with mud and their footing less sure. They entered the city shrouded by rain and hooded cloaks. The horses picked up their pace a bit when their hooves struck cobblestone and the promise of fresh hay and dry bedding was near.

Nahleen did not expect to see many people in the streets, but she did not expect the streets to be deserted. Rain did not usually deter vendors from opening their shops but most lay dark and empty. A dispirited atmosphere hung over the city. Something was not right. She turned to Dar'Kayel but he just shook his head. Near the end of the street a dim light drew their attention. They dismounted and Nahleen handed her reins to Dar'Kayel when she approached the shop. A bell rang when she pulled open the door. She was greeted by the warm scent of baked goods and spice.

A female voice called out from the back instructing her to wait a moment. Nahleen thought the voice sounded strained, as though the woman was trying to cover being upset. She heard the sound of water splashing and some rustling then a petite woman she guessed to be around the same age as herself emerged from the back of the bakery wiping her hands on her apron. Nahleen pulled back her hood to address the young woman.

The woman gasped and took a step back then made a rather flustered attempt at bowing. "My apologies, Naid Sharrana, I did not realize..."

Nahleen motioned her to stand. "No need to apologize." She paused for a moment. "What is your name?"

"I am Serena," the young woman answered, again with a short bow.

"Serena, can you tell me why there are so few shops open?" The young woman came out from behind the counter and Nahleen could see she had been crying. "What has you so distressed?"

Serena's face scrunched into a pained frown and her gaze dropped to the floor. Nahleen thought the woman was going to burst into tears and she waited patiently while Serena struggled to compose herself before she answered. "Last night..." She paused and drew a deep breath. "Last night the dark ones from the temple came." The woman paused, the words caught in her throat. "There was a cull." The words came out as though speaking them aloud would bring the priests back again.

"And who from your house was taken?" Nahleen did not think the woman was old enough to have a child of age to be taken in a cull.

"They took them all." She choked back a sob. "All the children past ten turns and all the men still able to work. They left only the very young and the old and sickly." Her face paled and she crumpled. Nahleen reacted quickly and caught the fainting woman before she fell and eased her gently to the floor. She called out for Dar'Kayel.

The door burst open and Dar'Kayel entered drawing his sword. Nahleen watched with some amusement as he quickly surveyed the shop looking for any threat then down at her and the young woman. He snorted and sheathed his sword.

"That was an impressive entrance."

He puffed out his chest and bowed slightly. "Yes, thank you." A wry smile crossed his face.

Nahleen suppressed a laugh. "Please check in the back for a place to lay her down."

Dar'Kayel stepped over the woman and went to the back of the shop. He returned a moment later and gathered the woman in his arms and carried her to a small couch in a room adjoining the bakery. Nahleen found a cloth and some water and brought them to the back. She placed the dampened cloth on the young woman's forehead and motioned for Dar'Kayel to follow her back to the storefront.

She indicated the woman who was now beginning to stir in the other room. "She ... Serena ... said there was a cull last night and the priests took all the young people, females as well, and any able-bodied men that were in the village." She could hear Serena moan and lowered her voice. "That is not a typical cull. I have had a strange feeling ever since we entered this village. Perhaps it is because of the cull and the people are devastated, but I fear there is something more."

Dar'Kayel nodded in agreement. "I did happen upon others in the village and they say the same thing. I have also been told there are some here from outlying villages that came this morning; they too have had the same experience. Word is they are gathering in the main hall this afternoon hoping to find an answer or make a plan."

"A plan for what?"

"Of that I am not certain, but I fear some more overzealous villagers would try to storm the temple. That would not bode well for them. Even an army of trained soldiers could not breach the temple. It would only end in blood."

"We must go to the hall. I will speak to the people." The sound of movement interrupted them. Serena had awakened and was standing in the doorway studying them. "There is to be a meeting this afternoon in the main hall," Nahleen told her. "There are those here from other villages who tell the same story of a cull where none but the very young and frail have been left. Dar'Kayel and I will go and see what news there is and try to prevent any unnecessary bloodshed." She went to Serena and ushered her back to the couch. "You need to stay here and rest. The child you are carrying will need you to remain strong and healthy."

Serena looked up at Nahleen. "How could you know I am with child?"

"If what you say of the cull is true then you should have been taken as well, for you are young and fit. There would be few reasons for you to be passed over." She turned to leave and motioned for Dar'Kayel to follow then turned back to the young woman. "I will return later to see that you are well and inform you of what the meeting brings." Then the pair pulled up their hoods and stepped out into the downpour.

CHAPTER 24

THE TOWN HALL WAS FILLED BEYOND CAPACITY WITH people and noise. An elderly man was standing on a raised platform trying in vain to bring the crowd to some kind of order. Nahleen and Dar'Kayel kept their hoods drawn low over their faces and made their way along the perimeter of the room, watching the crowd and listening to the voices that rose above the rest. When they neared the platform where the older man, whom they had heard addressed as Ko'Pell, stood, they waited quietly to see if he would be able to bring the room to order. While they waited, they listened and observed. It did not take long to determine who the leaders of the group were and the plan they were formulating. They planned to storm the temple; an act that would surely see every one of them killed. It quickly became apparent Ko'Pell was fighting a losing battle so Nahleen threw back her hood and stepped up onto the platform. Ko'Pell was first to notice the sharrana and, once he composed himself, he made a bow and stepped aside. Dar'Kayel threw back his hood and stood beside Nahleen. Silence fell over the hall in a wave when they saw Sharrana Nahleen before them and they bowed on bent knee.

"Rise," Nahleen spoke to the townspeople gathered before her.

As one, the people rose. Several struggled to regain their feet and needed the assistance of those around them. Yet, somehow, they were going to storm the temple? This did not surprise her, for the Rhue maintained strong family ties. It was not unheard of for several generations to live in close proximity. Some of the adolescents would venture to travel throughout Rhuna before returning home to marry and settle on land that was near their parents or even move in with grandparents or great-grandparents and care for their elders while assuming responsibility of the household and eventually inheriting it when the family members died. They were quick to rally and defend family, friend and neighbour, and they viewed this latest cull as an attack.

Nahleen let the silence brew for a few moments while she studied the faces of those before her and formulated a plan that would satisfy them. Most faces were filled with the pain of loss, though some held hope and expectation at the sight of their sharrana before them. Most were well beyond their prime and some had young children with them whose parents had been taken so they were left to be tended by elder family members. Nahleen did not know why the Sacerdos'helige had taken all the young, but she knew she had to find a way to bring these people to understand they must not move against the temple.

"I understand your pain and loss at this most recent cull. I cannot speak to why the Sacerdos'helige took so many, but I have to believe there is great purpose to what they have done." A murmur trickled through the crowd then quickly dissipated. Nahleen continued. "I wish no hardship to befall you, so I pledge I will send one hundred of my guard to each village affected by this cull to aid in maintaining your homes and assisting with the planting and harvest this cycle and ensure you have the help you need to ready for winter."

"But this does not bring our children and husbands back!" a voice in the back of the hall called out. Others spoke in confirmation and more added their voices to the growing din. Nahleen raised her hand to bring the crowd to silence. She looked to Dar'Kayel. He placed two fingers in his mouth and let out a shrill whistle. The crowd once again fell into silence and focussed their attention on Nahleen. She started to speak when she noticed something had drawn Dar'Kayel's attention. She followed his gaze to a hooded figure making its way through the crowd toward them. Dar'Kayel drew his sword. Some in the crowd gasped at this action and looked to see what or who had caused him to perceive a threat. Those nearest the hooded figure reacted and quickly restrained him. Dar'Kayel jumped from the platform and made his way through the crowd and pulled back the hood. The pair that held him let go and backed away.

Nahleen gasped. It was Kian'Huard, but something was different about him. "Bring him to me," she demanded.

Dar'Kayel gave Kian'Huard a small shove in Nahleen's direction. Kian'Huard readily complied and crossed the hall to stand before her. Nahleen stepped down from the platform. Their eyes locked for a brief moment. She knew it was Kian'Huard, but something had changed within him. She could sense he felt more conflict from the power that possessed him. And he had aged. The copper of his hair had turned silver and his face was now the well-weathered map of a long life. But his eyes remained clear and sharp and still held the depth that only one who had lived as long as he could contain. He bowed low before her. "You summoned me, Naid Sharrana?"

Nahleen pulled him aside, out of earshot of the crowd. "Indeed I did, Kian'Huard. Perhaps it is good fortune that you have arrived here at this time. I trust you are aware of the cull that took place here last night?" She still was not certain if she could trust him completely, but something about him told her she could trust him more now than she did prior to whatever happened to change him.

"For certain I have learned of what has taken place and what these good people wish to do. You must prevent them from going to the temple. It would not bode well for any of them. But this is not why you summoned me."

"No. This is an unexpected turn of events that I have no explanation for. Never during my reign or anywhere in the historic records have I been made aware of such an event. They took all the able-bodied; it is as though they were conscripting an army, but to what end? We have no threat. We are completely cut off from the rest of Mythos and there has never been any record of the perimeter being breached by anyone, let alone an invasion that would warrant assembling an army."

"No one except my brother, Ko'Resh. Your time with me was cut short, Naid Sharrana. Had you returned, I would have told you of the prophecy that continues beyond my brother and I releasing the Sem Lukos Resh into this realm. Know this: war is coming to Rhuna and I fear none have the power to stop it. I will explain all, but first you must address the people and convince them to stand down."

Nahleen nodded in agreement and returned to the platform though, as usual, conversation with Kian'Huard generated more questions than answers. She stood on the platform and waited. Quickly a hush settled over the crowd and once again the people turned expectant faces to her.

"I understand your need to do something to bring your loved ones home, but I fear that is impossible. There has never been a time when one of the chosen have returned from the Temple of Osiris, and I do not believe this will be any different. The Sacerdos'helige have served under the sorelige in the temple and have served Rhuna since the time of creation and their actions have never been questioned. Trying to take the temple can only end with bloodshed." A murmur of discontent percolated through the crowd. Nahleen raised her hand and the people returned their attention to her and once again fell into silence. Nahleen glanced over to where Kian'Huard stood and drew a deep breath and continued, "I am prepared to make a decree that any who approach the Temple of Osiris with the intent of trying to free those taken will be arrested and charged with treason against the temple and the House of Rhuna."

This time the discontent in the crowd flared to anger and Dar'Kayel moved to position himself between the people and Nahleen. "I am sworn to protect Sharrana Nahleen at any and all cost!" he shouted over the growing ruckus and unsheathed his sword. The scrape of metal brought the closest to him to retreat a few steps back. As others became aware of Dar'Kayel's stance more resigned themselves to surrender to the situation. One man forced his way through the crowd and lunged at Dar'Kayel. Dar'Kayel easily sidestepped the man and struck him with the hilt of his sword. The man crumpled and Dar'Kayel caught him before he fell and assisted him to one of the benches. He motioned for two of the women to tend the man then turned his attention back to the crowd. "I am but one man trained to fight for the house of Rhuna and I could easily dispatch all of you myself, for you are farmers and shopkeepers and not trained for conflict. What chance do you have against the temple guards who number in the hundreds, perhaps even thousands?" The crowd had fallen silent and looks of anger turned to despair and sorrow as realization took away hope.

Nahleen stepped forward. "I travel now to the temple, for that was my journey when I came to Kephas. I will speak on your behalf if I am granted audience with the sorelige. Know this, if there is any way to have your kin released, I will find it. But if this cannot be changed, you must remember, those in the temple can see farther than even myself and, if they have taken your families, then be certain there is a higher purpose than we can know. I will take my leave now and will send word as soon as I have any news." She stepped from the platform and motioned for Kian'Huard to follow. Dar'Kayel took up the lead and the people bowed as the trio made their way through the crowd.

Once outside, they found the rain had slowed to a fine drizzle and the solid grey of the sky was broken with patches of white. Occasionally the clouds would break apart to reveal a hint of blue. Dar'Kayel and Kian'Huard went ahead to the stables to bring the horses, leaving Nahleen to gather her thoughts.

Could war really be coming to Rhuna? How could she convince her people of such a thing when they had been cut off from the rest of their world almost since the beginning of its creation? How could she bring herself to believe Kian'Huard? She recalled her encounter with the being who called himself Saal. She knew what she experienced was real and so was the threat that he would somehow return. And Kian'Huard—what had happened since they last met that would age him after so many centuries when time did not touch him?

The sound of hooves on cobblestone claimed her attention and she watched the men approach with the horses. She studied Kian'Huard as he led his mount. For certain his posture was more stooped than she remembered and his gait slower and less deliberate. A far cry from the man who frequently bested her during their sparring matches in the mountain only a few turns ago. One thing she did know was his return generated far more questions than answers.

Dar'Kayel handed Nahleen the reins to her mount, pulling her from her thoughts. She took the reins and motioned for Dar'Kayel to step closer, out of earshot of Kian'Huard. She lowered her voice so only he could hear her words. "This cull has affected four villages. I want you to go back to the castle and bring back one hundred men for each of the villages to help those left maintain their farms and businesses. I am going to continue to the temple with Kian'Huard." Dar'Kayel began to object but she stopped him. "He is an old man; I am sure he poses no threat, but rest assured I will not let my guard down. I know he has important information about what is happening, but more than that, I feel he is at the centre of it." She paused to glance over at Kian'Huard then returned her attention to Dar'Kayel. "I do not think it is a coincidence that this cull happened shortly after I was taken by Saal. I do believe Kian'Huard when he says war is coming. I don't know how, but something is going to happen that will bring down the barrier that has separated Rhuna from the rest of Mythos, and when that happens we are all in great peril. If what Kian'Huard has told me about the Sem Lukos Resh is true, then his twin Ko'Resh intends to reunite the seven in one body and I will be the vessel that brings that body into the world. That cannot happen."

Her skin prickled when she recalled her encounter with Saal and his intent to possess a child born of her and Rhandor. She did not yet fully understand how that would come to be, but she knew she was in the middle of a power struggle between Ko'Resh and Saal. An outcome that saw either as victor would be disastrous for the entire world and that could not be allowed to happen at any cost. She placed her hand on his arm. "That is why I need you to remember your vow to take my life should I become a threat to this world."

Nahleen saw pain cloud Dar'Kayel's eyes before he shifted his attention to his horse. Sadness pulled at her heart, but she pushed it aside. There was no room for remorse. She had been put on this path and, for good or ill, she had to see it through to be sure none would ever be able to possess the power of the seven. Even if it meant her life was forfeit. Her journey to the Temple of Osiris was to seek out any information she could find on how to destroy the Sem Lukos Resh and prevent Saal or Ko'Resh from gaining full control over their power. Even if she were not sharrana, if this burden fell on her she could do nothing less then find a way to stop Saal and Ko'Resh. She knew Dar'Kayel understood this and knew his duty to the people of Rhuna above all else. If the time came, she knew he would carry out her order.

Dar'Kayel gathered his reins and moved to mount his horse. Nahleen turned him to face her. "When you have returned with men to assist the villages, seek me out at the temple. I want…," she paused, "…need, you at my side." Nahleen tried not to let her feelings show, but she knew he could see she was afraid.

Dar'Kayel nodded once then climbed on his horse. Nahleen could see he struggled with his own emotions as he reined his horse east toward Althena and spurred her into a full gallop through the still-empty streets of Kephas. When finally, distance and fog swallowed him from her sight, she turned to Kian'Huard. She studied his face and how it had changed over the past days. It was not more than twelve days since last they met but he looked as though decades had passed. But the fire that burned in his eyes remained bright and he easily swung his leg up to climb into the saddle. Nahleen followed suit and they guided their horses to the road that led to the Temple of Osiris. Nahleen saved her questions until they were clear of the narrow streets and had passed through the archway that marked the outermost town limits. Once they were beyond the confines of the town and into open countryside Nahleen drew in a deep breath. She was trying to find a starting point to her questions when Kian'Huard started for her.

"I know you have many questions, Naid Sharrana, and I will tell you all I know of what the future will bring. Know this—if I had the power to change what is to come I most certainly would, but I cannot. Ko'Resh is preparing an invasion of Rhuna and he brings with him an army that is battle-hardened and well trained. Our guardsmen have grown soft in the peace that has prevailed for so many cycles. Ko'Resh will be here in less than three full cycles and we must be prepared for what he brings. He has enslaved the mind of the leader of the Krit nation, Sharram Rhandor, and his sole purpose is to bring forth a child that will be Sheth, the chosen one who will be able to harness the power of the Sem Lukos Resh. That child will be of yours and Rhandor's blood, for both you and Rhandor are descendants of the line of Saal through manipulation and trickery. I confess I am as guilty of this deceit as my brother, for I did go to your grandmother at a time when Sharram A'Rhan was absent from the castle. The power of the Sama Lukos guided by the desires of Saal himself shrouded my true identity and she saw only Sharram A'Rhan during our encounter. Your mother was the product of that night." Kian'Huard paused and took a drink from his flask.

Nahleen felt her chest tighten with feelings of betrayal that threatened to spur her to anger and lash out at Kian'Huard. She did not think him as a victim, nor did she entirely regard him as the villain. If what he told her was truth, and if the vision he gave her of what happened in the caves those millennia ago was truth, then his possession by the Sama Lukos was an attempt to prevent even greater disaster from manifesting. Nahleen reined her horse to stop and Kian'Huard followed suit and turned to face her. She chose her next words carefully. "What if Saal was manipulating the events that occurred in those caverns? What if he needed the Sem Lukos Resh divided between you and your brother because it was the only way to bring the Sheth back into one embodiment through his selective breeding? What if his intent all along was to bring a new bloodline into the mix to further strengthen the power of the Sheth? Perhaps there was something in the Krit bloodline that has faded in the Rhue over the centuries of confinement." She watched his face intently for a reaction. Several moments passed before he ventured to speak.

"Nahleen..." His voice was heavy and it softened her anger as she waited for him to continue. "These questions are the same I have asked myself every day since my brother and I entered those caverns so many lifetimes ago. It has only been the past few cycles of rhuna when the planets have aligned enough to shift the energies of our world that I have been able to understand fully what is about to happen. Something in the energetic changes has awakened a part of my mind to allow me to see things that have not yet come to pass. I have spent considerable effort to see if my vision could show me a way to prevent the inevitable, if not forever, at least long enough to cause Saal to miss the window of opportunity that will occur when the planets are fully aligned." He nudged his horse to resume their journey and Nahleen followed suit.

"This window of opportunity...how much time will he have before the energy shifts and he cannot achieve his goal?" she asked. She didn't know why she couldn't bring herself to say out loud that he intended to impregnate her with Rhandor's child. It all seemed too surreal. For as long as recorded history the Rhue had been alone and unchallenged and now, in less than three full cycles, the barrier that separated her country from the rest of the world would fall and an invasion force would reach the shores of her land.

"I am not certain, but I fear it will be much longer than your army can hold back the forces that Ko'Resh brings with him. And even if the army is forced back, it is only Sharram Rhandor who needs to be successful in infiltrating the castle and taking what he needs." He stopped talking. The colour had drained from Nahleen's face at the realization she would be the unwilling vessel who would be forced to bring a child of destruction into the world.

"Is there anything we can do to prevent Ko'Resh and his army from landing in Rhuna?" Her question sounded more like a plea than she wanted. She was not prone to overreacting and did not feel she was in this instance; her fate would determine the future of an entire world, not just hers.

"I am afraid there is nothing that can be done to prevent the child from being conceived. Ko'Resh himself and, through the Sharram Rhandor with the aid of the six spirits, Saal, will hunt you relentlessly; there is no safe sanctuary. I will do what I can to prevent the ships from being completed or at the least try to destroy them before they reach our shores. But understand, I have tried to destroy one of the ships already and I was not able to complete my efforts. As the alignment grows near, Saal is able to gain more control over the Sama Lukos. If I am not able to disable the ships soon, I will not possess enough power over the Sama Lukos to call it to do anything that is not within Saal's plan."

Again, Nahleen felt as though the world fell away from under her. She gripped the reins tightly and drew in a deep breath to ease the sick feeling that rose in the pit of her stomach. It occurred to her that even though Kian'Huard truly wished to help her to defeat Saal and prevent the Sem Lukos Resh from being reunited, Saal somehow was connected to the Sama Lukos that possessed Kian'Huard and, most likely, would be aware of his thoughts and actions. Any plans they might make to defeat Saal would be made known to him through that connection. This realization gave her an idea, but first she would have to meet with the sorelige alone and it would take them most of the day to reach the temple.

They had travelled in silence for some time when Kian'Huard motioned her to stop and pointed to the road ahead. Nahleen could see a glimmer of gold shimmering on the horizon above the roadway then, as they drew nearer, she could make out a contingent of Sacerdos'helige, the temple guards, heading toward them at full gallop, the gold of their helmets gleaming in the light of resha that was finally breaking through the cloud cover. Nahleen and Kian'Huard quickly dismounted and led their horses to a safe distance off the road, but it was not necessary. When the company of Sacerdos'helige approached they came to a halt before the pair.

One of the riders dismounted and approached Nahleen, but his attention was clearly focussed on Kian'Huard. "Sharrana Nahleen." His tone was courteous though he did not bow, and it was not expected. Though she was ruler of the people of Rhuna, the Sacerdos'helige, under the governance of the sorelige, had ultimate control. "I have been sent by our sorelige to escort you to the temple."

Nahleen gave a nod to show respect, but her instincts were on high alert. She was not surprised to learn the sorelige knew she journeyed to the temple, but she did not expect the regiment of Sacerdos'helige to be sent to escort her. Even if she were to change her mind about going to the temple it wouldn't matter. This show of force was the sorelige's way of letting her know she was, in fact, being summoned and had no choice but to continue to the temple. She knew Kian'Huard spent his many years avoiding the temple and those who dwelt there. Though he showed no outward signs of concern, Nahleen knew he would not be comfortable in the company of the Sacerdos'helige, let alone that of the sorelige himself. Or perhaps it would be the other way around.

Kian'Huard held great power within him and much of what the temple held true acknowledged that power. If the visions he had shown her were true, then the Sacerdos'helige and the sorelige would fear the beast that he harboured within him and the connection with Saal, and they would be trying to find a way to destroy it. She could not let that happen, not yet. She needed Kian'Huard. He was the only one alive, with the exception of his twin, who could give her the tools she would need to defeat Saal should he be able to complete his plan to return to Rhuna. She also knew she was the key to his return and would be the vessel that brought the Sheth Child into the world. She was certain the sorelige knew that as well. She wondered if the sorelige knew they all sought the same outcome, to prevent Saal's return, and that she would gladly forfeit her life it that was what was needed, but not yet. She hoped there was another way. Her death would only delay the inevitable. Saal would find another way. A shiver ran up her spine. Perhaps it was she who should fear the temple.

Nahleen mounted her horse and the others followed suit. The contingent parted as she moved toward them then closed behind her until she was sur-rounded and separated from Kian'Huard. She strained to see if she could spot him among the sea of gilded helmets but was unable. She had no recourse but to continue to the temple and hope Kian'Huard remained nearby. She straightened her shoulders and held her head high. She would enter the temple as sharrana, and not as one who had been summoned. She would not be intimidated by the sorelige's show of force. Somehow, she had to maintain control of her meeting with the sorelige and not allow him to manipulate her into a course of action that was not agreeable to her.

The clouds had finally emptied themselves, the wind and resha had swept the sky clean. The air was crisp and noon was upon them. The contingent stopped long enough to water their horses and take some nourishment.

Nahleen excused herself under the pretence of needing to relieve herself. She ducked around a small outcropping of rocks and found a slightly elevated vantage point from where she could scan the group and look for Kian'Huard. She let out a sigh of relief when she saw him sitting near the creek that ran beside this stretch of the road. He appeared unrestrained and unharmed. In fact, he appeared to be in deep conversation with the Sacerdos'helige who approached them when they first encountered them on the road. A twinge of uncertainty pricked at her as she lowered herself from the knoll, but before it took hold she was jarred from her thoughts by one of the Sacerdos'helige. "Sharrana Nahleen, if you are ready, it is time to leave."

"Yes, of course," she replied as she pushed her way past the young man and made her way back to her horse.

The company resumed their trek without further delay and within three paces of resha, the Temple of Osiris could be seen gleaming white against the backdrop of mountains and heavy forest. The building was an architectural masterpiece that predated everything else in the country of Rhuna. It stood as a sentinel above the city of Kephas even though is was a full day's journey from the city to the temple. It's size and location, perched midway up the mountain face, gave it a vantage point where none could approach unseen and those who lived below in its shadow felt its presence looming over them, silently watching as they went about their daily business, ever mindful of the fact that at any time another cull could take place. They lived knowing those they loved who were snatched from them were so very near but impossible to reach.

Nahleen found herself looking up at the gleaming white pillars that supported the entrance to the temple. She tightened her grip on her reins. A palpable energy pulsed from within the temple and washed over them. Her horse grew skittish and she struggled to bring her under control. They pushed forward, passing under an ornate archway and down a narrow alley. They had to go single file. Nahleen strained to see if she could find Kian-Huard behind her but there were too many of the Sacerdos'helige filing in, blocking her view, and exit, behind. She pressed forward and soon the alleyway opened into a very large, sheltered courtyard that housed an impressive compound of stables and what appeared to be barracks. From these, several young children clad in simple green tunics hurried to take the reins as the contingent dismounted. Nahleen watched as a girl of no more than ten full cycles approached. Nahleen dismounted and handed the reins to the girl, who looked up, her green eyes growing wide when she recognized her sharrana. She made a short bow then a flicker of fear crossed her face and her eyed darted about to see if any had witnessed her action. Nahleen knew it was forbidden to acknowledge the House of Rhuna within the temple complex. She surmised the child was one taken in one of the most recent culls and was still learning her place among the Sacerdos'helige and the many rules and restrictions that were associated with serving in the temple. "Fear not, child, for none saw and I shall keep your secret." The child looked visibly relieved and the unmistakeable glimmer of hope shone in her face as well. Nahleen could only assume the child mistook her arrival as hope she may be rescued and returned to her family. Nahleen knew that was not possible, for she had no influence or governance over the temple or its practices. She handed the reins to the child and surveyed her surroundings for Kian'Huard.

She caught a flutter of green disappearing through a doorway to her right. A sinking feeling crept over her then deepened when she saw a group of six Sacerdos'helige moving toward her. She mustered her inner strength, straightened her shoulders and held her chin up. Her hands trembled in contrast to the air she tried to maintain. She folded them in front of her and faced the contingent as they approached. There was no courtesy shown as they closed around her and shepherded her toward a double row of ornate marble columns that towered several measures overhead. Their crowns supporting row upon row of gothic arches between which a tapestry of stained glass splashed its vibrant colour over the gleaming white-and-green checkered floor as the resh broke through the last cloud to succumb to its radiance. Her gut told her she had made a mistake in coming to the temple for guidance. She looked about at the faces of her escorts; they were stiff and emotionless, duty bound to deliver her to the sorelige. There was no way for her to turn back. She wondered if Kian'Huard was experiencing the same feelings of dread.

Her thoughts were interrupted when they came to a halt. She expected to see a great ornate entry but instead they stood before a small wooden door, plain in construction, no different then one would find in any home in Rhuna. One of her escorts knocked once on the door. She heard a latch click and the door opened enough for a head, shrouded in rough grey fabric, to peer out. Pale green eyes glanced at Nahleen and the head nodded, then a pale, thin hand reached to take her by the wrist and pull her through the doorway. She did not try to struggle; she knew it would be a wasted effort, so she let herself be taken from the guards and into whatever lay beyond. The door was opened only wide enough for her to pass through and was closed as soon as she cleared the threshold. It took her eyes a few moments to adjust to the dim lighting inside but her nose was filled with the scents of spices and herbs. She could hear water running nearby and the air in the room was heavy with moisture. Once her eyes adjusted to the lighting she saw she was in a bath room. Already she was being swept forward toward a steaming tub and three grey cloaked figures, who she could see now were young women, perhaps in their early adolescence, were quickly loosening her clothing and removing her riding cloak. She understood what was happening, and though the thought of a bath was very enticing, she needed to convey her feelings of urgency in meeting with the sorelige.

Another young woman, though a bit older than the others and garbed in a pale green cloak, approached. "None are permitted to have audience with the sorelige without being properly cleansed and attired. It is the custom of the temple and none are exempt." The woman gave Nahleen a cold stare. "Not even you." Contempt flowed through her words.

Nahleen pushed aside the resentment directed at her and addressed the young woman. "It is not my intent to break with protocol. I am more than happy to cooperate with the customary preparations; however, I am quite able to undress myself for a bath." She tried not to sound condescending.

"As you wish, *gaiethea.*"

The use of the word "gaiethea" was her way of completely depersonalizing Nahleen. There was no doubt the girl knew who she was and referring to her as "woman" was her way of letting Nahleen know her position held no special privilege inside the walls of the temple.

The three younger girls that were assisting Nahleen had backed into a neat row with their heads down during the exchange. Nahleen gave a short nod of understanding to the green robe, turned her back to her and continued to undress. As she removed her clothing it was taken by one of the grey-cloaked initiates and placed in a large sack. Once all of her clothing as well as her boots were placed in the sack, much to her surprise, the sack was thrown into a furnace and burnt. Before she could react, the blue-cloaked girl spoke up. "Within the walls of the temple there can be no remnants of the outside world. No distractions of past life or thoughts of what has been left behind. The bathing ceremony is to cleanse the body of any outside impurities, for only the pure can go before the sorelige. The water is blessed by the Sacerdos'helige and then further purified by our sorelige. It is anointed with rare herbs and oils that draw out impurities and cleanse the outer body. The drink you will be given will cleanse the internal body and free your mind of thoughts that clutter and distract." With that, she motioned the others to assist Nahleen into the tub. Two of the girls disrobed and each took her by an arm and moved her down the stairs into the pool of water.

The water was hot, as expected, and at first felt soothing. But as she was immersed deeper she felt her skin tingle then burn with the different herbs and salts in the water. She tried to identify them from the scent that wafted up in the steam but most were unfamiliar, either on their own or in the combination in which they were being used—whichever it was, she did not know. She tried not to appear alarmed as the water crept over her midsection and the burning sensation increased. She also noticed the deeper they submerged, the tighter a grip the two who held her applied. She was surprised at the strength they seemed to have. She noticed as she was moving into deeper water, her escorts were rising above her. Then, with no warning, they forced her head under the water. Her natural instinct to struggle kicked in as she tried to regain the surface. The two continued to hold her under. She felt the last bit of oxygen in her blood become depleted and panic took over. She thrashed about, trying to gain the surface. Her mind filled with blurred images then she felt a wave of darkness sweeping over her. Her struggles slowed and just before she succumbed to unconsciousness, they grabbed her by the hair and pulled her head from the water.

Nahleen drew in a deep breath and with it a spray of water. She coughed and sputtered, trying to clear her lungs of the burning water. The pair seemed not to notice as they continued to shepherd her forward in the pool and up the stairs on the other side. There was no reprieve. They walked the short distance to the next pool. The water in the second pool was equally warm but lacked the herbs and oils of the first. Her escorts led her to the centre of the pool then gathered small bars of soap that they worked into a lather in the water with coarse brushes. They began to scrub Nahleen's skin until it was red and raw, and scrubbed her hair as well. Again they immersed her, but only for a short time to rinse the soap from her hair. The third pool was filled with clear, cool water and Nahleen felt relief in its embrace. This time the two laid her back to float while they allowed the water to swirl through her hair, rinsing the last remains of the previous pools from her. When they helped her back onto her feet and out of the pool the other girl wearing grey dried her and dressed her in a similar grey robe.

The green-robed woman had returned with a steaming cup of some sort of herbed tea. Nahleen was reluctant to drink it when she identified one of the herbs as a strong laxative, but she was more reluctant to do anything that could be misconstrued as non-compliant so she took the tea and with a forced smile, drank it. The green robe took the cup from her and led her to a small chamber outfitted only with a small cot, a side table with a water jug and a wash basin and a waste port. Before she could ask how long she was to be detained, the door closed behind her and the unmistakable sound of a lock being engaged was the only answer to her unasked question. She tried to make herself as comfortable as possible. She knew she was in for a rough few paces of resha when the tea started to do its job. Apparently, the cleansing process was to be very thorough.

CHAPTER 25

KIAN'HUARD WAS ROUGHLY USHERED AWAY FROM Nahleen and toward another area of the temple. The room he was taken to was sizeable but sparsely furnished with only basic comforts. The only window overlooked the courtyard that housed the stables. Already the area was empty, with no indication of the contingent that had so recently arrived. Kian'Huard moved from the window and poured himself a long drink of water. He was being treated with a certain level of respect, not that of rank or position, but respect born of fear like one would respect a venomous serpent, and he was not made to suffer the same indignities of the "cleansing process" as Nahleen. Instead, his attendants offered him a basin and clean clothing then allowed him a modicum of privacy while he cleansed himself and changed. When they left the room, the unmistakeable sound of a lock being engaged could be heard. He did not relish being in the temple and recalled the last time he was brought here. Much blood was shed and much fear was instilled in those who survived the day he and his brother slashed their way from the temple to the false freedom that awaited.

Kian'Huard let out a heavy sigh. He knew the sorelige felt he had a plan to stop what was coming, but he also knew there was no stopping the inevitable. He was no longer sure of his own ability to be of assistance to Nahleen and the people of Mythos. As the time of the alignment drew near, he felt Saal's presence strengthen and did not know if his thoughts remained his own, or if Saal was able to read them through the beast that possessed his soul. He was not entirely certain if his attempts to help were being guided by his mind or if they were guided by Saal to see *his* plan come to fruition. Nor did he know how to prevent the Sheth Child from being conceived and brought into the world, or if it would be possible to destroy it after it drew breath.

He suspected that was the plan of the sorelige—to destroy the child after it was born. Avoiding the creation of the Sheth Child would only postpone Saal for another 2500 years. Kian'Huard did not relish the thought of remaining trapped on Mythos for that time. They would have to make their stand now. Somewhere there had to be the knowledge of how to trap the Sem Lukos Resh once again and perhaps even destroy them and free the beasts that had been bound against their will since the creation of their world. They were trapped once before. Kian'Huard wondered if the key was hidden deep under the temple in the caverns where he and Ko'Resh unleashed their horror so many millennia ago. Often, he returned to where they stumbled on the cave that led them below the temple, but he never found the entrance. It remained hidden from him, by some magic, no doubt, designed to protect the Sem Lukos Resh from being trapped again. Perhaps the sorelige knew of another passage into the depths of the mountain.

Footfalls outside his door claimed his attention. He turned as the lock was released and the door opened to reveal the sorelige himself. Though he was not the same man who imprisoned Ko'Resh and him those many years ago, his rank and station brought back the memory of that time. He felt the beast within him stir and pressed it back to its place of slumber. The two studied each other.

The sorelige spoke first. "For certain this will be a very tenuous alliance. If it were to be one at all." He stepped further into the room and closed the door behind him. He crossed to the small table in front of the window, sat in one of the chairs and motioned for Kian'Huard to sit in the other. "I know you do not wish to see the Sheth Child born into the world, and nor do I, but we both know it is necessary."

Kian'Huard sat across from the sorelige. "Necessary with hope the birth would create a window of opportunity to stop Saal." Kian'Huard did not wish to see Nahleen used in such a manner, but it seemed the sorelige had no concern for her wellbeing as long as the end result was to his liking; even if it meant killing her in the process. Kian'Huard poured himself a drink and continued, "We both know Nahleen would willingly give her life for the safety and wellbeing of her people and all of Mythos, but something about this equation does not add up. It seems too easy a plan to simply kill a child as it draws its first breath."

"Perhaps, but there are none who have given any other option to consider."

Kian'Huard nodded; it was true no other option had been made known to them. "First, the child has to be created. I know Ko'Resh has planned for many centuries how he would bring it about. And soon he will be on his way back to Rhuna with an army the likes of which have never before been seen in this quiet country. They will pass over the land like a wave of death straight to the temple and he will bring the Krit ruler to Nahleen to rejoin that which was separated when Ko'Resh and I were born." He sighed and leaned back in his chair.

"And when that child draws breath in this world and we are certain Saal has taken the body we will destroy it!" The sorelige could not contain his passion and slammed his fist onto the table to emphasize his point.

"It is too easy a plan. I feel something is hidden from us. Something only Saal knows."

"If Saal knows something, then your beast must know it. You must find a way to reveal the knowledge through the Sama Lukos you possess." The intensity in the sorelige's voice was unmistakeable.

"First, you must understand, I do not possess the beast, it possesses me, and each time I summon it, through good or ill, it gains more of my mind and soul and I am less able to discern between my thoughts and desires and its. I have tried to look inside the mind of the creature to seek answers but there is only darkness and pain. We cannot rely on using Saal's creations against him. We must find our answers here within the temple." He paused and drew in a breath. "And I must also caution you. My involvement may become a liability to you. As the alignment draws closer, Saal gains more of a foothold in this physical realm and is able to experience it through the beasts and I assume through mine and Ko'Resh's minds and bodies. He may already be aware of your plans to destroy the child or, if not now, may become aware very soon. Be cautious of what you speak of in front of me, for I may well be the means to bring your plans to an end."

The sorelige nodded. "Yes, that may be true. But we can also use that to relay misinformation as well, provided you are not already compromised."

"Perhaps," Kian'Huard replied, but something within him already knew deception was impossible. He shook the feeling and continued. He needed to see Nahleen. "I wish to see Sharrana Nahleen."

"I am not sure that is in everyone's best interest." Sorelige Garret Del Tolan's tone went cold.

Kian'Huard's face hardened, and his tone echoed deep authority. "I am certain it is."

Sorelige Garret Del Tolan's face grew slack, just for a brief moment, then reanimated. "Very well. Her cleansing ritual will be complete in two days; I will make arrangements for you to see her then."

Kian'Huard did not argue. He would see Nahleen on his schedule, not the temple's, but he needed to know where she was, and the cleansing rituals were held in that same part of the temple. He nodded in agreement to give the appearance of cooperation. "Thank you."

The sorelige rose from the table. "I will send one of the Sacerdos'helige to gather you to take your meals with them, unless you prefer to remain here and eat alone?"

"I fear I would not have anything to contribute to dinner conversation and do believe I make your Sacerdos'helige very uncomfortable. I think it would best serve if I took my meals here for the time being."

"As you wish," the sorelige replied. He looked down at Kian'Huard through sharp green eyes, as though sizing him up, then he turned and left the room.

The sound of the lock being engaged did not escape Kian'Huard. He smiled. The sorelige had no real idea how powerful he was. He listened as the sound of footfalls faded and only silence could be heard through the door. With a slight wave of his hand he was able to free the lock with the aid of the Sama Lukos. He cautiously opened the door. No guards had been posted at or near his room. He slipped into the hallway, pulled the door closed behind him and reset the lock. He was not entirely certain in which direction to proceed when the sound of someone approaching from his right made going left his only option. He tried to imagine the layout of the temple without drawing on the power of the Sama Lukos. The beast had grown extremely restless since he entered the temple and he was uncertain how long he would be able to control it if he summoned it. As he moved through the labyrinth of hallways he formulated a plan of sorts. His priority was to locate the Sharrana Nahleen and to determine if there were any within the temple still loyal to the House of Rhuna. Beyond that, he was going to have to improvise. He did not agree with the sorelige's plan to allow Nahleen to bear the Sheth Child only to have it destroyed. The more he considered the idea, the more uneasy he became. Saal would have some means of protecting the child after its birth and, with access to both the physical and non-physical realms, they could not be certain the child would be born on Mythos. Once the Sheth Child was conceived he could take Nahleen; he did it once already, and by the time Ko'Resh arrived in Rhuna with Rhandor, the alignment would be near its apex and Saal's power would be extremely formidable. Kian'Huard knew soon he would no longer have control over the Sama Lukos and he himself would become a slave to Saal's bidding. He prayed to Selam he would be able to intervene on Nahleen's behalf before that happened.

He was pulled from his thoughts by the sound of young female voices. As they drew near him he was able to pick up part of their conversation. They were discussing Sharrana Nahleen and whether her arrival meant they would be returning to their homes. One, who appeared to be the youngest, was explaining to the others her theory to why the sharrana had arrived, citing her wish to return home to her parents and baby brother. "Abby," the oldest said, firm but compassionate, "you must remember the teachings from this morning. The House of Rhuna has no sway over the governances of the temple."

"I *know* what it says, Jenella, but maybe Sharrana Nahleen has come to change the rules." Her voice carried as much hope as Kian'Huard imagined a young child could possess.

The one named Jenella crouched down to look directly at Abby and took her by the hands. She waited until Abby lifted her eyes to meet hers before she spoke. "I know this is difficult for you and you miss your family, but understand, we are your family now." She motioned toward the other two girls. "Petria, Ceecee and me." Tears welled up in Abby's eyes but Jenella continued while the other two each took one of Abby's hands to reinforce Jenella's words. "We were chosen because we are special and so are you. Somewhere inside you there is a special ability that only the Sacerdos'helige and the sorelige can see. It is an amazing gift that may not ever come into the world if you stayed at home with your parents. Here at the temple you will learn what your gift is and how to use it, then you will see how important it is for you to be here with us." She reached out and wiped a tear from the young girl's face. "Do you understand?"

Abby nodded, though Kian'Huard could see she was far from convinced. They rose and turned to continue up the hall. They were so engrossed in their conversation they did not notice him. He cleared his throat. The girls stopped short and their conversation ended abruptly. Four pairs of green eyes stared up at him, wide with fear.

"I mean you no harm," he told them. "I seem to be lost. You see, I am looking for Sharrana Nahleen. I have come to rescue her but I have gotten turned around in all these hallways. I could use some help."

The girls looked ready to bolt, but curiosity held them.

"Perhaps one of you could point me in the right direction?"

Abby lifted her hand to point but was cautioned by Jenella. "It may be a trap to see if we are loyal to the sorelige."

"I assure you it is no trick. Sharrana Nahleen is a dear friend of mine and I fear she may be in danger. I plan to rescue her." He bent down and looked into Abby's bright-green eyes. He saw the "gift" that caused her to be taken from her family. An excuse, mostly, to build an army. Abby's gift was her physical and mental strength. Though only roughly nine full cycles old, her destiny to become a fierce warrior was clearly etched in the energies around her. He could see her future as clear as any tapestry and, though it was honourable, it was very short. He also saw another path, one that, should she receive the right encouragement, would see her at the sharrana's side and free to be with her family. Jenella's future was bleaker and much shorter than Abby's. The other two girls' destinies were undecided to what their path would be, but being brought into the temple was one way to solidify one's fate.

"Will you help me, Abby?"

"You know my name?"

"Of course he does, he was listening in on our conversation earlier. He is no wizard come to liberate the chosen." Jenella grabbed Abby's hand and motioned the others to follow, but Abby pulled her hand away.

"I don't care if he saves me, but I want to help him save Sharrana Nahleen." She crossed her arms and planted herself defiantly.

"That, my dear Abby, is your gift." Kian'Huard smiled down at her and offered her his hand.

Kian'Huard looked to Jenella, and he could see she knew she lost this battle. She did not want to defy the temple but, when he looked into her heart, he saw she too had a deep devotion to the sharrana. Clearly, she was terrified at what might happen should they get caught, but as he studied her face he could see the courage rising in her. "Okay, we will all help you." She looked to the other two girls. "Petria, Ceecee, we all need to do this together. Are you in?"

The two girls looked at each other then at Kian'Huard, then Jenella. "Yes," they chimed at the same time.

"All right, then, let's go rescue the sharrana" He gestured them to lead and made a silent prayer to Selam that he did not just seal their fates to retribution by the sorelige.

"Sharrana Nahleen arrived here with me just three days ago. The sorelige told me she was in the purification chambers and would be for these three days. Can you take me there? It would seem the best place to start."

Abby Took his hand. "We go this way."

Jenella nodded in agreement.

"Okay," he replied, "but we must hurry. I don't think we should be in any one place too long."

Abby and the others led him through a labyrinth of passageways that intersected with other vast and ornate hallways. Kian'Huard followed, trusting the navigational skills of a child and her friends. They traversed the interior of the temple for nearly one full pace of resha before they found themselves peering down a rather plain hallway lined on both sides with equally nondescript doors.

"She will be in one of these rooms," Jenella whispered while she scanned the area for any signs of the initiates assigned to the purification chambers.

Kian'Huard counted twelve doors. He could not see if they continued beyond the bend at the end of the hallway. "Let's split up," he suggested. "Jenella, you and Petria check the doors on the left and Abby, Ceecee and I will check the right. Okay?"

The girls nodded in agreement and they set out, quietly opening each door. When they came to the end of the hallway, disappointment prevailed. "She is not here," Ceecee whispered.

The sound of a door opening caused the group to freeze. Quickly, Kian'Huard ushered them into one of the empty rooms, closing the door behind them. He motioned for them to be silent and he opened the door a crack to hear voices discussing his possible whereabouts since escaping from his locked chamber. One of the guards talking was certain Kian'Huard would be found trying to find Sharrana Nahleen. He was also certain that he would not be able to find her since she had been declared a threat to the temple and was slated to go to the catacombs to await trial.

That was enough for Kian'Huard. He closed the door and motioned the girls to come closer. "I am afraid our partnership must come to a close. I do not wish to put any of you in danger. Sharrana Nahleen is no longer within the temple proper; she is to be moved to the catacombs, a place I am famil-iar with," He paused when he recalled once more the fateful day he and his brother slashed their way out from the depths below the temple. "Right now, we must find a way to get you girls to safety."

Abby's face grew serious then brightened. "I know how we can get out of here and give you a chance to sneak past the guards."

All eyes turned to her when she went to a small grate at the base of the far wall. She pried at it and it easily gave way. "When I was first brought here I tried to find a way out. This was the chamber they put me in. This tunnel leads out to the hallway just around the corner. I think we can all fit." Her expression grew sad. "All except you, Kian'Huard. But when we get to the hallway we can cry or scream to get the Sacerdos'helige to come to us and then they won't see you leaving."

"You are brilliant, sweet Abby!" Petria exclaimed.

Kian'Huard agreed it was a sound plan. All four were new to the temple so could easily convince the Sacerdos'helige they became lost and fright-ened. Abby wasted no time removing the grate and crawling in to the small opening. The others followed and Kian'Huard replaced the grill behind them. "May Selam watch over you," he whispered quietly then rose to wait for their diversion. Kian'Huard moved to the door and cocked his head, straining to hear when it would be safe to leave the room. His chest tightened knowing the sorelige planned to imprison Nahleen in the catacombs, such a vile place to keep her until he could give her to Ko'Resh's progeny. There were still several full cycles of rhuna before the alignment was complete and, if he understood correctly, the energies would remain at a frequency that would accommodate Saal's plan for at least one full cycle of seasons. Kian'Huard did not have a plan as of yet, beyond finding Sharrana Nahleen and getting her out of the temple.

The unmistakeable shriek of young girls pierced the air, snapping Kian'Huard to full alert. He opened the door a crack and watched several Sacerdos'helige scrambling in the direction of the girls. He waited a few moments until he heard their voices and those of the Sacerdos'helige lending gruff responses to their excuse for being where they ought not to be. Satisfied they were in no immediate danger, he slipped from the chamber and down the hallway.

He knew he would have no difficulty in finding the catacombs. While following the young girls he noticed the unmistakeable gouges in the marble pillars and floor. He remembered the day those were made, when he and his brother tore from where they were being held prisoner under the enchantment of the sorelige and his Sacerdos'helige so many centuries ago. And how, when they perceived the slightest weakness in the binding spell, they were able to break it. He recalled their escape as though he watched it in a dream. He remembered seeing blood spewing from the throats of the robed Sacerdos'helige and his hand ripping their throats, but it was not just his hand—there was more to it, as though his hands became the clawed paws of a great lukos and his mind was overthrown by the mind of the beast and he slashed his way from the temple to escape into the wilderness with Ko'Resh. He knew Ko'Resh's hands were covered in as much blood as his that day. And much more since. The passing of centuries did little to diminish the memories.

He shook his head to free his mind and bring his attention back to the problem at hand. He had to make his way past numerous guards down through the main chambers of the upper temple then pass through the library to the passage that led down to the catacombs. There he would find the chamber he and Ko'Resh had been held in as well as other cells that held various prisoners of the temple, and Nahleen. It took much effort to keep his mind from straying back to his captivity. The pain and fear the memories generated distracted him from the present. He could not risk being captured. Once again, he pushed the memories aside and continued deeper into the heart of the temple. Still, something pricked in the back of his mind, something overlooked or forgotten about that day. The thoughts welled once again and he relived that terrible day, trying to remember what detail had escaped him that was so important to force him to endure the memories. Knowing his mind would not let him move forward until he succumbed to the memories, he sought out a place to hide while he followed the trail of thoughts back. He found a small chamber and slipped in, locking the door behind him. He could see the room was one of many used for privacy and meditation. A cup and water jug were on a small table to his left and a stack of reed mats were piled on the floor to his right. They were not large enough to lay on but would provide a comfortable enough place to sit and meditate. A tiny window several measures above his head provided the only light. He knew he would be safe there for the time being. He made himself comfortable on the mat and released his mind to the images, searching for what his memory had overlooked. He drew a deep breath and released it, clearing his mind of everything except the memory of that day:

Kian'Huard found himself laying on a table. He could feel the hardness of the wooden surface against his back. He looked about the room but his vision was blurred, shielded. He was aware of a soft glow around him covering him under a dome of pulsating light. He was aware of figures just beyond the light but shrouded under hooded cloaks. As the memory deepened, more details became clear as his other senses tuned in to that moment. The smell of spices and pungent herbs filled his head and then, as his hearing tuned in, the rhythmic sound of several voices chanting long, drawn-out syllables, varying in pitch and cadence. If he pressed deeper still, he could make out individual voices within the intonation and was somehow able to identify each person and where they were positioned around him. Going even deeper allowed him to see where Ko'Resh was lying and also identify those around him. He observed the chamber for some time, allowing the ebb and flow of the incantation to carry him, feeling how it bound him and the Sama Lukos within the dome of light. He did not struggle against it as his memory pulled him deeper into that moment. He felt the subtle wave when another joined the mantra and one took his leave, perfectly pitched and overlapped so no gap in the field was made. His attention was brought to the Sama Lukos and to the other six with Ko'Resh. They were lashing out against the barrier, gnashing their teeth and lunging at it.

He felt the sorelige leave the chamber, his tone being taken up by a novice Sacerdos'helige. The tone and inflections were perfect. There was no break in the spell that bound them. He became aware of the changing of the Sacerdos'helige. He was drawn to focus on that. He knew the sorelige returned with every sixth change. The fifth change had just blended. Kian'Huard waited. He felt a modulation gently incorporate itself into the invocation. He searched with his mind to the source of the tone, expecting to find the sorelige. It was not him. The new voice entered the chamber and replaced the figure at his head. Kian'Huard sensed a slight uncertainty. He knew the Sama Lukos sensed it as well. It gathered its etheric self into a ghostly form and sat before the newcomer. It remained still and fixed dark eyes on him. That was the moment the barrier faltered. The moment the Sem Lukos unleashed their fury upon the Sacerdos'helige. That was the moment Kian'Huard was forced to remember. The sorelige was not in the temple. He recalled how thorough the Sem Lukos were in their massacre. He recalled each body left littering the chamber and hallways. None were the sorelige. It was being made clear by the Sama Lukos that this was an important bit of information. But why, after so many centuries? Surely he was long since dead and buried. Then a thought struck him with absolute clarity. The Sama Lukos believed him to still be alive.

With that realization, Kian'Huard was thrust back to the present. He opened his eyes and stared silently. It took him a few moments to realize the resh had set, throwing the chamber into darkness, and it took a few more moments for his eyes to adjust. He could feel the Sama Lukos stirring, restless inside him. At first, he thought it was in response to the memories, but as he delved deeper he found it was more. Something was about to happen and it was readying for it. He could also feel Saal's presence in communion with the malevolent spirit. He focussed on his breathing, quieted his mind and drew on his inner strength to quell the unrest he felt in the Sama Lukos. It took several moments, but he was able to bring the beast within him into a more dormant state. He rose from the mat and retraced his steps from earlier to find the door in the near total darkness. He listened for a few moments then opened it a crack. Light poured in from the well-illuminated corridor. Again, it took a few moments for his eyes to adjust and, when he was satisfied no one was near, he slipped into the corridor and continued downward, deep below the heart of the temple. Very few Sacerdos'helige ever made their way this deep into the temple so he was able to continue to traverse the tunnels unchallenged. Though he had no recollection of ever being this far into the mountain, instinct told him he was somewhere below the chamber where he and Ko'Resh were held captive those many centuries ago. Though he did not expect to be confronted, he continued to proceed with utmost caution, keeping to the shadows wherever possible.

He had not gone far when a dim, pulsing blue light could be seen emanating from one of the side tunnels ahead. His skin pricked with a faint electrical charge and he felt a surge of energy sweep through the tunnel, radiating outward from the blue light then being drawn back toward the source. Cautiously, he crept closer to the illuminated tunnel. He had not gone far when the sound of someone approaching claimed his attention. He pressed back into a niche in the wall and drew his cloak tight to camouflage himself further. He peered around the stone buttress and held his breath. The hurried footfalls drew nearer, a soft shuffling of hide moccasins on the dusty stone floor. Then a figure suddenly entered the corridor and paused a moment as though deciding which direction to go. Kian'Huard leaned further into the hallway to get a better look. The man who emerged from the side tunnel was garbed as High Sorelige, but for certain he was not the sorelige who currently headed the temple. Something exploded within Kian'Huard's mind, evoking a long-forgotten memory. He shook it off, but there was a familiarity about the man he could not place. Initially, the man started toward Kian'Huard then stopped short. He was close enough for Kian'Huard to clearly see his face, but the man did not seem to notice him hiding in the darkness. Something else caused him to stop. Kian'Huard watched him as he once again surveyed the corridors around him as though he sensed Kian'Huard's presence but could not see him. The man threw back his hood and stared into the darkness of the corridor, searching for something. Then, with a sudden look of illumination, he turned on his heel and started making his way further down the tunnel and away from Kian'Huard.

Kian'Huard felt his mind cloud and his thoughts drift as though he was being forced into a deep sleep. He had felt this before when Saal's consciousness would take over his body and force him to do his will. Kian'Huard struggled to maintain control. He had to keep his mind clear and his body as his own. The invasion of his body by the spirit of Saal continued to force his own

234

consciousness deeper into a subconscious realm and he could feel himself losing control of his physical body. He felt a familiar stirring at the base of his spine, but his mind was already too restrained by Saal to stop the process. Then he was struck by a great power surging explosively inside him unlike any he had felt before. It caught him so off guard he nearly lost consciousness. His eyes widened with fear when he realized Saal had taken control of the Sama Lukos and was striving to move toward the man. In that moment, he also realized the man was Sorelige Kabit Del'Arran, the one who imprisoned him and Ko'Resh those many centuries ago. He did not know how that would be possible, but he was certain it was the same man.

He saw Sorelige Kabit Del'Arran stop and spin around, eyes wide with fear when they locked with his. Understanding of the threat the sorelige possessed overwhelmed him. Sorelige Kabit Del'Arran had somehow gained the knowledge of how to destroy the Sem Lukos, and maybe even Saal himself. Kian'Huard felt the power within himself mounting almost beyond his control. He struggled harder to force himself to stop advancing on the man who now seemed frozen on place. It was all he could do against the blinding surge of rage instilled in his mind by Saal to force out one word to the man— "RUN!"

Somehow that was all that was needed. The last thing Kian'Huard saw before he lost total control was the sorelige running and disappearing into the darkness of the catacombs. He was vaguely aware of his body clawing at the floor and walls, giant paws superimposed over his hands and feet, struggling to gain enough control to pursue their prey. He could hear his voice as a beast roaring and howling its anger and hatred, then utter frustration when the man was somehow able to elude him.

Kian'Huard felt Saal's wrath as his body was thrown about the catacombs and left, barely alive, in a heap of shattered bones and gaping wounds. He did not fear death, he welcomed, even prayed for it, but he knew it was not to be. Through the pain he felt the bones moving back into place, slowly and painfully, and the flow of blood from his wounds slowed then stopped as they too began to close and heal. Kian'Huard ebbed in and out of consciousness, vaguely aware of the cold stone floor and darkness around him, and for three days remained thus until a small group of Sacerdos'helige passed by to discover him in so vulnerable a state. They recognized him immediately and lifted him roughly from the floor to take him to the prison cells deep under the mountain. They sent news to Sorelige Garret Del'Tolan of his capture.

Kian'Huard was vaguely aware of being moved and more acutely aware of excruciating pain with every movement. Unconsciousness came and went, bringing brief periods of relief from the relentless agony. As though experiencing it from a distance, he was aware of being dragged into a cell and shackled to the wall. His legs, still healing from the beating bestowed upon him by Saal, failed to support his weight and he crumpled into a heap. His arms stretched over his head when the chains grew taught and dislocated his left shoulder. His captors left him there and slammed the cell door behind them with a resounding clang of metal on metal. Then there was the unmistakeable scrape of a key turning in a lock. Once more, Kian'Huard was a prisoner of the temple. His body pulsed with overwhelming pain then unconsciousness took him.

CHAPTER 26

NAHLEEN HAD FINISHED THE THREE-DAY RITUAL THAT was mandatory before having audience with the sorelige, though she felt the young initiates were a little heavy-handed with the cleansing tea. The plain grey robe they gave her was made of coarsely woven fabric that itched and chaffed her skin. A sound at the door to her chamber drew her attention. The door swung open and four young sacerdos'helige entered. Nahleen recognized the oldest girl, garbed in a green robe denoting some level of seniority, as the same one who oversaw her cleansing when she first arrived. The three younger girls were dressed in grey robes and positioned themselves to block the door. The older girl approached with scissors. "What do you intend to do with those?" Nahleen asked.

The girl gave a twisted smile. "I intend to cut your hair."

Nahleen drew herself up and looked down at the child. "You will do no such thing," she told her. "I have come for an audience with Sorelige Garret Del'Tolan, nothing more. Now I bid you take me to see him at once."

The smile never left the girl's face. "You have no power here, *Sharrana* Nahleen." The girl's bitterness was not lost on Nahleen. "You cannot bid me to do anything." She moved closer, holding the scissors as a weapon. Then the smile abruptly disappeared and the girl lunged. One of the three guarding the door moved to defend Nahleen but was pulled back by the other two. Nahleen easily avoided her attacker and quickly disarmed and restrained her. The girl struggled, flailing about like a wildcat trying to free herself, and it was some time before the girl settled and Nahleen could try to talk to her.

"I understand you are angry and frightened having being taken from your family and brought here." She adjusted her grip on the girl to be able to look her in the eyes. Deep green pools of emotion stared up at her. "You are

237

correct, I have no power here, but there is more happening here than what it seems. I think a war is coming and though I do not understand it fully, I came here to find answers." Then the girl's bottom lip began to tremble, tears welled and the child became a child once more. Nahleen held her for a few moments then addressed her and the others in the room who had witnessed the exchange. "I do not know what the future will bring or if that future will see you being returned to your families, but if somehow I can prevent any more children from being taken, then perhaps you can take some comfort in that?"

The air in the room lost its charge and Nahleen could see how affected they all were by her arrival, the hope it gave them and the frustration of the powerlessness they felt. That moment the door burst open and Abby, Ceecee, Petria and Jenella burst into the chamber, flushed and out of breath. Abby's eyes grew wide at the sight of Nahleen, and she nearly knocked her over when she ran to her and embraced her. Then she remembered herself and backed away, apologizing for being too forward, all the while holding the look of hope on her young face.

"Kian'Huard said you need help, and that Sorelige Garret Del'Tolan was keeping you prisoner and that you were going to have a baby and that the sorelige was going to kill it but that was not going to work and we helped him escape from the Sacerdos'helige and then he went to the catacombs to find you but you are right here…" She took in a deep breath and looked ready to continue but Nahleen interrupted her.

"You have seen Kian'Huard?"

Abby nodded with such enthusiasm her head seemed like it would fall off or at least give her whiplash.

"Do you know where he is?"

Abby continued her recant of how they helped him find the purification chambers and how they escaped being caught. When she finished her story, Nahleen thanked her and sat on one of the wooden chairs that lined one of the walls. With all attention focussed on young Abby, none noticed one of the older girls slip out of the room.

"So Kian'Huard has found his way down to the catacombs in search of me. But why?" She turned to Abby and her friends. "You are certain he told you I was being held prisoner down there?" All four nodded.

Nahleen stood and drew in a deep breath. "It seems I wish to cancel my audience with Sorelige Garret Del'Tolan and…"

At that moment, the door burst open and several Sacerdos'helige poured in to the chamber, weapons at the ready. The younger girls gasped and began to cry. Abby threw herself at Nahleen in an attempt to protect her, but one of the men grabbed her by the scruff of the neck and tossed her aside with the other girls. Nahleen moved to intervene but she was quickly subdued by two others. They unceremoniously shoved her from the room and locked the door behind them, imprisoning the girls within. She did not struggle against them. Her strength was diminished, a side effect from the purification process, and she knew, even at her best, she could not triumph against eight armed men. They surrounded her and shepherded her through the corridor. Apparently, she was not going to miss her appointment after all.

It was a short walk through drab, grey-stone passageways from the room where she was being held to stand before an enormous and ornate wooden door. It took two of the men escorting her to release the latch and pull the door open, exposing the marble-and-gold grandeur for which the temple was known. The passage they emerged from entered a main piazza. Nahleen had no time to appreciate the grand beauty of the architecture, the intricate gold inlays that bordered the passage entrances or the flawless marble floor. She did note that some of the pillars bore scars. As they moved across the square she could see where something or someone had passed through, slashing their way across the space, marking the marble and granite with deep furrows. She recalled the vision Kian'Huard gave her of when he first became possessed by the seventh of the Sem Lukos and how he and his brother escaped the temple those many centuries ago, and she knew it was he and Ko'Resh who had scarred the beauty of this place.

Her entourage turned sharply to the left, bringing her from her thoughts. They approached another door, this one even more ornate than the other, carved with a relief of the resh, its rays fanning out from the orb to tangle themselves into rows of intricate knot patterns bordering the door. The granite and marble arch that framed the doorway was equally embellished with the complex pattern. But what stood out were the three ragged grooves that cut across the frame deep into the hard stone. It appeared as though the door was replaced, because the lines did not cross the face of the door but resumed on the other side as if they were made by one great, sweeping motion.

Again, it took two of her wardens to unlatch and open the heavy door. Beyond it was the outer sanctum where the sorelige would take audience with those who were approved to see him. If the piazza was designed to impress, the outer sanctum was designed to overwhelm. The ceiling towered an impossible height above them, supported by enormous pillars each so big around that it would take a dozen people to encompass it with arms reaching fully. Gold, emeralds and all manner of precious minerals and gems were used quite liberally throughout the décor. The distance from the door through which they entered to where the sorelige sat was at least three hundred paces.

One of the Sacerdos'helige gave her a nudge forward; apparently conversation and courtesy were not high on their priorities. As she started across the distance between her and the sorelige the sound of the great door closing and being locked reached her ear before it was swallowed by the vastness of the space. She noted the guards stayed back. There was no seating within the great hall except that upon which Sorelige Garret Del'Tolan himself was seated. She resisted the temptation to look about for an escape as she moved toward him. Instead, she held her head high and focussed her attention on him. She did not hurry across the room nor did she hesitate. She moved with grace and purpose, even though in her heart she was extremely uneasy. As she neared, she saw the lavishness of the room was not spared on his garments. He was as ornately dressed as the chair upon which he sat, which was carved and embellished. One would think such decoration would only diminish the man shrouded in its splendour, but instead this man, Sorelige Garret Del'Tolan, seemed amplified by his surroundings and radiated with power.

Nahleen approached the throne and knelt briefly before mounting the three steps to where his feet rested. She touched the corner of his robe to her forehead as was customary then backed down to the floor to wait on her knees for him to address her. She kept her eyes down but was aware he had risen from his throne and approached her.

"Rise, Sharrana Nahleen of the House of Rhuna." His voice carried confidence and authority, and his tone was impersonal and neutral.

Nahleen rose and lifted her gaze to meet his. They remained thus for only a moment when his hand stuck her across the face, causing her to stagger back from both the blow and from shock. Nothing in his eyes told her he what he had been about to do. Then the neutrality left his voice and the true venom of his intent poured through his words. Nahleen stayed herself against a possible second strike, for now his eyes conveyed fear behind the venom. And his words were more than enough to subdue her more than any physical attack.

"You have been found guilty of treason and conspiring against the temple with a known enemy of the temple and the country of Rhuna." He continued to denounced her viciously, "Your existence is an abomination to the genetic line of the House of Rhuna and a threat to all who live here, and on the entire world of Mythos. You have been created to be a vessel whose sole purpose is to bring an ancient evil back into this world. You have been found to be meddling with the indoctrination of our newest initiates." He made a slight gesture with his right hand. His eyes never left hers when an opening formed in the wall to her right and four guards ushered Abby and her friends into the hall. They gave the girls a shove to have them fall onto their knees. Nahleen's ire rose. But she held it in check. A show of defiance right now would most likely mean death to one or all of the girls.

Sorelige Garret Del'Tolan read her well. A faint smile lifted one corner of his thin mouth for a brief moment. His green eyes darkened but never left her. "Take them to the indoctrination chambers."

Nahleen's heart sank. She'd heard rumours of how those who were not able to make the adjustment to life in the temple were sent deep into the core of the mountain to be locked in small rooms devoid of any light or stimulus other than the sound of someone reading the Book of Light repeatedly. None who were sent there were quite right when finally released. She looked at Abby's face, which was full of life and light. The indoctrination chambers would destroy her and the others. Sorelige Garret Del'Tolan continued, "They are to remain there for no less than six phases-." Even the Sacerdos'helige looked to each other and hesitated briefly. None had ever been sent to the chambers for more than one phase of rhuna.

The sorelige seemed to sense their hesitation. "Now." He did not need to raise his voice; the authority he possessed was all he needed to spur the Sacerdos'helige into action and the girls were taken from the room, their cries cut short when the passage closed behind them.

Though his gaze never left hers, Nahleen felt his attention shift fully back to her. "You will be detained within the temple as my prisoner until we find a way to destroy, once and for all, the Sem Lukos and their creator." He paused briefly then continued, "Understand, Sharrana Nahleen, your life is forfeit and I will do whatever it takes to bring Saal's existence to an end, even if that means allowing your destiny to be fulfilled and the Sheth Child to be born." His gaze left her and went to the back of the room to the group of Sacerdos'helige who brought her there. It was the only signal they needed, and they made their way toward her. Again, his attention was turned fully on her. "I am certain you know escape is impossible, but it bears telling. You need to know as well that we have Kian'Huard. He was found deep in the catacombs looking for you. He must have encountered some vicious animal, for he was quite badly beaten when the Sacerdos'helige found him. If you thought you would have an ally in him, you were mistaken. He is controlled by Saal, his only purpose now is to make available the vessel," he motioned toward her. "You; to the force that is making its way to Rhuna to complete the cycle and bring Saal back to this realm. Despite your rank, you are no more than a pawn in the battle that is to come, and I will make certain I am the one who uses you to my end."

The Sacerdos'helige had arrived. Sorelige Garret Del'Tolan turned his back to her, climbed the three steps to sit on the throne and glared down at her from his elevated vantage point. Nahleen was numbed by his words and though her instincts were to fight and escape, she had no will to do so. She was being led from the great chamber and made no attempt to defend herself or flee. Her mind seemed foggy and her thoughts unclear, and they remained so while she was being taken deep beneath the temple to the dungeons hidden within the catacombs. It was not until the clang of the steel door closing behind her that her mind cleared. But then it was too late. She did not know what solveige he used to subdue her mind, but it was powerful indeed. She looked about the cell. Though she was certain she was deep within the mountain there was light, but she could not see the source. Spartan was the only way to describe her prison. There was only a cot, a few blankets for warmth and a cistern in one corner to relieve herself, and nothing else. Two walls were solid stone, two were bars. One formed a partition between hers and the adjoining cell and the other faced a small chamber lined with similar cells, all of which appeared empty. She tried yelling, but no answer came except her own voice echoing back through the tunnels.

CHAPTER 27

THE DAWN BROKE WITH LITTLE PROMISE IN KO'RESH'S mind that the day would bring anything more than the usual snail's paced progression toward completing the great ships. His interaction with Saal and his threat to take away his power angered him. The Sem Lukos were his, and when he returned to Rhuna he would take the seventh of the spirits for himself. Saal would not take what was his. He would see Saal fade into myth as Ko'Resh became the most powerful being on Mythos. He was about to summon the beasts within him when Bartus burst into the chamber. "The garrison is back," he blurted then seemed to remember decorum and gave a short bow. "They have returned and have brought a prisoner with them. Rumour says it is a rephaim!"

Ko'Resh could see Bartus was out of breath and appeared to have run some distance to bring him this news. He went to his window to look down on the courtyard. Indeed, he could see the men in full parade regalia with coloured banners and leather breastplates assembled in neat rows below. To the right he saw what looked like it could have been a cage covered in several thick hides. Six of the men stood guard around it. Ko'Resh could see the hides move as though something was trying to escape. He sent Bartus to inform Sharram Rhandor of the news then hurried to dress. He had to gain control over the garrison before they had an opportunity to leave the courtyard and see the devastation that had occurred in their absence. Even as he hurried through the corridors and down to the main courtyard he was summoning the power of the Yanatramda Lukos to make the minds of the men pliable to his will.

When he arrived in the courtyard a light fog had rolled in, shrouding the men. The mist permeated their clothing, flowed into their lungs with each breath, taking away their will to resist the power of the Yanatramda Lukos and he who possessed it. A dark smile crossed Ko'Resh's lips. He could taste victory. He studied the ranks of the men before him. Such formidable warriors would easily overthrow any army the House of Rhuna could muster. But just as important was the fortunate capture of the rephaim. Ko'Resh did not believe in coincidence, but the chance that a rephaim was found injured and hiding in the darkness of a rock crevasse was too convenient. The warriors said he must have been injured when the earthquake opened the pass and most likely collapsed the tunnels he used to find his way back home. They were going to kill it, but for some reason they felt it important to bring the creature into the city. Very few had ever had the opportunity to see one and most eyewitness accounts were, to say the least, exaggerated.

Ko'Resh did not care how or why the warriors brought the creature. He would take it and be sure its injuries were tended and it was ready for the voyage ahead. He went to the cage and moved the hides aside. The creature huddled in a corner, blue blood oozing from a large gash on his leg. Ko'Resh studied the creature and found it both frightening and beautiful. Its skin was opalescent and favoured hues in the blue spectrum. Ko'Resh recalled hearing the colour of the scales was determined by the minerals that were most dominant in the particular caves where the clan lived. It made sense, because this particular rephaim was found in the Illuna Mountains where cobalt was abundant. The scales were very fine and reptilian, more of a leather than, say, a fish scale. He ventured to touch the creature to find the hide was indeed quite soft and pliable. The creature reacted to his intrusion by releasing his sensory tentacles, causing Ko'Resh to pull his hand away and take a step back. The layers of hides over the cage did not allow him to fully study the creature so he ordered them pulled back. Light poured in on the cave-dweller and it threw its arms over its face to protect huge, dark eyes that were designed to utilize even the faintest light over most of the spectrum to facilitate life in the near-total darkness within the mountains. Proportionately it appeared as human and if seen in the darkness as a silhouette could easily be mistaken for a man. But in the light his reptilian facial features were unmistakeable. The retractable tentacles that covered its head were designed to be sensitive to different subtle frequencies. This allowed it to sense electromagnetic changes in the air around it that would occur if prey or other living organisms were nearby. Every living thing emitted an energy frequency and, though the rephaim's eyesight was limited, especially in the light of day, it could determine what creatures were nearby either to avoid or to hunt. Ko'Resh knew the catacombs below the Temple of Osiris in Rhuna contained several passageways and chambers that were hidden behind subtle energy barriers that none could detect. Except maybe a rephaim.

He took one last look at the creature then ordered the guards to recover the cage. There was something below the temple that Saal wanted/needed, and he would find out what that was and keep it for himself. He ordered the creature to be taken to his apothecary where he would tend to its injuries and keep prying eyes at bay. He also sent Bartus to the shipyard with specific instructions on how to build a containment area for the cave-dweller and ordered the room be kept secret from everyone. The pieces were in place. Now the players had to make their way to the playing field.

The following months saw the ships completed and all who were able made their way to the shipyards to watch the launch. The spectacle was beyond anything ever seen before. The ships were massive, and once launched, had to anchor on the bay to wait as only one at a time could moor to the wharf to be loaded. The fifteen hundred warriors that compiled what was left of Rhandor's army were divided between the three ships and marched up the gangway in formation onto their assigned ship. When the third ship finally weighed anchor, the resh began to sink below the horizon. Smaller ships acted to tow the great vessels from the harbour and toward the open sea. Lanterns were lit and the harbour glittered as the lights flared and sparked in the gentle breeze, marking the shoreline and the dozens of small vessels that remained to escort the ships out to sea. Once there, the tethers were let go and the massive sails were hoisted. They ruffled for a few moments then the wind caught them, they snapped taught and the ships began to move toward their destiny. Captains shouted orders and the crew scrambled to comply. Ko'Resh stood on the upper deck, his gaze fixed on the distant horizon. "Soon we will be together," he whispered.

Barely three weeks had passed since the vessels left Krit to journey beyond where anyone, except Ko'Resh, had gone before when the weather turned. Storm after storm assailed the country of Krit, bringing almost as much destruction and illness as the drought while nature strove to return to balance after so many years of being artificially altered by Ko'Resh. But eventually these too subsided and after one last hurricane swept through the coastal city of Jordan, the energy meridians that flowed throughout the world of Mythos had returned again to a harmonious state.

CHAPTER 28

MONTHS PASSED WITH NO LAND IN SIGHT. IT TOOK
nearly all of Ko'Resh's power to keep his crew and passengers in a near-sleep
state, but the time was at hand to ready the troops and prepare for their attack
on Rhuna. He knew Saal was responsible for ensuring the winds remained
favourable, the trip uneventful and their hidden passenger alive and well. He
closed his eyes and allowed his inner vision to expand beyond the visible
horizon and knew they would be in sight of land within four more days.

He called Bartus to him to ready his quarters and see that his meal was
brought to him, and it did not surprise him when the boy emerged from
Rhandor's cabin. The two had bonded over the course of the voyage. No
doubt Bartus' relationship with Rhandor's dead son Arlon was the impetus.
Ko'Resh did not hinder the relationship, as it posed no threat to his own plans.

That night he watched the planets rise, forming a line that stretched deep
into space. The seven were nearly perfectly aligned. Lastly, rhuna rose full,
appearing as though she had sprung from the sea itself, casting a long light
across the water's surface marking a trail for them to follow. Ko'Resh knew
the forces that accompanied the alignment would manifest on their small
world in the form of extreme tides and earthquakes. He knew their ships were
at risk of being swept into the jagged rocks that protected his homeland from
the outside world and crushed into splinters. He doubted Saal would allow
that to happen, and he still had control over the six of the Sem Lukos that he
possessed. He retired to his quarters and let the gentle rocking of the ocean
lull him into a restless slumber. His dreams were more like visions of what was
to come and though they were, for the most part, as he planned, somehow he
never saw the end result. The Sheth Child continued to elude him.

The next days were spent in preparation of their arrival. His explosives

247

were gently moved from the cargo hold up onto the deck and then lowered onto several rafts. These remained tethered to the ships until they were close enough to the barrier to row in and plant them. It would take very little to set the explosives and the crew were more than a little nervous around them. Ko'Resh thought it strange that Saal had not been invading his thoughts over the past days. He took that as a good omen. A shout from above sounded above the din of the crew. "Land!"

Ko'Resh made his way to the bow of the ship. His heart skipped a beat at the sight of the jagged outcroppings that were home. He told the captain to bring the ship closer and drop anchor. They had to be close enough to set the charges but far enough away to not be affected by the blast. Each ship carried thirty bombs and each raft held two, with one person to row to put it in position. Ko'Resh had constructed a crude map of the barrier and showed each man where he was to set his charge to bring it down. He gave each of them a special flint that would spark even if it got wet. He did not tell them the fuse was very short and they would not have any time to escape the blast.

CHAPTER 29

BELOW DECK THE REPHAIM SHIFTED RESTLESSLY ON the crude mat that served as his bed then rose and turned his face to the west. He sensed a shift in the subtle energies in and around the ship. He knew land was near but with that realization came another stronger, more insidious understanding. His tentacles extended involuntarily in response to a powerful energy that was attached to the land. He allowed himself to follow the energy to understand its meaning and source and, for the first time since his capture, real fear gripped him. The energy was as ancient as Mythos herself. It encompassed the land before them, permeating deep into the ground and acting as a barrier, shielding those within from the outside world. But, as he probed deeper into the energy, he realized the opposite was true. The energy barrier was to protect Mythos from some ancient evil trapped within it.

Despite the general assumption the rephaim were primitive, almost bestial, creatures because they lived in caves and did not appear to have a social construct, they were, in fact, highly advanced. They had evolved beyond the need for material gain and chose to dwell within the shelter of the mountains in a symbiotic relationship with the land and the energies that flowed through all things. Their bodies evolved to support living in near-total darkness and on minimal food. They understood that everything, when broken down to its simplest form, was energy and learned to adapt to sustain themselves nearly completely on channeling subtle energies. When they did take organic nourishment, they respected that which they were going to consume and made blessing to ensure the vibratory pattern of the food was elevated to enhance their bodies rather than lower their own frequency by ingesting something out of "tune."

When he was injured he faded in and out of consciousness and was not able to consistently hide himself from sight and was captured by the Krit army. When he was taken into the city he felt the powerful force at work, interfering with the weather patterns and with the minds of the Krit people as well. He spent much of his own energy protecting himself from that force. When Ko'Resh came to his cell outside the palace, he sensed the power emanating through him, but it was not "of" him. And he also felt the disturbing presence of the six and understood the terrible evil attached to them. Now, as the ships drew near to land, and he allowed himself to "feel" the nature of the energy surrounding it, he understood the source of the power came from deep within the continent. He could also sense some interaction with the non-physical realm.

A very powerful entity was behind the tangled web of energies that swirled over and through the land. They drove deep into the core of Mythos and extended upward beyond Resha. But more then that, they crossed dimensions of space and time and between physical and non-physical realms. Some were connected, but others seemed out of sync, untouched by the evil that permeated everything. These were subtler and, he assumed, the entity that caused and controlled the other energy was not able to sense or tap into the subtler ones. He feared that was why he was brought to this place. He could harness the subtle energies, and in doing so could open the gate that would allow whatever evil was present to penetrate time itself. The barrier came to mind. Whatever caused that to be put in place to keep some ancient evil trapped within its boundaries, the rephaim instinctively knew it wished to return to that moment in time and prevent it from happening. That would subject the entire world of Mythos to the force of its power. He would not let that happen.

The muffled sound of footsteps penetrated the thick tarpaulin that shrouded his prison from view of the crew. He stood in the centre of his cage, closed his eyes and concentrated on the subtle frequencies around him. He was able to quickly distinguish the distinct energies of two men. Like the rest of the crew on board, he sensed another conscious energy surrounding them and holding them in a kind of mental prison that made them obedient. He sensed the connection between that energy and the energy that was imprisoned within the barrier surrounding the land ahead. He carefully shifted his thoughts to allow his mind to follow the path of energy native to the men and slowly synchronized his own to match that of one of the men enough so he could plant an idea but not so much to alert the one who controlled all aboard this vessel.

It was not mind control; the person could choose to follow the idea or not. The rephaim had no control over that, but he hoped the man's curiosity would be piqued enough for him to make his way to the cage and pull back the cover. He had been listening to many conversations during his captivity and had been able to interpret the words against the energetic intent behind them. Often he would be confused, as many words held vastly different intentions behind them. He hoped he had learned enough of their vocabulary that he could have these men understand what was truly happening and sway them to help him. Their footfalls drew near and he could make out more of their conversation.

"I tell you, it wasn't there before." The man kept his voice in a whisper but that did not diminish the earnestness in it.

"And I'm telling you there is no way it just arrived. We have not made port anywhere since we left Krit. We have just not noticed it before." This voice seemed to belong to one older than the other man, though neither seemed to carry a note of strong intellect, which may be why they were selected for this voyage.

"It can't hurt to take a look at it. Must be important to be hidden way at the back and covered like that," the younger man's loud whispers continued.

"I don't know. It may be dangerous and that is why it is hidden away at the back and covered. Besides, if we get caught we might be tossed overboard … or worse."

"What could be worse than being tossed overboard?"

"Having a hand cut off for touching something that was none of our business to be touching."

"I don't think that's worse than being tossed overboard. At least you are still alive, and I know a lot of people who get by with only one hand."

"Well, I heard Domini Ko'Resh has some strange disease and he peels the skin off his victims and somehow attaches it to his own body to replace the bad skin. That would be worse then being thrown overboard."

There was silence for a few moments then the other agreed that would indeed be a worse punishment.

During this exchange, the rephaim lowered his head, and his expectations, while he waited for the two to finish their debate and get to the task of opening his prison. After what seemed an eternity, the tarpaulin shifted. The rephaim sunk into the shadows at the back of the cage. He heard the distinct sound of a key turning in a lock followed by the squeak of metal on metal.

In that moment a thunderous explosion was heard and the ship lurched sideways against the force of the blast. The rephaim was thrown back against the rear bars of his prison and the two men were thrown clear of the cage and rendered unconscious when they landed against a stack of wooden crates. The tarpaulin fell back over the cage, pinning the open door to the bars.

It took the Rephaim a few moments to recover then he made his way to the opening of his prison. He crouched low to peer under the tarp to see if the way was clear for him to escape. He saw the two men begin to stir. They sat for a moment assessing themselves and each other for injury then scrambled to their feet and climbed the ladder to go above deck. The ship continued to rock dramatically with the aftershock of the explosion. The rephaim knew the detonation had to be very near the ship and very powerful for it to cause such a large vessel to be tossed thus. He sensed a shift in the subtle energies around him. Without even being able to see the sky, he knew there was a powerful alignment of planets that further affected Mythos and her people. Then he felt the floor drop away from beneath him. He grabbed onto the bars of his cage and just as suddenly the great ship rose. He felt the force of acceleration when something took the ship and thrust it forward toward land.

The rephaim braced himself and prepared his body. He did not know if the ship would withstand the forces that were hurling it toward land so he needed to be ready. Though the rephaim had evolved to dwell primarily on land, they retained an inherent ability to revert to an amphibious state and could remain submerged for several minutes, but he would have to hyperventilate then forcefully expel air through the dormant gills behind his ears once he was submerged. The gills were too underdeveloped to sustain him in a fully aquatic environment but would give him enough oxygen to escape the ship and reach land.

He did not wait long when a deafening scraping sound came up from beneath the hull. This was punctuated by the sound of wood splintering as the momentum of the ship thrust it forward, deeper onto land, ripping its way through trees and some outlying houses. Eventually the wave receded and the ship came to rest with a moan as the timbers adjusted while she listed slightly onto her port side before coming to a full stop.

The rephaim waited for a few moments then made his way toward the ladder that would take him above deck. A glimmer of light behind the ladder ahead caught his attention. He made his way toward it, climbing over debris that had been scooped up by the ship where a hole was torn into the hull just above the water line. He pushed his way forward and paused at the opening and listened. As far as he could tell, the crew were all still on the ship. He ventured to look through the opening. The hole was several measures above the ground. It would be risky to jump so far. He saw a tree leaning against the ship to his left and the forest canopy shielded him from view of the upper deck. A branch hung a few feet in front of him. If he could make the branch then he could climb down the tree to escape. He took a moment to look about for a rope to throw over to the branch. The sound of men at the ladder alerted him. He had no choice. He returned to the opening, quickly gauged the distance, took a few steps back then launched himself through the gaping hole. He flailed briefly then felt the rough bark against his hands. He grabbed with all his strength. His momentum swung him around the branch and he caught himself and clung there, pushing himself flat against the branch. He reached and pulled some of the smaller branches to shield him from view of the ship and waited, his heart pounding in his chest. He slowed his breathing and calmed himself while he listened to the sounds around him.

He realized the crew did not know who, or what, was being kept in the cage so he allowed himself to relax a bit more; very few on Mythos had ever seen a rephaim and to most they were a myth. Unless they were given specific direction, which he doubted considering the secrecy with which he was being held captive, none would be looking for a creature such as himself.

Shouts from the ship caught his attention. He ventured to move a branch enough to watch the opening through which he made his escape. He saw two men leaning forward through the tear in the side of the ship and look about. He could make out their comments that whoever was being kept below decks was probably swept out and killed. He waited another full pace of resha before slowly making his way down the branch and descending the tree to finally feel solid ground beneath his feet. With one last quick glance at the ship he turned and disappeared into the forest.

CHAPTER 30

KO'RESH WATCHED AS THE MEN ROWED THEIR SMALL rafts to the barrier and set the charges. A twisted smile brushed his lips. His breath quickened and his hands trembled with anticipation. When the explosion thundered through the barrier it sent shards of rock and water in a giant plume into the air that came crashing down all around them. He had to grab onto the rail to keep on his feet when the concussion waves tossed the ship. His breathing was laboured with the excitement he felt. Once the fallout settled, Rhuna lay before him like an emerald jewel ripe for the taking. A deep rumbling sound rolled over the water from the land. He watched as parts of the shoreline fell into the sea. Saal's voice sounded in his mind: "Weigh anchor now!"

Ko'Resh gave the order, and it was passed to the other ships. The unmistakeable rattle of the huge chains dragging against the hull could be heard. Then a voice from high above shouted. Ko'Resh looked up to see a man pointing back out to sea. He scrambled to the stern of the ship. His mouth dropped at the sight of a giant wave rushing toward them. The ship listed as the water level dropped beneath them. Panic set in. Again, Saal's voice sounded in his mind and he gave the order to turn the ships to face away from the approaching wave and to hang on.

The wave smashed into the ships and lifted them up onto the crest. There was nothing they could do but ride it out and pray. Ko'Resh felt the bile rise in his throat at the speed with which they were lifted and surged forward. He clenched his jaw and forced himself to remain calm. He found it difficult to move but slowly made his way back to the bow of the ship. There he clutched the rail and watched as they raced inland. The tsunami wave carried them toward the mountain, destroying everything in its path. He could see the city of Kephas in the distance. Part of him hoped it would be spared. The ship shuddered and listed dangerously to the port side when the hull scraped against a rocky outcropping. All hands rushed to check for damage. The hull bore a deep furrow along the starboard length but it did not puncture through. Ko'Resh's heart was pounding in his chest and his ears buzzed. He could feel the savage instincts of the six he possessed stirring within him. He fought to keep control and put them back to rest. The adrenaline rushed through his system, sparking nerves and intensifying the fight or flight response. He drew in several deep breaths and focussed on remaining calm.

He could see the water that bore them so deep inland was growing shallower. It would not be long before the ships ran aground. The captain noticed it as well and Ko'Resh could hear him barking orders above the roar of the water and debris it carried. All hands braced themselves. The sound of the ship scraping bottom as it ran out of enough water to keep it afloat was sickening. Beams groaned as the weight of the vessel came to rest. Momentum continued to carry the ships for several more measures, plowing through mud and the remains of the forest. Trees and branches snapped and fell over the deck, taking some of the men with them as they passed. There was nothing anyone could do except watch helplessly as crew members were swept overboard and wait for their screams to diminish and cease.

Ko'Resh scrambled to his quarters and huddled in a corner until the ship, with one final crash, came to a stop. The force threw him across the chamber against a wall. He tried to get up but as he gathered his feet under him the ship began to list once again to the left. Furniture and dishes slid toward him and he threw his arms over his head to protect himself. Eventually the movement stopped. There was a moment of silence, like the world took a deep breath and let it out slowly. Then voices started shouting and the sound of cargo being moved broke the silence. He could hear some of the Krit warriors addressing Rhandor.

In his state of self-preservation, he had forgotten about his most valuable cargo. Then he remembered the rephaim locked in the cargo hold in the lowest deck of the ship. He gathered himself and used the furniture piled beside him to help make his way up the awkward angle to the door. Once on the main deck he instructed four of the crew to bring the rephaim up from below deck and onto land. The crew had already dropped a ladder over the side and many had disembarked. At once, Ko'Resh was filled with a deep feeling of nostalgia. So many centuries had passed since he last set foot on his native Rhuna. He looked north toward the mountain and the Temple of Osiris. In his mind's eye he could see his twin looking down from where he stood in the temple courtyard. And the sharrana Nahleen at his side.

He had done the impossible. He had returned home.

He called Rhandor to him. "Assemble your warriors. We will make camp here tonight and march on the temple at dawn."

The Krit wasted no time establishing a base camp, sending scouting parties to hunt for food and information and posting sentries to keep watch. Their arrival was not likely overlooked, and Ko'Resh was certain the Rhue forces would be amassing in the nearby city of Kephas. He wondered if the port city of Althena remained intact but, judging by the range of destruction he could see and how deep inland they had come, he doubted there would be anything left of the coastal cities and villages. He wondered how many of the Rhue army were in Althena when the tsunami hit. Using the crow's nest on the second ship, which remained upright and wedged between two giant oak trees, as a vantage point, the sentry posted there had a clear line of sight to the temple and toward the city of Rainier. They may be exposed, but they were not vulnerable. There would be no way to launch a sneak attack on them from any direction. The third ship did not fare quite so well. At some point it had turned and plowed portside through the forest. The bow was torn open, and some of the cargo had spilled out and was taken back to sea by the receding waters. More of the cargo littered the muddy ground where the ship lay on its side like a great wounded wooden beast. Much to Ko'Resh's surprise, most of the five hundred warriors aboard her survived and only a handful were badly wounded—a testament to the strength and endurance of the Krit people.

They took stock of what supplies and manpower they had, and once camp had been established the cooks set about preparing the evening meal. That night they had to rely on rations. Any game that would have been in the forest when the water struck would be long gone from the area and probably would not return for some time. But the joy of being once again on land and among living trees seemed to be more than enough to lift the spirits of the Krit, and it was not long after the meal was taken that wine and song began to ripple through the camp. But that joy was short-lived when news of the missing rephaim was brought to Ko'Resh. He unleashed his fury on the men who brought him the news. More would have fallen to his temper had Rhandor not stayed his hand.

"We are here to fight a war. We are far from home and have no allies here. We need these men." Rhandor released Ko'Resh's arm.

Ko'Resh nodded briefly then retired to his tent and closed his eyes. He did not know if sleep would come or if he would lay awake subject to the visions that Saal plagued him with each night. Each time, the visions grew more dark and ominous to remind him Saal was the one true lord over the Sem Lukos and anyone who dared stand in his way would reap the consequences.

CHAPTER 31

THE TREMORS BECAME MORE FREQUENT, AND THOUGH Nahleen was not certain whether it was day or night, she was certain there were several in the span of what she thought was a day. The dim lighting remained constant, though she still could not find the source. She imagined it was the same as the light Kian'Huard had in his caves. She had been imprisoned under the mountain for months and, though she was not mistreated or neglected, her spirit was waning. Another tremor shook the ground beneath her. She heard the rumble of stones being shook loose down one of the tunnels to her right. She strained to listen for any sounds coming from the tunnels on her left. It was from those tunnels anyone bringing food or fresh clothing came. Another tremor, this one was stronger, and she held onto the bars of her cell to steady herself and tried not to imagine how much mountain was above her. The shaking passed.

Surely the sorelige would not keep her down here with the risk the entire system of catacombs could cave in. The sound of footfalls reached her and she breathed a sigh of relief. She backed away from the bars and waited in the centre of her cell. Two figures emerged from the tunnel, one bearing clean clothes and a blanket, the other a tray with bread, cheese and fruit. The smaller of the two looked up, and Nahleen gasped; it was Abby. Face drawn and pale, eyes sunken and dark. Their eyes met briefly then the girl looked away. They unlocked the cell and motioned for Nahleen to stand back against the wall. When she complied, her fresh clothing was placed on her bed and the food was placed on the table. The older girl turned and left the cell. Abby turned to look at Nahleen and gave a little wink and a slight nod toward the food then quickly turned and left the cell. Nahleen stood in place for some time before she went to the tray. She moved aside the bread to find a key.

She smiled at the thought of how strong young Abby was and how dedicated. Another tremor shook the mountain.

Nahleen ate what she could then tore a square from the fresh blanket and wrapped the remaining food. That was when she found a note with a crude map drawn on it. Abby was showing her where Kian'Huard was being kept. She took a long drink of the water. She listened for any sounds coming from the tunnels then tried the key in the lock. The latch released and the door swung open. Nahleen looked at the map. It indicated she go to the right. She knew those tunnels were beginning to collapse with the tremors. She thought of Abby and the risk she took bringing her the information, and though she was not certain of Kian'Huard's ability to remain loyal to her with his connection to Saal, she headed down the tunnel to her right. One thing she did know for certain was that for whatever purpose served their end, they all wanted her alive— for now.

As she traversed the tunnel she tried to formulate a plan but being locked up for the past months made it difficult to know what resources she had nearby. She decided not to try to make a plan, but to focus on freeing Kian'Huard and the two of them escaping the temple before the mountain came down on them.

Abby's map may have been crude, but it was very accurate. Within minutes, Nahleen found the chamber that contained the cell where Kian'Huard was being kept. It was obvious his internment was less pleasant than hers. She cautiously approached the chamber. Abby's map indicated there were four guards posted. She pressed herself against the wall of the tunnel and surveyed the area. She could not see any guards. She noted a table and chairs in the centre of the room. The table had been smashed by a falling rock. Three of the chairs were tossed back as though whoever was seated upon them was in a terrible hurry to get up. The fourth chair was crushed by another large rock, its occupant not so lucky. She heard a feeble groan coming from Kian'Huard's cell. She found him chained against the wall, hands and feet locked in thick iron shackles. His clothing was ragged and bloody, as was his face. Nahleen looked about for the keys and prayed the guards did not take them with them. She found them on the floor beside the table.

Nahleen fumbled with the lock, trying to find the right key out of the dozen or so on the hoop. She was so focussed on what she was doing that it took a moment for her to realize he was trying to tell her something.

"You must leave me and get out of this place." His voice was weak and the effort of speaking caused a coughing fit. He spat blood from his mouth and drew a ragged breath.

"I will not leave you. Abby sent me to get you, and if she feels you are worth saving then who am I to argue." She found the right key and went to him.

"Young Abby is most remarkable." His voice was strained.

Nahleen found the key and released him from the shackles. He crumpled and she caught him and helped him out of the cell. Another tremor brought the ceiling of the cell down behind them. The ground shook so that Nahleen lost her balance. She felt Kian'Huard's body grow rigid beside her. She felt she was falling to the floor but realized she was being pushed. She tried to free herself, but somehow his strength returned. They fell to the ground. She tried shoving him away and rolling out from under him but he held her down. And when she looked in his eyes it was not him but Saal who stared down at her.

"The time is at hand, Majha. Soon we will be together again." He bent closer, burying his face in her hair and smelling the scent of her.

Nahleen struggled harder. Kian'Huard let go his hold. She pushed him off and sprang to her feet. She paced for a moment to catch her breath then returned to stand over Kian'Huard.

"I told you to leave me, Naid Sharrana," he said. "The time of Saal draws near and with each passing day he grows more powerful and can descend more easily into this physical realm. My connection with him through the Sama Lukos is stronger as well. It is becoming more difficult for me to resist his control over the Sama Lukos, and now my own flesh as well. I will do what I can to assist you, but you must understand. With him so close, I fear whatever we may devise to conquer him he will know of and be able to counter." He drew another deep breath but this time he did not have a coughing spree, nor did he cough up blood. Nahleen could see his body healing before her eyes and though the wounds were healing, the age that now showed in his face did not change.

"I will decide who I leave behind." She reached a hand to help him to his feet. "Abby sees something about you she feels is important and put herself at risk to show me where you were. And even though she is a child, for some reason I trust her instinct."

Kian'Huard's face was soft when he looked at Nahleen "For now, that is enough but you must know I will, eventually, betray you to Saal. I have no choice." His voice echoed the sorrow she knew he felt in his heart.

"I understand, but I also know nothing is carved in stone except these caverns, and even they are collapsing under the pressure; if we do not get out of here soon we could be trapped." She motioned toward the tunnel where she came from. "This is the way out."

They made their way through tunnel after tunnel, always on an upward incline, of grey- green rock following the map provided by a ten year-old girl and eventually found themselves standing before a door. Nahleen opened it a crack to listen for any sign of activity in the hallway beyond. After a few moments, she felt confident no one was close by and they slipped into the midday brightness of marble and granite and resh-light. Nahleen breathed a short prayer of thanks to Selam, kissed the back of her hand and touched it to her forehead. Then she felt she gave thanks too soon. Once above ground she could see the devastation the earthquakes were having on the temple and the nearby town of Kephas. Smoke could be seen in the distance.

The pair made their way, unchallenged, to mingle with the sea of people hurrying to escape the mountain. Then movement caught her eye. She looked toward the sea on the horizon. She stopped short and Kian'Huard bumped into her then followed her gaze. It took a moment for her brain to make sense of what her eyes were seeing. She stood paralyzed at the sight. In the distance, a wall of water rushed toward them carrying what looked to be three enormous ships. Others around her stopped to see what held her attention. Within moments, panic swept through the crowd and they turned to scramble back up into the mountain to higher ground. Nahleen and Kian'Huard stood their ground and waited. Both knew what was coming.

Nahleen was jarred from her paralysis when Kian'Huard grabbed her by the wrist and pulled her back toward the temple. "We must hide in the catacombs."

She tried to pull free but he held tight. "No, they are not safe! Remember, they were coming down around us every time the ground shook." Something in his eyes told her Kian'Huard was no longer in charge; Saal had taken full control.

She struggled harder to free herself but could not. He dragged her back toward the temple. With a wave of his hand an opening formed in the wall before them. She struggled harder and he pulled her against him to half-carry, half-drag her into the tunnel. The opening closed behind them. She continued to resist him, but he was too strong. He waved his hand again and a chamber opened. In the centre she could see a mist beginning to swirl about, gathering in on itself and becoming denser. A form began to take shape in the fog. She recognized the beast; it was he who bore her to the mountain when Saal pulled her from her bedchamber. The beast swatted at the ground and raised its giant head to let out a blood-curdling howl. It turned and lowered itself on its haunches, then rested his head on his front paws, his clear yellow eyes fixed on Nahleen.

Kian'Huard pushed her toward the giant lukos and up onto his back. He climbed on behind her and held her tight. The beast stood then leapt forward through the solid rock. Nahleen let out a scream but stopped when she saw they were unharmed. Her mind could not comprehend how it could be possible to move through solid rock. She began to feel queasy. She tried desperately not to pass out. She gasped, gulping in air that tasted heavy, like minerals, as though she was breathing the mountain itself. They passed through a barrier and they were in a huge chamber with marble pillars and a flawless black marble floor. She recognized this place for the vision Kian'Huard gave her, and she knew the tunnel ahead led to the room where he and his twin were possessed by the Sem Lukos.

The great beast stopped and crouched down so they could dismount. Nahleen slid down from his back. Kian'Huard hesitated briefly then followed suit. Nahleen saw his eyes change and knew Saal was no longer in control of his body.

"I don't know long I can maintain control." His voice was strained and she could see he was fighting against Saal's invasion in his mind. "You have been here before. With me. You must run. I can no longer help you." With that, he turned and ran. She followed after him and stopped short. They were in the chamber where the beasts took control of the twins. The centre platform remained where it had for a millennium, but the outer ledge was crumbled and broken in several places and no longer looked safe. Kian'Huard ran headlong toward the edge and did not even hesitate when he got to it. Nahleen stood dumbfounded for a moment, staring at the place where he disappeared into the chasm.

CHAPTER 32

SAAL HAD FLED KIAN'HUARD'S BODY WHEN HE THREW himself into the abyss, another testament to the strength of the man. He changed his focus and was now fully in control of Rhandor's physical body and stood at the bow of the ship where he fixed his attention on the temple in the distance. Rhandor's consciousness was buried deep within the layers of consciousness that connect the physical with the non-physical. His essence remained intact, but he was unable to find his way back to his physical body. Ko'Resh stood beside him, both watching the temple. They could see the movement of people hurrying to higher ground, terrified of the water that had carried the ships so far inland. He looked down at Ko'Resh and felt disgust at the vile man. Drawing a deep breath, he allowed himself a moment to relish the feel of the air moving through his nostrils, and the rhythmic thump of his physical heartbeat. In fact, all physical sensations that had been denied him for eons flowed through neurons giving sensations of heat, cold, taste, smell. And the physical body that was Rhandor's was strong and powerful. He turned his thoughts inward and sought out the thread of DNA that would bring his beloved spirits back to one body and, with the power of pure intent, activated it to ensure control over the six that Ko'Resh thought he controlled.

"We must go at once to the temple." Ko'Resh interrupted his thoughts.

He did not have to repeat himself or even make any explanation. Saal feigned obedience. Ko'Resh did not take notice of the men around him when he and Saal disembarked from the ship and headed toward the temple. His focus on his goal blinded him to the changes about him. Saal was withdrawing his control over the men, as they were not part of his plan. He had indulged Ko'Resh to lure him into believing he had control over the spirits that possessed him. It was Ko'Resh who needed the army to lay siege to

Rhuna and claim her for himself. Ko'Resh was but a pawn needed to mani-fest people and events in the physical realm when Saal was unable. The time was at hand when he no longer needed Ko'Resh to act as a conduit between himself and the physical. The Rhue were his people, and he would not see them slaughtered by the Krit to feed Ko'Resh's hunger for power. Many Krit mulled about, confused as to where they were. They turned to who they thought was Rhandor for direction, not knowing he was fully controlled by Saal. He ignored their queries as he disappeared into the forest toward the city of Kephas and the Temple of Osiris.

CHAPTER 33

WHEN DAR'KAYEL LEFT NAHLEEN IN THE CITY OF Kephas to return to Althean he did not return to gather men to aid the villages as he was instructed. The information he received at the tavern in Rainer, coupled with what Nahleen told him about the coming alignment that would make Rhuna accessible and possibly a target for invasion, gave him reason to believe assembling a larger army would be prudent. If what he was told was true, the sorelige was doing just that. What he did not know was who, or what, the temple army would be defending. He pushed his horse and rode almost nonstop back to Althean. When the city walls finally came into view he had formulated most of a plan.

Once Dar'Kayel had seen to his horse, he requested an audience with Domini Val'Raslin. He did not wait for the guard to respond; he made his way to the main hall and threw open the doors. "My apologies for the intrusion, Domini Val'Raslin, but I have urgent news that requires your immediate attention."

Domini Val'Raslin looked up from his desk and nodded. He did not give the appearance of being surprised. He motioned for the others to leave the room and waited until the doors were pulled shut. "I have been waiting for your return, Dar'Kayel, for I too have news and I fear it may be far worse than what you have discovered." He moved from behind his desk to stand before Dar'Kayel and kept his voice low. "My contact in the temple has informed me Sharrana Nahleen has been taken prisoner by Sorelige Garret Del'Tolan."

Dar'Kayel tried to restrain his anger, mostly at himself for leaving Nahleen. His gut had told him to stay at her side even though she insisted he return to Althean. And though she seemed to trust the one called Kian'Huard, instinct told him the man could not be trusted. "What of the old man that was travelling with her, Kian'Huard—does your contact know what has become of him?"

"It is my understanding he is being held as well. Initially he was given a guest chamber but," he paused and moved to his desk, "from what information my contact could gather, it seems he too is now a prisoner somewhere within the catacombs." He poured a glass of wine and offered it to Dar'Kayel then poured another for himself. "I do not know what exactly happened to cause Sorelige Garret Del'Tolan to imprison the old man, but it is said Kian'Huard was found in the catacombs gravely injured, as though by some large beast." Val'Raslin downed his drink and poured another; he was clearly agitated. "Sorelige Garret Del'Tolan, I am told, intends to use Nahleen to lure the beast. He has made it clear her life is forfeit." He paused again. "I believe he intends to take the castle."

Dar'Kayel let the domini's words sink in for a few moments. "How long until this alignment that Nahleen spoke of? She believes when that occurs, Rhuna will be accessible to the rest of Mythos. She told me a great army will cross the Aevitas Ocean and attack."

Val'Raslin nodded. "My contact has heard this rumour as well. That is why the sorelige has ordered all able-bodied be collected. He has amassed a huge army. Enough to divide his forces between defending the temple and taking the castle. I have been told the sorelige believes the ships will set ashore at Kephas. It makes sense if they are coming for something at the temple."

"Yes, and that something is Sharrana Nahleen." Dar'Kayel paced the room. "She told me Kian'Huard has a twin who somehow was transported across the Aevitas Ocean. They are of the house of Rhuna and his twin, she called him Ko'Resh, intends to return to Rhuna with his progeny so he can mate with Nahleen and bring about a child that would see the destruction of Rhuna and, most likely, all of Mythos." Dar'Kayel suddenly felt a bit helpless. "We do not have the resources to defend both Kephas and Althean."

"And we can trust Sorelige Garret Del'Tolan has nothing but his own best interest in mind," Val'Raslin added

"How long till the alignment?" Dar'Kayel asked.

"Six full cycles of Rhuna," Val'Raslin replied.

"Then Selam be with us, that is not much time to build an army." Dar'Kayel gave a slight bow and left the castle. There was much work to be done.

Six full cycles passed far too quickly and Dar'Kayel found himself leading an army of very inexperienced soldiers through the thick forest that bordered the southernmost reaches of the city of Kephas. Dar'Kayel signalled the battalion of Rhue to come to a stop and take cover. He crouched low to the ground and crept forward to find a vantage point using a small bush as cover and motioned for his second-in-command, Ra'Dalan, to move to position with him. It did not take him long to note how disorganized the Krit army was, or how great in stature they were. Then his eyes fell on the ships. He kissed the back of his hand and touched his forehead for protection from Selam.

Dar'Kayel turned to Ra'Dalan. "Have you ever seen anything like it?"

"You know I haven't, for no such vessels could be constructed. Rhuna does not have the forest that would be necessary to mill that amount of lumber."

"That explosion we heard and the great wave that washed over the land; they came from beyond the barrier." Dar'Kayel shifted to try to gain a better view of the ships. "There must be at least a thousand warriors."

"They seem very disorganized, and we have two thousand warriors."

"This doesn't make sense. Sharrana Nahleen told me the old man, Kian'Huard, told her an army was coming to Rhuna from across the Aevitas Ocean and it could bring about the end of the world." He turned his attention back to the ships and the disorganized army. "They are big and they are many, but I think if we surround them and take them by surprise we will be able to defeat them with little bloodshed." He studied the Krit army again, noting their leather armour, when he noticed something else that put a faint smile on his lips.

"I know that look, Dar'Kayel. What have you in mind?"

"None of them have their weapons. If we strike now, they will not have time to assemble themselves."

Ra'Dalan looked to the ships and the men surrounding them. Dar'Kayel was right—none had weapons on them, and he could not see where any had been placed to be on the ready. "We still do not know if there are more within the ships."

"True," Dar'Kayel agreed. "Send two scouts to each ship to see if there are others. Have them use extreme caution; I do not want these men to know we are here. Meanwhile, we will ready our men into position to keep watch over their movements."

With a nod of agreement, the pair returned to their battalions and gave instruction to surround the ships. They would wait until the scouts returned to be certain the ships did not hold any significant numbers of soldiers then they would close in and subdue the army. They hoped with a surprise attack the invaders would be quick to surrender, but the Rhue were ready to do battle if necessary. Dar'Kayel hoped it would not come to that. Even disorganized, the Krit army would be formidable. Their stature alone made them intimidating and the Rhue army, though they trained regularly, had no real combat experience; in fact, there would not even be an army except the temple insisted there be one. There simply was no need.

Perhaps the sorelige knew this day would come and Rhuna would need to be defended. He also knew the temple would be well defended. The Sacerdos'helige, though their primary duty was in service to the temple and in maintaining the historical records, were also trained in combat. Dar'Kayel could understand the temple may, at some time, come under attack when enough families became distraught at losing their children to a cull. The most recent cull nearly had the whole city of Kephas storming the temple. Had Nahleen and he not been there to stay the crowd he was certain the streets would have run red with blood. His thoughts returned to the Krit army and the great ships. He felt certain the Krit were well versed in combat experience. He made a prayer to Selam then signalled the troops to advance.

Though the water had receded, it left the ground thick with mud and debris, making it difficult for the Rhue army to advance in total stealth. Once Dar'Kayel and his men broke through the wooded area he was able to see the true extent of destruction that was carved in the land from the sea to end at the ships. It destroyed a vast amount of precious forest that would take decades to regrow. He then turned his attention to the three ships that lay twisted and out of place so far inland and knew there was more lumber in them than would be harvested in all of Rhuna over ten seasons. Dar'Kayel returned his attention to his men and watched as they efficiently surrounded the ships. Once each battalion gave the whistle of a bird call to signal they were in position, Dar'Kayel gave the signal to hold their places. He studied the ships, looking for any indication of the whereabouts of his scouts, when movement caught his eye. Two scouts were making their way back from the centre ship. They lacked the cover of forest but were using the debris to hide their movements. It seemed like an eternity passed before he caught sight of the other four scouts finally making their way toward him.

Dar'Kayel waited patiently while the men were given water and a plate of food then beckoned them to follow him to a secluded area where they could talk uninterrupted. "What did you find?"

"The ship on the far right was very damaged when it was pushed ashore. There are several bodies and some supplies scattered through all the decks but from what we could see, everyone who is able has left the ship for land." The scout ran his hand through his hair, pushing it out of his eyes; his voice sounded forced, as though he did not wish to speak of what he saw. He hesitated a moment before resuming. "We watched the men for a while, trying to get a feel for what they intended. We crept as near as we thought would be safe to try to listen in on their conversations but it was no use to us. Their words make no sense; we cannot understand them."

His partner then came forward. "Maybe we could not understand their words, but the tone of voice and the look on their faces speak as loud. They seem lost, as though waking from a deep sleep. They mill about as though they have no idea where they are or how they got here."

The other scouts nodded in agreement, for they observed the same. Most of the contingent had abandoned the ships and were trying to make camp in the forest but they were keeping the ships within sprinting distance. A few had armed themselves, but most were still suffering the after effects of whatever trauma they all experienced in their journey there.

"There is one more thing," Kar'Galan spoke up. He was one of the two who investigated the ship on the left. "We found an empty cage below decks. It looked like it contained something powerful that they were afraid of or were keeping hidden. The cage appears to have been torn open and whatever was in it, we assume, has escaped."

Dar'Kayel's head bowed slightly as his thoughts raced. They had to gain control of the Krit army as quickly as possible and with as little bloodshed as possible. And they had to find whatever had escaped that cage. He drew a heavy sigh and studied the men before him. "Kar'Galan, you are a skilled tracker. Do you think you can find where the creature escaped the ship and track it? Take someone with you. I don't want you to engage it, just find it and follow it then send word back when you have located it. I want you to study it to see if it is indeed dangerous and what about it made it necessary for the Krit ruler to decide to bring it on such a long and perilous journey." Dar'Kayel looked to the west. The resh was past zenith and they had about six paces left until dusk. "If we are going to engage the Krit, the time is now."

The Rhue army swarmed quickly over the Krit giving them little time to arm themselves or to gain any order. A few did manage to take up swords, but their minds were still clouded from the mind control Saal had over them so they were easily disarmed. Dar'Kayel breathed a sigh of relief as he watched the Krit come forward and surrender. He moved to face the warriors on bent knee before him and knew the day could have been so much worse. He studied their faces and could see how they were so easily subdued. Most appeared as though they were recovering from a night of heavy drinking. It did not make sense to him that an invading force would construct such massive ships and travel across the ocean to lay down arms once they arrived. There was something more to this. He called Ra'Dalan to him. He was about to have him send word to the temple when a crashing sound advanced through the forest. The resh, now hanging low on the horizon, caught the gleam of gold helmets. The Sacerdos'helige had arrived.

Dar'Kayel surveyed the men before him. "*Ren telthadar gana dai prin dain dregault?*" he shouted, looking for one in command of the Krit army. He did not expect they would understand his language but he made it clear he was addressing them and gestured to try and clarify his intent. Again, he repeated, "*Ren telthadar gana dai prin dain dregault?*" He motioned to himself and then his warriors. "*Ren vodan applenta gana?*" He almost gave up when a man a few measures from him stood. Dar'Kayel felt just a little intimidated at the sight of the battle-hardened man before him, but he held his ground and disguised his discomfort. He hardened his gaze then motioned the man forward to follow him. He intended to initiate some form of dialogue. He gave Ra'Dalan a short signal to have him follow as well. The Sacerdos'helige would not be left out so one of the senior initiates joined the company.

Night was beginning to fall and the Krit had become fully aware of their surroundings but most had little idea as to how they came to be on the ships that carried them so far. They were easily outnumbered two to one, and though they were physically superior, they did not know what skills their captors possessed and their weapons had been taken so they remained yielding. Fires were lit around the makeshift camp and rations were handed out while their commanders tried to find common ground.

Dar'Kayel studied the giant of a man standing before him. He stood head and shoulders above Dar'Kayel and his demeanour remained calm and calculating. Dar'Kayel knew the man was studying him as well. Looking for any sign of weakness; it was what he would do. He motioned for Ra'Dalan to bring him the maps of Rhuna and unrolled them on the table. He motioned to the map. "*Haeth dai Rhuna.*"

He handed the Krit commander a paper and ink. The Krit warrior nodded that he understood then drew a crude map of Krit and some of the surrounding lands. "This is Krit, my homeland." He handed Dar'Kayel the paper.

Dar'Kayel put the two maps beside each other then moved them apart, indicating he wanted to know how far they journeyed. Again, the commander nodded. He thought for a few moments then started to draw. At first Dar'Kayel did not understand, but then as a pattern emerged he realized the Krit was drawing phases of the moon, rhuna. If he was understanding correctly, it took the Krit five full cycles of rhuna to cross the Aevitas Ocean.

The Krit then tapped himself on the chest to indicate he was referring to himself. "Montero." His voice was as big and booming as he.

"Montero," Dar'Kayel repeated.

Montero nodded then motioned to Dar'Kayel to indicate he wanted to know his name.

" Dar'Kayel."

"Dar'Kayel," Montero repeated.

Dar'Kayel nodded. Montero reached out his hand in an open gesture indicating a desire for peace. Dar'Kayel was about to do the same when the guard he posted burst into the tent

"The Sacerdos'helige are killing the Krit!"

Dar'Kayel turned to the Sacerdos'helige who joined them in the tent. "Order your men to stand down!" he shouted at him.

The Sacerdos'helige drew his sword. "I will do no such thing," he said and he charged at Montero.

Dar'Kayel drew his sword and lunged between the Krit and the temple soldier. The skirmish was brief and ended when Dar'Kayel's sword found its mark in the man's heart. Dar'Kayel wasted no time in getting to the door. Without thinking, he pulled the sword from the hand of the dead Sacerdos'helige and tossed it to the Krit. Montero caught it by the hilt and gave it a couple of practice swings. Dar'Kayel noticed how the sword seemed to shrink in the Krit's hands and prayed he did not make a mistake in arming the giant. Too late to second guess himself, he charged out into the fray followed closely by Montero.

As soon as he emerged from the tent, Dar'Kayel started shouting orders to his men to defend the Krit. There was a split second of confusion before the Rhue army sprung into action against their countrymen to protect those who, until a moment ago, were considered their enemy.

The Krit were, as Dar'Kayel assumed, fierce warriors. Outnumbered and without weapons, they were still able to hold their own and dispatch several Sacerdos'helige. Whatever solveige clouded their minds when they first arrived apparently had cleared. Dar'Kayel could hear Montero shouting orders to his men and once they armed themselves with the fallen soldiers' weapons, they were unstoppable. Dar'Kayel sent a pray to Selam giving thanks he was able to establish a diplomatic dialogue with Montero before the Sacerdos'helige started their attack.

Krit and Rhue fought side by side against the Sacerdos'helige. The night was filled with the sound of steel on steel and the last gasps of the dying. The air was tainted with the smell of blood and bodily fluids that covered the ground. Dar'Kayel and his men had never truly experienced real battle, and the sounds and smells were overwhelming. Darkness shrouded the grisly sight that littered the ground around them. Eventually, the night grew quiet as the last of the Sacerdos'helige retreated back toward the temple.

Dar'Kayel called his men to gather to him. Their faces held haunted expressions in the firelight. In that moment, war became real to the Rhue.

The Krit seemed to sense no Rhue steel had tasted blood prior to this night. Montero called his men to order. Dar'Kayel and his men watched the Krit fall into line with as much precision as the terrain allowed. Montero counted his men. He still had roughly eight hundred warriors. Each held a blade that he knew had never seen real combat. He was determined each blade would be honoured for the life it took and the life it saved. He shouted an order to his men and motioned for Dar'Kayel to stand beside him. As one, the Krit warriors moved forward and presented their weapons. Montero shouted another order and, as one, the Krit swung the swords to point the blade down and hold the hilt with both hands to their chest at heart level. Then they were grasped in their right hand and extended to arm's length and the blades were turned to point to the sky. The soldiers then bowed their heads, swung the blade back to face the ground and brought the hilt to their forehead, switched hands and, in a sweeping motion spun the blade two full turns and plunged the blade into the ground on their left. Then the Krit made an about face and marched back behind the rows of weapons. Montero barked another order and his men broke ranks. He turned to Dar'Kayel and did his best to explain their tradition called for the weapons to remain thus until resh rose in the morning to honour those fallen in combat.

Somehow Dar'Kayel understood and relayed the message to his men.

The mood remained somber through the night as the Rhue came to terms with drawing sword against the Sacerdos'helige. Against Rhue. A makeshift infirmary was set up and the injured were brought to be tended. One of the Krit warriors was half-dragging, half-carrying a wounded Sacerdos'helige who seemed bent on escaping, which only served to cause his wounds to bleed more profusely. Finally, the Krit brought his fist down on the injured Rhue's head and knocked him unconscious. Montero barked something at him, the man grinned sheepishly, then threw the unconscious Rhue over his shoulder like a sack and carried him to the infirmary. Dar'Kayel ordered the Sacerdos'helige restrained while physicians closed his wounds. So far, he was the only one they were able to capture alive and Dar'Kayel intended to interrogate him when he regained consciousness. There was no more for him to do until then so he retired to his tent to try to get some rest.

The morning dawned bright, but the weather did little to soften the sight Dar'Kayel and the others woke to. Bodies littered the ground lying in blood-soaked mud. Rows of weapons, still standing where they were sunk into the soil, lay testament to how many lives were lost. The tremors that shook Rhuna had continued through the night, growing in intensity, often making it difficult to walk. As the resh warmed the air, insects were drawn to the scent of death. The Krit, working side by side with the Rhue, had already begun removing the bodies of the fallen and had set funeral pyres to cremate the remains. Dar'Kayel also noticed the Krit warriors had armed themselves through the night. He called to Ra'Dalan, who had just emerged from his barracks tent, "I fear we may be on precarious ground." He cast a glance toward the Krit.

Ra'Dalan followed Dar'Kayel's gaze. "Indeed." He turned back to Dar'Kayel. "Let's hope our new allies continue as such. I do not think we would farewell against them in combat."

"I agree," Dar'Kayel replied. "And I am sure they know that as well." He watched the Krit warriors for a few moments when he saw Montero exit the middle ship carrying a large cask. He assumed the ship was where their weapons had been stored and it looked like several other supplies as well, including what looked to be some form of spirited beverage, for many had gathered around another wooden cask filling cups and whatever other containers they could find. That was when he noticed several of his men gathered with the Krit warriors sharing drink and some form of conversation. Montero spotted Dar'Kayel and a huge grin spread across his face as he made his way toward him with a cask over his shoulder. It occurred to Dar'Kayel the Krit would be valuable allies should the temple decide to try to overthrow the House of Rhuna. But first, drink and conversation.

CHAPTER 34

SAAL AND KO'RESH QUICKLY MADE THEIR WAY
through the remaining layers of forest to step onto a dirt road that would
take them into Kephas. The resh was at midday by this time and the heat of
the day struck them when the emerged from the cool shade of the forest.
Saal drew a deep breath and looked around at his kingdom. His people had
prospered despite being cut off from the rest of Mythos. From his vantage
point he could see the city rising before him in tiers carved into the foothills to end at the base of Mount Gillrest. From there the Temple of Osiris
took over, sprawling up the side of the mountain, an impressive example of
Rhue architecture and stone masonry. Saal knew as much, or more, remained
hidden within the mountain as could be seen from the outside. Much of it
he designed when Mythos was new and creation was merely a thought away.
He looked down at Ko'Resh. "We need to go to the crystal cavern where you
and your brother freed the Sem Lukos Resh. Your brother will have taken
Sharrana Nahleen there." Another tremor shook the ground. "And we must
hurry; these tremors will soon make the catacombs unstable."

Ko'Resh thought for a moment. "Perhaps one of these outlying farms has
horses. I am sure we could acquire two."

Saal shook his head. "I have something a little quicker in mind. Perhaps
you can summon two lukos to carry us." Being careful not to let Ko'Resh
see what he was doing, he made a gesture with his hand as though slowly
beckoning someone to him. Within moments two giant lukos appeared out
of nowhere to leap down from the sky and land softly on giant paws before
them. Ko'Resh took a step back. Saal grinned down at him. "Surely you are
not afraid of that which you possess."

Ko'Resh straightened and composed himself. "Of course not. I was startled at how quickly they arrived."

Saal made a discreet motion with his hand and the beasts lowered themselves so the pair could climb on their backs. He would continue his charade allowing Ko'Resh to believe he still had control over his creation. Once they were in the cavern he would strip Ko'Resh of what he has coveted for so long. Still, he cautioned him. "Understand, Ko'Resh, with the alignment comes a shift in the energy patterns of Mythos and the distance between thought and manifestation is greatly reduced. I caution you to be wary of what you focus your attention on." He motioned toward the temple. "It is time."

With that, the beasts sprung forward and carried them toward the temple. Saal turned to Ko'Resh. "We travel just outside the frequency that would allow those in the physical world to see us. To them, we would be as a strong breeze passing."

Within moments they reached the temple and, much to Ko'Resh's surprise, they did not ascend the stairs to gain entry. The stone wall ahead of them shimmered as though heat radiated off it then it thinned and an opening appeared before them. The lukos did not slow as they made their way ever downward toward the centre of the mountain and the place where Shista Ko'Resh's life changed forever. They slowed once they reached the platform that surrounded the dais where Ko'Resh took unto him six of the Sem Lukos Resh. Saal looked over at Ko'Resh. He thought it arrogant of him to think he was ever in control of the spirit lukos, or that he would be able to take them from him. He was so easy to manipulate to bring about a protégé that would reunite the Sem Lukos. Had his twin found the dais first, it would have been a different story. Kian'Huard was much stronger than Ko'Resh. He proved that by being able to resist using the power the Sama Lukos afforded him. Fortunately, Saal was still able to manipulate Kian'Huard enough to ensure he had what he needed to create a Sheth Child. He lifted his head and started chanting a mantra. Within moments the entire chamber resonated with the sound. Then he shouted, *"Nayer betice gan nune gan naidrae altheaneir!"*

Ko'Resh shifted nervously on the back of the giant lukos when four more lukos appeared around the chamber, all massive in size. Their fur was deepest ebony and their eyes emerald fire. All six were now with them. Ko'Resh tried to remove himself from atop the lukos on which he had ridden but was unable. Saal watched with smug satisfaction at Ko'Resh's obvious panic. Once more

Saal focussed his attention on the centre of the chamber and began another chant. This time six small vortices began to form in the very spot Ko'Resh lay over two millennia ago when he took six of the Sem Lukos Resh for himself. Saal watched quietly while the vortices gained strength. Once they reached a specific frequency he shouted, "NUNE!" as one the six giant beasts leapt the distance from the platform to the centre dais.

Saal dismounted and indicated Ko'Resh do the same. He led him to the very centre of the platform and turned to face him. Saal drew himself up and towered over Ko'Resh. He could see the fear in his eyes as he pulled one of the vortices he had summoned to surround them. Ko'Resh's eyes opened wide with fear as the vortex pulled the first, the Amladhar Lukos, from him. Saal watched Ko'Resh struggle and scream as he tried to keep it from abandoning him. Then the fear changed to anger and contempt as he watched helplessly while Saal drew the beast to him within the body of Rhandor. Saal just stared down at Ko'Resh, his expression calm and powerful at the same time. He called the second, the Sadishtana Lukos. Another vortex surrounded them and the power of the second lukos left Ko'Resh. This continued until all six had been reclaimed by Saal. Each time another of the lukos fled Ko'Resh, his body became frailer and more aged, so by the time all six had been taken, he was no more than a pathetic, frail remnant of a man with no trace of how powerful he once appeared to be. Saal took him by the throat and lifted him up until Ko'Resh's eyes met his. *"Na'vai greyan dern val rand dai naidre!"* "I have taken back that which is mine!" he growled. Then he tossed Ko'Resh from the dais and into the abyss that surrounded them.

Only moments later he sensed Nahleen was near. He made a grasping gesture with his hand as though he was gathering something then tossed it before him toward the abyss. A bridge formed before him as he strode across the abyss to search out Nahleen.

CHAPTER 35

NAHLEEN STOOD FROZEN, FOR JUST A MOMENT, staring at the place where Kian'Huard disappeared then turned to find her way out. The ground shook and more of the surrounding tunnel buckled and crashed into the abyss that surrounded the platform. She made her way back along the tunnel to where the giant lukos left them. She hurried forward when a slow rumble sounded behind her. She did not have time to finish her thought when a giant of a man emerged from the shadows. Her jaw dropped at the sight of the man. When she looked in his eyes she knew. "Saal!" she exclaimed.

She looked around for an escape but there was none. The only way for her to run was back to the chamber.

Saal advanced toward Nahleen, his eyes never leaving her. She turned and ran back toward the chasm. She was not sure if she had the courage to throw herself in as Kian'Huard did, but she was certain she would know very soon. The ground shook again and she stumbled and lost her balance. She staggered forward, holding the cave wall for support. Again, the ground shook and she fell to her knees. She looked back to see Saal was virtually unaffected by the tremors. Ahead, the platform was giving way all around the chasm. Water was spraying in through small fissures in the rock. Nahleen struggled back to her feet. She glanced behind to see Saal was nearly upon her. She made her way to the edge of the tunnel that now opened to the gaping abyss; she had nowhere to run. Saal was closing the gap between them. Another tremor caused a large chunk of the cavern wall to break away. Water spewed in through the opening. The floor of the tunnel was becoming slippery from the spray. Nahleen took another look back at Saal, and he was almost in arm's reach. She took a step back. She could feel the edge of the floor under her feet. The flow of water broke through another fissure in the rock. The spray caught her just as Saal reached to grab her. The water enveloped her and pulled her down and away from the ledge. She flailed, trying to grab onto something, but it was useless. She was freefalling deeper into the heart of the mountain. Water filled her nose and mouth. She tried to take a breath but couldn't. Her body screamed for oxygen. A peaceful calm flooded her mind. Blackness shrouded her vision then took her completely.

Saal clenched his fists in rage. Veins stood out in his neck and his face went crimson as he raised his head and opened his mouth to let out an enraged howl that brought the mountain crashing down around him.

THE END

ABOUT THE AUTHOR

LAURIE WAS AN INQUISITIVE KID AND A BORN STORY-teller! She apparently started talking at a young age and was quite adept at expressing herself. Our mom said she used to make up stories all the time when she was quite young, embellishing here and there about her life and her family. Her teachers were always curious to meet our parents as they had been hearing about Laurie's creative version of our circumstances. Of course, this ensured she received the extra school supplies she had convinced them she was sorely in need of!

There are six kids in our family Laurie being the second oldest and I the third girl of 4 and then 2 younger brothers to round us out. When we were kids Laurie and I spent a lot of time together playing outside using our imaginations to build awesome forts, rafts to sail on the mighty Nogies Creek, fishing rods to go fishing, construct whole towns in the sand and walk miles to do more of the same with friends. She was a fearless tomboy who would try anything once, so of course I went along for the adventure, because back then you had to entertain yourself with your imagination. My sister was the best playmate, so I was rarely bored when school was out in the summer.

As Laurie got older her creative talents were displayed in anything she tried her hand at, which was many things, as she seemed to love the adventure of living spontaneously! I always admired that quality about my sister, as she was never afraid to manifest her talents in a variety of ways. She is one of those people who can do many things well; she is a Jill of all trades! She is the kind of person you would like to have present in a crisis situation because not only is she a nurse, she could build you a house, grow you some food, cook an amazing meal, decorate the most beautiful cake, sew you some clothes, serenade you with her trumpet and sing Karaoke with you ... I think you're getting the picture, right?

And even though Laurie had all those talents there was yet another one waiting to be explored. One that had been waiting patiently in the recesses of her inquiring mind…this book. I remember it was probably 15 years ago when Laurie first told me about this idea she had for a book, she was so excited about it. She had even written the first few chapters. She wanted me to read them and let her know what I thought. I read it over and thought, wow what an amazing imagination! I told her she should continue, as I'm sure it would be a best seller, plus I wanted to read it myself! However, as life goes other adventures popped up and begged for her attention and Laurie, being the spontaneous person that she is, had to shift her priorities leaving little space for book writing. Laurie's enthusiasm and inspiration for getting the book done dwindled as a result, so she had to put the book on the back burner, however she left it on simmer and kept stirring it every once in a while.

Then one day some 15 years later it had simmered long enough and she was ready to add the rest of the ingredients. Inspiration and creative excitement once again compelled her to take whatever steps she needed to allow this story in her head to spill out onto paper and become an extraordinary tale of fantasy and adventure. A story that will take the reader on an epic journey in their imagination creating an alternate reality to escape to as they watch in their minds eye the adventures unfolding in a faraway land!

Laurie's gift for storytelling, from when she was a little girl, has blossomed and grown into an intricate and complex imagination that she is now able to express within the pages of this book. I hope you have as much fun reading it as I did! Enjoy!

With love,
Kimberly Ross

Printed in Canada